The Kind of Girl I Am

Julia Watts

Spinsters Ink
2007

Spinsters Ink
P.O. Box 242
Midway, Florida 32343

Printed in the United States of America on acid-free paper
First Edition

Editor: Christi Cassidy
Cover designer: KIARO Creative Ltd.

ISBN10: 1-883523-89-3
ISBN 13: 978-883523-89-3

For Robin Lippincott, who made me believe in this book again.

Acknowledgments

Growing up in rural Southeastern Kentucky, I thrilled to hear tales of the lurid activities in Knoxville, that sin city a mere hour across the state line. One name that particularly caused raised eyebrows among us small-town folk was that of Hazel Davidson, Knoxville's most notorious, flamboyant, and unapologetic madam. *The Kind of Girl I Am* is a work of fiction, and Vestal Jenkins, the novel's flamboyant and unapologetic protagonist, is not Hazel Davidson. That being said, I must admit that elements of Davidson's feistiness and fearlessness as the proprietor of a brothel in Bible-besotted East Tennessee definitely inspired some of Vestal's spirit. My hope is that in some other realm, Vestal's imaginary spirit and Hazel's departed spirit will get together for a few laughs.

The Southeastern Kentucky and Knoxville locations in this novel are either fictional or used fictionally. However, some savvy Knoxville readers might recognize some fictionalized ghosts from Knoxville's past. Though I attempted to be faithful to the spirit, if not the letter, of Knoxville history, I did consult one invaluable work while preparing the Knoxville sections of the manuscript, William Bruce Wheeler's *Knoxville, Tennessee: A Mountain City in the New South*. One other work that proved very useful for other reasons was the magnificent Pauline Tabor's book *Pauline's*, which provides an account of her years running a brothel in Western Kentucky.

The creation of this novel owes a debt to many other sources as well. I revised *The Kind of Girl I Am* during my time as a student in Spalding University's M.F.A. in Writing program. My special gratitude goes to my faculty mentors Robin Lippincott, Mary Clyde and Crystal Wilkinson, each of whom became very closely acquainted with Vestal Jenkins. I also greatly appreciate all the workshop leaders and participants at Spalding who read chunks of the manuscript and provided thoughtful comments. Thanks also to Linda Hill, Christi Cassidy and all the terrific women at Spinsters Ink. My love and appreciation goes to my parents on a daily basis and for many reasons. And of course, I always gratefully acknowledge Carol, Don, Ian and Alec, who, in the words of Frankie in *Member of the Wedding*, are the "we of me."

About the Author

A native of Southeastern Kentucky, Julia Watts is the author of eight novels, including *Women's Studies*, *Phases of the Moon*, *Piece of My Heart*, and the Lambda Literary Award-winning *Finding H.F.* She lives, writes, and teaches in Knoxville, Tennessee, a city that seems less sinful than small-town rumors led her to believe.

PART I: COAL DUST

CHAPTER 1

Mother and Daddy didn't have any business making another baby during the Depression, but I got made just the same. After all my years of living (and I'll leave it up to you to figure out how many years that is), there's just one thing I know to be true: no matter how bad off people are, they will still screw. Their bellies may be empty, and their bodies may be half worn out from years of hard labor, but somehow they'll still find the energy to get their clothes off and perform the one act that says, 'We may be poor and sick and exhausted, but damn it, we're still alive.'

I'm sure Mother and Daddy weren't surprised when a squawling little bundle of need showed up nine months after the small act of joy they allowed themselves, and even though they didn't have any place to put me but a bureau drawer, they shrugged and accepted my arrival just like they accepted every other hard fact of their hard lives.

I'll tell you one thing about me that did surprise them, though: I was beautiful.

The Bartlett Coal mining camp, where Mother and Daddy lived with us kids in a four-room house that was identical to every other house in the camp, was no place for beauty. Don't get me wrong: the mountains of southeastern Kentucky are beautiful when you drive past them on a fall day and the leaves on the trees are on fire with color. But to live in a coal camp back in a hollow on one of those mountains is no scenic Sunday drive, believe you me.

Bartlett camp was situated on the flattest spot on the side of the tallest mountain in Morgan County, and 'flat' is a relative term here because the whole camp was a little lopsided. The little houses, the church, the one-room school and the company store all leaned a little to the left, as though a strong gust of wind might topple them right over. The people in Bartlett leaned, too; like cows that graze on the side of a hill, they were used to walking favoring their left to make up for the unevenness of the ground. It was always easy to spot visitors to Bartlett the rare traveling salesman or circuit preacher, because they stumbled around like drunks.

There was no beauty in the buildings of Bartlett, which were whitewashed but had turned dull gray from coal dust, and not much landscape to enjoy because we were so far back in a hollow we couldn't see out of it. Come to think of it, the people in Bartlett weren't much to look at either. The wiry men got spat out of the mines every day and came home black from head to toe, the whites of their eyes the only white thing about them. When they cleaned up they were as raw and pink as newborn rats, their eyes squinty because when you spend most of your days in darkness, it's hard to get used to the light.

Sometimes there were cute girls in Bartlett, not beautiful, but cute and lively with bright dresses they'd made themselves and hairdos they'd copied out of magazines. But then they'd get married, and any love of lipstick and laughter would be choked to death by the endless days of getting up at four-thirty, cooking a big miner's breakfast and packing a dinner bucket, then sweeping up the coal dust that reappeared within hours and tending baby after baby.

Being beautiful in Bartlett was beside the point. What use is beauty in a dull, dreamless place like that, where, if a thing can't be eaten or spent, it's not any good? My mother regarded my looks as useless and ignored them (and me, for the most part) and gave all her love to C.R., my hell-raising older brother.

Daddy, though, was carried away with my looks from the start. When I wasn't much more than a baby, he'd take me down to the company store in the evenings to show me off. He'd taught me how to roll cigarettes with my tiny hands, so I'd roll smokes for all his buddies, and they'd give me a nickel for an orange pop and talk about how I looked just like Shirley Temple, who was big back then.

But really, I didn't look a thing like Shirley Temple. Shirley was an adorable child, with her curls and dimples and pouty lips. But watching her as a little girl, it was obvious that she'd already hit the height of her looks. Though Shirley didn't grow up to be ugly, it was still all downhill for her after she turned twelve.

With me, the same things that made me a beautiful child were going to make me a beautiful woman. I wasn't all baby fat and dimples like Shirley. Even as a little girl, my looks leaned more to the exotic. My eyes were as green as a cat's and lined with long, sooty lashes. My skin was so fair I had to be extra careful not to burn in the sun, but my hair was so black and thick and heavy that an old woman in the camp suggested that a gypsy had marked my mother when she was pregnant with me. I was a beautiful child who was going to grow up to be a beautiful woman, and everybody, especially Daddy, knew it.

By the time my sister, Myrtle, was born when I was four and a half, I was Daddy's little princess, and his lap was my throne. With Daddy spoiling me rotten and Mother crazy about C.R., poor, plain Myrtle didn't stand a chance.

One thing I do want to clear up right now, though, is that I don't want you to think I'm stuck on myself just because I say I'm beautiful. Over the course of my life, a lot of people have taken a dislike to me because of my looks, Mother and Myrtle being two of them. Actually, I probably should say, that a lot of women have taken a dislike to me because of my looks. Some men have publicly denounced me or made rude jokes about me, but I don't think there's ever been a man alive who disliked me. No man, straight or gay, can truly hate a beautiful woman.

Beauty is luck. Some people are born beautiful just like some people are born double-jointed or smart. Beauty's nothing to be proud of because whether you have it or not doesn't really have anything to do with you. It's luck and genes and nothing else.

The beautiful women who get on my nerves are the ones who pretend they're not beautiful...you know, the ones who'll stare at their perfect images in the ladies' room mirror and say, "I'm so fat" or "I hate my hair." Now, these women know damn good and well that their figures and hair are far superior to nearly everybody's; they just want to pretend otherwise so you'll jump in and tell them how gorgeous they look. Not me. I don't pretend to be anything I'm not, and that includes poor-mouthing about my looks.

Granted, I'm not much to look at now, sitting here in my housecoat and fuzzy house slippers, but before Father Time bit me on the ass and everywhere else, I just accepted my beauty as a fact. I never used it as a pole to fish for compliments or a stick to whack people with.

Except for Daddy's adoration and the orange pops I charmed out of his friends, growing up beautiful in Bartlett was no different than growing up ugly. I ran to the company store with enough scrip to buy a bag of cornmeal so Mother could fix cornbread for supper. I helped wash dishes and clothes. I learned how to kill and pluck a chicken, even though I threw up the first time I saw the chicken's head hanging down loose from its wrung neck and again when I smelled the feathers that Mother scalded to make them easier to pluck. In between helping Mother around the house, which was supposed to be the most important job a girl could do, I attended the camp's one-room schoolhouse, where Miss Hackett, who looked like one of those dolls whose face is made from a dried-up apple, terrified us into literacy.

Occasionally I played with Myrtle, but our playing was usually cut short by a temper tantrum on my part. Besides being too young to make a good playmate, Myrtle only wanted to play one game: house, with her as the mommy and me as the daddy and our two battered dolls as the children. Myrtle always said I hated playing house because I didn't want to be the daddy, but really, I didn't want to be the daddy or the mommy either. I thought there had to be better games to play, but what those games might be, I hadn't the slightest notion.

I had never been outside of Bartlett, not even as far as the county seat of Morgan, where, I had been told, there was a real movie theater. I didn't know any books except our dull-as-dishwater school reader, and what little education I had was based on memorization and discipline, not imagination. It wasn't that I had no imagination; it's just that your imagination is like your stomach, if you've got nothing to feed it, it can't do anything but grumble about how empty it is.

The only other games my grumbling imagination could come up with other than house, were school and church. Myrtle would agree to these occasionally, as long as I didn't make her play a boy. School and church were a little better than house because I always played the teacher or the preacher. In either role, I got to have the fun of screaming and hollering at Myrtle while she crouched in terror that was only half fake.

But the fun of these games wore off quickly. Like everything else in Bartlett, they lacked excitement, a word I probably didn't even know at the time, but you don't have to know a word to crave its meaning, and sooner or later, I'd stalk off from our game to sit in the woods and sulk.

If you've got an eight-year-old who's already an accomplished sulker, by the time she's a teenager, she's going to be holy hell. And I guess I was a hellish teenager, even though I never meant to cause trouble. Sometimes I've thought those words would be good to put on my gravestone: I never meant to cause trouble. Nobody would believe me, though.

By the time I was fourteen, there was only one thing I wanted: to get out of Bartlett. Not only could I stand on my porch and see every building in the camp, I could also tell you what was inside every building, right down to what was on each shelf in the company store. I knew everything there was to know about Bartlett and the people in it, or so I thought, anyway. Everything that lay beyond the mountain on which Bartlett was perched was as big a mystery as if it was in another solar system. Since I knew that because of my age, I was trapped for the time being. I desperately wanted to meet somebody who could clear up a little bit of the mystery for me, who could at least tell me what life was like in the county seat and beyond. And for a little while, Miss Taylor was that person.

In the fall of my eighth-grade year, old Miss Hackett started slowing down considerably. Arthritis stiffened her knees and turned her hands into rigid claws that were useless for her two main functions: writing on the blackboard and hitting children.

When we came back to school after Christmas break, the woman standing in front of the class looked as different from dried-up old Miss Hackett as two creatures of the same species can look.

"Good morning, children," the young woman sang. "My name is Miss Taylor, and I'll be your teacher for the rest of the year." And then she did something unbelievable: she smiled. Not one soul in Bartlett had ever seen Miss Hackett smile. If she'd tried, her face would have probably torn like crumpled-up paper.

Miss Taylor smiled a lot, though. The little children weren't scared of her like they had been of Miss Hackett, because Miss Taylor never raised her voice or hit them. The older boys fiddled with their overall galluses and looked down at the ground when Miss Taylor praised their strength for bringing in buckets of coal for the stove, and all the older girls worshipped Miss Taylor because of her blond beauty-shop hairdo, her store-bought dotted Swiss dresses and her rose-colored lipstick and nail polish.

I worshipped Miss Taylor for those reasons, too, of course, but there was more to my feelings for her than the fact that her dresses weren't stitched together out of old flour sacks. Miss Taylor, who was just twenty-two years old when she came to teach at Bartlett School, had three qualities I'd never seen in a woman her age: she was single, she was educated and she was happy.

Unlike the other seventh- and eighth-grade girls, I didn't just want Miss Taylor's hairdo or clothes or nail polish. I wanted her life. Well, I wanted her life with one exception: I couldn't figure out why somebody with her brains, looks and personality would be wasting her time in the little patch of hell that was the Bartlett coal camp.

My question was answered one day when Miss Taylor asked me to stay after school. I sat at my desk as the rest of the kids filed out of the classroom, looking down at my homemade dress and feeling ashamed. The fabric was an ugly dirt brown with little green flowers—who ever heard of green flowers? The dress itself didn't fit too good anymore, not because I was growing taller (I had already hit my towering height of five feet even), but because my titties were growing so big so fast that the darts Mother had sewn in the bustline were threatening to pop out. Even though she was never anything but nice to me, Miss Taylor's presence always made me aware that my things weren't as good as hers, my education wasn't as good as hers, maybe my whole personality wasn't as good as hers.

As soon as the other kids were all gone, Miss Taylor pulled up a chair and sat right across from me. "Vestal?"

"Yes, ma'am?" The way she said it, my name sounded almost pretty. I wondered what Miss Taylor's first name was. Whatever it was, it had to be prettier than mine.

"I've only known you for a short time, of course," Miss Taylor began. "But over the past several weeks, you've proven yourself to be a very clever student."

I felt my face go hot. I wasn't used to getting compliments about my brain. I had always gotten good marks on my tests from Miss Hackett, but she wrote the grade on my papers without any comments, and when she spoke directly to a student, it was never to pay a compliment. Now I know I should've said thank you to Miss Taylor when she called me clever, but I didn't know to do it back then. I may have been clever, but I sure was ignorant.

"You do plan on going to high school next year?" Miss Taylor asked.

Not too many Bartlett kids kept going to school after eighth grade, but for those who did, a bus stopped at the head of the hollow at six a.m. to pick them up and take them to Deer Creek High School. It was a full mile walk to the head of the hollow, but I figured if there was a bus that would take me just a few miles out of Bartlett, I'd get on it.

"Yes, ma'am," I said.

"I'm happy to hear that, Vestal." Miss Taylor favored me with one of her rosy-pink smiles. "A girl with your obvious gifts owes it to herself to get a high school diploma. And I must admit that sometimes I pray that you will go on to college and maybe even follow my path."

It's safe to say that nobody in the Jenkins family had ever even thought about going to college. "You mean being a schoolteacher?" I asked.

Miss Taylor smiled again, and I seem to remember her folding her hands and casting her eyes downward, but that may just be my memory painting in details.

"Teaching is a part of my path," Miss Taylor said, "but I was put on this earth for more than just making sure mountain children know their letters and numbers. Vestal" and here she sang my name, "do you know Jesus?"

I've always had a smart mouth on me, and so even though I was talking to the person I loved above all others in my life, I still almost said, "Yeah, I saw him buying an orange pop at the company store the other day. He said to tell you hey." But instead I said, "I go to church pretty regular."

Mother and Daddy didn't make it to church much, but every third Sunday or so they'd make us kids go. Of course, C.R. would just walk Myrtle and me to the door; I never knew him to sit through a service.

"Going to church is a good thing, a wonderful thing, Vestal, but what I mean is, do you know Jesus in your heart?" Miss Taylor's blue eyes sparkled when she talked about Jesus. I nodded my head yes, but I only did it to make Miss Taylor happy.

The truth was, I'd never thought much about Jesus, even during the times I was sitting in church, when I'd start thinking about how Nettie Marlow was wearing that sad old gray dress again, or I'd get myself giggling because the bald spot on the back of Arlis Ellison's head was shaped just like a person's behind. I'd keep looking at the people around me and thinking about them, and before I knew it, the sermon would be over, and I hadn't thought of Jesus once.

"I don't know if I can explain this to you," Miss Taylor was saying, wrinkling up her nicely tweezed eyebrows. "But when I was a girl growing up in Ohio, I kept seeing the girls around me throwing their educations away and marrying skinny little high school boys so they could spend their lives cooking meals and cleaning house, and I thought, that's not for me."

Hearing those words, the clouds in my heart parted to let in the sun for the first time. "That's just how I feel."

"I don't want you to think I judged the girls who were content to become homemakers, because I didn't," Miss Taylor went on, smiling her peaceful smile. "The way I felt, though…the way I still feel…is that cooking and cleaning don't last. You sweep a room, and an hour later, your husband tracks more dirt in. You cook a meal, and in fifteen minutes, all your hard work's been eaten up. I can't bear to think about that kind of impermanence; it makes me want to cry."

I sat on the edge of my chair, waiting to see if Miss Taylor was going to cry or not. But she didn't. She just kept talking.

"I decided when I was just about your age, Vestal, that I didn't want to spend my life cleaning and re-cleaning, cooking and cooking again for some man who wouldn't even appreciate my efforts. I wanted to do the kind of work that lasts."

I didn't know what to say. In my family, nobody talked about the kind of work they wanted to do or the kind of life that they wanted to have. For my family and every other family in Bartlett, the life you were born with was the life you got, and the work you did was the work other people said you were supposed to do. If you weren't content with the life you'd been handed, it must be because there was something wrong with you.

What Miss Taylor was saying was different than anything I had ever heard before. She seemed to be describing a kind of life that involved choice, and as ridiculous as it seems to say, at that time I had never really thought about having choices before. Until Miss Taylor took me aside that day, I had been trapped in Bartlett like a wild animal locked in a cage. I wanted out but didn't know there was a means to escape.

Because Miss Taylor had stopped talking, I guessed that she wanted me to say something. I was so flabbergasted the best I could manage was "yes, ma'am."

"There's only one man who wants a woman to do the kind of work that lasts," Miss Taylor half-whispered, her blue eyes growing misty. "And that man is Jesus."

"Is that a fact?" Like I said, I'd never given Jesus much thought one way or another.

Miss Taylor smiled and reached for my hand. The last hand I had held was Myrtle's when she was a toddler. "Vestal, it's the truest fact I know."

I kept waiting for her to take her hand away, but she didn't.

It was soft and smooth and cool.

"When I was just about your age," she said, her hand still in mine, "Jesus spoke to me. He said, 'If you give your heart to me, I'll take you places you've never dreamed of going.' And I did, Vestal, I gave my heart to Jesus right then and there, and since that time, he's never hurt me or disappointed me. He's never brought me anything but a peaceful heart and happiness. He truly is the only man for me." Her eyes misted over again. The way she talked about herself and Jesus, you would've thought they were newlyweds.

"And of course, Jesus always keeps his promises." Miss Taylor dabbed lightly at her eyes with a hanky embroidered with roses.

"Since I let him into my heart, my mission work has taken me places you wouldn't believe, and in each place I've done the most lasting work there is: winning souls for Jesus. Bartlett is just one of the many places my Lord has led me, —Africa, China, South America."

"Ain't we in South America right now?" I asked.

I told you I was ignorant. Our schoolroom didn't even have a globe. Why should we have a map of the world if all we were supposed to do was stay in the coal camp?

Miss Taylor smiled and squeezed my hand. "No, dear, we're in the southern part of the United States of America, which is part of North America. South America is an entirely different continent."

I nodded like I understood.

"You have a lot to learn, Vestal, but you have a good mind. I would like to teach you, if you'll let me, to teach you beyond the basic lessons you learn during school time. I would like to teach you about the people of other lands and their languages, about the Bible and God's love, about how to be a truly educated woman, so you can go forth into the world and do God's work."

I think I only really heard two of Miss Taylor's phrases, which spread themselves deliciously over me: 'educated woman' and 'go forth into the world.' Miss Taylor was smiling at me, and I smiled back.

"But before I agree to teach you, to really teach you, you have to give me the right answer to one question." This time, she took both of my hands in hers. "Will you give your heart to Jesus?"

I thought about how my mother's hands were cracked and calloused from years of hard work, while Miss Taylor's were soft and smooth and cool. I looked at her beaming, lightly powdered face and her perfect golden beauty-shop curls, and I thought: this woman is educated, she has been to countries I've never even heard of, and for some reason she thinks that I'm special, that I'm worth saving. And I did want to be saved—just not quite in the way that Miss Taylor meant it. Her China blue eyes were looking at me, searching for an answer in my face, so I finally said, "Yes, ma'am."

Miss Taylor jumped out of her chair and grabbed me up in a hug. I couldn't remember the last time somebody hugged me. Daddy hugged me all the time when I was little, of course, but after I started filling out, he wouldn't lay a hand on me and always looked at me like I embarrassed him. Mother had never hugged me that I could remember.

Miss Taylor's hug felt good. Her perfume smelled like lilacs, and I rested my head on her shoulder. She held me close, and I liked the way we fit together. "Oh, Vestal," she breathed into my ear. "Let's pray." She pulled me down to the floor where she knelt and held me, my head pushed up against her bosoms. She started saying things like, "Oh, Jesus, please accept your humble servant Vestal Jenkins," and going on the way praying people do. My thoughts were whirling all over, from the places I'd go, to the things I'd learn, to the fact that I was lying in a pretty woman's arms while she cried and praised me and touched me with what felt like love.

And that's how I gave my heart to Jesus, even though, at that moment, there were a thousand different things on my mind, and Jesus wasn't one of them.

CHAPTER 2

"Shall I say grace?" I tried to make my voice have the same lilt as Miss Taylor's.

"Go ahead on," Daddy muttered, but he didn't look like he was planning on bowing his head and closing his eyes. He was too busy crumbling cornbread over his soup beans. I looked around the table. Mother and Myrtle had their heads bowed, but C.R. was slicing an onion with his pocketknife.

Remembering Miss Taylor saying that mission work begins at home, I bowed my head and intoned, "Heavenly Father, bless this food for the nourishment of our bodies, and make us fit for Thy service. In Jesus's name we pray, amen."

When I raised my head, C.R. grinned at me and said, "Good bread, good meat. Good God, let's eat."

Mother laughed. She laughed at everything C.R. said whether it was funny or not, but I hissed, "Blasphemer."

Of course, that just made C.R. laugh harder. "Lord, Vessie, it's bad enough you've turnt into a little missionary girl, but do you have to get all high church with us? All them 'thees' and 'thys' and 'blasphemers.' Why can't you just be a regular old holy roller like everybody else in this goddamn holler?"

"Watch your mouth, honey," Mother said gently. You can bet if I had used that kind of language at the table she wouldn't have called me 'honey.'

"Vestal just talks that way 'cause that's how Miss Taaaaaylor talks," Myrtle said, drawing out Miss Taylor's name all long and nasty, which seemed like blasphemy, too.

"You're just jealous on accounta her liking me better than she likes you." I was debating whether it would be unchristian to pinch Myrtle under the table.

"Well, I reckon she'd like me, too, if I spent as much time as you do being the teacher's pet."

"I can't help it if Miss Taylor happens to recognize my potential."

"Listen at her!" Myrtle interrupted. "Don't nobody 'round here put on airs like that but Miss Taylor."

"I ain't putting on airs, you little rat-face."

"Teacher's pet!"

"Rat face!"

Daddy set down his spoon. "Can't a man eat his supper in peace?"

We shut up, at least until it was time for Myrtle and me to argue over whose turn it was to wash the dishes. After I finally convinced Myrtle it was her turn (I usually won our arguments because my abilities in both length and loudness outdistanced hers by miles), I went out on the porch to read the little Bible Miss Taylor gave me. It was pretty, white with pages lined in silver, and I tried to read it every day like Miss Taylor said I should.

The only problem was, and in my time of religious devotion, I never would've admitted this to anybody, the book bored me stiff. I knew there were good parts in it, with killing and fornicating and all kinds of juicy gossip about long-dead people, but it seemed like every time I opened it up, I came to one of those sections about who begat who else, and by the time the sun set, I'd be snoring on the porch swing.

This evening, though, my Bible reading didn't have time to 'beget' sleep because before I even picked a page to start on, C.R. came out on the porch, sat down beside me and started rolling a cigarette. "You go right ahead on and read, Vessie. I won't bother you none."

I kept on looking at the page in front of me, but I knew that C.R. would start back to talking any second because he'd never gone a full minute without talking in his life.

"Vessie?"

"Uh-huh?"

"I'm sorry I'm a blasphemer."

When I saw his grin, I had to grin right back at him. I couldn't stay mad at C.R. "It's all right. Miss Taylor says mission work starts at home, so I reckon if I've got a blasphemer for a brother, that'll give me lots of practice."

C.R. blew some smoke rings, and we watched the hazy Os float off the porch. "Well, it's good to hear you say something wise-assed. You've gone and got too good on me, Vessie. Just 'cause you've found Jesus, that don't mean you've got to lose your sense of humor."

I didn't know it at the time, but C.R. had a good point there. Miss Taylor, like a lot of do-gooders, was a serious woman. When she smiled, it was out of kindness, not humor, and of course, there was no laughter at all when it came to talking about God and Jesus.

I wonder if Jesus would've wanted his little cheerleaders to be so serious all the time. After all, he ran with a pretty fast crowd, what with Mary Magdalene and them? And if you believe what the Bible says about him, he was always doing party tricks: turning water into wine, a few pieces of bread and fish into an all-you-can-eat buffet.

"Of course," C.R. said, "I reckon being a missionary's about the only way a girl can go off and see the world. And that, I can understand. I'll tell you this, Vessie. I don't want to die with the only part of the world I've ever seen being the inside of a coal mine."

I closed the Bible. I had never heard C.R. talk about going off before. "What got you to studying on that?"

"I don't know. Turning eighteen, I reckon. And talking to Les. You know how Les is."

Les Tipton was a couple years older than C.R. and was famous for his love of gambling. If Les saw two crows sitting on a fence, he'd bet you a nickel that the one on the left would fly off first. He'd pitch pennies with ten-year-olds or bet on checker games at the company store. I had always liked Les, but my new religious zeal made me deplore his habits. Miss Taylor said gambling was a sin.

"Les talks big," I said.

"He sure does. But he got me thinking the other day. He says to me, 'C.R., I might make my living as a coal miner right now, but I ain't dying no coal miner. There's more to this life than a hole in the ground.'" C.R. lit another cigarette and stared off the porch for a minute. "You know, Daddy ain't forty yet, but he already looks like an old man."

It was true. Years of crouching underground had made Daddy's muscles so stiff that he moved like arthritic old Miss Hackett. Every morning I woke up to the sound of him coughing up coal dust.

"Vessie," C.R. almost whispered. "I'm thinking about enlisting."

"Are you crazy?" I hollered, before C.R. slammed his hand over my mouth. When he took it off, I said, "You'll get yourself killed. And besides, miners don't have to fight, right?"

We all heard the news on the radio, but the war didn't really touch Bartlett because mining was considered a necessary industry, and so our boys didn't have to enlist. For most people in the camp, the war seemed like just another radio program.

"Miners don't have to fight, but I might do it anyhow." C.R. shrugged. "It'd be something different."

"But it's so dangerous."

"Don't you go telling me how dangerous it is, Vessie. You're the one that wants to be a missionary. You're liable to get yourself boiled in a pot. Some feller with a bone in his nose'll be sopping you up with his cornbread."

I play-slapped him. "You're awful! I don't have no idee why Mother likes you best."

"Oh, speaking of Mommy, don't tell her I'm thinking about joining up, all right? I don't want to tell her nothin' till I've decided for sure."

Only a few people in Bartlett owned cars, so when a car was approaching, you could hear it for a long time before you saw it.

"That must be Les," C.R. said. "Me and him's going to the cockfight tonight."

"Miss Taylor says cockfightin's the sinfullest kind of gambling on accounta it being cruel to poor, innocent chickens."

C.R. slapped his thigh, laughing. "Is that what she says? Well, I bet Miss Taylor comes home from church on a Sunday and eats her some poor, innocent fried chicken just the same as everybody else." He grinned extra wide. "I can just see her with them prissy little lips all wet and greasy, sucking the marrow right out of the bones."

C.R. was cut off by the sound of the door of Les's Ford, which everybody said he must have bought with his gambling money. Les was one of those tall, skinny boys that people call a beanpole, and even though he was just in his early twenties, his hair was already a thing of the past. He wore a pair of thick, ugly, black-framed glasses, the only kind of glasses anybody wore back then. "Hidy, neighbors!" he hollered, throwing his hand up in the air.

I was sulking over C.R.'s blasphemous description of Miss Taylor eating fried chicken and so didn't say hello, even after Les walked up on the porch and sat down on the railing.

"Vestal here was explaining to me why cockfightin's a sin," C.R. said. "She's in training to be a missionary."

"Missionary, huh?" Les cackled. "Well, that's a good position to be in, ain't it?"

Les and C.R. commenced to laughing till tears rolled down their faces, but I couldn't figure out why. When C.R. could finally talk, he said, "Yessir, Vestal's been learning all kinds of do-gooder stuff from that new yeller-haired schoolteacher over at the schoolhouse."

"Oh, I've seen her," Les said. "You reckon she might teach me somethin' about the missionary position...if I asked her real nice?"

Now, of course, C.R. and Les were just being boys acting like idiots together, like boys will do, but as a holier-than-thou fourteen-year-old, I had no patience for that kind of foolishness. Though I was too naive to know what they were really saying about Miss Taylor, I did know that they were making fun of her, and that made me mad.

I clutched my Bible to my chest, stood up and said, "The two of you'uns don't have no respect for religion or common decency. You boys is already on the fast road to hell, so you might as well get in that car and go play with your cocks!"

I marched into the house, slammed the door behind me and wondered why in the Sam Hill Les and C.R. were laughing even harder than they had before.

CHAPTER 3

Every day after school, I'd sit alone in the classroom with Miss Taylor while she tried to cure my ignorance. On this particular afternoon, we were working on grammar. "Remember, Vestal," she was saying, her rose-colored lips making each word clipped and perfect, "ain't is not a word."

"It ain't?" I joked, but she didn't laugh. Like I said, C.R. had a point about Christians falling short in the humor department.

"No, it is not." She folded her nicely manicured hands in front of her sky-blue dotted Swiss dress. "If you are going to be a missionary, you must learn the proper way to speak the beautiful language God gave us. You don't hear anyone saying 'ain't' in the Bible, do you?"

"No, ma'am, I reckon not."

My answer must not have sounded too convincing because she asked, "You have been doing your daily Bible reading, haven't you?"

"Yes, ma'am," I said. "Only." I stopped myself short. If I admitted that the Bible bored me, Miss Taylor would give me up as a godless heathen.

"Only what, Vestal?" Her blue eyes were kind and trusting.

"Only...sometimes...I feel like I don't understand it too good. I was thinking...maybe I could go see if Brother Suggs could help me with it a little." Brother Suggs was the preacher at Bartlett Missionary Baptist Church, whose sermons I'd sat through but never heard.

Miss Taylor hopped up out of her seat. "You will not talk to Brother Suggs. I attended a service in which he opened his Bible and read aloud at the same rate that some of our slower third graders would. He finally hit one word that he stumbled over so badly that he said, 'Pray with me that the Lord will get me through this word'! Honestly, Vestal, what could you learn about God's word from that man?" She was pacing back and forth, her sky-blue dress flouncing prettily, until she clapped her hands and said, "I know!"

I had lost track of our conversation because I had been thinking about how her dress would look on me. "Ma'am?"

"I know whom we can engage for your Bible study...an acquaintance of mine, Reverend Moore. You'll like him, Vestal. He's young...right out of the seminary in Louisville. He's got a church over in White Oak right now, but that little church is just one short stop on the glorious path that God has laid out for him. He's the kind of man you should learn from, Vestal...someone who's educated in the Lord."

The next afternoon Miss Taylor took me for a ride in her car. I was surprised that a schoolteacher could afford her own automobile; I knew the Bartlett Primary School didn't pay much. When I asked her about it she said her daddy, who ran some kind of factory in Ohio, had bought it for her when she graduated from college.

We corkscrewed down the winding road that led down the mountain, then found ourselves on a bigger road. I was excited to be in Miss Taylor's car and out of Bartlett, even if we weren't going any farther than White Oak.

Reverend Moore met us at the door of his neat little white frame house, which sat next to his neat little white frame church. I had never been in a house that wasn't owned by the Bartlett Coal Company, and even though Reverend Moore's house was small, I couldn't get over how many things it had in it: a couch with two matching armchairs in the living room and a whole bookcase full of books.

"Sit down, ladies," Reverend Moore said, flapping his long-fingered hands in the direction of the couch. He was very young and very small—so thin that his dark suit hung on him pretty much the same way it would hang on a clothes hanger. "May I offer you ladies some refreshments? Coke? Coffee? Water?"

Miss Taylor asked for water, but I took Coke. A free Coke was too good to pass up. I looked around the room some more and studied the framed copy of the Ten Commandments hanging on the wall. Unlike at my dark, black-dusted camp house, sunlight streamed through the windows of Reverend Moore's living room.

"It's nice here," I leaned over and whispered to Miss Taylor, who smiled and patted my knee. That was nice, too.

Reverend Moore returned carrying a tray with two bottles of Coke, a glass of water and a plate of store-bought cookies. He set the tray down on the table, took a Coke and a cookie for himself and sat down in the armchair in front of us.

"Well," he said, "that takes care of the nourishment of the body. Now for the nourishment of the spirit."

I was just getting started on the nourishment of the body. Store-bought cookies were such a rare treat I had to remind myself not to cram them into my mouth three at a time.

"Vestal," Reverend Moore said, looking at me with beady eyes. "Miss Taylor tells me you want to be a missionary."

Both my jaws were bulging with cookies. I swallowed enough to say "yessir" without spitting crumbs.

"Well, Vestal," Reverend Moore smiled at me the same patient way Miss Taylor did (although his smile was nowhere near as pretty)—"I hope you realize that being a missionary is hard work that requires a lot of study, faith and courage. If you want an easy life, you shouldn't be a missionary; you should be a wife and mother."

You think it's easy being a mother? I thought. I would never have said these words aloud to Reverend Moore, but I couldn't help thinking them. I pictured my mother, scrubbing clothes on the washboard, wringing chickens necks, crying over the baby she had a few years after Myrtle who died while she was giving birth to it.

"I don't want to be a wife and mother," I said. "I want to go places I ain't never been before and see people I ain't never seen before."

"And when you see these people," Reverend Moore prompted me, "what are you going to tell them?"

"About Jesus, I reckon." I wasn't particularly comfortable

with the idea of walking up to complete strangers who might not even speak English and trying to tell them about Jesus, but when it came down to it, I would've been willing to tell people the sky was green if it meant I wouldn't have to spend the rest of my life in Bartlett.

"Yes!" Reverend Moore cheered. "You will travel to dry, parched, godless lands and bring the word of Jesus, which to pagan hearts will be as cool and clear and refreshing as the water that Miss Taylor now holds to her lips."

Miss Taylor smiled prettily and set down her water glass.

"Amen," she whispered.

"But you must learn in order to teach," Brother Moore said, "and that is why Miss Taylor has asked to bring you to me for weekly Bible study. You will learn the Word so that you may spread it to others."

And so every Friday after school Miss Taylor would drive me to Reverend Moore's house, where we'd eat cookies and read the gospels. I looked forward to Fridays—the car ride with Miss Taylor, the Coke and cookies in Reverend Moore's sunny living room. Even reading the gospels wasn't so bad.

With Reverend Moore's help, I had come to the conclusion that Jesus was a right nice fellow. I wasn't sure the world would be greatly improved if everyone worshipped him, but I did think life would be more pleasant if more people acted like Jesus had— nice to everybody, helpful to folks, not snobby or hypocritical. Now, I wasn't sure that Jesus was the Son of God any more than we're all God's children, but still, my missionary lessons were coming along pretty well until the Friday afternoon that Miss Taylor had a doctor's appointment in Morgan. She said she'd drive me to Reverend Moore's house on the way to town, and the Reverend would drive me back to Bartlett when the lesson was over.

My attitude wasn't the best it could've been that Friday because, to be honest, I would have rather gone on to Morgan with Miss Taylor. Being with her was the main reason I looked forward to Fridays, and I didn't like the thought of being without her. Also, having never been to Morgan, I could only imagine all the sightseeing I could've done to entertain myself while Miss Taylor was busy with the doctor.

Despite my wishes to the contrary, Miss Taylor left me with Reverend Moore, who let me in with a smile and bustled around getting my Coke and cookies.

"So, Vestal," he said, sitting down at the opposite end of the couch from me, "I thought that instead of going right into our Bible study today, we might spend some time talking about what you can expect a few years down the road when you go into the mission field."

He smiled that patient smile, which, if I was going to be a professional Christian, I reckoned I was going to have to learn.

"You see," he began, "You've never truly been in a godless country before. Here in Kentucky, you can be pretty darn sure that just about everybody has at least heard of Jesus. But if you go over to China or Africa..." He shook his head sadly. "It's tragic what never having heard of Jesus does to a nation of people, Vestal. Their souls are so black and twisted that it's hard to bring them to the light." He twisted his hands together like he was twisting a human soul. When he looked back up, his beady eyes gleaming, he said, "They'll want to drag you into the darkness, too, Vestal, but no matter what they try to make you do, just tell 'em you love Jesus." He clapped his hands and jumped up from the couch. "I'll tell you what. Let's play a game."

An adult had never asked me to play a game before, so out of curiosity, I said, "All right."

"Good, good." Reverend Moore's smile seemed to be one of genuine pleasure instead of just patience or kindness. "Vestal, this game will teach you all you need to know about being a missionary. It's a role-playing game. Now, you be the missionary, and I'll be the heathen."

Years later, playing different versions of this little game would earn me thousands of dollars, but at the time, I had no idea what the good Reverend was getting at. "All right," I agreed.

Reverend Moore then commenced to jumping up and down, stomping his feet, waving his fists in the air and singing something that sounded like, "Ooga booga, ooga booga."

He looked like such a fool I couldn't help laughing. "Reverend Moore, what in the Sam Hill are you doing?"

He beat his fists on his skinny chest. "Me heathen native.

Who you?"

"Uh..." I said, trying to be serious even though my voice was cracking with the threat of giggling. Teenaged girls are prone to giggling at the slightest provocation anyway, so it was hard to control myself at the sight of a grown man—a preacher, no less—behaving like a complete jackass. "I'm a missionary," I finally managed to say. "I've...uh...come to tell you about Jesus."

Reverend Moore wrinkled his brow and cocked his head like a hound dog. "Who...this...Jesus?"

"Uh..." This missionary thing was pretty hard, or at least it was hard to keep a straight face while you were doing it.

I wondered if I would do better talking to a real jungle native, standing shirtless in front of his grass hut, instead of a skinny white preacher doing a crude impression of a native, which I discovered later, was straight out of a Tarzan movie.

"Well," I began, "he's the...uh...Son of God who came down to earth and died on a cross for our sins." I wondered how that statement would sound to somebody who had never heard of Jesus before. Nutty as a fruitcake would be my guess.

"This Jesus..." Reverend Moore was crouched on the floor like an ape. "You...love him?"

"Yessir," I said, even though I wasn't sure whether or not I was supposed to call a heathen native 'sir.'

"What if I..." Reverend Moore seemed to have lost his heathen native accent all of a sudden. "What if I said I'd do terrible things to you, and the only way to stop me was to say, 'I don't love Jesus'?"

This game wasn't too hard, I thought. "I wouldn't say it because I'd still love Jesus," I said.

"What if I say I'll take the cookies away unless you say you don't love Jesus?"

I stood confident and strong. "Take 'em away. I still love Jesus."

Reverend Moore put the cookies up on a shelf where I couldn't reach them. I didn't care. I had already eaten six of them.

Reverend Moore looked at me with beady heathen eyes, and when he spoke, his jungle native accent was back. "What if I say...

I tickle you unless you say you don't love Jesus?"

This one was harder because I've never liked being tickled; it's always made me laugh so hard I come close to peeing myself. But Reverend Moore obviously wanted to test my faith, I thought, and I wasn't about to lose my missionary spirit over a little thing like tickling. "I still love Jesus," I said.

He came toward me with a silly, stomping walk, which was his idea of a native gait, and started goosing my ribs. He just did it for a few seconds, but I laughed so hard I fell backward onto the couch, tears streaming down my face.

When I finally caught my breath and looked up, Reverend Moore was kneeling on the floor in front of me, looking at me in a way I knew meant something, but at the time I was too young and ignorant to know what. "Vestal," he said, his voice sounding different somehow, "unless you say you don't love Jesus, I'm gonna...I'm gonna…"

But he didn't let me take my turn because before he even finished talking, he had mashed his mouth up against mine. One of his arms was holding my back; with the other, he was snaking his hand up to one of the well-padded spots above my rib cage.

I didn't even think. Before I knew what was happening, Reverend Moore was doubled over on the floor, clutching the front of his pants and gasping for breath. I reckon I must've kicked him.

I stood up and stepped over his squirming body on the way to the door. As I opened it, I heard him say my name—he kind of squeaked it, actually. His face was terrified, but I'm not sure what the source of his terror was—whether he was afraid I was going to tell somebody or afraid I was going to kick him again.

"Jesus was a right good feller," I said, looking right into Reverend Moore's watering eyes. "And I don't reckon he'd have tried to take advantage of a girl like you just done. But I tell you one thing. No matter how nice Jesus might have been, I don't love him enough to let the likes of you crawl all over me."

I marched out the door and headed in the direction of Bartlett, even though it was five miles down the road.

My experience with Reverend Moore was my first lesson that a pretty girl has to watch out for herself. When you're a beautiful little girl, men want to pinch your cheek or buy you an orange pop. But once you've grown up and filled out, they want to do much more than that.

It probably took me longer than it should have to catch on to the fact that when a man sees a beautiful girl, he wants to do things to her. But back in that day, girls didn't get much in the way of sex education. Unlucky girls got screwed and pregnant, and that was their education. The rest of us got by with what little the grown women saw fit to tell us.

In my case, Mother told me how to use rags to soak up the blood when my time came, but that was all. She never told me what men wanted when they looked at me with gleaming heathen eyes.

After about a mile and a half of walking, my feet ached, and my hair was damp with sweat. Still, if Reverend Moore had come driving up beside me and told me to hop in, there's no way I'd have done it.

I thought of Miss Taylor. She never would've dropped me off at Reverend Moore's if she'd known what he was really like.

I trudged on another half mile, past cow pastures and farmhouses. My shoes were pinching me so bad I finally took them off and walked barefoot. My feet had grown a half-size since Christmas, but it would be Christmas again before anybody would buy me new shoes.

I was thinking about what a terrible predicament Reverend Moore had put me in when I heard a car pull up beside me. I was amazed that the reverend would come to my rescue, since I didn't figure he'd be able to look me in the eye again after the stunt he pulled.

But when I turned around, I saw that it wasn't Reverend Moore at all. It was Les Tipton.

"I thought that was you, Vestal," he said, leaning over to open the car door. "Hop on in."

My encounter with Reverend Moore had left me less than trusting. "Thank you, but I'm doing fine on my own. Besides, Mother says I shouldn't get in a car alone with a man."

Les cackled. "You're a proud little thing, ain't you? Missy, it seems to me that if a girl finds herself out on a country road, miles from home and barefoot, then it's time for her to swallow her pride and get in the car."

He had a point. I jumped in the car before he had the chance to change his mind.

"You don't have to worry about riding in the car with me, Miss Vestal," Les said as we headed down the road to Bartlett. "If I laid so much as a hand on you, your brother'd skin me alive and throw my hide to the hound dogs."

I couldn't help grinning. "So," I said, "what are you doing out running the roads today when you're supposed to be at the mines?"

"Proud and nosy both," Les said. "Have you noticed me asking what you was doing plum out in White Oak, walking down the road barefoot and sweaty?"

"No," I snapped, a little offended that he called me sweaty, even though I was. "It ain't none of your business."

Les grinned. "I couldn't have said it better my own self."

We rode the rest of the way to Bartlett in silence.

That night at supper, I kept thinking I should tell somebody about Reverend Moore's little touchy-feely missionary game. But as I looked at the faces of my family members, I knew exactly how they'd react if I told them.

Mother and Myrtle would say I must have misunderstood what was happening because preachers were called by God, and a man called by God would never do something like that. Daddy would say that if a fellow did something like that, it must be because the girl brought it on herself. C.R. would be the most sympathetic, since he trusted me and distrusted preachers, but as soon as I told him, he'd track down Reverend Moore and kill him, and I'd have to face life with a murder on my conscience and a brother in jail.

Miss Taylor was clearly the only person I could tell. I would let her know that it wasn't her fault that she misjudged the reverend—that she was just being a trusting Christian. Miss Taylor was my friend, and I knew she would understand. The trouble was, it was Friday, and I'd have to wait until after school on Monday to talk to her.

On Saturday morning the house was heavy with silence. Mother and Daddy had been arguing about something or another the night before. Daddy had left the house to shoot pool in the back room of the company store. Mother was doing her chores in stony silence, and Myrtle was sulking because the only words that had escaped Mother's lips that morning had been harsh ones aimed at her.

Even C.R. was quiet, which he was more frequently as he gathered the courage to tell Mother and Daddy that he planned to leave the coal mines of Kentucky for the battlefields of Europe.

That morning, I wanted noise and activity and distractions, and so, like Daddy, I snuck out of the house to wander around the camp. Not that the camp was that interesting, mind you, but at least I could watch people other than the members of my own family: women hanging out their washing, men sitting on the porches, kids playing in the little front yards. I wandered past the company store, past the church, and then stopped at the school, where I saw Miss Taylor's car parked beside the building.

It was a sign, I was sure of it—a sign that I was meant to talk to her, to end the smoldering silence and tell her that Reverend Moore wasn't the purely spiritual being he made himself out to be. Miss Taylor would listen and understand, would hold my hands and kneel with me to pray.

The door of the schoolhouse was unlocked, so I pushed it open.

I heard them before I saw them. As I stood in the little foyer where the schoolchildren left their coats and lunch buckets, I heard a male voice saying, "Do you still love Jesus?" And a female voice gasping, "Yes! Yes! Yes!"

I couldn't help but look. Anybody would have.

Miss Taylor was leaned forward over her desk, the top of her dress unbuttoned so I could see the dark line of her cleavage peeking out from beneath the lace of her princess slip. The skirt of her dress was hiked up around her waist.

Reverend Moore was behind her, shirt and jacket on but britches down, with his teeth gritted and his hands gripping Miss Taylor's tiny waist.

I had heard my parents' hushed couplings after they thought

I was asleep, but the only creatures I had seen in the act of sex prior to this educational event were a couple of hogs feverishly rutting in their pen. Miss Taylor and Reverend Moore looked just like them.

The reverend must have felt my eyes on him because his own eyes snapped open, and he stopped in mid-rut. Miss Taylor also looked up, startled, and then looked worse than startled when she saw me looking at her.

I was jealous to the point of hatred of Reverend Moore, who had been crawling all over my beautiful Miss Taylor, and yet part of me hated Miss Taylor, too. She had betrayed me. She had flat-out lied to me, saying the only man in her life was Jesus.

"Vestal!" Miss Taylor screeched, dismounting the desk and buttoning her dress while Reverend Moore fastened his pants behind her. "We backslid!" Miss Taylor cried, her voice shaking with fear. "We were overcome by temptation! We…"

"I reckon it's hard when Jesus is the only man for you," I interrupted, "because no matter how much you love him, he ain't gonna come down from heaven to screw you."

"Now, there's no need for you to blaspheme, young lady!" Reverend Moore wagged his finger at me. He had zipped part of his shirttail up in his fly. "You ought to get down on your knees…"

"You got down on your knees in front of me yesterday, but it wasn't to pray," I said. "I reckon I'll just leave being a missionary up to folks like you'uns and try to find me a more honest line of work."

I turned to walk out, but like Lot's wife, I did look back once when Miss Taylor cried, "Don't tell anyone, Vestal. And… and don't give up on the Lord. I can still help you. I can educate you to be a proper Christian lady."

But it's hard to believe you can learn how to be a proper Christian lady from a woman who's talking to you with her drawers down around her ankles.

CHAPTER 4

When Myrtle was five and I was ten and our little brother died at birth, Mother cried. You wouldn't have known it if you hadn't been looking at her, because she never made a sound. She just sat still with tears sliding down her face and not a sob or a whimper escaping her clamped lips. When C.R. finally screwed up the courage to tell her he was enlisting, though, she howled like a coyote in a trap. She fell to the floor, wrapped her arms around his knees and wailed, "No, baby! No! No! No!"

Myrtle and I went out on the porch, uncomfortable because we weren't used to seeing such displays of emotion in our house. "Bet she wouldn't take on like that over me if I was to take off somewhere," Myrtle said as we rocked back and forth on the porch swing listening to Mother beg and bawl.

"Bet she wouldn't take on like that over my dead body," I said.

Myrtle didn't contradict me, probably because she knew I was right.

Mother's begging did pay off, at least for a little while. When it became clear to her that C.R. was set on going, come hell or high water, she struck a deal with him about when to go. C.R. agreed that he would wait till the Fourth of July, and if the war hadn't ended by then, he could go.

Mother spent the spring and summer listening to the news of the war on the radio. She listened day and night, waiting for one of the announcers to say that the war was over.

From what I could make out, it sounded like it was getting worse instead of better, but when I made this observation to Mother, she told me to shut my mouth. When she looked at me, it was with something close to hate.

I spent spring and early summer finishing up eighth grade, but without Miss Taylor as my teacher. The Sunday after I had caught them in a compromising (not to mention nonmissionary) position, Reverend Moore apparently didn't show up for church. The day after that, old Miss Hackett, who by that time was hunched over a cane, was teaching at Bartlett Primary instead of Miss Taylor.

Miss Hackett never acknowledged that she had been replaced for a while by another teacher who was now gone, but some of the older girls whispered that Miss Taylor had run off with a preacher late Saturday night. They speculated that the two of them wanted to get out of town before she started showing.

I always figure Reverend Moore and Miss Taylor ended up married and living in some little dinky town. I figure he had a church, and she stayed home tending the house and kids and living the exact kind of life she told me she didn't want to live, all the while desperately telling herself that her endless days of changing diapers and cooking meals and washing dishes somehow fit in with God's plan.

Miss Taylor made me decide that I'd never pick another woman as my role model. Women, I thought—and at the time, I thought this of all women because I'd never met any who were different—would talk a good game until a man came along, at which time they would forget about everything except how to make that man love them. They'd forget their friends, their dreams, their futures in order to do whatever it is that would make that man happy at that moment. And most of the time it's not that hard to figure out what you have to do to make a man happy at any given moment.

Women, I decided, let their passions get the best of them. That had been Miss Taylor's mistake, and it was one I swore I'd never make.

Nobody, I decided, be it Miss Taylor or Reverend Moore or Jesus, was going to take my hand and lead my out of Bartlett and into a better life. I would have to find my own way.

The war had not ended by July 4th, which I guess turned out to be a real Independence Day for C.R., since that was when he finally cut himself loose from Mother's apron strings. She begged him not to go but he said, "Now, Mommy, you done made me wait four months to go, and I waited out of respect for you. But now I've got to pay my respects to my country."

Of course, there's no other word for what C.R. said than bullshit. But like a lot of bullshit, it sounded good—like his love of country was the only thing that outweighed his love of his mother. Now, I know that C.R. did in fact love Mother—how could you not love somebody back who loved you that much?—but I also knew that patriotism wasn't the real reason he wanted to fight in World War II. Like me, C.R. craved excitement, and he was using patriotism as a way to get out of Bartlett just like I had tried to use Jesus.

Silently, as Mother took to her bed and cried, I wished him luck.

On July 5th, Les showed up in his car to drive C.R. to Morgan, where he'd get on a train and head for the army base in Georgia. Earlier that morning, I had asked C.R. if I could ride in with him and Les. I wanted to see the town and to see a train that hauled people instead of coal.

But C.R. refused. "I can't let you, Vessie," he said, shaking his head. "If you go, Mommy'll want to go. And she'd make a damn spectacle of herself at the train station. She'd probably throw herself under the wheels if she thought it'd keep me from going."

So later that morning, we all said good-bye to C.R. in the front yard, while Les sat in his car, waiting. C.R. grabbed Myrtle and me both in a big, three-person hug.

"You girls be good," he said.

C.R. shook Daddy's hand. Men didn't hug each other back then, unless they were too drunk to know better. Daddy said, "I talked to the foreman, son. He says when you come back, your job'll be waiting on you."

I always figured that was the closest Daddy could come to telling C.R. that he loved him.

When it was time for C.R. to hug Mother good-bye, she let out a wail and ran into the house, slamming the screen door behind her. C.R. made a move to go in after her, but Daddy grabbed his arm and said, "She'll be all right directly. You go ahead on."

When C.R. got into the car next to Les, I saw Les hand him a small metal flask. C.R. drank deeply as the car headed down the gravel road.

Les didn't stop coming by, even though C.R. wasn't there anymore. He'd still come by once or twice a week. Sometimes he'd sit and talk to Daddy, but if Daddy wasn't around, he'd sit and talk to me.

He never spent much time around Mother and Myrtle because they were always busy piecing a quilt or listening to some silly soap opera on the radio and so never said much more than hello to him. Also, sometimes the way Mother looked at Les, I wondered if she was a little mad at him...as if him agreeing to drive C.R. to the train station made it his fault that C.R. was gone.

One Saturday evening I was sitting on the porch swing, daydreaming about faraway places. Myrtle was off to spend the night with one of her stupid little friends, and while I was glad to have her gone, I was also a little jealous that she had a friend and a place to go. I was wondering if going to high school might make my life better (since it could hardly be worse), when Les pulled up in his car.

"Hidy, neighbors!" he called.

"They ain't but one neighbor setting out here."

"Well, then, hidy, neighbor!" Les said, bounding up the steps two at a time. He leaned against the porch railing. "What are you up to this evenin'? Setting out here waiting on a feller?"

"Lord, no. I'm just setting."

"Well, it don't do no good for a pretty girl to be setting by herself on a Saturday night. Listen, I'm about to drive down to Morgan. There's a poker game they got going every Saturday night down at the hardware store after it closes. Yesterday was payday, so I thought I might go down there and try my luck. Then when I was driving by, I seen you setting here, watching the paint peel, and I thought you might like to ride with me."

"Les Tipton, you ain't trying to court me."

"Vestal Jenkins, I am twenty-one years old. If I was aiming to court, do you think I'd be so hard up I'd have to go after a fifteen-year-old? The truth is, missy, I told your brother I'd look after you while he was gone. He said your mother and daddy never paid you no mind, and somebody needed to 'cause you was a girl who was going places." He lit up a cigarette and squinted at me through the smoke. "So, you wanna go or not?"

I was out of the swing and halfway off the porch. "You bet I do. We better take off now, before Mother and Daddy find out. I reckon I'll get my hide tanned later, but it'll be worth it."

"Now hold on just a second, missy," Les said. "I ain't taking you without your mother and daddy's permission."

Disappointment hit me like a wet washrag across the face. "Then you ain't taking me nowhere. There ain't no way Mother and Daddy are gonna give me permission to go to a poker game with you."

"Well, they don't have to know just what it is they're giving you permission to do." Les's eyes twinkled. "They inside?"

"Yeah."

"Well, let's go in and talk to 'em."

I wasn't hopeful, but I still swung the door open and hollered, "Les is here."

Daddy was peeling an apple with a pocketknife he could always make the whole skin come off in one long ribbon, and Mother was sewing a button on a shirt. I was always amazed how Mother and Daddy could sit together on the same couch, sometimes for hours, and never say a word to each other.

"How do, Les," Daddy said, popping a piece of apple into his mouth with the blade of his knife. "Set down, why don't you. *The Barn Dance'll* be on directly." *The Shady Grove Barn Dance* was a country music radio program that came on every Saturday evening. Daddy never missed it.

"No, thank you, sir, I can't stay," Les said, holding his hat in his hands. "I've got some business to take care of down in Morgan, and I was just telling Vestal about the special church program they got down there on Saturday nights."

This was news to me, but I kept my mouth shut.

"It's a special service for young people, over at Main Street

Baptist," Les said. "They've got a young preacher that does a sermon and a choir of young people that sings. And after that, they put on a big ice cream social. I figured Vestal must be awful lonesome tonight, what with being the only young'un in the house, so I thought she might like to come with me."

"They got chaperones at this church social?" Mother asked a little suspiciously.

"The meanest old chaperones you ever did see!" Les hooted. "Old-maid Sunday school teachers that look like walking prunes... they won't let them young'uns get by with nothin'!"

Even Mother had to smile at that. Daddy laughed and said, "Well, I reckon a little church and ice cream never hurt nobody. Vestal can go if you'll keep an eye on her."

"Don't you worry about that, Mr. Jenkins. What C.R.'s about to do to them Japs in the war ain't a patch on what he'd do to me if I let somethin' happen to Vestal."

For a second I just stood there in shock, not believing that I was finally getting to go to Morgan. Then I snapped to attention, said, "Just give me a minute," ran into the bedroom and slammed the door.

"Now, you hurry up!" Les called. "We don't want to be late for church."

I knew that the only church Les was thinking of was the First Church of Poker, and I knew better than to make him wait for anything that had to do with winning money.

"I'm hurrying," I hollered, and quick as a rabbit, I shucked out of my old brown dress and put on a yellow checked one Mother had run up for me a couple of months before. I tied back my thick black hair with a yellow ribbon. I wouldn't have looked any more like a rube if I'd had a corncob pipe stuck between my teeth, but at the time, I didn't know that. I was just doing the best I could with what little I had to work with.

As soon as I got in the car with Les, I burst out laughing. "I can't believe you told them you was taking me to church! And they believed you! You could talk the ears off a billy goat."

"I reckon I could," Les said, looking pleased. I was pleased, too. Nothing pleased me more than being in a car spiraling down the mountain, away from Bartlett.

"You're a right brave feller," I said. "Most folks'd be scared to lie about going to church like that."

"Not me." Les grinned. "Me and the Lord got an understanding."

"Oh, yeah?"

"Yep. Before she got knocked up and run out of town, did your missionary friend teach you what Luke eleven:nine says?"

"I don't recollect if she did."

"Ask and it shall be given you, seek and ye shall find, knock and it shall be opened unto you," Les quoted. "So the way I see it, the Lord's saying, 'Les, if there's an opportunity out there for you, and you ain't out there taking advantage of it, then you're one sorry son of a bitch.'"

"So," I was trying to understand his reasoning—"the Lord wants you to go to that poker game?"

"Damn straight he does! 'Seek and ye shall find.' Well, I'm gonna find me some money tonight! 'Course, the Lord also says it's easier for a camel to get through the eye of a needle than for a rich man to get into heaven, but I figure if I get rich, the Lord'll let me squeak through anyhow, on accounta me starting out so poor." He drove for a minute in silence while I looked out the window. We passed the place where you turn off to get to White Oak, which meant I was officially farther away from Bartlett than I'd ever been.

Suddenly Les said, "I'll tell you what else the Lord don't want."

"What's that?"

"He don't want you setting on the porch of that camp house ever night like somebody's half-dead hound dog. The Lord don't want a pretty girl like you hiding her light under a bushel. He wants you to have fun when you're young, have yourself a big ole' time, as long as you don't make a damn fool of yourself."

I grinned, figuring "making a damn fool of yourself" was code for getting pregnant. "How do you know that's what the Lord wants?"

"Like I said," Les took his hands off the wheel long enough to light himself a Lucky Strike, "me and him got an understanding. And besides, the Lord runs how things happen, right? If he hadn't wanted you to get off the porch and go to Morgan, your parents wouldn't have believed that fib I told them." He held out his pack of Luckies, and I took one, feeling very grown up.

Les's brand of theology was a little hard to figure. It seemed to say that the Lord wanted you to do any damn thing you wanted so long as you didn't do anything worse to anybody than lying to them or taking their money. One thing you could say for it—with a religion with so few absolute prohibitions, you ran less risk of being a hypocrite.

Even though I felt very adult for being offered a cigarette, I still had a hard time striking the match to get it lit. And when I took my first drag, I coughed so hard I was afraid I was going to upchuck all over Les's dashboard. When I finally stopped gagging enough to talk, I said, "So does this mean the Lord don't want me to smoke?"

Les laughed. "Not at all, missy. He just thinks you need more practice."

Morgan was a town built by coal money. It was not owned by a coal company, but all the coal companies in Kentucky— Bartlett, White Diamond, Double H and Argon—were the reason Morgan thrived. Morgan was where the company owners, managers and clerks did their shopping and where the miners and their families, who were not so stubborn as to think they had everything they needed right there in the coal camp, came to have a little fun.

It was a small town, Main Street was the street, but to my fifteen-year-old eyes, it looked very grand. The marquee of the Hippodrome theater was alight with glowing yellow bulbs. It was so beautiful that I didn't even care that the movie they were showing was a Western. (Even to this day, if a movie doesn't have pretty women in pretty clothes in it, I don't care to see it.) Goldstein's Department Store was right next to the Hippodrome, and its big window was full of mannequins wearing the stylish kinds of dresses that Miss Taylor used to wear. Next to Goldstein's was the City Drug, with a sign reading 'Soda Fountain' illustrated with a painting of an ice cream sundae.

The sidewalks were packed with people, most of them better

dressed and better fed than the folks I was used to seeing in Bartlett. They smiled as they strolled their way toward a new dress at Goldstein's or a milkshake at the City Drug.

Les drove us past Needham's Grocery and the Dixie Diner and found a place to park near Dabney's Hardware. We got out of the car, and a paunchy, middle-aged man waved from inside the hardware store as he put up the 'Closed' sign.

"I ain't never been to a poker game before," I said.

"And you ain't going to one now," Les said. He reached into his pocket and pulled out a roll of bills held together with a rubber band. He peeled off three ones and handed them to me.

Mother always sent me to the company store with scrip, so I wasn't used to handling paper money. "Les, I can't take all this money from you."

"Three dollars ain't nothin'," Les said, "especially if this poker game turns out like it ort to." He looked across the street, where the red brick courthouse stood. "You see that clock over there?"

I looked at the clock tower and nodded, crumpling up the three one-dollar bills in my hand. It was right at seven o' clock.

"When that clock says nine, you're gonna be waiting for me at the car. You have fun now. Go buy you a root beer float or somethin"

I was out for the evening, free of my usual humdrum life, but with an eye on the clock. I would've felt like Cinderella, if anybody had ever told me that story.

The first place I went was Goldstein's Department Store. I knew my three dollars probably wouldn't buy anything there except maybe some socks or drawers, but I longed to look at the dresses. Now I know that Goldstein's was probably pretty close to a place like J.C. Penney's in quality, but at the time it seemed so elegant that I was shaking when I walked in the door. I was sure that somebody would see me and tell me to go back to the coal camp where I came from. Nobody did, though.

As I looked at each dress in ladies' apparel, sometimes sucking in my breath at the beauty of a canary yellow shirtwaist or an emerald green sheath, a girl who wasn't much older than I was said, "May I help you, miss?"

I surveyed her beauty-shop curls, pink lipstick and chic

summer suit. She was smiling at me, but I still felt her judging eyes roam over my long, untamed hair, my homemade dress and my clodhopper shoes.

"No," I said, too sharply, and walked out of the store so fast she probably thought I had been trying to steal something.

The City Drug was less frightening. It was crawling with boys and girls about my age, most of them crowding around the counter of the soda fountain. I squeezed the three dollar bills in my hand and walked up the aisles, past shelves of aspirin and razor blades and soap and shampoo. When I got to the cosmetics section, I stopped dead.

At the company store, they sold loose face powder and bobby pins, but that was as far as the Bartlett Coal Company went in catering to women's vanity. The City Drug, though, could've been renamed Vanity Fair. Lipsticks from kitten-nose pink to brazen red, mirrored compacts filled with pressed powder and soft puffs, pots of rosy rouge, eye pencils and eyeshadows, glass bottles filled with clear and rose and red nail polish, their exotic names called out to me in a sultry whisper: Maybelline. Max Factor. Winx. The tubes and pots and pencils talked to me of transformation, promising me I could paint bright colors on my outside to match the bright colors that flamed inside me.

I knew it made me a bad person, and I knew if there was a hell I'd burn in it, but still...the sight of those powders and pencils and paint moved me more than the thought of Jesus ever had. I could never have been a missionary, mud-covered and slogging through the bug-infested jungle. I was in love with glamour.

It only took a second to pick out which shade of pressed powder was closest to my skin tone, but I probably took thirty minutes picking out my lipstick. They had the shade of rose Miss Taylor had worn, and a month before, that would've been my choice. But now I wanted to find my own shade—something that went with my hair and eyes but also said something about who I was.

And who was I? If I had known the answer to that question, it probably wouldn't have taken me a half an hour to pick out a damned lipstick. All I knew was that I wasn't like Miss Taylor or Mother or Myrtle, and I wasn't going to spend my life sweeping up coal dust. Finally, I chose a color called Cherries Jubilee because it was darker and bolder than anything Miss Taylor or any woman in the coal camp would wear. It wasn't quite a true red, which was the color I was most drawn to, but I decided to stop just this side of brazen.

The woman I paid for my purchases didn't put on the brakes on the right side of brazen. Her hair was a blatant bottle blond, her lips were brightest red, and her eyelids were a shocking blue. I know my mother would've thought she looked like the Whore of Babylon, but to me she was pretty. Her long nails were as red as her lips, and I promised myself that I'd let my nails grow long and buy a bottle of polish to celebrate. When she bagged my purchases she said, "Does your Mama know you're buying lipstick that dark?"

"No, ma'am," I said, irrationally afraid she would look up my mother and tell her.

She smiled, her teeth yellow against the red of her lips. "Well, I reckon what she don't know won't hurt her none."

Clutching my tiny bag of cosmetics, I wandered over to the soda fountain. I had enough money left for a sundae or float, but I ordered a cherry Coke instead, figuring I'd save the little bit of change I got back to buy another lipstick or some nail polish. I hadn't even tried out my new purchases, and I was already an addict.

I sat at the counter and sipped my cherry Coke, which was damned good, and looked at the soda fountain customers. A miner and his family sat at one table. I could tell the man was a miner because his fingernails were black underneath just like Daddy's. He sat in his clean overalls next to his long-faced wife who was wearing what was probably her best dress even though it was pretty sorry-looking. Their two kids were with them, a little boy about ten, wearing overalls like his daddy, and a pimply-faced girl about my age, whose homemade dress was made from the same pattern as mine.

The family ate their spoonfuls of ice cream solemnly, as if it was medicine. They were enjoying it, though. I knew by looking at them that those hot fudge sundaes were the best things they'd put in their mouths all week, but they weren't going to let the town people see their pleasure. Too much visible joy over the ice cream would tell the town people what a rare treat it was and serve as evidence of the family's poverty. I knew that fact all too well, as I sat sipping my cherry Coke indifferently, as if it was the third one I'd had that day.

The miner's family's table was silent, but the table next to it was raucously loud. Four teenagers hunched over it, two girls and two boys, probably on a double date. The girls wore the skirts and bobby socks that were fashionable at that time, and the boys wore stiff new high school letter sweaters. They laughed and joked about people they knew from school, not noticing the miner's family or anybody else. As far as they were concerned, the place belonged to them.

Part of me wanted to be one of those giggling, stylish girls, but another part of me hated them like poison. Their faces were as wide and innocent as babies, babies whose every whimper is cut short by the attentions of a devoted mother. Those girls had always had everything they wanted, and I simultaneously wanted what they had and hated them for having it. I knew that even if I found a way to get some of the comforts those girls were used to, I still wouldn't be like them. Unlike a person who is born into money, I would never have the ultimate luxury, the luxury to take all my comforts and pleasures for granted. Like the miner's family at the nearby table, I would always know just how good a hot fudge sundae tastes when you've eaten nothing all week but beans and cornbread.

Fortunately, I was too happy to waste much time on envy. I finished my Coke and walked down Main Street, soaking up the lights and colors. There wasn't time to catch the next show at the Hippodrome, but I studied the movie posters carefully and decided that with my new lipstick and my hair twisted up, I could look like a prettier Dolores Del Rio.

I was at Les's car at nine o'clock as instructed, and he came running out of the hardware store so fast you would've thought he'd just robbed it. This impression was not contradicted by the brown paper bag he threw into my lap.

"Count that," he said.

I looked in the bag and saw that it held piles of one and five-dollar bills, with the occasional ten thrown in. "Good God a-mighty, Les!" I gasped. "Did you win this?"

"Yes, ma'am!" he said. "And I done it by staying sober. All them fellers was passing around a bottle of whiskey, but I didn't take nary a sip of it. A man ort not to drink when he's gambling... makes him muzzy-headed. You count that now."

I counted up the bills. I'd never had my hands on so much money. "I got one hundred and seventeen dollars. Does that sound right?"

Les cackled. "Right as rain. I'll tell you what, missy. You take you one of them five-dollar bills outta there. You can buy yourself somethin' pretty when we come to town next week."

I didn't know what to respond to first, the five dollars or the invitation. "You...you want me to come back with you next week?"

"Damn straight I do. I just won me the most money I've ever got at that poker game. The way I figure it, you're my good-luck charm."

In the role of Les's good-luck charm, I rode with him every Saturday night. We always left Bartlett around six o'clock, letting my parents think that I was going to the church social while Les went to see some girl he was sweet on. I was always back home and in bed by ten. That time, however, between six and ten on Saturday nights, I lived for those four hours all week long.

Town was changing me. I studied the stylish Morgan High School girls. I knew I had more natural beauty than any of them, but they had the money to buy things to fix themselves up with, so they still had the advantage over me. I don't care what those bare-faced feminists say; even if you do have natural beauty, it still needs to be helped along. I did the best I could with what I had, saving my powder and lipstick for Saturdays and putting them on in the car so Mother and Daddy wouldn't know I was. 'Painting' nail polish, I decided, would be too hard to hide, but I did let my nails grow, and I bought a file to shape them.

One Saturday, walking down a side street in Morgan, I saw a shop window with 'Louise's Beauty Shop' painted on it in flowery pink cursive. I had heard of beauty shops but had never seen one. When the women in Bartlett needed a haircut, they did it themselves, and by God, their lack of experience showed. At best, the poor things wore their hair chopped off to an approximately even length. At worst they walked around looking like they'd stuck their heads in an oscillating fan.

The women in Morgan, though, wore their hair in soft layers and curls like the models in the magazines I pored over in the City Drug. There was no question that my hair, which hung heavy down my back, was beautiful. But I also knew that it was country-girl hair, merely naturally beautiful.

I had no idea how much a haircut cost, but I knew I needed one. Then I saw the other sign on Louise's Beauty Shop window, the one that said 'Closed.' I could see a girl inside sweeping up, so I knocked at the door. She looked up from her sweeping and pointed at the 'Closed' sign, but I kept right on knocking. Finally, she rolled her eyes, propped her broom against the sink and opened the door. "What is it?" she said, out of patience with me before I had even said a word.

I tried to turn on the charm. "Are you Louise?"

To my surprise, she laughed. And once I got a look at her, I could see why. She was wearing a sophisticated periwinkle blue summer suit and high heels, and her hair was swept up in a little pouf on top of her head, but for all this adult elegance, she wasn't much older than I was. "Lord, no," she finally said. "Louise is my aunt. She pays me to clean up the place after she closes."

I couldn't hide my disappointment. "So you ain't a beautician?"

"No." She let herself smile a little. "I might be when I finish high school, though. If I don't get married first."

I know your kind, I thought. Another one of the zillions of women who would spend over half their lives cooking for and cleaning up after some man. "Well, I was hopin' you was a beautician because I need to get my hair cut."

"Well, Louise'll open back up on Monday morning."

"I won't be here Monday. I'm from...out of town." Suddenly my long country-girl hair was weighing me down so much it felt like it would snap my neck. An idea popped into my head. "Say... what's your name anyway?"

"Susie," she said like she couldn't figure out why I was still talking to her.

"All right, Susie. I know you ain't a real beautician nor nothin', but do you know how to cut hair?"

She grinned. "Well, sure. Aunt Louise has been teaching me. She just won't let me work on customers, 'cause I don't have my beautician's license yet."

I reached into the front of my dress and pulled out the five-dollar bill Les always gave me as my cut of his poker winnings. Five dollars was way more than a haircut in a hick town beauty shop cost back then, but I didn't know that. Hell, back then I didn't even know that Morgan was a hick town. "Look, Susie," I said, "if I give you this here five-dollar bill, will you give me a real fashionable haircut like you see in the movie magazines?"

"Gosh, I don't know," she said, but her eyes stayed on the money. "Aunt Louise'd kill me if she found out."

Grinning, I held out the bill. "Then let's not tell her."

Within seconds I was lying back in a beautician's chair feeling like a queen with Susie massaging shampoo into my scalp. When I sat back up, she brushed my hair out to its full length, which, given that it had never been cut except for a quick snip on the ends with Mother's sewing scissors, was pretty impressive.

"Look at that." Susie sighed. "Virgin hair."

"What did you just say?" I was pretty sure Susie was getting more personal than I was comfortable with.

She just laughed. "Your hair...it's what Aunt Louise calls virgin hair. It's never been dyed, it's never been processed, it's never even been layered. You don't hardly see hair this pure these days. Wigmakers pay top dollar for it."

"Virgin hair, huh?" For the last time, I ran my hand down the length of my natural tresses. "Well, I reckon it's time my hair lost its innocence."

Susie laughed and picked up the scissors, but when she got them near my head, she turned serious. "Are you sure you want to do this?"

"If you don't go ahead and do it, I'm gonna grab them scissors and do it myself."

"Okay, here we go." Susie sighed and made the first cut.

She gave me bangs that brushed my eyebrows and cut the rest so it fell in soft waves just below my shoulders. I was astonished by my reflection in the mirror. I might not have become a woman just because my hair had lost its virginity, but I sure looked like one.

"Well, look at you," Susie said, smiling. "I might just be a beautician after all. You want me to tie up the hair I cut off in a ribbon so you can keep it?"

As I shook my head no, I felt the lightness of my shorter hair. It felt like freedom, and I was happy to leave those long, country-girl locks on the floor for her to sweep up. I've never been the kind of person who makes a change and then gets all sentimental about how things used to be.

Mother and Daddy each acted just the opposite to the way I thought they would when they saw me. Daddy said I looked like a harlot, which probably shouldn't have surprised me. He'd been awfully hard on me since I started looking like a woman, but I still sometimes expected him to be the devoted daddy he was when I was a little girl. Mother, though, said I was getting to be the age where it was natural for me to worry over my hair and clothes. She even told me I could buy dress patterns for my school clothes in Morgan instead of Bartlett, so I'd look more up-to-date. She didn't care how I looked, she said, as long as I wasn't boy crazy.

And I wasn't. I noticed the girls in Morgan, and what they were wearing and how they were fixing their hair, but I never gave boys there so much as a glance. A boy was the last thing I wanted. The first thing I wanted was to pass as a town girl instead of a rube.

My trips to Morgan were changing me on the outside, but they were changing me on the inside, too. As I watched the movies at the Hippodrome with heroines who were nightclub singers or newspaper reporters or glamorous socialites, as I sneaked and read the paperback novels on the racks at the City Drug, I was discovering that the world and its opportunities were big beyond my imagining. I was too ignorant to realize that movies and cheap paperbacks might offer an overly romantic view of the world. I bought the fairy tales those books and movies were selling, and in them, I started to discover a word I had heard about but had never known the meaning of: joy.

It was joy I felt as I sat in the darkness of the Hippodrome, joy as I leafed through the movie magazines and sampled the lipstick at the drugstore, joy as I watched Morgan's streetlights flick on at dusk. I was an innocent, joyful girl, and I had no idea that even as I flitted from place to place in Morgan like a moth fluttering from light to light, I was being watched.

CHAPTER 5

He first approached me at the soda fountain. I was sitting at the counter, sipping on a cherry Coke and writing a letter to C.R. C.R. had never written a full letter home, but every week or two we'd get a postcard with phrases scrawled in pencil. His first card from the army base had read: "Arrived at base yester. Nice fellers. Bad food. C.R." When he went overseas, his postcards were like horrifying snapshots taken by a photographer on the front lines: "Them Japs is mean. Saw a guy shot today just wounded tho. Don't worry, Mommy. C.R."

I figured C.R. didn't write real letters because he was too busy fighting a war, but I had no excuse not to write him some. So every Saturday night since C.R. had arrived overseas, I had taken to spending fifteen minutes at the counter of the soda fountain writing to my brother. Mother and Myrtle sent him packages once a month, which were usually filled with socks. Apparently, they considered warm socks essential to fighting a war, but I figured C.R. might appreciate a weekly letter more than a box full of socks. Socks can't keep you company the way a letter can. Les always attached a P.S. to my letter, usually something touching like 'Don't get your ass shot off now. Your buddy, Les,' and we'd mail the letter on the way out of Morgan on the theory that letters mailed from town would reach C.R. sooner than ones mailed from the coal camp.

So there I was, filling up a page with chitchat about my days at Deer Creek High School (which, disappointingly, was just a big country school in the middle of a field, populated by miners' and farmers' kids), when a soft male voice said, "Excuse me?"

The only time I'd heard someone say "excuse me" was when

they burped, so I looked up and said, "Oh, that's all right. I didn't even hear you."

The tall, thin young man had hair as dark as mine and dark eyes that seemed to want to look at everything in the room except me. "Uh," he stammered, "you didn't hear me? I just said, 'excuse me.'"

"Oh," I said, honestly having no idea why this nervous person was making the effort to speak to me. "I heard you say 'excuse me'; I just didn't hear you burp."

He looked confused for a second, then his lips spread into a smile. His teeth were very white compared to the tobacco-stained choppers of the young men in Bartlett. "Oh," he said, laughing. "Oh. No, I didn't burp. I was trying to find a polite way to get your attention."

He didn't talk like anybody else around there. Like Miss Taylor, he didn't seem to have an accent of any kind. Also, unlike the miners in their overalls and the schoolboys in their letter sweaters, he wore a dark suit and tie. I looked him up and down. He had on the shiniest shoes I had ever seen. "Well," I said, "I reckon you have it."

His forehead wrinkled in confusion, but he was still smiling. "Uh...what is it I have?"

I smiled back. "My attention."

"Oh...well...in that case...I've seen you around...in my store once and here several times, and I was wondering..."

I don't usually interrupt people, but the wheels in my mind were turning so fast that my mouth flew open. "Your store? What store is that?"

"Goldstein's Department Store. It's my father's store, really, but I'm the manager." He reached out a slender, long-fingered hand. "I'm David Goldstein."

I took his soft hand; apparently, managing a department store wasn't hard enough work to make calluses. "Vestal Jenkins. A pleasure to meet you."

"The pleasure's all mine," David said. A couple of weeks before, I had heard a handsome actor in a movie say that when he met the leading lady; I figured David had seen that movie, too. "Say, uh...if you'd care to join me, I'd be happy to treat you to anything you'd like."

I moved to the table and scanned over the menu board that hung above the counter. The banana split was the most expensive thing on the menu, so I decided I'd ask for that. If he balked, I figured he wasn't worth my time.

He didn't balk. And I wish I could say I was as subtle as that miner's family in enjoying my treat, but oh, when the first bite of banana and vanilla ice cream drenched in chocolate syrup touched my tongue, it was so good I closed my eyes so I could shut out the world and do nothing but taste.

Of course, the ice cream wasn't the only sweet thing at the table. I can't say that David made my insides shiver and my heart go pitapat, because there's only one person in my life who ever had that effect on me and we're not to that part of the story yet, but he was sweet. He looked at me like I was an angel who just fell down from heaven. And I liked that.

"So," I said, since he seemed to be so busy watching the ice cream spoon disappear between my lips that he forgot to strike up a conversation, "you don't talk like you're from around here."

"Hm? Oh!" he said, like I had just startled him out of a dream. "No, I'm from Kentucky, but I'm not from around here. I grew up in Louisville, which, as you can imagine, is pretty different from a little town like Morgan."

"Yeah," I said, but of course I couldn't imagine what a place as big as Louisville was like. "So how come you decided to move to a place like this?" I sucked off some chocolate that was stuck to my spoon, and David watched me.

He smiled sheepishly. "I guess my pop decided for me. See, Pop worked in a big department store in Louisville for years, but he worked himself as high in the company as he could go. He was the manager of haberdashery, which was fine, but he had always wanted to own his own store. He figured the only way he could make his dream come true was to open up a store in a small town because there's too much competition in the city. So after the Depression lifted, he and Mom sold our house in Louisville and moved down here. They used up every penny of their savings to open up the store."

I pushed my empty ice cream dish away. "And you moved

down here with 'em?"

"Not then. I lived with my aunt and uncle in Louisville while I finished high school. Then I started classes at Kentucky College of Business. I went there for two years, and after I graduated, Pop told me if I'd move to Morgan he'd make me the manager of the store. How many fellas get to be store managers before their twenty-first birthday?" he said. "And so I came down here to help run the store. Which, Pop is always reminding me, will belong to me after he's gone."

I didn't say anything. I had a hard enough time being able to imagine owning a dress from Goldstein's, let alone owning the whole store.

"I'm sorry," David said. "I don't know why I'm telling you all this business stuff. You couldn't possibly find it interesting, heck, I don't even find it interesting. It's just that right now, it seems like all I do is work, so work is all I have to talk about. Why don't you talk to me instead? Tell me what you like, what you like to talk about."

I dabbed my mouth with a paper napkin, a little self-conscious that all my lipstick was probably gone. "Oh, I found what you was...what you were saying very interesting," I said, smiling. "Tell me what it was like living in Louisville."

Part of the reason I answered him that way is because I really did want to know what it was like living in Louisville, a big city I'd only vaguely heard of. But there was more to my evasiveness than that. I didn't want him to know I was just in my first year of high school, since my overripe curves had probably led him to believe I was older. And even more than that, I didn't want him to know I was some ignorant girl who lived in a coal camp.

The skirt and blouse I had on were from a pattern I had picked up at the Morgan five-and-dime. I had two other decent-looking outfits at home that Mother had sewed for me to wear to school. My scuffed, too-tight shoes were a dead giveaway to my poverty, but they were hidden under the table.

Actually, I think David liked me more because I didn't give him a straight answer when he asked me to tell him about myself. Men are like that. They don't like a woman who reveals too much of herself. A woman who knows how to make a man adore her is like the Hippodrome Theater, some glamour and bright lights to attract them on the outside, then once they get in the door, all they see is a blank screen on which they can project their fantasies.

That's how it's always been with me and men. I start out as the blank screen until I figure out what their fantasy is. Once I've figured out the fantasy, I seem to become it. And the way most men deal with women, 'seeming' is enough. They don't know that all they're seeing is the light show of their fantasies being played out on the blank screen that separates them from my real personality. They never get to see what's behind the screen.

When it was almost time for me to meet Les, David escorted me out of the drugstore and onto the sidewalk.

"I like you, Vestal," he said, as we stood outside the door. "And I'd like to see you again, if that would be all right with you."

I looked down at his clean fingernails and thought of the racks of beautiful dresses in his daddy's department store. "It's all right with me."

His face lit up like the Fourth of July. "When, then? Tomorrow?"

He couldn't very well drive up to Bartlett and pick me up. He'd see where I lived, for one thing, and then there was my mother's warning about not going boy crazy. "Well, see...I live... out of town. The only time I come here is Saturday nights. A friend of my brother's brings me."

"Is he your boyfriend?"

"Lord, no." I laughed. "Les is like a second brother to me. Besides, he's too old for me anyhow." Of course, right after that was out of my mouth, it occurred to me that Les was a year younger than David.

"Well, why don't we meet at the Dixie Diner a week from now...around seven?"

"All right."

David's face got all serious. "Vestal, would it change your mind about going out with me if I told you I was Jewish?"

"Told me you was what-ish?"

"Jewish. Goldstein, it's a Jewish name. I'm not that religious or anything, but in terms of who my people are, I'm a Jew."

An old couple walking down the sidewalk turned to look at him.

I'd never met anybody Jewish before, but I didn't see why it should be a problem. The Bible was full of them, after all. "A Jew, huh?" I said. "Wasn't Moses one of them?"

David raised up his eyebrows and said, "Yes. He was."

"Well," I said, "Moses was a right nice feller. I reckon I would've gone out for a hamburger with him if he was to ask me."

David grinned, then laughed. "Saturday at seven, then?"

"I'll be there."

So Saturday nights I started spending with David. We ate hamburgers at the Dixie Diner and saw movies at the Hippodrome.

The movies were my great love. I'd sit there, my eyes fixed on the screen, and in my mind I was at the same glamorous supper club where the actor and actress were ignoring the lobster and champagne in front of them and staring into each other's eyes. Sometimes while I was watching I'd feel somebody's eyes on me. I'd look over to discover that David was watching me instead of the movie.

Sometimes when David and I were out together I thought people might have looked at us unkindly, but nobody ever went so far as to say anything to us, probably because David's family was rich, and I wasn't from Morgan so nobody knew me. Mostly, though, I didn't notice if we got looked at funny because when I was with David, I was happy. That makes me sound romantic, I know, like I was head over heels in love with him. I wasn't. I liked him well enough, though, and he adored me, and feeling his adoration made me happy.

One night late in the fall, driving back to Bartlett, Les said, "A feller at the game tonight told me you was running around with that Jewboy whose daddy runs the department store."

I was a little afraid of what Les might say next, that he might say he wasn't going to drive me to Bartlett anymore, but I acted brave, anyway. "What if I am?"

"Well, I ain't got no quarrel with it," Les said. "They say the Jews was the ones that killed Jesus, but I don't reckon your little friend was the one that nailed him. Is he a nice feller?"

"Yes."

"He ever try any funny business?"

Assuming 'funny business' meant physical contact beyond holding hands, I said, "No." Unlike the supposedly morally upright Reverend Moore, David's hands had never tried to explore uncharted territories of my anatomy.

"Well, I reckon there ain't no harm in it, then. 'Course, if I was you, I don't believe I'd go around Bartlett telling everybody I had a Hebe for a feller."

"I won't say a word if you won't."

Les cackled. "You ain't got nothin' to worry about there, missy. I don't tell folks nothin' but what they want to hear."

Les's statement was the whole truth. He was a pleasant fellow to be around, and everybody in Bartlett, even the folks he had won a lot of money off of, liked him. Les always made friendly conversation, but he never said anything revealing about anybody else or himself. Nobody, not even C.R., who was supposedly his best friend, knew anything about the whereabouts or character of Les's family or anything about Les's likes and interests beyond his obvious one in making money.

Mother was a casualty of World War II. Ever since C.R. had left home, she had been one of the walking wounded. She cooked and cleaned in silence and never said a word to Myrtle and me but "hush" when we got too loud. She didn't say much to Daddy either. Sometimes, at night, lying in the iron bed I shared with Myrtle, I could hear Mother crying.

Deer Creek High, which was packed to the gills with kids who were even bigger hicks than I was, had been a disappointment, but even so, I looked forward to getting on the bus because home was unbearable. Mother pined away for her precious baby boy, and while I got sick of her showing us that C.R. was the only child she loved, I missed him, too, and worried about him now that he was actually fighting the war. C.R. was the only member of my family who could always make me smile, and the house was a sadder place without him in it.

Lately, too, the house was a sadder place with Myrtle in it.

At the age of eleven and a half, Myrtle had found all the religion I'd lost.

I've never been one to believe that there's a place in the afterlife where you're punished for all the mistakes you made. It seems like there's no need for such a place because most of the time you reap what you sow and get your comeuppance right here on earth. My punishment for driving everybody crazy with missionary talk the year before was having to put up with Myrtle's newfound religious devotion, which was a hundred times worse than mine had ever been.

My godly phase had been about loving Miss Taylor, wanting to be like her, and most of all, wanting to get out of Bartlett. Myrtle was different; she bought the Father, Son and the Holy Ghost hook, line and sinker. I figured since Myrtle had never been either Mother or Daddy's favorite, she figured that if she played her cards right, she could be God's favorite. At the rate she was running, she was going to be the world's first Baptist nun.

One Saturday afternoon, I was sitting on the porch swing wrapped up in a quilt. Everybody thought I was crazy for sitting out on the porch in the cold, but I liked the nip of the fresh air better than the stale air of the house. I was immersed in what had become my new Bible, The Tinseltown Tattler, which was packed full of news about all the Hollywood stars: what they were wearing, where they were going, who they were dating. This particular magazine had been a gift from David, who had taken to showing up for our dates bearing gifts (usually movie magazines or candy), a habit I highly approved of.

I was just reading about Rita Hayworth dancing the night away at the Coconut Grove, wearing her shimmering silver gown without nylons to show her support for the war effort, when Myrtle plopped down beside me on the swing.

"That magazine's of the devil," she said with her typical charm.

"This magazine ain't got nothin' to do with God or the devil either one, and right now, I ain't got nothin' to do with you." I kept reading about how the champagne at the Coconut Grove 'flowed like water.'

"Well, if it ain't got nothin' to do with God, then you can bet it's got somethin' to do with the devil."

I was beginning to wonder if the preacher who baptized Myrtle had held her under too long. "Myrtle, is there some reason you come out here, other than to pester me?"

Myrtle smiled and folded her hands in her lap, nice as pie, which always meant she wanted something. "Is Les coming to take you to church this evenin'?" Her voice was so syrupy you could practically see the flies gathering around her.

"He always does."

"I was just thinking that maybe I could go with you'uns."

It's a wonder she hadn't asked before then, and I should've seen it coming, but even so, my heart just about blew to smithereens at the thought of Myrtle finding out that there was no Saturday night youth service at the Morgan Main Street Baptist Church, and that the real reason I had been going to Morgan every Saturday night was so Les could play poker and I could hold hands with a Jew.

"They...they won't let you go to the youth service." My mind was moving at top speed. "It's just for teenagers. You've got to be thirteen to get in the door."

"Now, how are they gonna know I ain't thirteen?"

"Because your chest's as flat as an ironing board, for one thing. Besides, even if you did go and they let you in, you'd be lying—you'd be saying 'I am thirteen' just by being there. And you know what the Bible says about bearing false witness."

Myrtle sat for a moment, letting her lips draw into a thin, tight little line, then she narrowed her eyes at me. "You know what I think? I think there ain't no Saturday night church service, and even if there is, I don't think you've been going to it. I think you and Les is up to somethin'!"

"And what, pray tell, do you think we're up to?"

"Somethin' sneaky," Myrtle said. "Somethin' sinful."

I had just raised my hand to slap her self-righteous little face when a male voice said, "Excuse me?" For one crazy moment I thought it might be David, even though he had no idea where I lived, but when I looked around I saw it was a boy not much older than me.

"I have a telegram for Mrs. Zed Jenkins," he said, sounding a little nervous.

"I'll get her!" Myrtle hopped up off the porch swing and ran into the house, probably to get away from me before I could hit her.

I stood up, waiting for Mother to come outside, knowing the news in the telegram was about C.R. and fearing what it might be.

Mother walked out onto the porch, took the telegram in her shaking hand and then, to my surprise, handed it to me. "I can't read it," she said. "I'm all to pieces."

I was all to pieces, too, knowing the main reason that soldiers' families received telegrams during wartime, but I also figured that knowing is always better than not knowing. I looked down and read aloud:

SHOT IN SHOULDER STOP
AM OKAY STOP
HOME IN TWO WEEKS STOP

Myrtle and I, who had been on the verge of blows mere seconds before, hugged each other in relief that our brother was wounded but alive. Mother, who had never been a hugger, hugged Myrtle, hugged me, and then hugged the telegram boy for good measure.

CHAPTER 6

"You're all smiles tonight," David said, sliding into the red vinyl seat across from me at the Dixie Diner. "You're beautiful."

I looked down at the table, blushing. I could still blush back then. "C.R.'s coming home. He got shot in the shoulder, but he's all right."

"He's lucky. The only way a lot of guys get home is in a box." He shuddered like it was cold. "I don't like to talk about the war. I hear enough about it at home. You should hear Mom talking about what's going on in Germany. She comes up with all these crazy stories about Hitler and the horrible things he's supposed to be doing to the Jews. I think she's just letting her imagination run wild with some of that stuff. Nobody could really be as crazy as she makes that guy out to be."

I didn't know much about what was going on in Morgan County, let alone Germany, but I still said, "There's some crazy people in this world." I guess I've always taken kind of a dark view of humanity.

The waitress came and David ordered two hamburgers and a milkshake for me and a Coke for him. He'd never drink a milkshake with his hamburger on account of Jews not liking to mix meat and milk. He may not have been that religious, but some of the rules he'd learned as a kid still stuck.

After the waitress left, he looked me straight in the eye and said, "Vestal, I've been thinking…" And then he trailed off. He always lost his train of thought when he looked straight at me like that.

"Mm-hm?" I prompted him, looking back into his dark, serious eyes. He had to break my gaze before he could talk again. "I've been…uh…thinking it might be time for you to meet my family."

I was already overexcited at the thought of C.R. coming home, but when David said that, my belly did backflips. I felt flattered because he thought I was worthy to meet his folks and guilty because here he was wanting to introduce me to his mother and daddy when he barely knew me himself. "David...there's some things you need to know before you decide to introduce me to your mother and daddy."

"I've already decided."

"Well," I said, "I'm giving you the chance to change your mind."

The waitress set our food down in front of us, and we both stared at it like we didn't know what it was for.

"Are you going to tell me you've killed a dozen people and thrown their bodies down mine shafts all over southeastern Kentucky?"

"No." I grinned. "I ain't killed but half a dozen people."

"Well, then, I'm not going to change my mind, but go ahead and say what you have to say."

"All right." I was trying to decide where to start. "Well, first of all, my family ain't got much money." I had already worn each of my three good outfits three times, so I guessed he had already figured that one out.

"So? What do I want with money? I've got plenty."

"And my family, David...I ain't even met your family yet, but I know mine ain't a bit like yours. My daddy's a coal miner, and we live in the Bartlett camp up on the side of a mountain way out in the country. Except for C.R., there ain't a person in my family that's been outside of Morgan County."

"I don't care about your family, Vestal. I care about you." His brown eyes were as devoted as a hound dog's.

"But you don't hardly know a thing about me. You know how I told you I was still in school, but I was looking forward to graduation? Well, I am looking forward to graduation, but I won't be doing it for another three and a half years!"

"Is that all you wanted to tell me?"

I thought of other things I could tell him, how I hated Bartlett so much that sometimes I thought I'd do anything to get out of it, how my mother and my sister got on my nerves, how I didn't believe that Jesus was anybody special other than a regular nice person (though I don't guess that would've bothered him, being a Jew and all) but I decided I'd sprung enough on him for one night. "That's all."

"So would dinner at my parents' house next Saturday be all right?"

For a minute I was confused because 'dinner' meant what town folks call lunch at our house, and I couldn't figure out how I was going to get to Morgan in the middle of the day. But when I remembered from the movies that fancy people sometimes called supper 'dinner,' I said, "Dinner next Saturday sounds good."

We paid attention to our hamburgers for a minute, then David said, "You know the new movie at the Hippodrome is a Western, right?"

"Ugh." I stuck out my lip in a pout. "I don't understand why people around here like them things. Seems like after working some dull job all week, you'd want to look at somethin' prettier than dust and horses."

"I know I would," David said, looking at me. He seemed a little more sure of himself since I had agreed to meet his parents. "Listen, I was thinking, since you don't care for Westerns, maybe we could go for a drive instead of going to the movie."

However naive I was, I had sense enough to know that when a boy asks you to go for a drive, he's more interested in how far he can go with the car stopped than with the car moving.

"Oh, that's okay," I said. "We can go see the cowboy picture if you want to." Of course, I knew damned good and well that what he wanted to do in the dark wasn't to watch a movie. "I know how you fellers like to think of yourselves wearing them big hats and shooting them big guns."

"Not me," David said. "I have yet to see a Jewish cowboy. So how about it, Vestal? We could drive out to the lake. You've... you've never seen my car before."

It was true. And I bet his car was nicer than Les's. "They got ducks out at the lake?"

"Sure. I mean, I think they do."

I let him sweat it out for a few seconds, then said, "Well, I reckon we could go feed the ducks."

David's car was nicer than Les's. Much nicer—only a couple of years old, long, black and shiny, still with traces of that fresh store-bought smell that a clean, new car has.

The lake wasn't much more than a pond, really. There were ducks, though, and I fed them from a bag of hamburger buns David had bought at the Dixie Diner. I fussed over the ducks a long time, knowing David was getting more and more restless.

"You know what I love about ducks?" I said.

"No, what?" He was trying to sound interested, but I could tell he was distracted.

"When they're on the water, they're the gracefullest things alive, but on land, they move like they've been tacked together out of spare parts." I threw a wad of bread at a fat mallard, and he caught it in midair in his bill.

"Aren't you getting a little chilly, Vestal?"

"Lord, no. I like the cool air."

"Because if you are...I thought we could sit in the car."

"Oh, I'm fine." I was shaking crumbs out of the empty bag. "We should've brought more bread, though. These poor ducks is starving to death." Of course, the truth was, the things were so fat it was a wonder they didn't sink to the bottom of the lake.

"I just thought if we sat in the car, we'd have some privacy."

"What?" I laughed. "You got somethin' to say to me you don't want these ducks to hear?" Poor David. While I was enjoying torturing him, I was also starting to feel a little guilty, so I said, "Of course, I reckon it ain't safe for us to stand out here with this empty bread bag. The ducks is liable to eat us."

David hurried to the car, and I followed behind at a leisurely pace.

Once I was in the passenger seat beside him, David said, "You know, I had a few girlfriends back in Louisville. But there's never been a girl..." He got flustered, trailed off and banged his head against the steering wheel.

"Careful now. You're fixing to knock your brains out."

"I just...I can't find the words to say what I want to say." He took my hand and held it tight in both of his. "I think about you all the time, Vestal, and that's no exaggeration. I think about you when I'm supposed to be working, when I'm supposed to be listening to Pop...no matter what I'm doing, I'm thinking of you...of what you must be doing, of when we'll see each other again. At night, in bed, I think of you in bed, too, lying there, with that blue-black hair all spread out on your pillow..."

He reached out to stroke my hair and then leaned forward to kiss me. His kiss was completely different than those quick, close-lipped good-night kisses he had bestowed the past couple of times we'd gone out. His lips were open and locked to mine, and he wrapped his arms around me so I was pressed against him. My titties pressed against his chest, his tongue darted between my lips, and I felt a hard bump against my thigh that took me a second longer than it should have to identify.

At that time I didn't even have a name for that part of the male anatomy. I knew the doctor's term for it was 'penis' but that was a downright unfriendly-sounding word. I had heard some girls at school giggling about boys 'things,' but 'thing' was one of those words for something that's so polite that you don't know what the hell it means. One time when Daddy thought I wasn't listening, he told a dirty story to his friends where he called the male organ a 'jimdog' but that sounded like what a rube would call it. These three names were the only ones I knew, even though a few years later I could've probably filled up a whole book with the names I knew for it. But in the early days with David, I hadn't quite made the connection between dicks and my destiny.

In fact, as the part of David that at the time remained nameless poked against me, I was a little afraid. Living in a house without any doors that locked, more than once I had accidentally walked in on C.R. naked, his dick hanging limp and harmless as a just-wrung chicken neck. But David's was different, so hard that it was impossible to imagine it in a relaxed state, bigger than it seemed like it needed to be for where he wanted to put it. This dick wasn't anybody's old floppy chicken neck; it was a body part with an agenda. Which made me realize I'd better make sure to keep an agenda of my own.

I pulled back from his kiss and gently pushed David away. He was as sweaty and short of breath as if he'd just run a mile. I was amazed, to tell the truth. The kiss had been all right, but it hadn't had anything like that effect on me. It was just as well, I thought. Losing control was dangerous, it made you weak, and if one of us had to be weak, I was glad it was him and not me.

"Vestal," he breathed, then he started kissing my neck. It kind of tickled, but I was careful not to laugh.

While he kissed my neck, his hand, which had been around my waist, started to scoot up toward my right breast. Just before it reached its destination, I picked it up and gently placed it back at my waist. He kept it there, but leaned up to kiss my lips again.

After a few more minutes of kissing, he whispered, "Don't you think we'd be more comfortable in the backseat?" I pictured us in the backseat, me lying down, skirt pushed up, drawers pulled down. If I let him lose control and put it in me, it would be no surprise what the doctor would be pulling out of me nine months later.

"I'm fine where I am," I said.

"Oh—okay," David said. "Hey, I almost forgot. There's something for you in the glove box."

I opened the glove compartment and reached in to find a small box covered in red velvet. I took it out and petted it like a kitten. I had gotten presents before, a doll when I was little, new shoes at Christmas. But this was the first present I had gotten that looked like a present was supposed to look and that was given to me with the appropriate amount of ceremony. That's why they're called presents, you know, you're supposed to present them.

"Open it."

I lifted the lid off the box. Even in the dark, I could see it was a silver bracelet, made up of chunky little links, with a single heart-shaped charm dangling from it. I had never owned a piece of jewelry before, and I couldn't believe it was mine. "Oh, David…"

"Look at the heart. There's a little keyhole in it, see? That's because you have the key to my heart."

God love David. He could say crap like that and mean it. I knew I was supposed to say something mushy back, but all I could come up with was, "Help me put it on."

He hooked the bracelet around my left wrist, and I reached up with that hand to touch his cheek, and then kissed him on the lips, the first kiss I ever initiated. It turned out to be a long, wet kiss, and when David reached his hand up to try to cup my breast again, I did a quick count of, "one, two, three" in my head before I reached down and moved his hand away. I figured he ought to get a quick thrill since he had bought something nice for me. Tit for tat. Or something to that effect.

I let him kiss my neck some more, and he trailed kisses down the hollow of my throat to the point just above the top button of my scoop-necked blouse. When it seemed like he might be thinking about undoing that button, I whispered, "David?"

"Hm?" He didn't look up.

"What time is it?"

"Time?" he said, like it was a concept he was unfamiliar with. Then a light went on behind his eyes, and he checked his wristwatch. "Quarter till nine."

"Good God a-mighty!" I yelped, straightening up so suddenly that I knocked him backward. "You've got to take me downtown. I'll miss my ride."

"Are you sure you don't want to stay here with me a little bit longer? I could drive you home myself."

It sounded like a gentlemanly offer, but I knew if I stayed I'd be in danger of getting a different kind of ride than I'd get from Les. "Of course I'm sure. My daddy'll tan my hide if I'm not home by ten."

"Okay." David sighed. He gave me a long look and a longer kiss, made a few adjustments below his waist and started the car.

The game I learned to play with David was one I was good at. I was a natural, just like a boy who's never held a baseball bat before, but manages to hit a home run on the first try.

David's role in the game was to cautiously test the limits. If an open-mouthed kiss was okay, then was a hand on the knee also acceptable? How about the thigh? The breast? My job was to resist, just enough, to let him kiss me and touch me enough to titillate him, but not to do anything that would lead to the satisfaction of his desires.

These were the days when girls who gave boys what they so desperately wanted were considered not to be 'nice,' but my reputation wasn't what concerned me. I knew that if I let David do everything he wanted to do to me, then the spell would be broken, and I would never get another present from him again.

The secret I learned with David is one a lot of girls never learn. Some girls, and a lot of girls were like this when I was young, wouldn't let a boy touch them on the theory that boys only marry girls they respect. Of course, most of the time, the boyfriends of these girls got so frustrated they went hunting for the other type of girl, the kind who'd give it up on the first date sometimes even before the boy had the chance to buy them so much as a Coca-Cola. Both of these types end up losing their boyfriends before they'd gotten the good out of them, the good girl because she sent her man off for one too many cold showers, the so-called bad girl because she satisfied her man's desires...and curiosity...too soon.

Now me, I learned to split the difference. I say, in a strictly personal, non-business relationship, it's best to spend as many dates as you can giving the man just a taste of what he wants. It's the Baskin-Robbins principle. They give out those tiny little spoonfuls of ice cream for you to sample, and that little spoonful tastes so sweet that it makes you want to pay for the whole pint.

Later on, many people would say I was a cold-blooded golddigger for the way I treated David. But the way I saw it was this: he and I were using each other in a mutually beneficial way. I know David would have denied this and said he loved me, which he thought he did. But he didn't. David didn't know me well enough to love me. He may have loved the idea of me he had in his head, but would he have mooned over me if I had the exact same brains and personality but had been plug ugly? Of course not. He loved my looks just like I loved his car and the silver bracelet he bought me and all the other things he might buy me in the future.

I was poor but beautiful; he was rich but average-looking. We each had something the other person wanted, and it seemed like a fair trade to me.

That night, when I slid into the seat of Les's car, he fingered my new bracelet as he set his bag of newly won money on my lap. "Well, I'll be dogged, missy!" He cackled. "Looks like both of us done hit the jackpot tonight!"

CHAPTER 7

In the days since C.R.'s telegram, Mother had gone from being a zombie sleepwalking through her household duties to a housewife so happy she could've stepped out of a women's magazine, if only she'd had the nice house and nice clothes to match her mood. She spoke to Daddy, Myrtle and even me in a pleasant manner, and when she wasn't talking she was singing like she had more happiness in her than she could hold and she just had to let some of it out.

The funny thing about Mother was that even though she only sang when she was happy, the songs she sang were as depressing as all get-out. She knew all the murder ballads: the one about the girl who gets drowned by her boyfriend, the one about the silver dagger, and that real strange one about the girl who discovers her boyfriend is a cannibal. Mother may have sung out of joy, but what came out of her mouth was pure morbidity. I know she sang those terrifying songs to Myrtle when she was a baby, so I figure she must've rocked me to sleep on them, too. It's a wonder I didn't grow up to be a serial killer.

Daddy was happy, too, at the prospect of C.R.'s return, although he was a little worried that C.R.'s shoulder injury might impair his coal-mining abilities. Myrtle was deliriously happy because she believed that her prayers and love for Jesus were what was bringing C.R. home. I was happy C.R. was alive, but I wondered how he felt about coming back to Bartlett so soon after he'd left it. I hoped when I left, it would be more permanent.

Despite the cheerful mood of our house, I still felt suffocated sometimes. When it got really bad, I'd wait until Myrtle was asleep and reach under the mattress where I had hidden the silver bracelet David gave me. I would slip it from its hiding place and hold it up so that the moonlight from the window hit it. The silver chain gleamed with a promise I did not yet understand. All I knew was that it felt good to have a secret bracelet and a whole secret life outside of my family and outside of Bartlett.

One afternoon I was sitting on the porch wondering if David would present me with another piece of jewelry on Saturday. I wondered with what frequency a girl could expect jewelry. I figured two weeks in a row was too much to ask, but maybe if I put on a good show meeting his family, he might spring for something else shiny.

I was nervous about meeting his family, though, and wasn't sure my conduct with them could win me any prizes. Unlike David, they wouldn't ignore every ignorant thing that came out of my lips just because those lips happened to be full and kissable. Besides, I didn't know anything about Jewish people. What if there was some special set of rules you were supposed to follow in a room full of Jews, and nobody had ever told me about them?

I was swinging and worrying, swinging and worrying. I didn't even realize how hard I was swinging until Myrtle came out on the porch and said, "You trying to swing plumb up to heaven?"

I dragged my feet on the porch to slow down. "I guess I let my mind wander away from me."

"Where was it wandering to?"

There was no way I was going to tell her the truth, so I said, "Different places. I was thinking about C.R. and about...church." I figured if I said I was thinking about something godly, she'd leave me the hell alone.

"Well, if you think about church so much, then how come you don't come to church with me on a Sunday mornin'?"

"Because I'm too tired from going to church Saturday night." I thought about David and me in his parked car and figured that God must not listen to everything people say, or else he'd smite me for calling that 'church.'

"Well, I'm fixing to go to church right now. Why don't you come with me?"

"What kind of a holy-roller church do you go to on a Thursday night?"

"It's a tent revival out on the edge of the camp. They started it last night, and they're keeping it going through Sunday. Vestal, you should get a look at the young preacher they got. He's so... devoted."

Looking at Myrtle's shining eyes, I could tell she had a crush on this preacher boy. For some reason, I was kind of curious to get a look at him. Besides, it was either go to the tent revival or sit home reading the same movie magazines I'd already read umpty dozen times. "Yeah, all right, I'll go with you."

"You will?" Myrtle looked so happy that I started thinking, well, I am her older sister; she probably looks up to me. Maybe I should start paying more attention to her and, do things with her more. But then I remembered that our house was temporarily awash in love and goodwill because of C.R.'s return and that Myrtle was extra happy because this tent revival was feeding her religious mania. Despite the temporary shift in mood, Myrtle and I usually got along as well as a pair of wet fighting roosters.

I followed her off the porch. "Yeah, I'll go with you just this once. Don't get all excited thinking I'm gonna do stuff with you all the time."

Myrtle crossed her arms over her chest. "I'm not all excited about doing anything with you. I just thought hearing a real preacher might do you some good. I don't trust that church you've been going to over in Morgan; last night at the revival they was saying how them downtown Baptists ain't right with the Lord. I'm trying to save you, Vestal." Myrtle had that same misty look that Miss Taylor used to get.

"If you want to save somethin', try saving your breath."

We walked the rest of the way in sullen silence.

The white tent had been pitched on the edge of the woods. The wooden folding chairs underneath it were already filling up with women in flowered dresses and a few men in overalls, some of whom I recognized from Bartlett. The others must have come from the few other houses on the mountain. There was a nip in the air, and it occurred to me that late fall was a strange time for a tent revival. Usually, the traveling preachers just came around in the hot months, not when the nights were chilly and there was no use for the pasteboard fans decorated with blond-haired, blue-eyed Jesuses that helped cool off overheated worshippers.

Myrtle led me to the front row of chairs, and while I didn't much want to sit right in front of the pulpit, I sat anyway.

A little upright piano was set up in front to the left of the pulpit, and soon a pretty, chestnut-haired girl who had been sitting behind me walked up to the piano, sat down and started playing with gusto. It was the kind of song that I later came to refer to as 'jumping Jesus music,' with a fast, plinky piano tune and belted-out lyrics that seemed unnaturally concerned with Jesus's blood.

Soon everybody but me was singing, Myrtle and all the flowery dressed women and the men in overalls. I didn't know the words, although I did catch on to the chorus pretty fast, which was something like, "The blood, the blood, the blood, the blood—His precious blood is mine." It sounded like a hymn written by vampires.

After everybody got through the third chorus, the chestnut-haired girl hollered, "Clap your hands for the Lord!" She started playing louder and faster, and everybody started clapping along.

I heard a man behind me shout, "Praise God!" I turned my head for a second, and when I turned back, a young, sandy-haired man in the whitest suit I had ever seen stood before us, his arms stretched upward and outward in an arrogant gesture that was probably supposed to look humble.

"Oh, yes!" the man shouted over the piano and clapping. "Oh, yes! We are gathered here in the name of the Lord tonight!"

Several people said, "Amen."

"Yes, brothers and sisters, we are gathered in his name in the woods tonight, but since I don't know no songs about gathering in the woods, let's sing that song about gathering at the river...if you'll play it for me please, Sister Helen."

Sister Helen looked to be about the same age as the preacher, I wondered if she was his sister or even his wife. Or maybe they had the same kind of hog-rutting relationship as Reverend Moore and Miss Taylor. I stifled a giggle. Myrtle elbowed me in the ribs and whispered, "Sing."

I shot Myrtle a mean look but then moved my lips like I was singing. After we finished gathering at the river, the preacher hollered, "Brother Bobby is happy in the Lord tonight! They say Brother Bobby ain't supposed to be traveling around having tent revivals when it's getting cold outside, but Brother Bobby doesn't care what people say because Brother Bobby is happy in the Lord the whole year through!"

For a second I wondered who Brother Bobby was, but then I realized he was talking about himself.

I could see why Myrtle had it bad for Brother Bobby. He didn't do much for me, mind you, but since Myrtle went for the Godly type, I could understand why she would find his neat, sandy hair and zealous blue eyes striking. And even I was fascinated by the whiteness of his suit. Nothing in a coal camp was ever that white. No matter how much bluing you put in the wash water, white shirts and underwear always came out dingy with gray flecks of coal dust.

"Are y'all happy in the Lord tonight?" Brother Bobby shouted.

Several voices, my sister's included, said, "Amen" or "Praise God."

"Are you happy in the Lord tonight, Sister Helen?" Brother Bobby asked.

Sister Helen smiled. "I'm always happy in the Lord, Brother Bobby."

"Oh, wouldn't this world be a fine place to live if everybody was happy in the Lord? There'd be no more killing, no stealing, no gambling, no forn-i-catin', just everybody loving the Lord!"

There was a chorus of amens.

"And if you love the Lord, brothers and sisters, there ain't nothin' he won't do for you. If you give your heart and soul to Jesus, then he will bless you every day of your life. So if Jesus tells you to jump, what are you gonna do?"

"Jump!" Myrtle yelled, along with everybody else but me.

"Well, I don't see you jumping! I wanna see you jump. Jump for Jesus!"

Everybody got up and started jumping up and down like jackrabbits, fat old women with their big, heavy titties flopping up and down, old men in overalls solemnly hopping in place. I half-hearted bounced on the balls on my feet without leaving the ground, but Myrtle was jumping so high I thought she'd hit the roof of the tent. Brother Bobby was jumping, too, like he had springs in his shoes. Meanwhile Sister Helen had started up on the piano again, playing in time with everybody's jumping.

After a while Brother Bobby said, "And what are you gonna do if Jesus tells you to run?"

"Run!" Everybody but me yelled, and the younger folks started running laps around the tent.

"Go on now," Brother Bobby coached. "Don't you say, 'I can't run on accounta my body's too old and broke down to run. Jesus wants you to run, and He will give you the strength and the power to run!"

Soon just about everybody was up and running. The men who were coal miners could barely get their wind, and some of the ladies, who were clearly used to moving at a more leisurely pace, reminded me of cows when they try to run. I was debating whether I should run, too, since I was clearly younger and healthier than many of the people who were exerting themselves, when Brother Bobby started singing,

"I'm gonna jump up and down and run around
And give my heart to Je-sus.
Gonna jump up and down and run around
And give my heart to Je-sus,
Gonna jump up and down and run around
And give my heart to Je-sus,
Gonna give...my heart...to God."

I looked at Brother Bobby's flushed and sweating face; his eyes were so dilated there was only a slim ring of blue around the black pupils. When I looked around me, I saw everyone else was pretty much the same, faces flushed, eyes wide, bodies quivering. My little sister ran up to me and took my cool hands in her hot ones. "Can you feel it, Vestal?" she breathed. "Can you feel the power of the Lord?"

"Sure," I said, but I was lying. All that Jesus talk seemed to run through my soul like water through a sieve. Not for the last time, I wondered if I had the same feelings as normal people.

Of course, I may not have felt anything at that tent revival, but I sure as hell thought some things. Looking at my sister, flushed and breathless, then looking at the inflamed face of Brother Bobby as he started to shout out words that weren't even English...looking at the faces of those Jesus-happy people was just like looking at David's face a few nights before when he had kissed me long and hard and then pulled away, out of breath.

All of a sudden it seemed funny to me, how preachers are always going on about the sins of the flesh when what I was seeing in this tent wasn't much different than what David had been going after in the backseat of a car. Ecstasy.

There's two kinds of ecstasy to choose from: sexual ecstasy or religious ecstasy. People take sides on which one is better, and the ones who choose religion will call the ones who choose sex sinners. But really, there's no difference. Teenagers in a car and Christians in a tent are both after the same thing: that momentary wave of feeling that rushes over you and sweeps you away from your pitiful, everyday life—those few seconds when it's not just you, but you and the person you're touching awash in sex or you and the people around you awash in God.

But you know what? When you wake up the next morning, it'll be just you again. You in your little camp house in Bartlett, Kentucky, trying to think of one good reason why you should get out of the warm bed so you can do the same thing you did yesterday. Ecstasy doesn't last, and that's why I wanted no part of it. Girls who got caught up in sexual ecstasy found themselves trapped by pregnancy, and girls who got caught up in religion threw away their real lives to get ready for a perfect future life that might just be imaginary.

But not me. I wanted more from my life than the occasional rush of feeling. I wanted the good things in my life to be as real and solid as the weight of a silver charm bracelet in my hand.

I looked at the people dancing around me, jabbering and singing in a frenzy of religious delight, and in my mind I flashed forward to the following morning, when they'd rise early for another day of backbreaking labor. I prayed, not to Jesus, but to myself, that I would come to lead the kind of life I wouldn't long to escape from.

CHAPTER 8

The Saturday I was supposed to eat supper with David's family I was a nervous wreck. After an hour of agonizing, I finally decided to wear my baby blue blouse and a dark blue skirt. I brushed my hair and tied it back into a respectable-looking ponytail and wished my shoes weren't so scuffed and cheap. I shoved my charm bracelet, lipstick and compact of powder into my brassiere so I could put on my secret finishing touches in the car. I didn't figure anybody in my family paid enough attention to notice if my bosom looked bumpy.

As Les drove us toward Morgan he said, "Well, ol' C.R.'ll be getting home in a week or so, I reckon."

I reached into my bra and pulled out my lipstick and compact. "Reckon so," I said, dabbing powder onto my nose and cheeks.

"I was thinking when he gets back I just might have a little business proposition for him. A boy with C.R.'s smarts ort not to have to go back down in the coal hole."

"Daddy wouldn't like him not mining," I said through pursed lips as I checked my lipstick in the mirror. "Daddy thinks a man's either a coal miner or nothin'."

"Well, missy, if you don't mind me saying so, your daddy has his limitations."

"Mother and Daddy both," I said, reaching back down into my bosom. The bracelet got hung on my bra, and I had to give it a good tug.

Les craned his neck and peered down my shirt. "Lord God, what are you gonna pull outta there next? I'm kinda hungry. You wouldn't happen to have a pork chop in there I could gnaw on, would you?"

I play-slapped him on the arm. "There ain't nothin' in there for you to gnaw on, boy."

Les hooted. "You ain't the innocent little thing you used to be, missy! I remember when I could make you blush to beat Moses. So...what are you getting all dolled up for? You and the Jewboy going someplace special?"

"I'm eating supper with him and his parents."

"Eating with the Jewboy's mam and pap, huh?" Les was quiet for a second, then started chuckling. "Well, I reckon I'm not the only one who ain't gonna be gnawing on a pork chop tonight."

David had said to meet him in front of the drugstore, and when I got there, he was already waiting. "Hey," I said.

"Hi." His face lit up like it always did when he saw me. "You ready to go meet my folks?"

"I reckon," I said, but my stomach was doing cartwheels. We walked to his car and he opened the passenger door for me. His mood was unusually solemn, which made me think he was also nervous, that this meal with his parents was a test for him, too.

We hung a right on Poplar Street and climbed a hill that went past the Methodist church that was, I noticed, much smaller than Main Street Baptist. The houses on Poplar Street were mostly of the white-frame variety, small but neat, with fresh, clean paint and nicely groomed shrubbery. When we climbed to the top of the hill and turned onto Walnut, though, the houses were suddenly larger and finer-looking: two-story houses, some of them brick, some Victorian, though I didn't know that's what they were at the time.

David's family's house was of the Victorian variety, but to me it looked like a castle. With its two huge stories, its tower overlooking the street and its gingerbread trim, it looked like the home of a princess. I couldn't get over how big it was.

"So you and your mother and daddy are the only people that live here?" I said.

"Yep. Mom and Pop live on the first floor, and I live on the second. I have to have some space of my own...some privacy."

Privacy, to me, was as foreign as a Japanese tea ceremony. I'd never even had a whole bed to myself, let alone the whole floor of a house.

My heart thudding in my chest, I walked with David up to the front porch. He opened the door to a foyer with a beautiful curving staircase and then led me to the living room, where a balding, well-dressed man I recognized from the department store was sitting on the doily-draped overstuffed sofa. Beside him was an attractive woman with helped-along but pretty platinum blond hair.

When David's father saw us, he rose to his feet to greet us. "You must be Vespa," he said, his voice booming. "Well, David said you were lovely, but I never thought you'd be this lovely!"

I smiled while deciding not to correct him on my name. "Thank you, sir."

"I'm Ira Goldstein, and this is my wife, Marge. Say hello, Marge."

Mrs. Goldstein looked up hazily, said hello, and then looked away again, toying with the string of pearls around her neck. I couldn't tell if she didn't like me or just didn't notice me.

"You'll have to excuse Marge, Vespa. She's a little under the weather."

"Uh, Pop," David broke in, sounding more than a little uncomfortable. "Her name's Vestal."

"Of course, of course," Mr. Goldstein said, smiling. "That was what I said, wasn't it?"

 Mr. Goldstein gestured for us to sit down, and I sat in an overstuffed armchair that matched the couch. Actually, overstuffed is a word that could be used to describe the overall decor of the Goldstein house, it was overstuffed with expensive-looking knickknacks and doodads and bric-a-brac. The coffee table alone was loaded down with a cut glass candy dish (empty of candy), a cut glass ashtray that looked like it had never been used, a pair of china kittens frozen in a playful posture and a black china Scottie dog. Two glass-doored cabinets in the living room were stocked with more figurines of playing animals and children. I took every little doodad and bibelot as a sign of the Goldsteins' prosperity.

Everybody seemed awfully quiet, so I said, "This is a beautiful room."

"Beautiful?" Marge said, looking around her as if the room was filled with rotting meat.

"Marge was kind of attached to our house in Louisville," Mr. Goldstein said. "But I don't know...I rather like this house. It's old and full of character." He grinned. "Like me."

I laughed politely. I was starting to wonder if we were going to eat supper or just sit in the living room all night, since Mrs. Goldstein didn't seem to be lifting a finger to get food on the table. Just then, though, a black woman in an apron appeared in the doorway, which was surprising to me, since I could probably count on one hand the number of black people I'd seen in my life.

Mr. Goldstein looked at her and asked, "Is everything ready, Cora?"

She lowered her eyes and said, "Yessir."

"Well, then," Mr. Goldstein announced, "let's eat."

We followed Mr. Goldstein into the dining room, where two roasted chickens, huge bowls of mashed potatoes and green peas and a basket of rolls were spread out on a long, shiny table. Each place was set with real china and silver. I must've frozen for a second because I felt David guiding me to my seat.

I sat and briefly worried that they were going to say some kind of Jewish prayer that I wouldn't know the words to, but instead Cora started carving up the chicken and offering portions to everybody. When she asked me "Light or dark?" I felt my face flush because I couldn't help thinking that I was light and she was dark and that was the reason why she was waiting on me while I sat there.

Mr. Goldstein started passing the potatoes and then the peas and everybody dipped for themselves. I noticed that Mrs. Goldstein probably didn't put more than a teaspoonful of each on her plate. Like I always did on Saturdays, I had already eaten enough supper at home so as not to make Mother ask any questions. Still, I took good, healthy portions of everything that was offered to me. If you grew up like I did, if somebody sets a plate of nice food in front of you, you eat it.

"So, Vesta," Mr. Goldstein began. He still hadn't got my name down pat, but he was getting closer. "David tells me your father has a position with the Bartlett Coal Company."

"Yessir," I said. I was busy trying to watch how other people used their forks and knives. Apparently, I was going to have to study up on table manners.

"What does he do for the company?"

"He mines coal," I said. I wished I could think of a lie, but what was I supposed to say? That he owned the company?

"Well," Mr. Goldstein was smiling a little too widely—"if it wasn't for coal, we wouldn't be down here, would we, Marge?"

Mrs. Goldstein pushed away her untouched plate.

I had drunk most of my tea and suddenly, Cora, who I hadn't realized was standing behind me, was refilling my glass. It made me nervous to think of her just standing back there waiting for somebody to need something so she could run and get it, so I looked at her and said, "Ain't you gonna set down and eat a bite?"

Her face twisted up for a second like she was trying to keep herself from laughing. "No, miss," she said finally. "I done eat in the kitchen."

Like I said, I'd never been around black people before, and I'd sure never been anyplace that had servants, so I didn't know all the rules I was breaking by asking her to sit down and eat. But the way I see it is, if they're stupid rules, then it's all right to break them. It doesn't make a lick of sense to say that somebody's good enough to cook and serve your food but not good enough to sit down and eat it with you.

After that, Mr. Goldstein changed the subject to the store, and I sat politely and listened all the way through the pound cake and coffee.

Mr. and Mrs. Goldstein got up from the table after dessert, Mr. Goldstein saying it was nice to meet me and Mrs. Goldstein saying nothing, and David said he'd be gone a minute, but he'd meet me in the living room. I stayed at the dining room table and reapplied my lipstick while Cora cleared the dinner dishes. My ears were burning because I knew David and his parents were talking about me. To keep from worrying myself to death, I said to Cora, "You make that cake?"

"Sure did," she said.

"It was real good."

"Thank you." She looked genuinely pleased. She had a nice face, round and sweet-looking.

"You want me to help you clean up?"

This time she let herself really smile. "No, honey. They pay me for this, you know, and the pay's better than what most colored folks in this town makes. Some of the white folks in town might talk bad about me, say the only thing worse than a nigger is a nigger that works for a Jew, but I'll tell you the truth: a Jew'll pay you a sight better than a Baptist will. I do all right for myself, but you..." She looked me up and down. "I seen the way young Mr. Goldstein was looking at you. You play your cards right, country girl, and you'll really do all right for yourself." She cleared up the rest of the dishes and disappeared into the kitchen.

"So," David said when he found me still in the dining room, "got time to sit for a few minutes before I drive you back to town?"

"We could set a spell."

David took my hand and led me into the living room. We sat down on the couch, but he didn't let go of my hand. "Pop thinks you're charming," he said.

"Well, that's good, I reckon." Since then, I've thought a lot about that word. 'Charming' is what city people say when they're antique shopping and see something quaint and out of fashion, like an old butter churn or washtub. "Your mother don't think much of me."

"Don't take her personally," David said. "She acted the same as she would've if you weren't here. She's been sick a lot since we moved down here, though the doctor can't seem to find anything wrong with her. And I don't know..." He lowered his voice. "The war's hit her hard, too. Reading about Hitler in the paper and then living in a town where most people have never seen a Jew before...that's why she dyed her hair blond, so 'they' couldn't tell, she said. Pop said, 'Your name's Goldstein, Marge. They'll still be able to tell.' But there's no talking to her. Of course," he said, smiling and letting his voice get normal again. "I don't want to talk about my parents."

"No?" I said. "So what do you want to talk about?"

He let go of my hand and reached up to cradle my cheek. "You," he said. "And me."

I smiled. "Oh, is that all?"

"That's all," he said. "That's all I ever think about, you and me together, kissing and touching." He leaned over and locked his lips to mine, kissing me so long and hard I finally had to push him away.

"We'd better be careful," I said. "Your mother and daddy could walk in."

"You're right." David's mouth was smeared with my lipstick. He pulled a white hanky from his pocket to wipe it off, then stared down at the red-stained cloth. "It's just you, Vestal. I can't control myself when I'm with you. And when I'm away from you, I can't control my thoughts." He reached into his shirt pocket. "I was going to wait a month or two on this...that was Pop's advice: 'Wait a couple of months, make sure you still feel the same way.' But like I said, I can't control myself. Here." He held out a tiny, red, velvet-covered box.

I smiled, took it from him and opened it. I should've been expecting a ring, but I was too ignorant to know what to expect. That's what it was, though: a thin, gleaming band of gold with a clear, sparkling one-and-one-half carat diamond.

"David," I breathed. "It's the prettiest thing I've ever seen."

"You," he said, "are the prettiest thing I've ever seen. Take it, Vestal. Take it, and be my wife."

"Oh!" That's when it occurred to me that this wasn't a present with no strings attached like the silver charm bracelet. You could get silver just for batting your eyelashes and being pretty. For gold and diamonds, you had to make a commitment. The ring was beautiful, but I held it in shaking hands. Words started pouring out of my mouth. "I...I don't know, David. I mean, I ain't but fifteen years old. I ain't even halfway through high school. My mother and daddy don't know you from Adam's house cat."

"I've thought about all of that, of course," David said, his voice serious. "And I know you're young. We won't even start trying to have children for three or four years, and in the mean time, you could still finish high school. I could set you up for tutoring with some of the Morgan City High teachers if you felt funny about going to regular school and, you know, being a married lady."

"And what about my mother and daddy?"

"You know them best. If you want me to drive up to Bartlett and talk to them, I will. If you think it's better that I don't, I won't. They're your parents, Vestal. Whatever you decide to tell them, I respect your decision."

I looked down at the ring. I couldn't concentrate with that big diamond winking at me, so I closed the box, gave it a little squeeze and then handed it back to him. "Keep it till next Saturday, then offer it to me again. I need a week to think."

David's lips clamped into a straight line, and I could tell he was hurt.

If he started to cry, I knew I'd say yes just to make him stop, so I said, "I ain't turning you down nor nothin'. I'm just asking for a little time. A week ain't long."

David threw his arms around me and crushed me up against him. "A week without you is a long, long time." He was holding me tighter than I liked and burying his face in my hair, and all I could think was that if his mama walked in, I'd want to disappear in a cloud of smoke.

I hugged him a little, gave him a few little pats on the back and said, "Now, now, there ain't no need to take on." When I looked into his eyes, they were like a crazy man's.

"I'm sorry," he said, putting the ring box back in his pocket. "I...I try to hold back. It's just that I've never met another girl who's had this effect on me. I...I love you, Vestal."

I knew it would make him feel good if I said it back, but instead, I looked down at his expensive wristwatch and said, "Lord, David, it's a quarter till nine! You'd better get me back to town."

We rode in silence, and his good-night kiss was short and tight-lipped. I could tell I had hurt his feelings. An ordinary girl would've said yes the second she saw the size of that diamond and the look on David's face.

When I got in the car with Les, he didn't drop a paper bag of money in my lap. "How was the game?" I asked.

"Not so good," Les said. "I just broke even. I sure hope this ain't a sign my luck's running out. How 'bout you? How's the little game you're playing?"

"I don't know." I sighed, looking out the window at the darkening sky. "I think he just raised the stakes."

CHAPTER 9

We heard about it on the radio before we got the telegram. Even now, it still amazes me how horror can strike when you're doing the most ordinary things. Mother was peeling potatoes to fry for supper, and Myrtle and I were at the kitchen table with our schoolbooks open when the radio announcer's voice said, "A train carrying soldiers derailed in Burnside County this afternoon, sliding off an embankment and landing in the river below. The number of dead and injured has not been determined yet, and the names of the passengers are not yet available."

It seems strange that we didn't run for the nearest telephone and call the sheriff of Burnside County to find out who was on the train, but we didn't need to. We knew. As soon as she heard the radio report, Mother dropped her knife and crumpled to the floor, sobbing. She must have lay down there half an hour before Myrtle and I stopped our own sobbing long enough to help her to the bed.

Later that evening, when there was a knock at the door, Daddy glanced down at the telegram he was handed like it was a newspaper he had already read.

Myrtle and I stayed awake all night, sobbing into our pillows. We could hear Mother doing the same. I never heard Daddy make a sound, but the next morning, his eyes were rimmed with red.

Mother didn't get out of bed for three days straight. Myrtle and I didn't go to school, and Mother didn't seem to care. I knew how she felt. I didn't care for much of anything. C.R. was the only member of my family who I understood and who understood me. All he had wanted was to get out of Bartlett, and now his remains were going to be planted on a mountainside just a quarter-mile from the coal camp.

With all the womenfolk out of commission, the house fell into disarray. Washday passed by unnoticed, and the floor and furniture were soon covered with a gritty layer of coal dust. Mother didn't eat and didn't care whether or not we did, so no meals were cooked. Daddy seemed to be the only one of us with any appetite, so he took to stopping by the company store for a bologna sandwich and an orange pop on the way back from work, since he knew he'd be coming home to an empty table.

I felt like the black dust that settled inside our house had coated my heart, too. Maybe it would've been better if C.R. had died in battle instead of a freak accident. At least the families of those who died in war can convince themselves that their brothers or sons or husbands died for a heroic cause. The best I could wrap my mind around it, though, the only reason for C.R.'s death was that the world is a place where good people suffer and die for no reason, and that fact made me feel my life was as dark and dangerous as the inside of a coal mine.

Myrtle and I had to wash and dress Mother for the funeral, the same as you'd do a baby. At the service, on the muddy patch of land beside C.R.'s open grave, Daddy and Les stood on either side of her, their arms linked in hers, supporting her with their weight. Mother's face was red and swollen and crumpled, but Daddy's jaw was set firm, and his eyes stared straight ahead. He was a man determined not to cry, even at his own son's funeral.

Les didn't seem to be ashamed of his tears, though. With his free hand, he reached into his pocket, pulled out a hanky and dabbed at his eyes.

The preacher, who had just finished saying something about how C.R. had died in the service of his country, called on us to pray. Myrtle bowed her head, but I didn't. How could I believe in a God who would let my brother die before his twenty-first birthday? And even if I could believe in a God like that, how could I feel anything for him but hate?

I looked down at C.R.'s open grave and wondered if I jumped into it while everybody else was praying, would they notice? I could just curl up in the cool earth, close my eyes and rest beside my brother. What was the point of trying to get out of Bartlett, of trying to do anything, when death could snatch us away at any second? Best to just lie back and give in.

Of course, everybody had stopped praying and had opened their eyes before I got up the nerve to jump in the grave. After the service, Les said to my father, "Zed, why don't you help the missus to my car and I'll drive her home? It don't seem like she's in no shape to be walking." He took my hand then and squeezed it. "How you holding up, missy?"

"Not too good." There was a hitch in my voice. "How bout you?"

"Well," Les said, "I reckon you seen me a minute ago bawling my eyes out. I been doing a lot of that lately. That, and drinking a lot more than I probably ort to. I figure it's all right 'cause C.R. would want us to miss him. Now that he's in the ground, though, I reckon he'd want us to keep living our lives, too." Les took out his hanky and wiped his nose. "And that's why the day after tomorrow, you're gonna be waiting for me on the front porch, just like you always do on a Saturday evenin'."

"Not this Saturday night. Maybe some other time."

"Some other time, my hind foot. You're gonna be on that porch Saturday evenin', and if you ain't, I'm gonna bust into the house and drag you out by the hair of your head. C.R. told me I had to look after you for him while he was gone, and that's what I aim to do. There ain't no reason to let your life get derailed just like C.R.'s train."

Les put on his hat, then doffed it at me and Myrtle and went to drive Mother and Daddy home.

Myrtle watched Les leave, then looked at me. "The girls at school say they bet once you turn sixteen, you and Les'll get married."

"Well, then the girls at school's all a bunch of hare-brained fools, 'cause I ain't getting married to nobody."

But just as I said it, a picture flashed in my mind: a one-and-a-half carat diamond winking against a slender band of gold.

CHAPTER 10

Would my decision have been different if C.R. hadn't gotten killed? How should I know? I try never to begin sentences with "if I had to do it all over again," because you never do have it to do all over again. I think that's why so many old people end up going crazy. They spend too much time looking back on their lives and wondering if they did the right thing and if their lives would've turned out better if they'd made a different choice about one thing or the other. You spend too much time thinking like that, and before long, you're blithering away about some boy who just asked you to the high school dance while the nursing home attendant is changing your diaper.

I refuse to think about changing things from my past. I did what I did when I did it, and there's no point in worrying about it now.

So that Saturday when Les came to pick me up, I was ready. And when David slid into the vinyl booth across from me at the Dixie Diner, I was ready then, too. Before I even said hello, I looked right into his nervous, darting eyes and said yes.

He grinned, but he still looked a little nervous, like he wasn't sure what I was getting at. "What was that?"

"I said yes, you silly thing. Yes, I'll marry you."

He jumped out of the booth, yanked me from my seat and grabbed me into a hug. I felt a little self-conscious because the place was packed, what with it being a Saturday night and all.

"David," I breathed, "people are staring."

"Let them stare!" he shouted. "Let them stare at me and my beautiful bride-to-be!" He pulled the red velvet box from his breast pocket, took out the ring and slipped it onto my finger.

Some people smiled at us, some people scowled, and some went right on eating their hamburgers. I smiled back at the people who smiled at us, then slid back into the booth.

David was grinning like an idiot. He grinned at the waitress when he ordered our food. After his hamburger came, he grinned even when his mouth was full. After he swallowed, he said, "This is the best damn hamburger I've ever eaten in my life."

"I'm glad," I said.

"I'm so happy, Vestal. Are you as happy as I am?"

"Well," I said, idly stirring my milkshake, "I'm real glad you asked me to marry you, but I can't be all the way happy right now."

"Why not, sweetheart? Is there anything I can do? Just name it, and I'll…"

"There's nothing you can do but be patient with me until I can feel happy again. C.R. is dead, David. He got killed in that train wreck in Burnside County." It was hard not to cry, but I managed. I had taken to wearing a little bit of eye makeup, and I didn't want it to get all runny.

David reached for my hand. "Vestal, I'm so sorry. If you want to wait, to have a long engagement, until the shock is over, I completely understand."

I thought about the dark house in Bartlett, about Mother crying in bed, Daddy silently working himself to death, Myrtle preaching about how the Lord's ways are not for us to understand. "I'd marry you tonight if I could."

"Well, let's do it as soon as possible, then. You can get married in one day in Morgan, did you know that? The license and the wedding all within an hour." He took a piece of paper from his pocket and handed it to me, then whispered, "The only catch is… given your age, you'll have to get at least one of your parents to sign this."

I looked down at the slip of paper and lost my appetite for my hamburger. "You don't think they'd know the difference if I signed it myself?"

"Vestal, you're going to be leaving home. Your parents will notice. They might as well know why."

"You're right." I folded up the piece of paper and stuck it

down my bosom. Even after I was done, David's eyes were still on my bosom.

"You think we could do it Friday morning? I could drive to Bartlett and get you."

"No, don't be driving to Bartlett. My daddy'd shoot you soon as look at you. I'll tell you what. I'll ride the school bus Friday mornin', then skip school and walk the rest of the way to Morgan. I'll meet you at the courthouse around ten o'clock."

David's eyes went soft and dreamy. "Do you want to go for a drive tonight?"

I thought a second. David would probably take new liberties with me now that we were engaged. Wouldn't it be better to leave him aching in anticipation of Friday night?

"Well," I said, sounding all innocent, "I was thinking we could go see the new Barbara Stanwyck movie at the Hippodrome."

I loved Barbara Stanwyck. She wasn't as pretty as some of the other movie stars, but she did absolutely everything that could be done with her looks. And she knew how to work it so she got just what she wanted.

David's voice was awash with disappointment when he said, "Barbara Stanwyck it is," but I knew he couldn't be too unhappy. Come Friday night, he knew he was going to have everything he'd been dreaming about.

Since Mother wouldn't hardly get out of bed, Myrtle and I took to cooking supper. We were still sad, of course, but we didn't want to starve to death either. So we'd fix a pot of soup beans and a pone of cornbread, which Daddy and the two of us would sit down at the table to eat in silence. One of us would always take a bowl of milk and bread to Mother. Sometimes she ate a few bites, but mostly she left it untouched.

On Sunday night after our sad little supper, Myrtle went into our bedroom to change clothes for church. I was washing dishes, scalding my hands in the hot water and feeling the nervous anticipation I'd felt ever since David had asked me to marry him, when suddenly Myrtle was standing behind me.

"Vestal, what is these?" she asked in that simpering, innocent tone that always meant trouble.

I knew what was in her hand before I turned around, but I turned around anyway. She had the charm bracelet stretched out across her palm so the heart was dangling where Daddy could see it from the couch. The diamond ring sat behind it, and just that one time, I wished it didn't shine so brightly.

I snatched them both from her hand. "Who told you you could snoop around in my things?"

"I wasn't snooping," Myrtle said. "I dropped a hair barrette on the floor down by the bed, and when I reached down to pick it up I saw somethin' shiny sticking out under the mattress. Now how was I supposed to know you had a whole jewelry store under there?"

My first impulse was to run out the door. I had been planning on telling Mother and Daddy about David, I had to, to get the consent form signed, but I had been going to wait until Wednesday night when Myrtle was at prayer meeting and I could have a little more control of the situation. Out of the corner of my eye, I saw Daddy rising from the couch.

"Who give them things to you?" he asked, real quiet. He always talked real quiet when he was mad.

"A friend of mine did, Daddy. His name's David, and…"

"And you're fixing to marry him, ain't you?" Myrtle butted in.

"Mind your own business," I said. "Daddy, David is the nicest feller you'd ever meet…"

"Who's his people?" Daddy's voice was as cold and hard as steel.

Here it came. "His last name's Goldstein. He runs that department store in Morgan. His family's real…"

"Vestal Jenkins," Daddy interrupted, "are you so all-fired ignorant that you don't know what kind of a name Goldstein is?"

"Well, I know it's a…"

"It's a Jew name." Daddy cut me off again. "What you been doing with that Jew for him to give you them things, Vestal?"

"A Jew!" Myrtle was clearly having the time of her life. "They was the ones that killed Jesus!"

"Jesus was a Jew, you fool," I said.

"He was not!" Myrtle snapped. "He was a Christian. What else would he be?"

Before I could argue further with Myrtle's theology, Daddy was in my face. "I said," he almost whispered, "what you been doing with that Jew for him to give you them things, Vestal? And don't you tell me nothing, a Jew ain't gonna part with his money unless he's getting somethin' for it."

I finally had all I could take. Tears were rolling down my face. "It ain't like that, Daddy. He's a real nice boy. He...he don't lay a hand on me, and he asked me to marry him."

Daddy drew his hand back and slapped me hard across the face. He looked at me like he could do much worse than just slap me. "I used to think you was the best young'un I had." His voice ached with regret for any love he had ever borne me. "But you ain't nothin' but a whore." He turned his back on me and walked out the door, slamming it behind him.

"What's going on?" Mother stood at the bedroom door, her hair unwashed and matted, wearing the same nightgown she'd had on for days.

"Vestal ain't been going to church on Saturday nights," Myrtle blabbed gleefully. "She's been courting some Jew instead, and he asked her to marry him."

Mother looked at me through narrowed eyes. "Is that a fact, Vestal?"

There was no reason to deny it now. "Yes, ma'am."

I'd never seen so much hate in my mother's eyes. "You've been nothin' but a sorrow to me since the day you was born, Vestal. I wish to heaven the Lord had seen fit to take you instead of C.R."

I could've stood there and cried some more, but I'd had all I could take. "Well, you finally got it said, didn't you?" I snapped. "I always knowed you hated me like poison, but that's the first time I got the pleasure of hearing you say it. I'll tell you what. You hate me so much, you want me gone so bad..." I pulled the consent form from my bosom and picked up a pencil. "Sign this. Sign this here piece of paper saying I can marry David, and you'll see C.R. in heaven before you ever see me again!"

I shoved the paper into Mother's hand, and she scrawled her

name across it.

"Nobody'll be seeing you in heaven," Myrtle said, going to wrap her arm around Mother, who was trembling.

I snatched the signed paper out of Mother's hand. "Well, Myrtle, if heaven's where you're gonna be, then hell sounds downright pleasant to me. I'll take me some weenies to roast."

I marched into the bedroom and shoved the consent form, my toothbrush, my makeup and my three good outfits into a paper sack. I put on my ring and bracelet, grabbed the sack and strode out the front door without ever looking back at Mother or Myrtle. I never set foot in that house again.

Once I was out the door, I started running. But then I thought, why waste my energy? It wasn't like anybody was about to come chasing after me. Also, there was the sizable question of where I was running to. My eventual goal was to get to David, but there was no way I could make it all the way to Morgan on foot. I stopped for a few seconds, caught my breath, and then started walking up to the camp house where Les lived.

Like many of the young, unmarried miners, Les shared his house with a couple of other fellows. I was nervous when I walked up to the front porch, which was identical to the front porch of the house I had just run away from. What if some other young man opened the door, one of the young men who had started to whistle at me when I walked by the company store? But when I knocked, the man who came to the door was Les, wearing a white undershirt and work pants and holding a half-eaten bologna sandwich.

"Well, look what the cat drug in!" he said, swinging the door open. "What are you doing over here, missy?"

"Got kicked out of the house," I said. You would think somebody would cry to have to say something like that, but my eyes were as dry as a bone. I guess after C.R. died, there wasn't anything for me at home anymore.

The inside of Les's house was plain, almost bare, like single men's houses often are. It was surprisingly clean, though.

"I was just finishing my supper," Les said, setting his sandwich down next to a cup on the kitchen table. "Let me fix you a sandwich and coffee."

"Just some coffee would be fine. I done eat before I got kicked out of the house." As soon as I said it, it struck me as funny, and I started laughing.

"Lord, missy, you're getting purt' near hysterical. Drink this." He set a mug of dark coffee in front of me. "That orta bring you to your senses. Charles, one of the old boys I live with, says my coffee's so strong you could trot a mouse across it."

I hadn't drunk coffee much in the past, but when I picked up the cup and sipped, I liked the dark, bitter, adult flavor.

Les sat down across from me. "So your mother and daddy found out about your feller?"

"Yeah. Thanks to Myrtle. She found this," I held up my hand so he could see my ring, "under my mattress and showed it to 'em."

"Let me see that thing," Les said.

I took off the ring and handed it to him. He held it up to the light and then squinted at it with his glasses down over the bridge of his nose. "You wouldn't happen to know how much he paid for this rock, would you?"

"Shoot, no. You think I'm trashy enough to ask him?"

"I'll tell you what." Les didn't look up from the diamond. "However much he paid for it, it's more money than anybody in this camp's ever seen in one place." He held up the jewel so the light hit it. "You know, a diamond like this starts out as a regular hunk of coal just like I dig out every day."

"Is that a fact?" Nobody had ever told me where diamonds came from, and this piece of information thrilled me. If a dull, dusty old hunk of coal could transform itself into a diamond, then surely a girl with good looks and good sense had a chance of transforming herself into something just as spectacular.

Les handed me the ring. "It's a fact, missy. Not everything ends up the same way it started out." He drank his coffee for a minute, then said, "I don't know what I'm gonna do with you tonight. If it was just me living here, I'd let you sleep on my couch, but the other fellers that lives here's out drinking and they'll be back directly. I know I'm a gentleman, but I can't speak for them."

I slipped the ring back on my finger. "Could you drive me to

Morgan then?"

Les looked at his watch. "Well, I don't see why not. I could have you there by nine o'clock. I wasn't gonna do nothin' but study, and I can do that any night this week."

"Study what?" Les was too old for school, and he didn't strike me as a person who would sit and study the Bible, not even on a Sunday.

"Business," he said. "I'm taking a correspondence course from the National School of Business Success. I started working in the mines before I could get much of an education, so now I'm trying to make up for that a little bit. I'm right ignorant now, but that don't mean I've got to stay that way."

I had always liked Les, but at that moment, I understood why I liked him.

I grabbed my sack of belongings and climbed into Les's car for our familiar ride to Morgan. This time it was different, though, because as we drove down the side of the mountain and away from Bartlett, I knew I wasn't coming back. Nothing had ever felt so good to me as the motion of that car going forward.

When we got to Morgan, I directed Les up the hill to David's house. I hoped David's parents wouldn't be mad at me for showing up on their doorstep, but I had nowhere else to go.

"Well," Les said, once he had parked the car, "I hope I run into you in town once in a while."

"We'll do better than just run into each other," I said. "After me and David gets settled in, you'll have to come over for supper."

"I don't know that your new husband will want me hanging around," Les said, avoiding my eyes. "Husbands gets peculiar about their pretty young wives having men friends."

"Well, if David wants me, he'll just have to get used to you coming around from time to time. You're the closet thing to a brother I've got now." I leaned over and kissed Les on the cheek.

He turned away, and I couldn't tell if he was hiding embarrassment or tears. I grabbed my sack and got out of the car.

As I walked toward the house, though, I heard him holler, "missy!"

I turned around. "Yeah?"

"If you ever need me, you know where I'm at."

Before I could say anything, he turned on the engine and drove away.

CHAPTER 11

Mr. Goldstein answered the door. His fuzzy eyebrows went up in surprise when he saw me. "Why, hello, Vesta." His greeting sounded like a question.

"Hello, Mr. Goldstein. I'm real sorry to be bothering you at night like this, but is David home?"

A streak of fear shot through me. What if David wasn't home? Where would I go then?

"He's upstairs," Mr. Goldstein said. "I'll go get him."

He left me standing on the porch, and I hoped I wasn't causing a big family scene. I sure didn't want to cause two in one night. Nervous as I was, I still knew I had been lucky; it would've been much worse if Mrs. Goldstein had answered the door.

"Vestal!" David was smiling, but he looked nervous. Instead of inviting me in, he walked out on the porch and shut the door behind him.

"You don't reckon there's somebody over at City Hall who'd marry us right now, do you?" I said.

He broke out in a big grin. "Did you get the…"

Before he could finish his sentence, I handed him the paper with my mother's name on it. David flung his arms around me and hugged me close. "So it went all right with your parents?"

I gently released myself from his embrace. "Well, I wouldn't say that, exactly, but I got the paper signed, didn't I?"

"I'd hate to think I'd caused any trouble between you and your family…"

"Then don't think about it. Listen, David, I need a place to stay tonight. I don't want to barge in and take advantage of your family's hospitality or nothin'."

"You can't stay here," David said quickly. "Pop is pretty

understanding about what's going on between us, but Mom's having conniptions. Besides..." He looked at me, and his eyes went all soft. "I can't have you under the same roof with me before our wedding night. Too...tempting." He kissed me, and as he pulled me against him, I was aware of the hard bulge under his britches. When he finally pulled away, he said, "See what I mean? I'll tell you what. I'll drive you down to the hotel by the train depot. I'll fetch you in the morning and take you to breakfast, and by lunchtime, you'll be Mrs. David Goldstein."

I smiled because I knew I was supposed to, but I also knew that deep down I'd still be Vestal Jenkins just like I was before. David wasn't a fitting name for a girl, even if you did stick a 'Mrs.' in front of it.

The hotel by the train depot was really just an old house with a sign reading, 'Rooms for rent, by the night or week.' David told the old lady who answered the door that his bride-to-be needed a room for the night. He paid her in cash and bade us both a gentlemanly goodnight.

The old lady led me through the musty-smelling old house and up the stairs to a little room with a single iron bed and a small dresser with a cracked mirror. The bathroom, she told me, was down the hall.

After she left, I lay on the bed a few minutes and enjoyed being in a room that, however small and shabby, was just for me. I listened to the walls to hear if there were any other lodgers in the rooms around me and couldn't hear anybody. Finally, deciding I was alone on the floor, I grabbed a towel and a bar of soap and my gray-from-coal-dust nightgown and made my way down the hall.

The bathtub was the big, claw-footed kind, and I ran it nearly to the brim with good hot water. Baths at home had consisted of quick scrubbings in a metal washtub. I had only seen big, deep bathtubs in the movies.

There was a bottle of Halo shampoo in the cabinet door above the sink, and I grabbed it and a razor someone had left behind. I stripped and submerged myself in the tub, lying back and letting the hot water unknot my tight muscles.

After a few minutes, I sat up and lathered my legs and armpits and ran the razor over them. I wanted my skin to be smooth and like the movie stars I had seen in their strapless evening gowns. I rolled the bar of soap around in my hands until they were white with foam and then rubbed my soap-slick hands all over my body—my belly, my breasts. This is what David wants to do to you, a voice in my head whispered. Touch you naked all over.

As I reached down to soap the soft fuzz between my legs, I thought of the hardness I had felt when David had pulled me against him earlier. A ripple of fear ran through me.

David wants to do more than just touch you. The voice in my head wasn't whispering anymore. He wants to stick his thing in your...your...I didn't even have a word for that part of my body. Mother always called it a bird. "Wash your bird," she would say when I was taking a bath when I was little. But I could never figure out why she called it that, since it didn't have wings or feathers.

I was scared when I thought of the size of the bulge in David's pants—about that big thing somehow burrowing its way inside me. It seems silly now, I know. These days most girls have had a speculum or a tampon or their own fingers up there long before they lose their virginity. But no doctor had ever examined me down there. I pinned rags to my underwear when my time came, and I had never had the privacy required to finger myself. And even if I had, I probably wouldn't have had the courage to do it. I thought about it. Sitting there in the tub alone, I started thinking, what if I hurt myself? What if I made myself bleed so I wouldn't bleed like I was supposed to on my wedding night? It's pitiful to say, but I was no more familiar with the hole between my legs than I was with the Black Hole of Calcutta.

I lay in the tub and felt nervous for a while, but then I decided to wash my hair and stop worrying. Surely no woman had ever died from having a man stick his thing in her.

David picked me up the next morning and took me to breakfast at the Dixie Diner.

"Pop says I've got to do a couple hours of work over at the store before I can take the rest of the day off," he said, buttering a biscuit. "Maybe you could come in with me. We could start an account for you, and you could do a little shopping. You're not going to get a real wedding gown the way we're doing this, but you can at least buy yourself a pretty dress to wear."

He didn't have to ask me twice. While David took care of business at the store, I tried on dress after dress. It being winter, I couldn't find anything white to wear, so I settled on a cream-colored, rayon two-piece suit dress which hugged my waist and hips but flared at the skirt's hem. Judy, the cute, blond shopgirl whom I'd run away from months earlier, helped me pick out a pair of pumps and a smart little hat (women loved smart little hats back then) to match.

"You might as well pick out another suit for traveling," Judy said. "You'll need it to wear on your honeymoon."

"I don't think we're going nowhere."

"Then how come I just heard your husband-to-be on the phone a few minutes ago making hotel reservations?" She pulled a soft green suit off the rack. It was rayon, too. Nearly everything was during the war; I think I've always been partial to rayon because the first really pretty clothes I owned were made of it. "Try this one," she said. "The jade color will bring out your eyes."

In the dressing room I found that the jade really did bring out the green of my eyes, and the green of the suit against the black of my hair made me look exotic.

"Now," Judy said, after my two new suits were draped over her arms, "we need to go back to..." She lowered her voice to a whisper, "Underthings."

I'd never given much thought to what my underwear looked like, but I guessed if I was going to be a married lady, somebody was going to be seeing my drawers besides me. I followed her to the back of the store, where the ladies' underthings were discreetly displayed under a sign reading 'Hosiery.' Of course, what with the war, there was very little real hosiery for sale.

"I've been trying to figure out a nice way of telling you this ever since you walked in the door," Judy said, her painted-on eyebrows crinkled with worry.

"Just tell me. I don't care whether you're nice or not."

Judy tittered nervously. "Vestal, it's your bosoms. They're so... big. I don't know what you wear underneath your blouses, but whatever it is, it's not enough. Honey, your boobies is bouncing around like two water balloons."

I laughed, and so did she, probably out of relief as much as anything. My titties probably did flop around something awful. The only brassiere I had was one Mother had sewed for me and, of course, it offered no support.

Judy took me in the back room and wrapped a tape measure around my titties. When I tried on the bra she finally picked out for me, both my boobies stood up straight like saluting soldiers. She picked me out a few pairs of drawers, too, and then kind of whispered, "So, Vestal, what are you planning on wearing tonight?"

I had no idea what she was talking about. "I don't know. Where am I going tonight?"

She got her case of the giggles back. "To bed, you silly girl. What are you wearing to bed?"

"Hmm. Nothin', I reckon. I figure that's what David would want me to wear."

Judy was blushing furiously. "No," she said. "That's not the way you do it. You've got to wear something pretty. You don't want your new husband to see everything all at once. You want him to unwrap you like a present."

I thought of the pretty boxes that encased the beautiful jewelry David had given me. Presentation was important. "All right," I said. "What have you got?"

Out of a drawer in a table, she pulled out a couple of nightgowns which were low-cut and lacy, with shoulder straps instead of sleeves. I wanted the black one because it looked like something I'd seen in a movie once, but Judy said the white one would be better because I was a bride.

Judy reached into a drawer in the same table and slipped a small package into my hands. "I want you to have these, too. They're the only pair in the store, and we're not supposed to be selling them because of the war. But I'm giving them to you as a wedding present."

I looked down at the package of tan stockings and gave Judy a thank-you hug. In the ladies' dressing room, I put on my new bra and panties and slid my new silk stockings up my legs and secured them with garters. I slipped on my cream-colored suit and buttoned up the matching jacket and stepped into my new pumps. I was a little wobbly at first, but if I kept telling myself to put one foot in front of the other, I did all right. I touched up my makeup and brushed out my hair.

When I was done, the person I faced in the mirror was not a fifteen-year-old from the coal camps, but a young woman who was at least stylish enough to pass muster in a town the size of Morgan. I stuffed my old clothes and shoes into the wastepaper basket, and when I emerged from the dressing room, Judy clapped her hands and said, "If I could make all my customers look that good, there'd be a line stretched all the way down Main Street." She handed me a shopping bag filled with my other purchases. "Now I want you to march upstairs to your fiance's office and tell him to put his damn papers away and get you down to that courthouse."

I didn't exactly march up the stairs, since I was still getting the walking-in-heels thing down pat. Walking through the store, though, I did notice that if I swung one leg in front of the other just so, it made my hips sway back and forth just enough to make men stop what they were doing to look at me. The clerk in the haberdashery department got so flustered looking at me that he knocked over a whole rack of ties.

I stood quietly in the doorway and waited for David to look up from his desk full of sales receipts. When he finally did, his eyes widened and his jaw dropped.

"So," I said, looking down at the floor but then looking back up at him real slow, "do you wanna work all day, or do you wanna get married?"

He jumped up from his desk, knocking several papers off it. "Well," he said, "I told Pop I'd work till noon." He glanced down at his watch. "But it's a quarter till eleven. That's practically noon, isn't it?"

I don't remember too much about the wedding except that wedding is too grand a word for what it was: a bored justice of the peace reading words out of a book and us agreeing to them, or paying lip service to agreeing to them, anyway. I do remember David's fingers pressing into my back during the 'kiss the bride' part. It was like he was using all his strength not to tear off my clothes right in front of the justice of the peace, the two strangers who were serving as witnesses, God and everybody.

I also remember that when we were walking out of the courthouse hand in hand, David leaned over and whispered, "I hope that was okay, Vestal. I would've given you a big fancy wedding if things were different."

"It was perfect," I said, but I wish I'd had the nerve to ask him what 'if things had been different' meant, so I wouldn't have to guess about it for years to come. He could've meant that he would've given me a big wedding if I hadn't been just fifteen years old. Girls in the hills got married that young all the time, but they always married boys who were from the hills, too, so nobody thought anything of it. But a twenty-one-year-old businessman, and a Jewish businessman at that, marrying a fifteen-year-old country girl would raise an eyebrow or two.

My other guess about what he meant was about my ethnic and religious background. His parents weren't going to flat-out tell him not to marry me, because you don't drag your son to a little town in southeastern Kentucky where even Presbyterians are considered exotic and then tell him he has to marry a Jewish girl. Still, his parents, especially his mother, would've probably supported our union more wholeheartedly if my name had been more like Rosenbaum and less like Jenkins. They might even have given us a wedding at their house or maybe at a synagogue in Louisville.

But really, the wedding didn't matter to me. I had always been the kind of girl who fantasized about evening gowns instead of bridal gowns. And even if I had been disappointed by the lack of a fancy wedding, what David said next would've made it up to me.

We were walking toward his car when he said, "So, ready to go on a little trip?"

"A trip? Where to?"

He stopped and took both my hands. "Vestal, I'd love to sweep you off to some sunny island and serve you fruit drinks on the beach. Unfortunately," he cleared his throat, "Pop wants me back at work at noon tomorrow. So…in lieu of a sunny island, we're settling for a night in a hotel in Knoxville. But it's a nice hotel, the Wemberley, with a lovely restaurant and a romantic atmosphere." He smiled. "Of course, any atmosphere with you in it is romantic."

I grinned. I'm sure David thought I was responding to the romance instead of the exciting prospect of going to a real city in another state. "Well," I said, "for a girl who ain't never been nowhere, Knoxville sounds just as good as an island."

Actually, it sounded better. You can't shop on an island.

Folks today don't have any idea what it was like traveling before the interstate highways connected one place to another and to another and so on. Driving on the interstate gets you from one place to the next, but you have no idea where you've been to get to where you're going. You miss the little grocery stores and post offices, the ramshackle houses perched on hillsides and the thin black ribbons of road that wind around mountains and dip through valleys.

Traveling on my wedding day on what locals now call 'the old road,' I saw a thin young mother in the yard of her tar paper shack, hanging diapers on the line to dry while her baby, sitting on the ground, scooped up some dirt in his tiny hand and jammed it into his mouth. We stopped at the A and B Grocery Store, which seemed to be held together by metal signs advertising Nehi and Kern's Bread, and bought a tank of gas, two orange pops (Nehi, naturally) and two bologna sandwiches wrapped in wax paper.

When we crossed the Tennessee state line, I clapped my hands with excitement because I had never been out of Kentucky before. David called me adorable and leaned in for a quick kiss even though he was driving.

Down the twisting road we drove, at one point stopping to let a mother hen and the line of fuzzy yellow chicks following her cross. "Why did the chicken cross the road?" David said. "To delay the man on his honeymoon."

David was a man with a goal. For him, this trip was about getting to the hotel in Knoxville and the privacy of our reserved room. Every slight delay, be it caused by a mother hen or the need for a tank of gas and a bologna sandwich, was a source of frustration.

I was different. I was enjoying the ride, the experience of being somewhere I'd never been before and on my way to somewhere I'd never been, a real city. The thought of being naked in bed with a man was still making me nervous, but I was also a little interested to find out what it was like. After all, that was somewhere I'd never been before either.

It took us about two hours to get to Knoxville. Now, with the interstate, it would probably just take an hour and fifteen minutes...less if you speed.

Even now, Knoxville doesn't have much of a skyline, and it had even less of one back in 1944. But the buildings were bigger than any I had ever seen before, and the streets were wider. It was the middle of a workday, and so the streets were lined with parked cars. Men in suits and overcoats bustled out of a diner, briefcases in hand, on their way back to work. A couple of young women, wearing pastel cloth coats that made them resemble Easter eggs, paused on the sidewalk to look in the window of a jewelry store. I wished I could see into the window, too.

This street in Knoxville had many of the same businesses as Morgan's Main Street: a drugstore, a department store, a hardware store, a movie theater. But everything was bigger and brighter and shinier than in Morgan, and I had to remind myself that this street, which was called Gay Street, was only one of several streets full of shops and theaters and restaurants in Knoxville. In Morgan, Main Street was the only street that was lined with anything other than houses and the occasional church. Gay Street. Back then, the only meaning I knew for gay was happy, and Gay Street looked like a gay street indeed.

"So what do you want to do?" David asked. "We can't check into the hotel until after four." He sounded disappointed; it was pretty clear what he wanted to do.

"We could just walk around a while if that'd be all right," I said, "since I ain't never been in a city before."

"Well, you're barely in one now." David laughed. "Someday I'll take you to New York so you can see what a real city looks like. In the meantime, he said as he pulled over into a parking place, "we'll settle for walking around Knoxville."

I must have been gazing lovingly at the bright polka dot

dresses in the window of Diller's department store because David whispered, "You want a dress like that, just let me know. When we get back home, I'll get it for you wholesale."

I smiled and squeezed his hand. I looked in amazement at the window display of Klein's jewelry store. The window was tiny, and its display shelf was lined with blue-velvet. A blue-velvet covered model of a lady's neck on the shelf displayed a string of pearls, each one round, luminous and perfect. A matching pearl bracelet sat on a pedestal on one side of the necklace, a pearl ring on the other.

"Beautiful, aren't they?" David breathed in my ear.

I smiled and nodded.

"You know, each one of those pearls started out as nothing more than a tiny piece of grit inside an oyster. Over time the oyster changed that little unformed thing into a perfect, shining pearl." He looked down at me and touched my cheek. "That's how it'll be with you and me, Vestal. I'll be the oyster, and you'll grow more beautiful and polished until you're the perfect pearl."

I smiled at him, thinking about how Les talked about a piece of coal transforming itself into a diamond over time, but as I thought about what my new husband was saying, I felt my smile turn into a mask. This was the first time I had heard David imply that I was something unfinished, unrefined, something he wanted to mold according to his own vision. Beautiful though I was, I wasn't a pearl yet in his eyes, but a piece of grit with potential.

He was right in some ways, of course. I was gritty and unrefined. I did gawk at every store window on Gay Street and look up to measure how tall the buildings were. My grammar and table manners were terrible, and I was ignorant on a wide variety of subjects. But with all this said, I didn't want somebody else to take the unformed lump of clay that I was and sculpt me into the shape he wanted me to be. I wanted to change myself, to sculpt myself into the person I wanted to be. I wasn't sure who that was yet, but I was determined to find out.

That moment in front of Klein's jewelry store taught me an important lesson about what men want. I had thought David had wanted to marry me because he wanted to screw me, and while the thought of screwing made me nervous, I knew deep down that I could handle it. And I still believe that David married me mostly because he wanted to screw me, although he would have labeled this desire as 'being in love.' But once a man marries you, he doesn't just want to screw you; he also wants to change you.

As I stood in front of the jewelry store, smiling at my new husband, I realized I had entered into a bargain that was more complex than the 'I'll let you screw me if you'll financially support me and buy me presents' deal that I thought I was entering into. Even though we hadn't gone to the hotel yet, I felt like I had already been screwed.

But I kept on smiling, and David was none the wiser, which made me feel a little bit better. I may have been unsophisticated about life, but David was unsophisticated about women: soft-hearted and romantic and uncomplex. Maybe it wouldn't be that hard to appear to change some of the ways he wanted me to on the outside, while working on being the person I really wanted to be on the inside. It's two-faced, I know, but it's the same thing a lot of married women do: they seem one way for the husbands while really being another way altogether. I was just honest enough to admit to myself what I was doing.

"That movie theater's just about the prettiest thing I ever seen," I said, nodding toward the theater up the street. "Let's go look at it."

The Tennessee Theater was a bigger, more opulent version of the Hippodrome in Morgan. The huge marquee wasn't lit up, because it was daytime, but it must've had a hundred light bulbs. The glass in the box office was trimmed in gold paint, and the big front doors were gold, too. It looked like a palace.

It was ten after two, and the movie started at two-thirty. I asked David if we could see it, partly because it was one of the glitzy women's pictures I liked, but mostly because I wanted to see the inside of the theater.

"Might as well." David sighed, reaching into his wallet and gazing longingly across the street at the Wemberley Hotel. It wouldn't be the first movie he had sat through while his mind was on other things that could be done in the dark.

The inside of the theater was opulent, too, with thick red carpet and a domed ceiling flocked with golden cherubs. As I sat in a red plush seat next to David and watched the actress in her glittering evening gown go out on the town with her tuxedoed fiance, I knew that I was a lot closer to that glamorous life than I had been a couple of months ago.

Of course, the heroine in the movie loved the man she was with, and I just liked David well enough. But what did love get you? I had only ever loved two people: Miss Taylor, who could never have lived up to my dreams of her, and C.R., who was rotting on a hillside in Bartlett. The second the words The End flashed on the screen, David jumped out of his seat and blurted, "Well, I guess it's time to head over to the hotel."

The hotel lobby was high-ceilinged and trimmed in dark wood...a far cry from the little boardinghouse where I had stayed the night before. I sat on a green camelback sofa while David talked to the man at the front desk.

Within a few seconds, David came back dangling a key. "I sent the bellboy to the car for our luggage. He's going to meet us upstairs."

My only luggage was the Goldstein's shopping bag, which held the clothes I'd bought that morning. I wondered if the bellboy would know to bring it. And I wondered what a bellboy was, exactly.

We rode the elevator up to the fourth floor. It made my stomach feel funny, but that could have been nerves.

Once we were in the room, David acted nervous, too. It was a big room, bigger than the living room and the kitchen at the camp house in Bartlett.

David sat on the edge of the bed, but I couldn't bring myself to sit there next to him, so I settled in the armchair in the corner. We sat on our little perches as stiff and nervous as strangers, which, in a lot of ways, we were. When there was a knock at the door, we both jumped about a foot.

It was the bellboy carrying David's suitcase and my shopping bag. David gave him a quarter and sent him on his way.

"So," David said after the bellboy had gone.

"So," I said, "ain't it getting to be about suppertime?"

"Ah," David said, "food," like he was a member of some species that didn't require it. "You know—" his voice brightened— "they have room service here. Anything you can think of, steak...oysters, we can just call downstairs and order it, and they'll send it right up to the room."

"Is that a fact?" I was stalling. I was nervous in a way I hadn't been when we'd been, say, in the backseat of his car. The rules of the game we had played when we'd been dating had changed. There was no stopping place, no gentlemanly behavior to call upon. "But didn't you say there was a real nice restaurant downstairs? I ain't never eat in a nice restaurant before."

"All right," David sighed. "We'll eat in the restaurant. Let's go."

"Just a second." I flashed him a smile. "Let me fix my face."

The tablecloths at the hotel restaurant were pure white. There were more glasses and forks and knives on our little table for two than my family had ever owned. A serious waiter in a bow tie showed us the wine list, and David ordered wine. I was impressed by how comfortable he seemed. I was thrilled to be in such a fancy place, but I was also terrified I would do something wrong.

The waiter uncorked the wine at our table, and David ordered us steaks, medium rare. This was in the days when the man got to say what the woman would eat. In this case, it was probably just as well. I wouldn't have had any idea what to order.

The wine didn't taste that good, I wondered if it had been let to go bad, but David drank it like it was good, so I did, too. Even though the taste wasn't so hot, there was a big payoff to drinking it. After the first glass, I felt like a warm, pleasant fire was burning in my belly.

The rare steak took some getting used to. Country folk tend to cook meat till it's 'good and done,' which means it's about as tender as a pair of work boots. But after a few bites and a few more sips of wine, I started to like the meat's juiciness.

I loved the restaurant with its dim lighting and clean tablecloths and well-dressed couples sipping cocktails, and when the waiter asked if we would care for coffee and dessert, I said yes at the same time David said no.

The waiter smiled at David and said, "It sounds like the lady has a sweet tooth. Shall I bring the dessert cart around?"

"Go ahead." David wasn't rude exactly, but he was a little short. Coffee and cake weren't high on his priority list.

I ate a big slab of chocolate cake. It was moist and gooey, and as I licked the frosting from my fork, David looked at me like I was a piece of cake he was dying to gobble up. When the waiter came around asking if we wanted more coffee, David said no, thank you, shoved a couple of bills in his hand and told him to keep the change.

When we went back upstairs, David scooped me up in his arms and carried me over the threshold. I yelped and giggled, but I was a little scared that he'd drop me. I figured he must not do much heavy lifting at the store because I could feel the muscles in his arms quivering. When he did drop me, though, it was on the bed. I landed with my dress hiked midway up my thighs so you could see the tops of my stockings. I started to pull my skirt down, but David said, "No. Let me look at you."

I looked at him looking at me. His eyes were all over my body, and I liked the feeling and didn't like it at the same time. "Just a second," I said, hopping off the bed. I grabbed my shopping bag, ran into the bathroom and locked the door behind me, which was probably silly. It wasn't like he was going to come in there after me.

Of course, I was just plain silly to be so worked up about a little thing like sex. But you can never be calm about something the first time you do it.

In the bathroom I took off my dress and bra and shoes and stockings and put on the flimsy white nightgown. I couldn't decide whether my panties should stay or go. Finally, I figured they were coming off sooner or later anyway, so I slipped them off, too.

For the second time that day, I surprised myself when I looked in the mirror. My hair hung lush and loose around my shoulders, and the thin white gown clung to the curves of my breasts and hips. I had never worn anything that showed off my cleavage before, and I had plenty of it.

When I stepped out of the bathroom David let out a gasp so sharp it sounded like somebody had just stuck a knife between his ribs.

"Are you all right?" I asked.

"Oh, I'm better than all right." He sat down on the edge of the bed. "Why don't you come over here?"

I walked across the room slowly and solemnly, almost like I was marching down the aisle in a church. But when I sat down beside him, it was clear that we weren't in a church.

His mouth mashed into mine, and after that I have a hard time piecing together what happened. All I know is that within what seemed like seconds I was flat on my back, and my slinky nightgown was in a heap on the floor along with David's shirt and pants.

The act probably took three minutes. David was on me, and then I felt his thing pushing against me. It pushed and pushed and pushed like a square peg trying to get into a round hole, and then I felt a short, sharp pain. David moved back and forth maybe four times, saying, "Unh, unh, unh, unh, unh," and then he pulled out and flopped over on his side, his eyes as glassy as a fish caught yesterday.

I laughed. I couldn't help it. I lay there laughing so hard my bare titties bounced up and down, and when I saw them bouncing, I laughed even harder.

"What's so funny?" David finally mustered up the energy to say.

"Nothin'," I said, even though tears of laughter were streaming down my cheeks. "I was just so scared of what was gonna happen tonight, but...well, it wasn't so bad at all."

It wasn't so good at all either, but I wasn't about to say that. The thing that made me laugh so hard was that...well, that was all there was. For months David had been pining away like a hound dog that had lost its master, losing sleep and missing meals, and all for three minutes' worth of grunting and groaning.

And it wasn't just men who got all silly over sex. I thought of Miss Taylor and all the wives in Bartlett who were sentenced to a life of fighting coal dust and dirty diapers, all because of sex. Based on the supposed wisdom that my one, three-minute sexual encounter had bestowed on me, I decided that sex was a drug that I was immune to.

"I can do it better," David said, stroking my hair. "Make it last, I mean. This time was just quick because I've been waiting so long."

"I know you have, honey," I said, somehow feeling like I was older and more sophisticated than him, even though he had a good six years on me and I had only lost my virginity five minutes before.

He leaned over and kissed me, then kissed me again, harder. And before I knew it, he was on me again. This time, though, before he put it in, he said, "Oh, I forgot before," and got up out of bed and walked over to where his pants were, his thingy sticking out like a crank on a wringer washer. He reached in his pants pocket and pulled out a little package. "I got so excited I forgot this before, but it'll be okay." He crawled back in bed, unwrapped the package, pulled out the first rubber I'd ever seen and rolled it down over his thing.

"Oh." I giggled. "But what about rubber rationing?"

He laughed, too, but just for a second because he was ready to get down to business again. This time it lasted longer and hurt less, but I still have to say the chocolate cake I'd had in the restaurant gave me a lot more pleasure.

After he pulled out, he looked down and said, "You're bleeding a little. You might want to go wash up."

"I think I'll take a bath."

"All right, darling." David picked up my hand and kissed it. "I love you."

"I love you, too." I figured I had to say it now that we were married. It was the kind of lie you tell to spare somebody's feelings, like when your friend asks you if you like her new outfit and you say yes even though it makes her look like a heifer.

As I lay in the big tub, a cloud of red rose in the water from between my thighs. I wondered if this was what some girls called losing their innocence. But of course, I hadn't really been innocent to start with. David was the innocent one.

By the time I was finished soaking, David was snoring away, his open mouth making him look dull-witted. I slipped my white gown back on and walked over to the window, where the lights from the Tennessee Theater were shining like a thousand tiny suns.

CHAPTER 12

The next morning we did it again and then had eggs and toast from room service. We took turns getting cleaned up in the bathroom, and I put on my green suit. "We'd better get a move on," David said. "I told Pop I'd be back at the store to add up the receipts before closing."

David held my hand as we walked down the sidewalk. All of a sudden, something across the street caught his eye.

"Come with me," he said, and he pulled me out into traffic. We ran across the street, with me in my high heels I was just learning to walk in and with sore thighs from the night before.

The middle-aged man in Klein's Jewelers was just turning around the sign on the door so it said 'Open.' He saw us, smiled and opened the door for us. I felt a little thrill of anticipation.

"Good morning." The man's voice was warm and friendly. "What can I do for you good-looking young people?"

"Well, there's only one of us who's all that good-looking," David said, putting his arm around me. "We're on our honeymoon, and I thought a little bauble might make a nice memento. We were admiring the pearls in your window yesterday."

"Yes, the pearls are lovely," the clerk said. "There are more in this case over here." As he was unlocking the case, he said, "Knoxville's an unusual place for a honeymoon."

"We had to go somewhere close by," David said. "I couldn't leave my store for too long."

"What store is that?" The man was spreading out lustrous pearl necklaces and earrings and bracelets on a blue velvet cloth.

"Goldstein's Department Store in Morgan, Kentucky."

"Morgan? That's one of those little coal towns, isn't it? Some friends of mine moved out to a little town like that to open a store. They say business is great...no competition to speak of."

"It's true," David said.

"I don't know if I could live in a little town like that, even with the good business," the clerk said. "I think I'd get lonely for my own people, you know?"

"Yes," David said, and it occurred to me that both of them were talking about being Jewish.

"But how can I talk to you about lonely? You've got a beautiful new wife to keep you company. Which pearls do you like, sweetheart?"

I looked at the perfect white beads spread before me. I didn't want to be a pearl formed by the oyster that was David, but I did want to wear pearls. "They're all so beautiful."

"What do you think of this one?" David picked up a necklace, a single pearl, perfectly round, dangling from a delicate gold chain. He fastened it around my neck, and the clerk held up a mirror so I could see what it looked like. The pearl hung just below the hollow of my throat.

"I love it."

David and the clerk did their business quietly, so I had no idea what the necklace cost. As we were leaving, the man called out something to us in a strange-sounding language. "Thank you," David called back to him. "Good-bye."

On the sidewalk I said, "What did he say to us just then?"

David laughed. "All I recognized was 'Mazel tov.' He was wishing us well in our marriage."

I felt sad leaving Knoxville. Morgan was better than Bartlett, but now that I'd seen Knoxville, I could put Morgan in perspective: it was a busy little hick town, but it was still a hick town. Of course, I'd feel the same way about Knoxville many years later when I went to Atlanta. Every place you go puts every place you've ever been into perspective, which is a far bigger loss of innocence than a little thing like screwing.

We didn't talk much on the way back to Morgan, but David hummed to himself and occasionally reached over to pat me on the knee. I could tell he was happy. Once we got about half an hour from town, he said, "I've got a little surprise for you when we get back."

"Another one?" I fingered my new necklace. "David, if you keep surprising me like this, you're gonna surprise yourself right into the poorhouse."

He smiled. "Don't worry about money. You had to worry about it enough growing up. I never want you to have to worry about money again."

This statement almost made up for the oyster and pearl speech the day before. I leaned over and kissed his cheek.

The surprise was that David had made a down payment on a house. I was happy and relieved. I had been dreading living under the same roof with his mother, even though I figured I was used to living with contrary females. Now I wouldn't have to.

The house was as cute as it could be, a freshly painted little white bungalow on Pine Street, with a big snowball bush in the tiny front yard.

"I figured we'll want something bigger when we start a family," David said, "but this should suit us for a couple of years."

My stomach knotted at the thought that I would be expected to have children, but I smiled as he opened the door of the house.

The inside of the house was also white and freshly painted, with hardwood floors, a modern kitchen and a shiny tile bathroom. While David was at work that day I went to the furniture store and picked out things for the house: a maple bedroom suite, a kitchen table and chairs, a gold upholstered couch and chair for the living room. Everything I picked out was in the most modern style I could find, all sharp angles and straight lines. Of course, nothing looks out of date quicker than something that's supposed to look modern, but I didn't know that at the time.

The next six months or so blur together in my mind. I spent a lot of time making the house look pretty, hiring an old lady to sew us some curtains and, special-ordering some lamps from the furniture store. It's hard to imagine me being such a little housewife, but I think that at the time I was in love with the idea of living in a place that could be pretty and inviting, a place that could look the way I wanted it to look.

And it wasn't like I was doing that much work. A house

without children doesn't require anything more than a little sweeping and dishwashing. Most days I'd have enough time to walk downtown in the afternoon to buy a magazine from the drugstore or check out a book from the tiny library that was in the basement of the courthouse. Or I'd get my hair done at the beauty shop and stop by the store to see if there were any new dresses I liked.

I'd go back home to cook supper, which was usually a disaster. As I said, David didn't practice his Jewish faith that seriously, but he still wouldn't eat pork. And the only food I knew how to cook was swimming in pork: soup beans with ham hocks or big chunks of salt bacon, potatoes fried in bacon grease. Even the cornbread Mother taught me how to make had bacon fat and cracklings in it. I read the women's magazines and threw together some truly disgusting concoctions based on their recipes: a casserole made with canned mushroom soup and canned tuna that wasn't worth feeding to a cat; a meatloaf that somehow managed to be leathery tough and floating in its own grease; slick, slimy baked bell peppers stuffed with a soggy mixture of ground beef and cornflakes.

David cleaned his plate without complaining, but he never asked for seconds. I don't think he minded that much, to tell you the truth. After all, he hadn't married me for my cooking. He married me mostly for what came after dinner, and I had gotten better at that.

I still didn't find sex to be thrilling, mind you, but I did like the fact that David found me so beautiful and that I could reduce him to jelly by breathing just one well-planned kittenish sigh. After David would pass out, I'd get out of bed and put my nightgown on and go into the living room to read whatever potboiler I'd checked out of the library that week. The books I liked were similar to the movies I'd insist on seeing at the Hippodrome when they came to town: full of beautifully dressed women who lived lives full of glamour and intrigue.

My life wasn't full of intrigue, but thanks to my account at Goldstein's and my weekly trips to the beauty shop, I did have a fair amount of glamour, small-town glamour, at least. And while I wasn't wildly happy with David, I remember being largely content, which is why the time is so hazy in my mind. In fact, there are only two real incidents I remember from that period of my life. One was a conversation with David's mother.

David and I had been invited to his parents' house for coffee and dessert, but when we got there his mother was nowhere to be seen. It was just Mr. Goldstein and Cora serving up the pound cake and coffee. For some reason, I couldn't get past calling David's parents Mr. and Mrs. Goldstein, even though I was supposed to be a Mrs. Goldstein myself. The real Mrs. Goldstein was just as happy with being formal, I think, but Mr. Goldstein wanted me to call him 'Pop,' which I couldn't quite wrap my mouth around. If David and I both called Mr. Goldstein 'Pop,' then it made it sound like we were brother and sister, and no matter what gets said about mountain folks and their ways, the thought of that made me queasy.

The three of us ate our cake and made small talk, and as Cora was cleaning up, Mr. Goldstein said, "Vestal," now that David and I were married, he got my name right about half the time, "I believe your mother-in-law wants to talk to you in her room."

He smiled and I smiled, but I felt like my insides were caving in. I had been feeling low that day anyway. Some days I just couldn't help crying, missing C.R. and Les, who might as well have been dead, too, for all I saw of him. A conversation with Mrs. Goldstein was about the last thing I needed to cheer me up.

But I was a dutiful daughter-in-law. I knocked on her door and came in when she told me to. She was propped up on pillows in her big four-poster bed and wearing a lacy pink bed jacket. Even though she probably hadn't gotten out of bed all day, her dyed blond hair was carefully arranged, and her makeup was perfect. She was holding a pair of scissors and cutting something out of the newspaper, something about the war, I figured, to add to what David called "her scrapbook of atrocities."

"Good evenin', Mrs. Goldstein," I said. In addition to reading lots of trashy novels, I had been studying different books on manners. I was getting good at greeting people and using the right silverware.

She looked startled to see me, even though she had told me

to come in. "Vestal."

"Yes, ma'am."

"Come closer."

I walked up to the side of the bed. She smelled of perfume, but underneath was the smell of somebody who hadn't gotten out of bed for a couple of days.

She sat there a moment as if she couldn't remember what she was going to say. Then, finally, she said very slowly, "You...need... to...hire...a...cook."

"Ma'am?" I said.

"I don't know if you know this or not, but David has made a habit of coming home...that is, to his family home...every day for lunch. The boy eats like a starving lumberjack. He's never said a word against your cooking, mind you, he's too much of a gentleman for that. But I do know that men go elsewhere when they're not getting what they need from their wives." She looked me up and down, focusing a little too long on my bust. "Food seems to be the need that you are not satisfying."

"Well, I'll think about finding somebody to help with the cooking."

"Do more than think about it." She smiled at me suddenly. From her, a smile was as shocking as if she'd just turned her face inside out. "So," she said, "are you enjoying your position as the wife of one of the wealthiest men in Morgan?"

It was a trick question, and I wasn't sure how to answer it. "I like being married to David."

"So, now that you've got your respectable little house and your respectable little wardrobe, have any of the other respectable matrons come ringing your doorbell, asking you to join the Garden Club or the Sewing Circle?"

I hadn't thought about that until she asked me, but why would I? There weren't any garden clubs or sewing circles in Bartlett. "No, ma'am."

She smiled again. "I didn't think so. Why do you think that is?"

"Well, I don't know. I reckon it's probably because I'm younger than most married gals."

"It's not your age." Mrs. Goldstein laughed. "The reason

you will never be included in any social activities in this town is because you married a Jew. And because you married one, you might as well be one."

I didn't know what to say, but as it turned out I didn't have to say anything because Mrs. Goldstein went right on talking.

"Five years I've lived in this town, Vestal, and I've never gotten anything more than a frosty hello from the town ladies, and that's only when I had them backed into a corner so they couldn't help but speak to me. And even then, I hear them whispering behind my back as I leave. They're all against us in this town, Vestal, and you should never forget that."

She opened the drawer of her nightstand and pulled out a small, pearl-handled revolver. "Take this. I've got one just like it. I sleep with it under my pillow. You never know when they'll come for you. Just look at what's going on in Germany."

"But we ain't like Germany, Mrs. Goldstein. Hitler ain't running this country."

"You don't think there are men walking the streets of Morgan with as much hate in their hearts as Hitler? Take the gun, Vestal."

I took it and held it carefully. I had held Daddy's shotgun before, but that was different. The gun I was holding wasn't meant for shooting squirrels and rabbits.

Mrs. Goldstein looked tired. "You may go now."

"Ma'am, I can't walk back out into the living room with a gun in my hand."

"There are some handbags in my closet. Take one, and put the gun in it."

Mrs. Goldstein's closet was packed with skirts and blouses, shoes and purses. It seemed a terrible waste when you considered that she hardly ever got out of bed. "Which one do you want me to take?"

"It doesn't matter."

I grabbed a cute one made of black patent leather and dropped the gun into it.

Mrs. Goldstein leaned back on her pillows. "Don't forget about the cook. And Vestal?"

"Yes, ma'am?" My voice sounded shaky.

"My son is a delicate boy. Be careful with his heart."

"Yes, ma'am." I walked back into the living room, clutching the purse with the gun in it, hoping I didn't look too rattled.

David talked about his father on the way home. "It would be nice if just once the old man would talk to me about something besides the store." But once we got home, he noticed the patent leather purse I was still clinging to fearfully, as if the gun inside it would go off any minute.

"Mom gave you a purse?" David asked. "I think she might be warming up to you."

I held the purse out to him. "Look inside."

He unlatched the purse and looked. "Good God! Where did she get this?"

"I never asked. She said she sleeps with one under her pillow. She said it ain't safe to be a Jew in this town, or to be married to one."

David just stood there, holding the purse the way I had been holding it seconds earlier. "Did she talk about Hitler?"

"No, but she had a newspaper on her lap. She was cutting something out of it."

David shook his head. "Pop and I tried to keep the papers out of the house, but she'd always manage to get one. She'd make Cora bring her one or pay some boy in the neighborhood to buy one." He pulled out the gun and handed the purse back to me. "Well, having a gun might not be such a bad thing. You might feel safer when you're in the house by yourself."

It had never occurred to me to feel unsafe. Morgan wasn't a high-crime town, and while I knew the townfolks might shun me for who I chose to marry, I didn't think they'd kill me for it. After all, who was I to them? Just some dumb country girl. It wasn't like the young Jewish businessman had managed to romance a girl from one of Morgan's finest old Southern Baptist families.

"No, this isn't a bad thing at all," David said, setting the gun on top of the grandfather clock in the living room. "We'll just keep it here so it'll be hidden but handy. When you think about it, Mom was doing a good thing, in her way. She wants you to be safe. Like I said, I believe she's warming up to you."

For all of David's chatter about what a grand thing his

mother's gift to me had been, this was still the first night of our marriage that he rolled over and fell asleep without screwing me first.

The second incident I can remember happened no more than three days after my conversation with David's mother. I was finishing gathering up the dirty laundry for Polly, the woman who washed and ironed for us. When there was a knock at the door I figured it would be Ed, Polly's sixteen-year-old son who always smiled at me sheepishly when he came by to pick up the clothes. I dragged the bulging bag to the door, opened it and said, "Here you go," before I even noticed who I was talking to.

"Do I look like a washerwoman to you?"

The lanky body at the door did not belong to Ed. "Les?"

"Hidy, missy. How's married life treating you? Must be pretty good...what with you wearing pearls and diamonds in the middle of the day."

I grabbed Les's hand and pulled him into the house. "Get in here and let me fix you a cup of coffee."

Les looked around like he was appraising how much everything in the living room cost, which he probably was. Finally he said, "Why don't we go sit in the kitchen? I don't want to get coal dust on your nice furniture."

"Don't be silly. Furniture's for sitting on. Besides, you don't look like you've got no coal dust on you except for the places it don't wash off." No matter how much a miner scrubbed, he could never get the black out from under his fingernails.

"I always did like to set in a kitchen."

In the kitchen, I made a pot of coffee and set some store-bought cookies out on a plate.

Les dunked a cookie in his coffee and said, "What time does your old man get home?"

"Not for another three hours or so. How come? You got indecent intentions toward me?"

Les grinned. "If I did, your brother's ghost would come back and whup my ass. I just thought if I was your husband, I wouldn't like to come home to find you with another man...even if you wasn't doing nothin' with him but eating cookies."

I sat down at the table across from Les. "David is awful

jealous. Sometimes he'll drag me out of a place just cause' he don't like the way some man's looking at me. One day he come home when there was a Fuller brush man at the door. I was just being friendly to him, you know, but David stomped up on the porch and hollered, 'I'm sure there are other ladies in this neighborhood for you to pester. Why don't you go find one?' Then he said, 'Vestal, never let one of those men into the house. They don't tell all those traveling salesman jokes for nothing.'"

Les laughed. "Well, he's probably right. You want to hear what's going on in Bartlett?"

"Does anything ever go on in Bartlett?"

"There was a cave-in in the mines last week. A boy that had just started working there got killed."

"Ain't it somethin' to be a boy around here? You can go off to war and get shot or stay home and get killed in the mines."

"I reckon women have it easier." Les slurped his coffee.

"Maybe, maybe not...you give birth to any babies lately?" I grinned at him, but then my mind turned serious. "Besides, you don't know what it's like for women like my mother...stuck in that little house, trying to keep it clean and cooking three meals a day. It's safer than fighting a war or mining coal, but I believe I'd rather die from a bullet or a cave-in than from boredom."

"There's somethin' to that, I reckon," Les said.

My mind was still in that closed-up little house in Bartlett. "You didn't come here to give me bad news from home, did you?"

"Oh, Lord, no. Nobody's sick nor hurt nor nothin'. Maybe you should make that husband of yours drive you to Bartlett to see your people if you're so worried about 'em."

"I ain't worried. And if my family wants to see me, they can climb down off that mountainside and come find me."

"Stubborn as a mule." Les shook his head and dunked another cookie. "The reason I come here was I wanted to see you before I took off."

"Took off? Where to?"

"Knoxville. At least to start with. I quit the mines. With C.R. gone, the little bit of fun that was in that job was gone, too. And when that boy got killed last week, I said, that's it. He wasn't but sixteen year old, Vestal. I figure you've moved on to a better place, and so has C.R. in a way. It's time I'd better be moving on, too."

"David took me to Knoxville on our honeymoon. It was real nice." Part of me wanted to grab my things and go with him. But marriage was a binding contract. You didn't just pick up and leave when the urge hit you...at least you didn't back then.

Les cackled. "I bet all you saw of Knoxville was the inside of a hotel room."

I slapped Les's arm. "See if you get any more coffee and cookies out of me, you nasty thing!"

Les rubbed his arm like it hurt. "Being a married lady ain't took away none of your meanness." He looked down at his coffee cup, and his face turned serious again. "I figure I can find somethin' to do in Knoxville. What I'd like to do is go into business...get me a job that pays real money, a job where when I go into work in the mornin', I know I've got a better than average chance of living to see the end of the day." He got up from his chair. "Well, I reckon I'd better get on the road."

I walked with him to the front door. "You stay out of trouble, now."

"Stay out of it? I was hoping to stir some up." Les put on his hat and touched the brim the way men used to do when they were talking to ladies. "If you're ever in Knoxville, look me up." I promised I would, and then I watched his little car putter down the street and wondered how it was that Les was the one going places and I was the one left standing on the porch.

CHAPTER 13

Winter wasn't all bad. We put up a Christmas tree that sparkled with store-bought ornaments, and David set out a menorah that had been his grandmother's. He decided that in the spirit of celebrating each other's holidays, I should buy him a Christmas present, and he should buy me Hanukkah gifts.

I have to say I did like Hanukkah. You get one, maybe two presents on Christmas, but Hanukkah lasts for eight whole days with a present for each day.

The presents started out small. David would bring me a box of candy one day, a paperback novel the next, but each day I knew I'd be getting something, and I'd spend the whole day wondering what it might be. The gifts got bigger as the holidays progressed, ending with a seafoam green cashmere sweater and big bottle of Chanel No. 5.

For David's Christmas, I went to the drugstore and bought a big red Christmas stocking and filled it with candy canes, chocolate-covered cherries and a pair of silver cufflinks I had ordered through the mail from Klein's jewelry store. He was as tickled with his stocking as a little kid.

After the New Year, I started to feel restless. I still liked going to town and getting my hair done and buying new dresses during the week and seeing the new movie at the Hippodrome on Saturday night, but I didn't get the same thrill out of those things that I used to. Plus, the little public library hardly ever got any new books in, and I had read everything on their shelves that wasn't a Western or a picture book.

Living in Bartlett, I never could've imagined that I'd be bored living in Morgan. But I was just a teensy bit bored, simply because

I didn't have enough activities to fill my days. The church ladies in town kept themselves busy getting together to sew clothes for poor children or to put together care packages for soldiers, but as David's mother had pointed out, none of those women were going to come knocking on my door asking me to join them.

One day, flipping through an issue of *Glamour* while I was waiting for my nails to finish drying, I remembered a promise David had made when he proposed to me: that if I decided I wanted to finish high school, he would make sure I could. I decided to take him up on his offer.

And so I became a born-again high school student. The principal of Morgan High decided it was inappropriate for me to attend regular classes since I was a 'married lady' and therefore too worldly to mix with the virginal high school girls. Of course, I had seen how a lot of these girls acted out on Saturday night dates with their boyfriends, so I wasn't sure I'd use the word virginal to describe them.

The principal arranged for me to come to the school from three to five every afternoon for tutoring. It would take a while for me to finish all my courses this way, but if I did passing work, I'd be allowed to graduate with a regular high school diploma. David arranged all this, so my guess is that some money changed hands in order to convince enough high school teachers, who are used to bad pay but good hours, to work late every day.

As it turned out, my going back to school was also how I came to follow Mrs. Goldstein's advice and hire a cook. The first day of tutoring, Miss. Mills, an English teacher who put me in mind of Eleanor Roosevelt, walked into the empty classroom and said, "Vestal, there is another young woman who would like to join our tutoring session. I told her she was welcome if you agreed to it. I wondered if you would at least be willing to meet her."

"Sure, I'll meet her."

Miss Mills nodded toward the door, and a girl about my age walked into the classroom. She was wearing a dress that didn't look much better than the clothes I had to wear in Bartlett, and her dishwater blond hair was pulled back in a lank ponytail. Her gray eyes met mine and shone with what looked like defiance. She was about six months pregnant.

"This is Florrie," Miss Mills said. "As you can see, Vestal, she is in no condition to attend regular classes."

My guess was that Florrie wasn't a 'Mrs.,' despite the fact that she was 'in the family way,' as people used to say back then. "Nice to meet you," I said to Florrie.

"So I can stay?" Florrie asked.

"I don't see why you need my permission. You've got as much right to be here as I do." Probably the reason Miss Mills felt I should give permission was that David was paying a pretty penny for this tutoring, and Florrie would be getting the benefit of it for free. But that didn't bother me a bit, and I didn't think it would have bothered David either.

"Very good, then," Miss Mills said. "If you will excuse me for just one moment, I'll get your textbooks, and we will begin."

"It's been a while since I've set in one of these desks," I said after Miss Mills was gone.

"It ain't been that long for me," Florrie said. "Course, now, I'm getting so I have trouble fitting in one. I was going to school right on up till I started showing. Then the principal called me into his office and told me I couldn't stay. I reckon he was afraid the other girls might catch what I've got."

I laughed. "They might catch it all right, but they ain't gonna catch it from you."

Florrie giggled. She sounded like a little girl. "Miss Mills was madder than a wet hen when I got throwed out of school. She said a girl shouldn't have all her opportunities took away because she makes one foolish mistake. And I got throwed out of the house for getting throwed out of school."

"I got throwed out of my house, too, when Mother and Daddy found out I was engaged."

"You married that Jew, didn't you?"

"I married David Goldstein, if that's who you mean." I hoped I wasn't going to regret letting her stay.

"It's funny," Florrie said. "Everybody wants to talk about how bad Hitler is and how awful it is the way he's doing the Jews over there, and it is awful. But then you do somethin' like marry a Jew over here, and people talk about how awful you are. It don't make no sense."

I let out a long, relieved breath. "It sure don't."

Florrie rubbed her hands over her belly. "Of course, the man I was gonna marry thought he was gonna go over there and bring down Hitler single-handed. The night before he left, I thought I'd give him a little good-bye present in case I never seen him again, which I never did. This baby turned out to be a good-bye present from him."

"I lost my brother over there."

Florrie nodded, and I knew she understood.

When our class was done, I walked out with Florrie. "So, if your parents kicked you out, where are you living at?" I asked her.

"I've got a little room at a boardinghouse up the road. Miss Mills paid my rent three months in advance. She said I couldn't be out on the streets, not knowing where my next meal was coming from, with a baby on the way."

"She's right."

"I know. But I hate taking charity. I've got to figure out how to take care of myself." She patted her belly. "And this one, too."

The order that David's mother had given me popped into my mind. "Can you cook?"

"Nobody that's eat my cooking has died or nothin'."

I grinned. "Well, that's somethin' anyway. I can't cook my way out of a wet sack, and David's mother thinks I'm starving him to death. She told me I ought to hire somebody to do the cooking."

"I can fry chicken and make biscuits."

"Well, as far as I'm concerned, you're hired. Let me talk to David tonight."

That night, after David had rolled off me and was lying there with a silly grin on his face, I told him about Florrie—about her fiancé getting killed in the war and her being pregnant and alone and, by the way, the best cook in Morgan County. Could we, I asked, afford to pay her a small wage to cook supper for us during the week?

David agreed quickly—partly, I think, because he was softhearted and felt sorry for Florrie, but mostly because he had barely been able to choke down my cooking for the past several months but had been too polite to say anything about it. Also, I think David liked the idea of having another woman around the house. He hated the thought of leaving me alone all day, not because he feared me being lonely so much as me not being lonely. I told David time and time again that I had no interest in other men, but he always acted like once he left the house, the men would be lining up around the block to have their way with me. "It's not that I don't trust you," he'd always say, "it's just that you're so beautiful...and I know firsthand what men are like." So with Florrie, I was getting not only a cook, but a chaperone.

She started coming over every day around noon. She'd help me with some light housecleaning even though I'd beg her not to because of her condition, and then we'd sit down at the kitchen table with a pot of coffee between us and do our homework. Sometimes she'd start cooking before we left for school, and we'd hurry back right after class so she could have everything ready when David got home from the store.

Florrie might not have been the best cook in Morgan County, but she was still awful good. She'd make things I could never even imagine making: chicken and dumplings, roast beef, fried chicken and mashed potatoes. I turned the grocery shopping over to her, too, and she usually bought and fixed a little extra food so that we'd have enough leftovers during the weekend. This way, my terrible cooking never had to touch anyone's lips. David and I both started to put on a little weight.

Florrie and I complemented each other well. I possessed qualities she didn't have, and she could do things that I didn't have the talent, energy or patience to do. I was 'book smart' in areas where she was just average, and I ended up giving her a lot of help with our math homework. On the other hand, I couldn't boil water, and she could produce chicken potpies and banana layer cakes from scratch.

I took pride in arranging my hair and makeup and clothes to show off my natural good looks, but after my first frenzy of buying things for the house, I found that I didn't really care if the tabletops were dusty or dirty dishes were piled in the sink. Florrie was neither pretty nor ugly and didn't seem to think about her looks beyond washing and keeping her hair out of her face, but she would scrub the house till it sparkled.

One time she looked up from washing the dishes while I was sitting at the kitchen table painting my nails and said, "You know, Vestal, if you could put the two of us together, we'd make the perfect woman."

"It's true," I wiggled my fingers in the air to dry them. "But there wouldn't be a man alive who deserved us."

Florrie and I were cozy in those days, with our schoolbooks at the kitchen table and a kettle of coffee between us and a pot of chicken and dumplings simmering on the stove. A white cat with one blue eye and one green eye had taken to hanging around the house, and I'd named him Snowball after the bush in our yard. Snowball would sit in my lap while I studied, and after Florrie's baby, a dimple-cheeked little boy she named Robert, was born, he'd sit in hers.

When I think about those months, I don't think about David much, and it makes sense that I wouldn't. He worked such long hours at the store that when he got home, he'd just have time to eat supper, read the paper or listen to the radio a little while, screw me, and then go to sleep. Like a lot of men back then, David seemed like a guest in his own house. Home was a place he visited during the few hours when he wasn't at work. I wasn't unhappy with him; I just wasn't with him much at all.

Overall, I'd say I was content with my life, maybe not jumping-up-and-down happy, but content. I could see things going on like they were for several years without getting real unhappy. I guess that's what being content means, thinking things will go on like this, and that'll be okay.

Of course, things weren't going to go on like they had been, but I was too blinded by contentment to see the big change coming. I was too lulled by the sound of the cat purring and the coffee perking to hear the foundation I'd built my life on crack and crumble. That's probably why since those days with Florrie, I've never let myself be content again. A contented person is too comfortable sipping her coffee and petting her cat to look over her shoulder and see the danger that's creeping up behind her.

David had gone to Lexington on a buying trip one Friday. If leaving me during the day made him uneasy, leaving me overnight gave him fits. He always called me a half a dozen times even if he was just gone for the night, and he always returned with armloads of presents to make up for his absence.

Florrie had stayed for supper that night but left right after to put the baby to bed. It was a little after ten o'clock, and I was stretched out on the couch, reading some trashy paperback I'd picked up at the drugstore, with the cat on my belly and a box of chocolates on the floor beside me. I was enjoying having the evening to myself and knowing that tonight, the bed would be just for sleeping.

Then I heard the noise. It was a soft rustling like somebody walking around in the yard. I told myself it was nothing, somebody's dog out loose or a possum out prowling for garbage, and kept on reading.

When I heard it again, the cat jumped off my belly and stared at the door with his fur prickled up. He had obviously heard it, too, and his instincts were telling him to be alert for danger. That was when I started to get scared.

Who could be out there? Somebody who knew David wasn't at home and who was ready to knock me out and steal all our valuables? I thought about Mrs. Goldstein's warnings. Maybe she wasn't so paranoid. Maybe there could be people who wanted to hurt me just because I had married a Jew. Florrie had told me about some Klansmen over in Taylorsville who had burned a cross in the yard of a carpenter just because he had hired a couple of black men to help him build a house. If the KKK considered a white man a race traitor for hiring a black man, what would they think of a white Christian woman who shared her bed with a Jew? Shaking, I reached to the top of the grandfather clock and grabbed for the gun.

It was there. When I held it in my hand, I wasn't comforted, though. Even if I was in mortal danger, would I be able to use the thing? And if I did try to use it, would I just end up shooting off my own toe?

I would open the door and see who it was, I decided, but I'd hold the gun behind my back just in case it was a robber or a rapist or a Klansmen. I crept toward the door and opened it a crack.

"Vesta!"

I had never been so relieved to see a familiar face. "Hey, Mr. Goldstein." I opened the door wide for him to come in. "I'm glad you're here. I heard somebody outside a few minutes ago, and I like to scared myself to death."

Mr. Goldstein smiled. "It was just me. I thought I might stop by and check on you since David's gone."

"Well, I'm glad you did." I tried to put the gun back on the clock as discreetly as possible. "I had myself plum spooked for a minute there."

"Did Marge give you that gun?"

"Yessir." I couldn't think up a lie about where I would have gotten it.

Mr. Goldstein sighed and shook his head. "Marge," he said, mostly to himself. Then he asked, "Do you mind if I sit down for a minute, Vesta?"

"Lord, I don't have the manners God gave a hog, do I? Of course you can set down. Let me make you some coffee."

"You wouldn't have anything stronger, would you?"

"There probably ain't much that's stronger than my coffee. Florrie says you could use it to strip furniture. I think David might have a few beers in the icebox, though. You want one?"

"Beer would be fine."

I brought Mr. Goldstein his beer and sat next to him on the couch. I guess I should have wondered why he had showed up at the house after ten at night, but maybe because I was so glad to see a familiar face instead of the murderous ones I'd been imagining, I didn't.

Mr. Goldstein took a long swig of beer. "I'm sorry Marge is... the way she is, Vestal. Giving you that gun, probably scaring you half to death about how you aren't safe in your bed at night."

"She don't bother me."

"Well," Mr. Goldstein took another long drink, "that makes one of us."

When he said "us," the *s* slurred into a *sh* sound. That's when it dawned on me that the beer I just gave him wasn't all Mr. Goldstein had had to drink that night. I hoped he didn't ask for another beer; I didn't want my father-in-law passed out drunk on my couch.

"So," Mr. Goldstein said, setting his empty beer bottle on the coffee table, "I've been dying to ask you this question since the first time I met you. What does a gorgeous girl like you see in a schmuck like David?"

I didn't know what Mr. Goldstein had just called his own son, but I knew it wasn't a compliment. "David," I began, "is the nicest feller you'd ever meet…"

"Yes, he's nice," Mr. Goldstein interrupted. "But you don't love him."

My insides went all cold. "Now, honestly, Mr. Goldstein, how can you know what a woman feels?"

"I just know. For instance, I know Marge used to love me, but she doesn't anymore. And I know that you've never loved David… not for one second. He's a weak man, and you could never love somebody weak."

"All right," I said, my voice getting high and thin, "if I don't love David like you say I don't, then how come I married him?"

Mr. Goldstein smiled and shook his head. "Do I really need to answer that question?" I didn't say anything, so he said, "Oh, all right. If you're going to make me state the obvious, I will. But if you tell me I'm wrong, I won't believe you. Money, money, money, 'That little Jew's got bags of money,' you thought, 'and if I can get him to marry me I'll have pretty clothes and shiny jewelry and a one-way ticket out of the coal camp where I had the misfortune of being born.'"

We sat in silence for what was probably a few seconds, but it felt like much longer.

I don't know how I must have looked, but it was bad enough for him to say, "Oh, don't look at me that way. I'm not criticizing you. You have ambition. Now David, he's never had a drop of ambition. He's always just drifted along, doing well enough in high school to get into a business college but not into a university, being a good enough businessman to work for me but not to work on his own. He's a dreamer, a romantic, always losing what little mind he has over some girl. But you and me, we're not like that, Vestal. You got another beer?"

"Yessir," I said, even though I had told myself I wasn't going to let him drink any more. If I told him I'd given him the last one, he'd know I was lying. The man could see right through my milky skin and straight into my selfish little heart.

He threw back some beer, then said, "David is damned lucky to have me for a father. If he hadn't been born into a family that was already successful in business, he would've been lucky to get a job pumping gas. He's too emotional, too delicate, to get ahead in this hard world of ours. It's because of me that David has a respectable job and the money to buy you those baubles you're so fond of. But I'll tell you a secret, Vestal." He leaned in close, and I could smell the beer on his breath mixed with another smell, whiskey?—beneath it. "I have more money than David will ever see in his life. But I'll tell you another secret it brings me no happiness. Money doesn't mean a thing when you wake up in an empty bed every morning and feel yourself one step closer to being a lonely old man."

"What do you mean about waking up in an empty bed? Mrs. Goldstein is in that bed more than she's out of it."

"That's her bed, Vestal. I sleep in a separate room. I have ever since we moved to Morgan. It's Marge's little punishment for me for bringing her to this place." He smiled feebly.

"I'm sorry," I said. But I'm not sure if I meant 'I'm sorry your wife won't let you screw her' or 'I'm sorry you're telling me this.'

"I know you are," Mr. Goldstein said, his voice sounding kind again. "So I've been asking myself, is there a solution to my problem? And tonight it occurred to me. I have lots of money, but without companionship, money means nothing to me. And you, you're still hungry from all those years of cornbread and coal dust."

I scooted away from him a little. "I don't think I understand."

He scooted toward me. "I think you do. You're the most beautiful girl I've ever seen, Vestal. More beautiful than Marge was in her prime. We would be very discreet...we would only meet occasionally. I'm not as young as I used to be, but I'm not so bad, am I?"

Before I could say anything, he was on me, pushing me

back on the couch, kissing my neck and mouth. Was this real? I wondered. Or was this a scene being played out in one of the Saturday night movies at the Hippodrome? But when I felt his spit on my mouth, I knew it was real. There were no slobbery kisses in the movies.

How could a man go after his son's own wife? And David was a good man, nice and kind, even if I didn't love him.

"Stop it!" I hissed at him when I finally got my mouth away from his. "You can't do this! I'm your daughter-in-law, and...and you don't even get my name right half the time!"

"Money," he whispered into my ear like it was a sweet nothing. "Money and diamonds and new dresses and a mink coat to keep you warm." And then his mouth covered mine again. I admit that for about two seconds he had me distracted, thinking about all those pretty things, but then David's adoring face flashed into my mind, and I knew this had to stop. I wasn't sure how I was going to do it, but I was going to push Mr. Goldstein off me and send him on his way.

I was going to, but I never got the chance because right at that moment, the door swung open.

I know it looked bad. Poor David, probably thinking he'd drive back from Lexington early so he could crawl into bed with his pretty young wife, only to find her on her back on the couch with his own father on top of her. He didn't say a word at first, he just made a horrible sound, a long, painful gasp like the sound of a tire deflating.

"David!" Mr. Goldstein stood up and straightened his clothes. "You were supposed to be in Lexington." He said this as though it was David, not him, who had been caught doing wrong.

David said nothing. He just stood there in horror. I did much the same.

"At any rate," Mr. Goldstein went on, "I'm glad you got here...before things went too far. Your little wife here is quite a temptress. Bringing me beers, batting her eyelashes. And you know how things are at home, son. I'm in a weakened state…"

David's face was a ball of fire. "Don't even try it, Pop. Can't I ever have anything that's just for me? All my life I've done what you told me to. 'Go to business school, David. Move to the

middle of nowhere, David. Work in my store with me, David.'
I've given my whole life to you, Pop. And now...my wife belongs
to you, too?"

"I don't belong to…" I began, but David interrupted me with
a 'shut up.' It was probably just as well, since what I was going to
say was, "I don't belong to nobody."

"Shut up, shut up, shut up," David chanted, even though
nobody was saying anything. He strode to the grandfather clock,
picked up the gun and aimed it at Mr. Goldstein. I had never seen
violence in David before, but at that moment I was sure he was
going to kill his daddy and me both. He waved the gun toward
the door. "Get out of my house."

Mr. Goldstein inched toward the door sideways, as if he was
afraid David would shoot him in the back if he turned around.
"We'll talk tomorrow, son. At the store. After you've calmed
down."

"I'll never set foot in that damned store again!" David yelled
at his father's departing figure. "And don't call me your son!"

If somebody had showed me a picture of David's face when
he turned around and looked at me just then, I wouldn't have
recognized him. His face was red and shiny with tears and sweat,
but it was also twisted-his brow wrinkled and his lips curled in
rage and fear. He was still holding the gun.

"David, honey, why don't you put the gun back on the clock?"
I took a couple of tiny steps toward him.

"Don't you come near me." He lifted the gun like he was
going to aim it at me, but then his arm went limp, and he started
bawling. Big, racking sobs shook his whole body. He still didn't
drop the gun, though.

He ran into the bedroom and slammed the door behind him
like an angry teenager. I waited a few seconds. I didn't want to
get too close to him in case he changed his mind and decided to
shoot me.

When I pushed the bedroom door open, he was sitting on
his side of the bed, cradling the gun in his hands. "This bed," he
muttered, "our bed...my own father."

"Now, David." I spoke as softly and soothingly as I could.
"Him and me didn't get nowhere near that bed. Let me tell you

what happened."

"I knew it would never work," David said, as though I hadn't said anything at all. "Somebody like me married to a beautiful girl like you. I see their eyes on you, you know, every man on the street looking at you like a juicy steak they want to sink their teeth into...even Pop. And you. You knew you could do better." He shook his head, shaking tears onto the sheets. "Pop, Pop, Pop."

"David, would you just listen to me for a…"

But I never got to finish that sentence. It felt like it happened in slow motion, but at the same time it was too fast for me to do anything to stop it. David lifted the pearl-handled revolver, aimed it at the side of his head and pulled the trigger.

I told you about the whiteness of our house: the clean white walls, the white curtains. Now the white walls and the white bedspread were sprayed with red, and David lay on his side of the bed, where he had lain so many times before, with a red stain spreading on his white pillow.

I couldn't find the voice to scream. When I picked up the phone and asked the operator to connect me with the hospital, I sounded strangely calm, like asking for a doctor for my husband who had just shot himself was an everyday occurrence. It was only on the second phone call, the one to Florrie, that my voice broke.

As I waited for the doctor and Florrie to arrive, I sat down on the couch and tried to make sense of what had happened. The cat jumped onto my lap, and I petted him automatically. How could it be, I wondered, that an evening that started out with the cat on my lap and a dime novel in my hands had ended with my husband dead in the bedroom? Sitting there, waiting, I understood that when David had pulled the trigger, he had ended not only his life but my life as I knew it.

I sensed right then that there would never be a comfortable, contented life for me again. I didn't know the half of it, though. I knew I was sure to be the center of a scandal that would keep tongues in Morgan flapping for months, but I didn't know that I was about to be arrested for murder.

CHAPTER 14

I can't remember much about the events that led to my sitting on a narrow cot in a cell in the tiny jail at the Morgan Police Department. I know that the coroner came, and some men took away David's body. And then the police came and took me away, too. My brain wasn't working right, the only thing running through it was the picture of the barrel of the gun at David's temple, the sound of the shot, the spray of red.

Apparently the police thought I killed David. At least that was the impression the sheriff gave when he questioned me the next morning.

The sheriff was a paunchy man in his fifties who was obviously excited to have a more interesting charge on his hands than the 'drunk and disorderlys' and 'disturbing the peaces' he was used to. He questioned me in his office, peering at me from across his cluttered, coffee-stained desk. The chair I was sitting in must have been four inches lower to the ground than his was, which came in handy to remind me which person in the room had all the power, in the unlikely event that I would forget.

"So, Mrs. Goldstein," he began. Was it my imagination, or did he say the name 'Goldstein' in a particularly nasty hiss, as if to show his feelings about Jews and the little gold diggers who marry them? "How long had you and the victim been married?"

I flinched at hearing David called 'the victim,' but I didn't argue with it. He was a victim, and at that time, I felt like David was my victim just as surely as if I had put the gun to his head and pulled the trigger myself.

"No, sir. I'm sorry. Let me think...almost a year, I reckon."

"So when was it that you'uns got married?"

I should've remembered the date of our wedding; our anniversary had been coming up, and David had said he was going to buy me a pearl ring to match the necklace he had bought me on our honeymoon. "I can't think of the date right now. It was in the fall, though."

"Well, Mrs. Goldstein," the sheriff chuckled, "I have to say it's a mighty unusual kind of woman that don't remember the date of her wedding anniversary. You can be danged sure my wife reminds me what ours is every year."

"Sir, if I was just sitting here having a normal conversation, I'd be able to remember when David and me got married. But this ain't a normal conversation."

"Well, you do have a point there, Mrs. Goldstein. It sure ain't a normal conversation when a wife's being questioned for murdering her husband."

"I didn't murder David. I…I…" I knew it would sound good to say I loved him, but I couldn't quite spit it out, so instead I said, "I could never kill anybody. If you'll just let me explain what happened…"

"We'll get to that in a minute, Mrs. Goldstein. But right now I want you to tell me a little bit about how you met your husband."

I wasn't really in the mood to tell him the story of our courtship, but I wasn't really in a position to say no either. So I told him I used to come to Morgan on Saturday nights back when I was living in Bartlett and that David first spotted me at the City Drug.

"Was it love at first sight?" He gave me an encouraging smile.

I shrugged. "I don't know." I've never understood that saying. How can you love a person when you first see them?

"It was for him, wasn't it?"

"I reckon." Actually, I figured lust at first sight was more like it.

"It wasn't for you, though."

I didn't like what he was getting at. "Well, not at first sight, no. But I did like him as soon as I met him. I'm slower to warm to people than David," and here I felt the pain of speaking in the past tense, "was."

"I bet after you found out how much money he had, you

warmed up to him right fast." The sheriff was smiling, but it wasn't a friendly smile, it was a 'now I've got you' smile.

"What are you trying to say, sir?"

"I ain't trying to say nothin'. What I am saying, though, is that a rich little Jewboy like David Goldstein must've looked like a pretty good catch to a girl from the coal camps."

"Me and David made each other happy," I said. And to an extent, it was true. Of course, the main way David made me happy was by buying me presents, and the way I made him happy was by letting him screw me whenever he felt like it. But I wasn't going to say that to the sheriff. He made everything sound so dirty.

"And one of the things that made you happy was his money."

"Well, it was one of the things, but I don't understand why you're making such a big deal out of it. Anybody would rather be rich than poor, wouldn't they? I don't remember hearing it was a crime for a girl to want nice things."

"That ain't a crime, but murder is. Why don't you tell me real slow about everything that happened last night?"

I told him about David going to Lexington, about lying on the couch reading, about hearing a noise and getting the gun down because I was scared. But when I got to the knock on the door, I realized I couldn't say it was Mr. Goldstein. I kept seeing his face and the desperation and the loneliness that made him throw himself at me. Sure it was wrong of him to come after his son's wife, but I didn't, and still don't, think he would've done it if he'd known his son's life would be the price he'd have to pay. Mr. Goldstein had been drunk, lonely and horny, and I wasn't about to ruin his and his wife's life any more than I already had by making his private mistakes public. Mr. Goldstein had already lost his son; I didn't want to cost him his wife and his business, too.

"I opened the door, and it was a friend of mine."

"What's her name?" the sheriff asked.

"It was a him, and I don't think he'd want me to tell you his name."

"I don't give a damn what he wants. If he was on the premises the night a man died, then I need to know the son of a bitch's name."

"Can I just...tell what happened for now?"

The sheriff looked irritated, but said, "For now."

"So my friend sits down and I offer him a cup of coffee, but he asks if I've got anything stronger, so I get him a beer. That was a mistake, though, because the more he talks, the clearer it is that he's had plenty to drink already. He keeps telling me how beautiful I am and how if we was to get somethin' going, David wouldn't have to know about it. And of course, I tell him no, but I'm trying to be as polite as I can on account of this person being a friend of mine." I took a deep breath. "But he ain't actin like a friend, and he ain't taking no for an answer. He's got his arms around me, and he's pushing me back on the couch, trying to kiss me, and just then David walks in, back early from his trip. And, well, you know how it looked."

"So then what happened?" the sheriff asked.

"Well, David started acting all crazy, he always was real jealous, and he gets the gun down from the clock and starts waving it around. He runs off...uh, my friend...and goes in the bedroom. I follow him in there to try to explain what happened, but before I get the chance, he shoots himself."

"You mean to tell me that a man caught his wife with another man, went crazy from jealousy and shot his own damn self instead of the son of a bitch fooling around with his wife? What kind of sense does that make?"

"You'd just have to know David. He didn't get mad. He got... hurt." For the first time since this awful mess happened, I felt tears in my eyes.

"Well, let me tell you what I think, Mrs. Goldstein. I think you've cooked up a nice little story that'll explain why your prints will be all over the gun, because you heard somebody outside and took the gun down because you were scared. And you've explained how it is that you didn't shoot your husband while he was in bed. Why, he shot hisself on accounta being so jealous of you and your made-up friend."

"My friend ain't made up. Like I said, I just don't want to drag him into all this."

"Well, you'd better drag him into it 'cause if it's just your word, I ain't too prone to believe it."

"I don't understand why you won't believe me. Why would I want to kill my own husband?"

"Mrs. Goldstein, it ain't that hard to figure out, is it? Your husband is worth more dead than he is alive." The sheriff gave a little smile when he said that line. Clearly, in his mind he was the hero of his own little movie about the smart, tough-talking detective who was about to send some murdering dame up the river. He signaled to one of his officers and said, "Lock her up."

"I'm telling you the truth," I yelled as the cop led me away.

"Well, when you decide you want to tell me who your friend is, we'll talk again. In the meantime, we're gonna hold you while we investigate the case."

In the cell, the tears spilled. I cried for the bullet through David's brain, for the train wreck that killed C.R., for the sudden, violent way men's lives ended. And I cried for myself, too, trapped in a gray box with no hope of getting out, a victim of my beauty just like David, just like his father. Mr. Goldstein. As much as I wanted out of this cell, out of this town, I couldn't bring myself to say his name.

Think, I told myself. There had to be a way out, but I was floating in so many tears that my thoughts were as blurry as images seen through a rain-streaked window.

At noon, a cop brought me a bologna sandwich, which I couldn't even imagine eating. But as he handed it to me through the bars, a picture flashed in my mind: a half-eaten bologna sandwich sitting on a table in a camp house in Bartlett.

I looked at the cop. He was young, with a faint fuzzy moustache that was barely visible on his upper lip. "Say," I whispered, "could I have a pencil and a piece of paper?"

"Uh, I don't know." He looked around, maybe for somebody who could answer my question. "I'd have to ask the sheriff."

The little cop couldn't have been much older than me. I was sure my eyes were puffy from crying, but I noticed that didn't stop him from stealing a glance down my top. "Now, really, officer," I said, leaning forward to give him a better view, "do you think I'd find anything real dangerous to do with a pencil and paper? About the best I could do would be to write 'help me' on the paper, make it into an airplane and sail it between the bars." I looked down the length of his uniform, then looked back up at him and smiled. "Please, officer. I promise to be a good little jailbird and do whatever you say."

His eyes glazed over for a second, and when he came to, he said, "I'll be right back."

I let my hand brush his for a second when I took the pencil and paper. "Thank you, officer," I whispered.

"Yes, ma'am." He gave me a goofy grin. I had him.

There was no table in my cell, so I stretched out on the floor and wrote.

When I read back through the letter, I wasn't sure if it would work or not, but I figured it was worth a try. I folded up the paper. I had a message. Now all I needed was a messenger.

My messenger turned out to be Florrie, who came in with the baby in one arm and a basket of fried chicken and biscuits in the other. Her eyes were swollen from crying; she looked as upset as I was. The officer opened my door long enough for Florrie to hand me the basket, then shut it tight again. After he left, Florrie shook her head. "That little man searched my basket. Said he had to make sure I wasn't bringing anything you could use to escape. I wouldn't have been a bit surprised if he'd searched Robert's diaper, too."

"I don't reckon he would've liked what he found if he had."

Florrie didn't crack a smile. "Vestal, I know you didn't do it. You couldn't kill David nor nobody else either. Lord, you get sick watching me cut up a chicken."

"He did it his own self, Florrie. Right in front of me."

Florrie winced like she was trying to imagine it. "Vestal, I'll do anything I can to help you. Right now all I've done is feed your cat and fry you chicken, but if there's anything…"

"There is one thing you can do for me." I handed her the letter. "You remember Les Tipton that used to play poker over at the hardware store on Saturday nights? He's down in Knoxville now, at least I hope he is. I need you to get an operator in Knoxville to find his phone number. And when you call him, read him this letter."

CHAPTER 15

The coffee in jail was ice cold, but I drank it anyway and nibbled on one of Florrie's biscuits, which was the first solid food that had passed my lips since two nights before. My neck hurt from another restless night on the metal cot. I was wondering how much longer they could hold me without charging me with anything when my little pet cop came in to announce that I had a visitor. I figured it was Florrie, coming to tell me she'd had no luck finding Les, but when I looked up the woman I saw was not frumpy Florrie, but an elegant older woman dressed expensively in a pearl-gray suit with matching pearl-gray netted hat. Muzzy-headed from lack of sleep, it took me a few seconds to recognize the pained but still carefully made-up face behind the net.

"Mrs. Goldstein?" I had never seen her outside of her house.

"My husband wanted to come speak with you, but I made it clear that seeing you again was not an option." Her voice sounded calm, but it was the kind of calm that comes after you've cried and screamed and raged so much that there are no more emotions left to bubble to the surface. "However, he did speak with the sheriff."

"What did he tell him?" In my mind I was hearing Mr. Goldstein telling the sordid tale of the little gold-digging slut who had murdered her husband only minutes after trying to seduce her father-in-law.

Mrs. Goldstein would not meet my eyes. "He told him it was probably suicide. There had been another attempt a few years ago…when David was in school. It was over another girl. He had to spend a month in the hospital in Louisville. I told you…he was delicate." I didn't have to look in her eyes to know there were tears in them.

My first, crazy response was jealousy that David had loved another girl enough to try to kill himself over her. Hadn't he told me he'd never loved a girl like he loved me? But after I told my vanity to hush, I understood what Mrs. Goldstein was getting at. If there had been no murder, then there was no murderer. "Thank you, Mrs. Goldstein."

"It wasn't me who talked to the sheriff. Personally, I would be quite happy to see you spend the rest of your life in this cell; it would certainly protect a great many of the poor, helpless men on this earth. You may not have killed David, but he killed himself because of you. As far as I'm concerned, that makes you no better than a murderess. Of course, my husband disagrees with me, but he seems to have a guilty conscience where you're concerned."

There are some things words just can't make right. Maybe that's why when I tried to speak to Mrs. Goldstein, the words that spilled out of my mouth were a useless jumble. "Your husband and me never…and David, I never meant to…"

"Don't try to explain yourself. I only came down here concerning a business matter. As David's widow, you would normally be entitled to inherit his property. However, given the circumstances, my husband and I feel it would be wrong to reward you for the misfortune you have brought to our family. Our attorney suggested that you sign a waiver, which I have right here." She opened her pearl-gray purse and pulled out a pen and a neatly folded piece of paper. "By signing this waiver, you agree to give up all rights to David's property in exchange for a single payment of one thousand dollars."

I didn't know how much money I'd be giving up, but it didn't take a genius to know which end of the stick I was getting. "What if I don't sign it?"

"Well," Mrs. Goldstein began, "that's certainly your choice. But I'd venture to say if you don't take the thousand dollars that's in my purse, it would go a long way toward persuading the sheriff to take his sweet time filling out the papers to get you released. How long do you think he'd keep you in here for a thousand dollars? Two weeks? Two months? Longer?"

Everybody knew the Morgan Police Department was especially partial to payoffs. The Saturday night poker game at the hardware store was illegal, but every Monday morning the sheriff would send a deputy to the store to pick up a percentage of Saturday night's ill-gotten gains in a plain white envelope. Les used to joke that the only sure winner of the Saturday night poker games was the Morgan Police Department.

The kickbacks the sheriff got from cockfighters, moonshiners and garden-variety bootleggers were also well known. If Mrs. Goldstein gave him a thousand dollars, I figured I'd be in the holding cell till my hair was gray and there wasn't a tooth left in my head.

I signed the waiver, and Mrs. Goldstein counted ten one-hundred-dollar bills into my palm. "That should be more than enough money for you to buy a train ticket and start a new life. Do you follow me, Vestal?"

"I'm no fool, ma'am."

"I didn't think you were." Mrs. Goldstein folded the paper and put it back in her purse. "I've called you many names, but 'fool' is not one of them." She clutched her purse in both hands, turned her back on me and walked away without another word.

The sheriff and the guard unlocked my cell ten minutes later. "You're free to go, Mrs. Goldstein," the sheriff said in such a pleasant tone that I wondered if a few dollars had passed from the older Mrs. Goldstein's hands into his.

I walked out of the building as fast as I could without actually running. I didn't want to give them the chance to change their minds and lock me up again. When I got outside and the bright sunshine hit my face after me being cooped up with no fresh air and no light, I felt relief for the first time in three days. I didn't think anybody or anything at that moment had the power to make me feel better than the sun on my skin, but then I saw somebody who did.

"Les?" He was leaned up against his car, smoking a cigarette and looking like he was deep in thought. He was also wearing a suit and tie, which was something I'd never seen on him before. He had just worn clean overalls to C.R.'s funeral.

"Missy?" He dropped his cigarette in shock, then stomped it

out. "You ain't supposed to be out here; you're supposed to be in there!"

"They let me out. David's daddy talked to the sheriff."

"Is that a fact? And here I was, practicing my speech for the sheriff. I was gonna tell him how I come over to your house the other night, knee-walking drunk on moonshine. I was gonna say how I knowed your husband was out of town and had got it in my head that I was gonna have you or die trying."

I laughed for the first time in days. "You was gonna say that with a straight face?"

"You bet I was, missy, and I was gonna tell how David busted in on us and it looked like we was sparking even though you was really fighting me off. I practiced my little speech all the way from Knoxville. I figured if I done a good enough job to get you out, I might just keep on driving till I got to Hollywood."

"They don't put bald men in the movies."

"Sure they do. They just put wigs on 'em." He opened his car door. "You want a ride back to your house?"

"It ain't my house no more, but I reckon I ort to stop by and get my things."

On the way, I told Les about how I had signed away my rights to inherit David's property. He kept shaking his head and saying, "You ort not to have done it," and he was probably right. But I was so glad to be out of jail that I didn't care.

The house didn't look like my house anymore. Nothing on the outside had changed, of course. The white paint was still clean and unchipped. The snowball bush was still in the front yard, and Snowball the cat was lounging in one of the front porch rockers. I knew that just a little more than forty-eight hours ago I had been lounging, too, lying on the couch in the living room of this now strange house and thinking of it as home. But it wasn't my home anymore. I had signed my right to it, and to everything else, away.

If I had any doubt that the house wasn't mine anymore, it would've been erased when I put my key in the door and it wouldn't turn. "It never stuck before," I said, stepping aside to let Les try.

Les jostled the key around in the hole. "They've changed the locks on you, missy."

I only cuss when the occasion requires it, and this occasion did. "Goddamn it to hell! I can live with not getting any of David's money, but can't I at least get my own damn clothes?"

"We'll get you your clothes, missy. I'll be right back." Les ran out to his car and came back carrying a hammer. "Now, which one's your bedroom window?"

"Les, we can't break into this house! I ain't been outta jail thirty minutes yet!"

"You ain't gonna break into this house. You're gonna stand there and beg me not to do it. That way, I'm the guilty one in case anybody comes by to hear us."

"Les, don't you dare break that window!" I hollered as he wrapped his hand in his jacket and hammered at the glass.

His arm and hand still covered, he knocked aside the sharp points of glass that jutted from the window frame.

"Don't you open that window!" I hollered as he opened it, and then I added, "Don't you dare go in there!" as he climbed on in. I leaned toward the window and whispered, "There's a suitcase in the closet you can put my dresses in, and my jewelry's in that rosewood box on the dresser," then I hollered, "You get out of there right this minute!"

Actually, Les was out of there in less than three minutes. As we threw the suitcase in the car and took off, I regretted that I had been too embarrassed to tell Les to fetch me some underwear from the top drawer of the bureau. Of course, Mrs. Goldstein had given me a thousand dollars, so I figured I could probably buy myself a few pairs of drawers when I got to wherever I was going.

"I thought I might take you to Knoxville," Les said as we drove away from the house. "A pretty girl like you ort to be able to find herself a job there. I might even know somebody to help get you one."

"Let's go," I said, but then I thought again and said, "But take me to see Florrie first."

"You'd better make it fast," Les said. "Your mother-in-law's gonna be madder than a wet hen when she sees that house has been broke into."

"I won't be five minutes."

As it turned out, I was right, because Florrie wasn't at the boardinghouse. I asked her landlady for a piece of paper and an envelope. On the fancy stationery she gave me I wrote,

Florrie,

I'm out of jail and am going to Knoxville. You can keep the cat.

Vestal

I folded the note and stuck it in the envelope, and when I was sure Florrie's landlady wasn't looking, I slipped two of the hundred-dollar bills Mrs. Goldstein had given me in the envelope, too. I ran up the stairs, slipped the note under Florrie's door and was back in Les's car in no time flat.

"So," Les said, "have you seen enough of Morgan?"

"Enough to last me two lifetimes."

We headed south on the same road David and I had traveled on our honeymoon, when I had spent the whole day knowing that my destination was the bed I'd share for the first time with a man. This time I had no idea what my destination was, but not knowing felt good. For the first time, nobody was telling me which way to go: not Mother or Daddy, not Miss Taylor, not poor, dead-and-gone David. As soon as Les got me to the city, I was going to find my own way.

PART II: DIAMONDS

CHAPTER 16

"Just drop me off downtown," I said as we passed a sign marked 'Knoxville.'

"Missy, I ain't dropping you off on the side of the road like somebody's old mangy dog. Let me stop by work a minute to make sure they ain't tearing the place apart, and then we'll find you someplace to stay."

I didn't want Les to do any more for me than he already had, but I also knew it would hurt his feelings if I turned down his help. "All right."

Les turned onto a side street lined with little frame houses with peeling paint that didn't look too different from the houses in Bartlett. Clothes and diapers were hanging on lines in yards that had more dirt than grass. I had never pictured city neighborhoods looking so poor. I had always thought of the city the way it was in the movies: all bright lights and supper clubs and lavishly furnished apartments. I never thought that some city folks might have it as hard as I did growing up.

We pulled over in front of a gray concrete block building, the windows of which were covered with brightly painted signs advertising JFG Coffee and chicken livers and cornmeal. I was so busy reading the little signs in the windows that it took me a minute to see the big sign that stretched across the top of the building:

LES TIPTON'S STOP 'N SAVE MARKET

'Save more with Les.'

My mouth dropped open. When I had asked Les where he was working, he just said a grocery store, leading me to believe that he was bagging groceries or stocking produce. "This...this is your store? How come you didn't tell me?"

"'Cause then I would've missed the pleasure of you looking

at it all slack-jawed."

"How could you afford to open up your own store?"

"I had me a little somethin' saved back. You think I spent all that gambling money on chewing gum? Besides, this place didn't cost much. When I first seen it, it wasn't fit for the rats that was living in it."

Inside, the Stop 'n Save was sparkling clean, lined with rows of bright boxes and cans. Then I noticed the shoppers, the loose-dressed housewives with a baby in one arm and a shopping basket in the other, a skinny old man at the counter buying a can of sardines and a box of crackers.

"Les," I whispered, "all the people that's in here is colored."

Les cackled and hollered at the old man with the sardines. "Hey, Edgar! My pretty friend over here was just noticing that you're colored."

Edgar, a soft-eyed old man with a neatly trimmed gray moustache, looked down at his hands in mock shock. "Now, how in blue blazes did that happen?" he said. "When I woke up this mornin', I was as white as you." He gave me a grin and a wink and walked out of the store.

"How come you embarrassed me like that?" I asked when Edgar was gone.

"I was just funning you," Les said. "So was Edgar. He's a good ol' boy. Just cause it's quare to see colored people in Morgan don't mean it's quare in Knoxville. This is the colored part of town. When I bought this place, they wasn't but one grocery store on this side of town, and their prices was so high I run 'em out of business in two months." He hollered over to the cashier, a pudgy white girl a few years older than me. "You doing all right without me today?"

"I didn't have much choice, did I?"

The pudgy girl stared at me like I had just killed her dog. I was staring back at her just as mean, but then Les said, "Why don't we go back to my office for a minute?"

Les's office was a back room stacked with fruit crates and cases of canned vegetables. "So," I joked, "why don't you fire that mean little heifer of a checkout girl and give me her job?"

"Because," Les said, looking me square in the eye in a way

few men were able to do, "that mean little heifer is my wife."

I wanted to apologize, but I was laughing so hard I couldn't breathe. Les was laughing even harder than I was.

Within two hours of hitting Knoxville, I had a place to stay and the prospect of a job. I felt a little bad because I'd said I'd make my own way once I hit Knoxville. I owed the place and the job to two phone calls from Les, one to the owner of the Mimosa Boarding House for Women and one to Diller's department store. Of course, a city like Knoxville's not that different from a town the size of Morgan; you can't get a thing done unless you know the right people. By letting Les use his connections, I was putting myself in a position where I wouldn't have to rely on him anymore.

My new life consisted of waking up in my narrow bed in my plain but clean room in the Mimosa Boarding House. I had bought a couple of things to make the room homier, a green oval rug with pink roses, so my feet wouldn't hit the cold hardwood floor first thing in the morning, and a little lamp with a frilly pink shade that I set on the nightstand. These feminine touches saved the room from total dreariness, but it still wasn't all that homey. There was no doubt that my little cubbyhole in the Mimosa was a place to stay, not a place to live.

After I would dress and fix my hair and makeup and take my turn in the bathroom down the hall, I'd go downstairs to eat the biscuits and gravy that Mrs. Henry, the owner of the Mimosa, had cooked.

I ate my biscuits and drank my coffee at a long table filled with plain-faced girls in dull, cheap suits who talked and giggled with one another but never with me. Sometimes I entertained the thought that the girls distrusted me because I was younger than them or because I was from a little wide place in the road in Kentucky, but I knew what it really was. They saw my shiny black hair and my long-lashed, cat-green eyes and my big titties and tiny waist, and they hated me for them. Even Mrs. Henry, who was too old to feel any competition with me, told me six times as I was moving in that she ran a "respectable home for good girls," as though my looks made me automatically suspect.

It takes a strong, confident woman to trust and befriend a woman who's beautiful, and real strength and confidence is much rarer than beauty.

Of course, I wouldn't have had anything to say to those boardinghouse girls anyway. The were all aged nineteen to twenty-five and were working as typists or file clerks or shopgirls or in the other low-paying positions that were left over for women after the war ended and the men who survived it wanted their jobs back. Those girls were just killing time, making a little money until they quit work, married and had babies. And with me, even though I was just seventeen, I had already been married and widowed and jailed on suspicion of murder. I was younger than those girls in years, but much older when it came to real living.

After breakfast, I'd take the streetcar to Diller's department store downtown. I liked being a part of the bustle of the city men and women on the sidewalks, hurrying off to their jobs in offices and banks and stores, and I liked walking into Diller's and seeing the new dresses and shoes and purses on display.

Once I settled into my post in the store, though, I was in for nothing but a day of boredom and pain, my throbbing feet trapped inside the high-heeled pumps women were expected to wear to work in those days. I worked at the costume jewelry counter, which was hard because I hated what I sold. I would occasionally use my Diller's employee discount to buy a new blouse or skirt or nylons, but I would never waste one thin dime on the shiny geegaws I was stuck selling. The paste pearls, the rhinestone brooches, the gold-painted necklaces all filled me with an aching sadness.

I'll admit that a lot of glamour is based on lies. You put some color on your lips so they'll look fuller and brighter; you put on some stockings so your legs won't look blotchy and stubbly. You might even put on a padded bra to make your bust look fuller, although I've always felt like that kind of false advertising leads to dissatisfied customers.

A lot of glamour is fake, but the things a girl uses to fix herself up ought to be real. Sweaters should be cashmere instead of Orlon, hair should be colored by a professional instead of dyed at home, and jewelry should be made of real gems and precious metals instead of paste and tin. One real cashmere sweater with no jewelry beats a closetful of Orlon sweaters and a drawer full of costume junk. Glamour means that a girl should turn herself into an elegant illusion, not a cheap trick.

Whenever a girl bought one of the worthless trinkets I sold, I felt sorry for her. Some of them, you could tell, wanted better things and couldn't afford them; others had no more taste when it came to shiny things than a magpie eyeing a piece of aluminum foil.

When men stopped at my counter, I had a hard time hiding my contempt for them. At least the girls were buying this garbage for themselves; these men were buying it for their wives and girlfriends. Each time I boxed up a string of paste pearls and handed them to a male customer, I had to bite my tongue to keep from saying, "I hope you don't plan on passing these off as real, you cheap bastard."

But of course, I never said anything like that. I smiled at the customers even though my blisters bled in my high-heeled shoes, and I kept my job, which paid me just enough to keep my little room at the Mimosa and go out for a hamburger and a movie on Saturday nights, which I did alone. It was sad to look up at those fabulous faces on the silver screen and know that even though I lived in the city now, I was no closer to that kind of life than I had been in Morgan. Maybe I was even farther away from it. At least when I was with David, there had been what seemed like an unlimited supply of money.

There was a story in one of the books back at the Bartlett School about a man who had done something wrong, and his punishment was to be tied up and starve while looking at and smelling all this delicious, juicy fruit that was just out of his reach. That's how I felt those first months in Knoxville. I worked all day surrounded by beautiful clothes I couldn't afford and walked down streets lined with restaurants and nightclubs and beautiful apartment buildings that were off-limits to a shopgirl like me. Like the man in the story, a feast was spread out before me, but it was just there for me to look at and want. I couldn't touch it. My hands were tied.

CHAPTER 17

I met Lucy in the 'employees only' ladies' lounge (back then, people were too genteel to say 'toilet') at Diller's. I had flopped down in the chair next to the mirrors where the shopgirls reapplied their lipstick and tied back their hair. My feet were so swollen I could barely slip them out of my pumps, and I was so sick to my stomach that I had nearly thrown up on a rude customer a few minutes earlier. Not that he wouldn't have deserved it. I leaned back in the chair and closed my eyes.

"Not that it's any of my business, hon, but you look like you ought to take the rest of the day off."

I opened my eyes to a girl in her twenties who was leaning over me and looking concerned. She wasn't pretty, exactly, but she knew how to make the most of her looks. Her hair was a dull mousy brown, but it was arranged in perfect, shoulder-length curls. Her nose was a little crooked, but she distracted from it with red lipstick and dramatic eyeliner.

"I'll be all right in a minute," I said. "I'm just having one of my spells."

"Spells? What are you, a witch?"

I couldn't help but smile a little. "I've been having these dizzy spells. Spells where I feel like I'm gonna throw up. If I can just set down for a few minutes, it passes, though."

She took a cigarette from a silver case and fired it up with a matching lighter. "Well, you can call 'em spells if you want to, honey, but it sounds to me like you went and got yourself knocked up."

"Knocked up?"

"Jeez, where are you from? The moon? Knocked up.

Expecting. In the family way. P-r-e-g…"

"Oh, my Lord!" My life had been turned so upside down I had forgotten about 'my time,' as Mother always called it. The last blood I had seen had been David's, not mine. "But I'm not just sick in the mornin'—"

"Doesn't matter what time of day it is." She reached over and put her hand on my forehead and then, to my shock, reached inside the top of my blouse to rest her palm just under my collarbone. "Nope. No fever. Just knocked up, I bet. You married?"

"Widowed."

She rolled her eyes. "Look, hon, the war's been over just a little too long for you to be using the knocked-up-by-a-dead-soldier story. If you plan on staying in that condition, you've got to come up with a better story than that."

I opened my mouth to say that I really was a widow, but what came out instead was, "I can't be having a baby," and then I just broke down crying, which I hardly ever do in front of people.

Lucy, who still hadn't told me her name, sat on the arm of my chair and held me. I cried about David, about my days in jail, about my lousy job, about how despite their best efforts women seem to fall into the same traps every time. Lucy rubbed my back and lit me a cigarette, then took it away from me after one puff made me gag.

"Listen," she said, "I'll tell you a secret. If you've got fifty bucks, you can take care of your problem."

Except for what I gave Florrie and what I used to pay my first week's rent at the Mimosa, I hadn't touched the money from David's parents. I had wanted to save it for my future. "I've got it."

"All right." Lucy was businesslike all of a sudden. She opened her purse, took out a slip of paper and started writing on it, her cigarette clamped between her red lips. "That's her address. She's home just about all the time, but you'll want to go see her on a Saturday so you won't have to go to work the next day. It's not a lot of fun, but a few minutes of pain beats years of changing diapers and wiping noses."

Back home, if a girl got pregnant she stayed that way unless the baby got born too early and died. I wanted to make sure Lucy was talking about what I thought she was talking about. "So if I go see this woman she'll fix it so I ain't pregnant no more?"

"That's what she'll do, all right. But you can't tell anybody because it's against the law. You can keep a secret, can't you?"

"Sure."

"All right then." Lucy snapped her purse shut and checked her curls one last time in the mirror. "You go get yourself taken care of, then. I wrote down my number for you, too. After you're all better, give me a call and we'll go out and celebrate. After an ordeal like that, a girl ought to go out and have a little fun." She grinned. "Of course, if you hadn't been having fun, you wouldn't have ended up in this situation in the first place." She winked and disappeared through the ladies' room door.

I looked down at the slip of paper. There was an address with no name and then under it, a phone number with 'Lucy' scrawled beside it.

Saturday morning I called a taxi and asked the driver to take me to Walnut Street, which was what had been written on Lucy's paper.

"What's the street number, miss?" he asked me.

I was afraid if I gave him the number, he would know what I was doing. "Uh, no number in particular. Just let me off on Walnut Street."

He looked at me like I was an idiot, but he drove anyway.

The farther he drove, the more scared I got about what I was about to do. My terror increased when I began to recognize the neighborhood where the cab was taking me. When I passed Les Tipton's Stop 'n Save, I ducked my head down in case Les might be where he could catch a glimpse of me. The driver made a left, then another left, then said, "You just wanted me to let you off at Walnut, right?"

"Right." I got out and paid him. I was too ignorant to know I was supposed to give him a tip, so I didn't understand when he scowled at me.

I walked down Walnut Street, where black children played in the tiny yards of the rundown frame houses. Once, I stepped off the sidewalk so as not to interfere with the two little girls who were turning a rope and solemnly chanting some nonsense rhyme while a third girl jumped, her pigtails bouncing. When I came to the building marked 237, I was sure Lucy had given me the wrong address. Two-three-seven Walnut Street was a plain white frame house with potted plants on the porch and clothes drying on the line in the yard. I had been expecting a building that looked more businesslike, a doctor's office, maybe, with a back room where the top-secret procedures were performed.

I stood on the sidewalk so long the little girls stopped jumping rope. Finally, the one who had been doing the jumping said, "How come white ladies always stare at that house for an hour before they go knock on the door?"

Well, I thought, this must be the place, and I'll be damned if I'm going to stand on the sidewalk all day so an eight-year-old can talk about what a fool I am. I walked up to the door and knocked. After a few long seconds, a well-padded black woman opened it. Her round face was the color of milk chocolate. At first it was easy to mistake her for fat, but when I saw the massive arms that bulged out from the short sleeves of her flowered housedress, I realized that a lot of her mass was muscle.

When she said hello, her greeting was a cautious question. In her business, you couldn't be too careful.

"Hello," I said, trying to sound polite and trustworthy. "My friend Lucy…" I tripped up for a second because I realized I didn't know Lucy's last name, but I finally finished—"said I should come see you."

"Did she now?" The woman looked me up and down, resting her eyes for a second on my belly, which was still flat as a plate. "Well, come on in."

I followed her through a clean living room with a picture of a blue-eyed Jesus hanging over a gold sofa and into the spotless white kitchen, where a man was tinkering around under the sink. I could see his slacks and loafers, but his head and shoulders were hidden under the sink cabinet. A toolbox sat on the floor beside him. I was a little nervous about talking about my situation with the plumber in the room, but my hostess didn't seem to notice him at all.

"What's your name, honey?" she asked.

"Vestal." I kept shooting nervous glances at the figure under the sink.

"Well, Vestal, why don't you just sit down at the table yonder, and I'll fix you a nice cup of tea. A girl in your state don't need no coffee; you're nervous enough as it is."

I was a little embarrassed that my nerves were showing.

"My name's Bertha, but your friend probably told you that. Folks round here call me Dr. Bertha." She turned on the sink to fill the teakettle, making the figure underneath the sink jump out backward and stand up, soaking wet.

"Now, Mama, why did you go and turn on the sink with me right under that leaky pipe?" When the plumber spoke, it was clear he wasn't a man at all. She was a girl a few years older than me, dressed in a man's crisp white button-down shirt and gray pleated pants. She was smiling despite her irritation, a crooked grin full of straight, white teeth which looked even whiter against her caramel-colored skin. Her short, black hair glistened with water droplets.

"This here's my daughter, Treasure," Bertha said. "She helps me out around here."

"Yeah, when Mama isn't trying to drown me." Treasure took a clean dishtowel from a drawer and patted her face dry.

"Treasure goes to school over at Frederick Douglass A and T," Bertha said, putting the kettle on the stove. "She's gonna be a real doctor one of these days, not just an herb granny like her mama."

"Now, Mama, you're more than just an herb granny." Treasure sat down on a kitchen chair backward, straddling it. I had never seen a woman who moved like she did, like a man, but graceful. She put me in mind of a cat. "You worked with old Doc Evans for years."

"He was a good man." Bertha set a steaming cup in front of me. "But his hands was never steady like mine, especially once he got the arthur-itis. I bet I put in and took out more stitches than he ever did. And I know how to do things nice and clean, just like he did. Vestal, you ain't got nothin' to worry about."

I sipped my tea and nodded, trying to look brave.

"Now, how far along are you?"

"I...I don't really know. So many things have happened. I've missed my time maybe twice."

"Well, that's good. You ain't that far gone, then." Bertha looked me in the eye like she was searching for something. "You ain't married, are you?"

I was about to say, "I'm widowed," but good sense stopped me. Most widows, it occurred to me, would be happy to discover they were pregnant with their dead husband's child, to know that this way, at least a part of their husband would live on. So why had I not even considered having the baby? Was it because I had never wanted to be a mother or because I wanted to put every part of my marriage to David, except the jewelry he gave me, behind me? And if the answer to that question was yes, what kind of person was I?

"No," I said. "I'm not married."

"And you're sure you don't want to be a mother yet?"

Not yet. Not ever. "I'm sure."

"All right. I ain't one to pry, so that's all I'm asking. Treasure, go on and get her ready."

Treasure led me into a bedroom that was just behind the kitchen. It looked like a regular bedroom except with no decorations, and the bed was covered with a clean white sheet. "Mama likes girls to leave the money on the dresser," Treasure said. "She gets funny about money changing hands."

I took two twenties and a ten out of my purse and laid them down.

"All right, Vestal, go ahead and get undressed and lie on the bed. You can cover up with the sheet if you get cold."

"Well," I said, "I reckon if I hadn't got undressed and laid on a bed in the first place, I wouldn't be here."

Treasure grinned. "Not too many girls that come in here have a sense of humor. I like you."

Her eyes, I noticed, were so deep brown they were almost black. like coffee. And then I felt strange because I had never noticed another woman's eyes before. Well, only one other woman's. Miss Taylor's.

"I'll be right back," Treasure said.

I undressed and crawled between the white sheets.

In a few minutes, Treasure came back carrying a tray with a

big basin of water. "All right, Vestal, I'm going to have to shave you."

I probably should've known what she was talking about, but I didn't. "Shave me? Where?"

Treasure raised an eyebrow. "Where do you think?"

"Oh. Oh."

Sometimes you have to tell modesty to take a walk so you can get on with your life. I pulled up the sheet and opened my legs. A few days before I had been uncomfortable talking to a black person in Les's store and now I was lying in a bed, trying to act calm, while a black woman, a most unusual black woman, besides, soaped up my pubic hair.

"So...uh..." I stumbled. "You go to college?"

"Uh-huh. I'm a sophomore."

"I was a sophomore in high school before I dropped out. I wish I hadn't done it, though."

"Aah, you'll do all right. Pretty white girl like you." Treasure rinsed her hands in the basin. "If a colored girl wants to do somethin' other than work in somebody's kitchen, she'd better get an education. And even then, she might end up washing dishes all the same." She picked up a shiny silver straight razor. "Here we go. Better be quiet for this part."

When somebody's shaving your pussy with a straight razor, you tend to sit real still. I listened to the blade go scrape, scrape, scrape and craned my neck to see. Treasure leaned over me in concentration. Her brow was crinkled, and her eyes were focused on a part of me I was sure nobody had ever looked at that close before. David had looked at it enough to know where to stick his thing in, but that was it.

Treasure worked carefully, her free hand resting on my right thigh to hold me steady. Her hand was fine-boned and long-fingered, with short, neatly trimmed nails. It looked like the hand of someone who was strong and competent yet gentle. And the sight of it, caramel-colored and spread like a five-pointed star against the soft whiteness of my thigh, almost made me shiver with a strange feeling. I held still, though. I didn't want to get hurt.

When Treasure set the razor down, our eyes met for a second, and then we both looked away. She busied herself getting a towel and patting me dry. "There you go," she said. "All done. Just as bald and pink as an Easter egg."

My face was probably pink, too. I could still blush then.

Treasure poured a glass of water from a pitcher on the bedside table, then squeezed a couple of drops of liquid from an amber bottle into the glass. "Drink this," she said.

"You ain't poisoning me, are you?"

Treasure laughed. "You think I'm some kind of maniac that shaves girls' pubes and then poisons them? This is just a little concoction I mix up to make sure you're feeling no pain while Mama fixes your little problem."

I drank, and in a few minutes, I was sure the bed I was lying in must have been the most comfortable bed in the world. In a few more minutes, I was just as sure I was floating above the bed. I vaguely remember Dr. Bertha coming into the room, and I remember closing my eyes. But after that, I can't remember anything except Treasure gently shaking my shoulder and telling me to wake up.

I couldn't talk yet, so I listened to Treasure tell me that everything was fine and taken care of, that I had bled quite a bit but a lot of women did that. The anesthetic had hit me hard, too, she said, but that wasn't surprising since I was such a tiny little thing.

She offered me a bowl of murky green liquid and said it was the pot liquor from some collards her mama had fixed and that the iron in it would do me good. Her hands were steady, and she tipped the bowl just enough that not a single drop ran down my chin.

When the mist in my head started to clear, I asked, "What time is it?"

"A little past six. We just had supper."

I sat bolt upright, then flopped back down from lack of strength. I had missed supper at the Mimosa and hadn't called Mrs. Henry to tell her not to expect me, which was practically a capital offense. For Mrs. Henry, part of running a respectable boardinghouse was keeping up with the whereabouts of all "her girls." More than one girl had been thrown out of the Mimosa for missing meals without calling or for staying out all night.

I must have looked scared because Treasure said, "What's the matter?"

I explained the situation to Treasure, and in no time she was on the phone with Mrs. Henry, talking in textbook English and claiming to be a friend of mine from work. "Vestal has fallen ill, ma'am," she said, her voice as pale and creamy as butter. "She'll be staying over at my home tonight."

"There," she said, after she hung up the phone.

"I've never heard the like," I said. "You sounded...you sounded..." I was afraid to say the next word.

"White? That's right, Miss Thing. That was what I call my special cracker telephone voice. It works like a charm every time." She sat on the edge of the bed and said, "Vestal, you look like if you closed your eyes, you'd go right back to sleep and sleep all night."

I did, and I did.

CHAPTER 18

The next morning Treasure brought me eggs and bacon and grits and biscuits in bed. After I cleaned my plate, she said, "Well, it looks to me like you've made a full recovery. If you can get up and get dressed, I'll call you a cab."

At the Mimosa that afternoon, I stayed in my room, stretched out on the bed, reading the latest issue of *Glamour*. Occasionally I'd slip down my panties and check my sanitary pad like Dr. Bertha had told me to do. There wasn't too much blood, but the blood that was there was shockingly red—much brighter and redder than what I was used to seeing on a monthly basis.

The bright blood on the white pad looked too much like the bright blood on the white sheets of David's and my bed. And here was a little part of David, too, this stain on this pad was all that was left of a part of himself that he put into me, only for it to end in more spilled blood. I didn't regret my decision, but I didn't like to think about it either, so I picked up my *Glamour* and focused my mind on a feature called "Spritely Spring Suits."

Mrs. Henry made me take an extra piece of chicken at supper because she said I still looked a little peaked. I took a wing, and as I picked at it, I looked at the other girls at the table and wondered if any of them had ever paid a visit to Dr. Bertha or somebody like her. Their plain, scrubbed, giggling faces were all the answer I needed. Virgins, every last one of them.

It was becoming apparent to me that the world was populated by two kinds of girls: girls who do and girls who don't. And no, you nasty-minded thing, I'm not just talking about screwing here. Girls who do are more likely to screw, but screwing is just one small part of it.

Girls who don't, like those plain, pasty-faced virgins at the Mimosa, are ladies-in-waiting. They sit and wait for something to happen to them. They work their boring jobs as typists and telephone operators, all the while waiting for something better to come along. When and if that something does come along, it's usually in the form of a man who says, "Quit your job, and be my wife." Then the girl turns into a different kind of lady-in-waiting. She stays at home, cleans the house, cooks the food and waits on her husband hand and foot.

Girls who do make things happen. That's not as hard now as it was back then, when most educated women didn't dare hope for a better job than an underpaid nurse or schoolteacher. I wanted something better, though. Looking at the girls around me, I felt like I was a completely different kind of animal. Their hopes and dreams were as transparent as cellophane, but mine were carried deep inside me, in a little red velvet box that nobody could see.

My short time as a wife had given me a small taste of what I wanted but not the way I wanted it. Even though every smiling virgin at the table would tell me I was too young to make this vow I knew I would never marry again.

So what did I want? I wanted to wear diamonds again, diamonds that weren't bought for me by a husband, at least not by my husband. I wanted money that wasn't doled out to me as an allowance but was all mine to do whatever I pleased with. I wanted to buy the real clothes that were splashed on the pages of fashion magazines every month, not the cheap knockoffs. I wanted to put on an emerald green evening gown and dine on rack of lamb and Champagne in an elegant supper club instead of gnawing on dry chicken wings at a boardinghouse. I wanted a beautiful apartment with gilt mirrors and a chaise lounge and a big tub for bubble baths.

A lot of people cluck their tongues in judgment at these dreams, I know. "How sad it is when somebody's dreams all revolve around money," they say. Or they trot out that old workhorse: "Money can't buy happiness." But the people who say these things were never poor. They don't understand what it is to spend your life looking at movie screens and at rich families when all you can feel is what you lack. It's like being hungry all the time. You don't have food to fill you up, so to keep from being empty, you let the hunger fill you up instead.

But it wasn't just money and things I wanted. I was also lonely. At the Mimosa I was lonely in a crowd, which is the worst kind of loneliness. I missed Florrie, and I missed C.R., only now I didn't have Les to comfort me because his jealous wife didn't like him seeing me. Once in a while he'd stop by Diller's and say howdy, always buying some geegaw for his wife as an excuse. I needed a new friend. I decided that when I went back to work the next day, I would find Lucy and tell her I was ready to go out and celebrate.

I went home with Lucy after work on Friday night. She lived in a red brick apartment building downtown. I followed her up two flights of stairs, and she let me into a surprisingly spacious living room with shiny hardwood floors and walls the color of fresh cream. There wasn't much furniture, but there was a nice powder-blue sofa and matching armchair, a low-slung coffee table piled with fashion magazines. "The perfume counter must pay better than costume jewelry," I said. "This is some place you got here."

Lucy flopped on the couch, pulled off her high heels and sighed with pleasure. "I got a good deal on this place from a guy I know. You wanna beer?"

"No, thank you. I've never cared for the taste of it."

"Well, what's your poison, then? You said you wanna celebrate, and I ain't no Baptist. I don't believe in celebrating with lemonade."

I laughed. "Well, what have you got that tastes good?"

"I'll make you a Seven and Seven, you mix the booze with Seven-Up; you can't even taste it." Lucy opened a cabinet beside the kitchen door. The inside was filled with all kinds of liquor bottles. If you listened to a Baptist preacher, there was enough sin in that one cabinet to send all of Bartlett, Kentucky, straight to hell. Lucy chose a bottle from the cabinet and carried it into the kitchen. She came back a couple of minutes later with a can of Schlitz for herself and a glass of something fizzy for me.

"You know, being where you're from, Vestal, I would've

thought you'd be able to drink moonshine straight from the jug."

I sipped my drink. It did taste just like soda pop, so I reminded myself to drink it slowly. "I drunk moonshine once, when I was twelve years old," I said. "It was my brother's. He had it hid behind the coal bucket on the front porch. I took one sip of it and threw up over the porch railing. C.R. come up the road about that time, and I thought he'd never quit laughing. 'I want you to look at that,' he hollered. 'Missy's been hitting the shine!'"

Lucy had a nice laugh; she put her whole body into it. "I used to sneak drinks of my daddy's beer when I was little," she said. "He'd yell, 'Bring me a beer, little bit.' I'd open up the beer for him in the kitchen and have three or four good swallows before I took it into the living room. I'd do that with every beer he asked for, and when he'd finally pass out, there'd always be at least half a can left for me. I guess that's why I'm still a beer drinker. When I'm out on the town, I'll wear my pretty dress and my high heels and order a Tom Collins or a Manhattan or some other little drinkie that looks pretty in a girl's hand. But when I'm home, I put my feet up on the coffee table and drink Schlitz right out of the can. I'm my daddy's girl, I guess."

I thought of a time when I used to be my daddy's girl, too, but it seemed like a thousand years ago. "Do you still see your daddy?"

"Yep." Lucy tossed her empty beer can across the room, landing it smack dab into the wastepaper basket. "I go to Mom and Dad's for dinner every Sunday. I drag in around twelve-thirty, hung over as hell. They ask me when I'm going to get married and settle down, and I say, 'Don't hold your fucking breath.'"

I had never heard a girl say 'fucking' before, and I liked that she had the guts to say it. I knocked back the rest of my drink, deciding if I wasn't going to be like those pasty-faced schoolmarms at the Mimosa, I was going to have to be less cautious.

"Well," Lucy said, "I'm about ready to get changed and go out. How about you?"

"Uh...well, I didn't bring anything to change into."

"Well, you can't go out on the town in your work clothes; people'll think you're wearing the only dress you own. Let's raid my closet and see what we can find. You're littler than I am, but I bet we can rig something up."

Lucy's bedroom floor was strewn with shoes, underwear and fashion magazines. I snagged my heel on one of the leg holes of a pair of drawers and tried to shake them off gently, but I kicked too hard and they sailed through the air, landing on the lamp on the bedside table.

"Well, Vestal, I have to say that's the first time a girl has ever slung my panties across the room." She didn't bother to pick up the flying undies off the lamp, and I found myself wondering how long they would stay there.

She opened the door of her closet and rifled through the rack of dresses. There were at least three dozen of them hanging there, and before I even thought, I said, "Lord, girl, how'd you afford all them dresses?"

Lucy smiled the kind of fake smile we used when dealing with customers. "Why, with my Diller's employee discount. But of course, I use the special five-finger discount."

"What's that?" I asked, green as a new apple.

"Let's just say if one dress disappears off the rack every two months or so, nobody makes much of a fuss. They just figure it was an outside job, somebody sneaky enough to get past the store detective. Because, of course, it couldn't be a Diller's employee who just happens to be on very friendly terms with the store detective." She batted her eyelashes, all innocence.

"You steal from the store?" I couldn't help sounding shocked.

"And you don't?" Lucky sounded just as shocked as I did. "As little as they pay us, I think we're entitled to some free merchandise." She pulled a dress out of the closet. "Here. See how this suits you."

It was a short-sleeved, V-necked black dress splashed with big red poppies. Back in Bartlett, I could have only seen a dress like it in the pages of The Tinseltown Tattler. "It's beautiful."

"Try it on. If you like it, you can keep it. I'm too small-busted to wear it. The damn thing makes me look like Olive Oyl."

Olive Oyl I was not. I stood in front of Lucy's full-length mirror, seeing how my breasts filled out the bodice of the dress, the line of my cleavage peeking out of the V neck. The dress hugged my narrow waist and flared with my hips, and its blackness brought out the fairness of my skin. Lucy pulled my hair back on one side and stuck in a red fake flower, and all of a sudden I could've been a girl in a movie: the exotic jungle princess, or the glamorous cabaret singer whose life is full of intrigue and heartbreak.

Lucy was looking at me in the mirror, too. "I swear, Vestal," she said, lighting up a Lucky Strike, "if I had your face and your body, I'll be goddamned if I'd be standing on my feet all day selling junk jewelry."

"Well, I don't think I could ever be somebody's wife again, be the pretty little birdie in a pretty cage. Pretty or not, a cage is still a cage."

"There's other things in this world for a pretty girl to do besides be a wife." I waited for her to explain what those things might be, but she just turned her back to me and said, "Zip me up."

Lucy's dress was baby blue with silver threads running through it, and her stockings were stitched with shiny silver bows at the ankles. We both looked like movie stars.

The Talk of the Town, the nightclub where Lucy took me, was not the fanciest nightclub in Knoxville, but it was plenty fancy for me. Because of the blue laws, the club was for members only, which sounded impressive until you realized you could buy a membership for two dollars at the door.

Inside the club, little round tables were draped with fresh white tablecloths and decorated with tiny little lamps. Well-dressed couples drifted around the wooden dance floor as the tuxedoed band played *I'll Be Seeing You*, that weepy wartime song about longing for a lost soldier. I had to swallow some sadness, thinking about C.R. and about David, too, who wasn't a soldier but was lost all the same. As I looked around the club, though, with its potted palms and glowing lights, I couldn't feel sad for long. This was the kind of place I'd always wanted to be, and I told myself C.R. would want me to be here. "Live it up, Sissy," he'd say. "You don't go around but once." David, being as jealous and protective as he was, probably would have disagreed with

C.R. on this count. But I was trying my hardest not to think about David.

When a waiter in a black bowtie came to take our drink orders, Lucy said, "Manhattan," and I said, "Seven and Seven," because it was the only cocktail I knew how to order.

After he was gone, I leaned over and whispered to Lucy, "I've always wanted to come to a place like this."

"I come here just about every Friday night. There's no reason you can't, too."

Our drinks came, and I sipped mine and listened to the band and watched a woman in rose silk lean over and let a middle-aged man light her cigarette. She exhaled and smiled smokily; the man stared at her like an adoring hound dog, but he was begging for something other than table scraps.

"Looks like we're about to have company," Lucy said, a smile spreading over her face. I had never seen that smile on her before, but it wasn't a smile that was meant for a female audience.

Two men approaching our table, one of them tall and fairly good-looking with sandy hair and a salesman's smile, the other neither ugly nor handsome but nervous as all get-out. His smile quivered around the edges. He fit into a specific category of men I would later name 'The Two Sh's': short and shy.

"Harold!" Lucy's face glowed more than the lamp on the table. "They decided to let you back in the city limits, did they?"

"Sure did." Harold laughed. "The city council decided I spend so much money on booze when I'm in town that it would be detrimental to the economy if they kept me away."

Lucy laughed uproariously at his little joke maybe a little harder than a man likes to see a woman laugh, and I smiled a little.

When Lucy finally quit hooting and snorting, Harold asked, "Mind if we sit down?"

"Be my guest," Lucy said, smiling. I was beginning to wonder if she had forgotten I was there. Come to think of it, she hadn't really acknowledged Harold's friend either.

Harold must have noticed this because he said, "By the way, ladies, this is my friend Norbert. He's the bookkeeper for my company. I thought I might bring him here this weekend and show him how we do things in the big city."

"H-hello," Norbert stammered.

When the boys pulled up their chairs, Harold scooted in next to me, and Norbert sat by Lucy. When the waiter came Harold ordered a bottle of champagne. I glanced over at Lucy to see if she was happy about the champagne. People were always drinking it in movies, and I was excited to try it. But she wasn't smiling. I wondered if she was regretting bringing me along, what with me being so much better looking than she was.

"So, Lucy," Harold said, "aren't you going to introduce me to your friend?"

"Her name's Vestal," Lucy said, her voice a lifeless monotone. "She works with me at Diller's."

"Vestal, huh?" he said. "What an unusual name. Well, Vestal, I'm in lumber myself. Work for a company out in Grainger County. I come here a few times a year to sell lumber to hardware stores, building contractors…"

And he was off, talking about his work the way men love to do. I clearly wasn't required to say anything in response or even really listen as long as I gave the appearance of listening. So I smiled and nodded occasionally and focused on the happy feeling of champagne bubbles popping on my tongue.

After ten or fifteen minutes of blah-blah-blah conversation, Harold changed his tone and said, "So where did you get such gorgeous green eyes?"

"Klein's jewelry store," I said. "They're emeralds. I can't see a thing, but don't I look pretty?"

"You sure do," he said, and for a second he couldn't look straight at me. The waiter came by, and Harold said, "Hey, buddy, how about bringing me a bourbon? This fizzy stuff gives me heartburn." He poured the rest of the champagne from his glass into mine.

I sipped from the flute and realized I was well on my way to getting drunk.

"I like the way you talk, Vestal." Harold was sipping his bourbon. "Where are you from?"

"Same place as that bourbon."

"Kentucky?"

I nodded.

"Well, that makes sense. You remind me of this bourbon—smooth and sweet, but with a kick to it."

It was an awful line, but I smiled anyway. It was strange. I didn't want Harold, but just like it was with David, I liked making him want me. I liked seeing him get flustered and fidget with his cigarette lighter and try to think of the right thing to say. On the job and in politics, men had all the power, but one-on-one like this, the power was all mine, and a captain of industry or powerful politician was as helpless as a just-hatched baby bird.

"Vestal, would you like to dance?"

"I don't know. I was raised a Baptist so I don't know much about dancing. Of course, I don't know much about drinking champagne either, but I seem to be pretty good at it."

"Dance with me then. Just do what I do backwards."

I knocked back the rest of my champagne for courage and joined him on the dance floor. His steps were kind of slow and jerky, so it wasn't that hard to follow. I looked over his shoulder at the band in their tuxedos and listened to the deep, rich sounds of the saxophone. The champagne and the music hummed together in my head, and soon I felt the rhythm in my shoulders and hips and feet, which all moved where the rhythm told them to go. Harold may have thought he was leading me, but the truth was I had almost forgotten he was there. I was Ginger Rogers in a beautiful, feather-trimmed evening gown, except I was even prettier because I wasn't big-boned and flat-faced the way she was.

I'm not sure how much time passed before Harold asked, "Aren't you getting tired?"

I was full of champagne bubbles and music and would have loved to dance even more, but Harold's face was red and sweaty and I didn't want to give him a heart attack, so I said, "Maybe a little."

When we headed back to our table, it was empty.

"Well," Harold said, sounding delighted. "It looks like ol' Norbert and Lucy hit it off. You think they went somewhere quiet to talk?"

"Maybe," I said, but I didn't think so. Lucy and Norbert hadn't exchanged two words when we were all at the table. "Harold," I said, "you and Lucy, you're not…"

He laughed. "Good God, no. Lucy's a fun gal, but she's not my type. So…do you want to go for a little walk?"

I agreed to walk with him mainly because I was stranded. My plan had been to flirt a little while to pass the time, but I had thought that by the end of the evening, Lucy and I would go home together and laugh about the men we'd met.

On the street, Harold took my arm. We walked past a late-night diner, and he asked me if I was hungry.

"Not really." I couldn't stand the thought of sitting in the booth of a diner while a man sat across from me, staring at me goggle-eyed. It would remind me too much of my early dates with David, and thinking about my beginnings with David would only make me think about the end.

We walked for a while longer until we stood outside the Bentley House. It was the fanciest hotel I'd ever seen. "Uh, this is where I'm staying," he said, his voice all shaky. "Would you like to come up and have one more drink with me before I drive you home?"

I knew Harold had no intention of driving me home, but I was drunk, and I really wanted to see what the inside of the hotel looked like. "Just one drink," I said.

The lobby was gorgeous, with plum-colored carpet and gold-framed mirrors. The golden elevator was beautiful, too, but riding it in my drunken state made my stomach feel queasy.

"Here we are," Harold said as he fumbled with the key to his room. The room had the same plum carpet as the lobby and a big bed with a fancy cushioned headboard. As pretty as the bed was, though, I avoided it and sat on the loveseat in the corner instead.

Harold poured me a drink, which was about the last thing I needed, and then after I'd had a few sips, he took the glass out of my hand and kissed me. Harold was just the second man I had let kiss me and touch me (that horny little preacher back in Bartlett didn't count), and I let him not out of desire but curiosity. Would it be different, I wondered, getting kissed, squeezed and screwed by a man who didn't love me? The answer was not that different, except the whole process from first kiss to screwing moved a lot faster. What happened on that loveseat was like David's and my whole courtship condensed into about twenty-five minutes.

I don't remember how we moved to the bed, but we did get there, and when we did, all the rest of it was over in five minutes.

Lying there next to him as he snored, I didn't feel trapped the way I had on my wedding night. I knew that unlike with David, this one screw wasn't the first in a series of screws followed by breakfast and small talk. In the morning, Harold would put back on the wedding ring he had only half-hidden behind the alarm clock on the nightstand and go on his way. That thought was a big relief.

So why, you're probably asking, did I let Harold go so far as to screw me when I wasn't even interested in him in the first place? Well, I'm no shrink, but my best guess is this: I wanted to see if there was more to screwing than there had been with David.

There wasn't.

I found no pleasure in lying under a man while he grunted and sweated and made funny noises for three minutes before passing out. I found no pain in it either. It didn't embarrass me or shame me; it just didn't do much for me one way or another.

The part of the evening that I liked was being out in a nightclub wearing a beautiful dress, dancing and feeling everybody's eyes on me. I liked feeling men's desire and women's envy, but the actual thing men desired me for was an anticlimax. Well, for me, anyway.

When I woke up the next morning, Harold was gone, which didn't surprise me at all. What did surprise me was what I found on the nightstand. The note said:

Vestle,

Thank you for a lovely evening. Buy yourself something pretty. Hope to see you again sometime.

Harold

The money was under the note, two twenties and a ten-dollar bill. This small-town businessman whose wife's thighs must've been glued together with rubber cement had actually paid me the same amount of money I made in two weeks at Diller's just for lying still for five minutes while he screwed me!

My first thought was, this beats the hell out of marriage. My second thought was that it also beat the hell out of working for a living. If there was this much money to be made lying comfortably on my back, then what sense did it make for me to stand around in high heels all day making next to nothing? I set my bare feet on the plush carpet and practically danced to the bathroom, where I filled up the tub. As I soaked I looked down and saw my fortune. The full, white, pink-nippled breasts, the tiny waist, the rounded hips they were all I needed to shake the coal dust of Bartlett permanently off my feet and start living the kind of life that flickered across the movie screen.

My looks wouldn't last forever, but if I didn't throw my money away on too many foolish things, they wouldn't have to. Pregnancy was a fear, but I knew there were things I could do to prevent it. I also knew from recent experience that even pregnancy was a situation that a little money could get you out of.

I watched the bathwater swirl down the drain and imagined that all my old worries were being sucked down with it. I never had to worry about being poor again because what I was selling had been in demand since the beginning of time.

I put on my dress and shoes and stockings. I brushed through my hair and finger-brushed my teeth and painted on a fresh coat of lipstick. I closed the room's door behind me and walked down the hall like I had never walked before, proud, with a swing in my hips. The dowdy maid shot me a look that said she noticed I was in my evening clothes in the morning, but I just smiled and looked her right in the eye so she'd know she couldn't make me feel ashamed. Her disapproval was nothing but envy, I thought. If she had what I had, she wouldn't be cleaning toilets for a living.

That Monday I went to work at Diller's, but I couldn't keep my mind on my job because I was too busy soaring with the possibilities of a new life. When my fifteen-minute break came,

I went to see Lucy at the perfume counter, since I hadn't heard from her since she left the club Friday night.

When I walked up to the counter, Lucy's back was turned to me. She was wearing a navy blue and white sailor dress and was rearranging bottles of Shalimar. "Hey, Luce," I said, "is it time for your break yet?"

When she turned around and faced me, her brown eyes seemed to darken to black. "You've got a lot of nerve, sister, to march over here and talk to me like nothing happened on Friday night."

"Nothing did happen, except you was there one minute and gone the next."

"Don't play all innocent with me. Your dumb little country girl act don't play with me."

"Is this about Harold? Because I asked him if he was your boyfriend, and he said he wasn't."

"Boyfriend? This isn't fifth grade, Vestal. All's I know is I said hi to Harold. I obviously knew him from before, and that didn't stop you from digging your claws into him."

"I can't help it if he liked me. I was just trying to be nice."

"A little too nice, if you ask me."

"Look, Luce, Harold don't mean nothin' to me. I'm sure I'll never see him again. I'd much rather have you as a friend than have anything to do with Harold."

"Having friends like you is a bad business, Vestal. I think from now on I'll just go out on my own."

"I swear, Luce, if I had knowed you liked Harold that much…"

"Damn it, Vestal!" Lucy's voice was getting loud enough that the shoppers were starting to stare. "This isn't about liking or not liking. Do you think I pay rent on my apartment with the money I make in this joint? I needed that twenty dollars Harold gives me when he comes into town."

The words that thoughtlessly bubbled out of my mouth next ended any hope Lucy and I might have had for salvaging a friendship: "Twenty? He gave me fifty."

Lucy and I were too busy glowering at each other to notice that the assistant manager was standing right beside us. He cleared his throat and ran his hand over the few strands of hair that covered his bald spot. "Ladies," he said, "this is not the kind of behavior we tolerate from our shopgirls. Miss Smitty, you get back to work. Miss Jenkins, you return to your station."

I walked wordlessly toward the costume jewelry counter, and then without a thought, I walked right on past it and out the front door.

CHAPTER 19

If I was going to pursue my new career path, I was going to have to live somewhere other than the Mimosa. Telling Mrs. Henry I had been at a girlfriend's every time I dragged in from an all-nighter would only work for so long. After scanning through the classifieds in the Knoxville paper, I used the fifty bucks I had earned from Harold to put a deposit on a pretty little one-bedroom apartment in a big building where people seemed to mind their own business.

To make the rent and pay for food, all I had to do was go out twice a week. But there was no point in earning my living on my back if it didn't pay for little extras, too, dresses and shoes and dinners out and movies and magazines. And since all I had to put in my new apartment was the rug and the lamp I had bought when I moved into the Mimosa, I was going to have to have some furniture, too. I decided I would work Wednesdays through Saturdays and take Sundays, Mondays and Tuesdays as my nights of rest.

Before I started my career in earnest, though, there was one thing I had to do. I put on my wedding band and a respectable-looking dress and went to the doctor.

I sat on his examining table and cried and said that back in Kentucky my doctor had told me I had a condition that would make it very dangerous for me to get pregnant. I said I knew I couldn't keep pushing my husband away every night because it was starting to hurt our marriage, but that I was so scared of getting pregnant I didn't know what to do.

The kindly, white-haired doctor patiently explained to me that there was a device a man could put on his...I believe he called it a 'member,' which struck me as funny, but I couldn't giggle because I was supposed to be upset. He gave me a brown paper sack filled with rubbers and told me I was a good wife to be so considerate of my husband's needs and to come back when we'd used up the sack.

Every night when I went out I carried a rubber in my purse. Forty years before anybody was preaching safe sex, I was practicing it.

I went to the Talk of the Town on Thursdays and Saturdays since Lucy went there on Fridays and had already accused me of horning in on her territory. I went to other clubs on other nights, the High Hat, the Kitty Kat, nice, members-only nightclubs frequented by respectable men with regular jobs. Soon I knew how to order all kinds of cocktails: Tom Collinses, Manhattans and gin fizzes. And not only could I dance to the swinging music the nightclub bands played I knew the names of all the songs, too. These brassy, peppy tunes, from Mairzy Doats to Rum and Coca Cola, lifted my spirits even more than the cocktails and were a big improvement over the church songs and murder ballads that had been the music of choice in Bartlett.

Once in a while I'd have a drink at one of the nicer hotel's bars and meet a man that way, but not too often. Hotel managers seemed to have a pretty good idea what a dressed-up woman sitting alone in a hotel bar might be up to, and more than once a manager came up to me and told me that if I was unescorted and not waiting for anybody in particular, I would have to leave.

Whatever nightspot I chose, I'd slink in, let my gaze wander across the room, and then sit at a table, noticeably alone. I'd always be looking my best, never crossing the line between looking like a Hollywood starlet and an outright whore. I was an outright whore, of course, but the kind of men I was after didn't want to walk out of a place with a woman everybody knew was getting paid. So I dressed just a little bit sexy, in dresses that showed just a little more cleavage than other girls', in heels that were an inch or two higher than most girls could comfortably walk in. I wore my hair long down my back instead of in the shoulder-length and shorter styles that were popular after the war because so many of my customers talked about how they loved to see a woman's long hair fanned out on a pillow.

I'd sit at my little table and nurse a drink, usually a Seven and Seven or a Tom Collins, until a man would approach the table and ask if he could buy me another. If he was nicely dressed and had good manners, I'd say yes. There would be a drink or two and some meaningless chitchat and maybe a dance or two.

Some men were quick to ask me to go to a hotel with them. Others were so shy you'd think they were trying to get up the nerve to ask me to marry them. With all of them, though, I'd ask the same question. I'd look them straight in the eye and say, "Do you know what kind of girl I am?"

If they seemed confused or said something like, "A real nice girl, I reckon," I'd plead a headache and go home and read a book. If they said yes, though, we'd proceed to a hotel room.

I always insisted on going to hotels. I figured if you got yourself in a bad situation, it would be a lot easier to get out of it in a hotel full of people than it would be in some fellow's house in the middle of nowhere. And I flat-out refused to do it in a car. If a girl's nice enough to let you screw her, even if you are paying her for it, the least you can do is find her a comfortable place to lie down.

Once we were in the hotel room, there was no special trick that I'd do. I'd take the rubber out of my purse and set it on the nightstand so the man could see it, then I'd take off everything but my stockings and high heels and lie down (I kept on the stockings because they looked sexy; I kept on the heels because I figured if a fellow got rough, a few swift kicks with a pointy-toed stiletto would get him off me). Back then, when it was harder for fellows to get laid for free, even a working girl didn't have to give a virtuoso performance in bed. As far as my customers were concerned, the fact that I was pretty and naked and willing to be underneath them for the five minutes it took was worth more than the twenty bucks an hour (or fifty for the whole night) that I charged.

Only a few of them argued about the rubber, but when it became clear that if they didn't put it on, then I'd put my clothes back on, they always gave in.

Most of the men I did business with were nameless and

faceless. Men tended to look alike in those days, with their dark suits and dark ties and close-clipped hair and clean-shaven faces, all of them with their good-paying but dull jobs and shiny, new, ugly houses tended by their homebody wives.

Most of these men had fought in the war and were confident that the freedom to live their peaceful, predictable little lives was why the U.S. had won. But these men had a war going on inside them, too. After the adrenaline rush of the battlefield, after the drunken thrill of their weekend leaves, these men's new, safe, suburban lives seemed a little boring. Sure, they didn't miss getting shot at, but how could they not miss those weekends when they had pumped every moment full of pleasure because they knew they could die on Monday? These close-cropped, polite, dark-suited men had animals inside them, wild beasts that wanted to forget the fears of the past and the responsibilities of the present in order to rut and wallow in momentary pleasure. And for twenty bucks an hour, or fifty for the whole night, I would set that beast free.

With one exception, all the men I did business with in the early days were so alike they could have been manufactured on the same assembly line. That one exception was Alex Winter.

I met him at the Talk of the Town. I had just finished my last sip of Tom Collins when a second one magically appeared before me. "From the gentleman in the white suit," the waiter explained.

It didn't take long to spot him. All men in those days wore dark gray suits or maybe navy blue if they were feeling adventurous. And so the beautifully tailored, white double-breasted suit Alex wore practically glowed, even in the dim lights of the club. I flashed him my "I'm available" smile and sipped from the drink he had bought me. Soon he rose from his table and sauntered over in my direction. As he drew closer, I saw that his thick, wavy, dark hair was streaked with silver.

"I can't bear to see a lady drink alone," he said when he reached my table. "But I'm guessing that a lady like you never drinks alone for long. May I join you?"

I nodded, and he sat. I had only heard accents like his in the movies. He put me in mind of one of those suave, middle-aged, tuxedo-wearing actors like Claude Rains. Without thinking about what a hick I was about to sound like, I said, "You ain't from around here."

He smiled as he took a cigarette from a gleaming silver case. "No," he said. "I ain't. You, however, most certainly is."

I was pretty sure he was making fun of me, but I didn't want to get into an argument because he was obviously dripping money, and I hoped to catch a few drops of it for myself. "I'm from Kentucky."

"Kentucky. Yes. That's the next one up from Tennessee, isn't it? The one with the horses."

Horses are what rich people think of when somebody says Kentucky. "So," I said, "what brings you all the way down here?"

"A speaking engagement at the little university you've got here. I was just at the most dreadful cocktail party, all these professorial types with their weak little eyes and their pointy little noses, it was like being in a colony of moles. And of course they all wanted to ask me about this line or that word or this syllable in one or the other of my poems. I am a poet, by the way. Alex Winter. Please tell me you've never heard of me."

"I never have." It was the truth. "I don't read poems much. Just magazines and novels."

He smiled like I had said something funny. "Which is why poets must supplement their incomes with dreadful speaking engagements. So tell me...who is your favorite novelist?"

"I like Olive Higgins Prouty real good."

Alex's mouth curled into another little smile. "Of course you do. You know, you haven't told me your name. It wouldn't be Stella Dallas by any chance?"

"Vestal."

"I beg your pardon?"

"My name is Vestal."

At this, Alex laughed so hard his whole chest shook. "Vestal, eh? But not a vestal virgin, I would warrant. Tell me, Vestal, am I correct in presuming that you are the sort of young woman who would be willing to accompany me to my hotel room, if I were to provide enough monetary...lubrication?"

You needed a dictionary just to figure out if the man was

asking if he could screw you. But since I had heard the words "hotel room," I went ahead and said yes.

"I thought as much. Well, shall we?"

He offered me his arm and walked me out of the club just like he was a gentleman and I was a lady.

With Alex Winter, there were no drinks or kisses to warm up with. As soon as he closed the door of his huge room at the Bentley, he said, "Off with the clothes."

I set the rubber on the nightstand, stripped and lay down. Alex didn't undress. He didn't even loosen his tie. He just unzipped his pants, daintily rolled on the rubber, climbed on top of me and stuck it in.

He wasn't dignified and prissy when he was screwing, though. He bared his teeth like a junkyard dog and rammed into me so hard I had to put a pillow on top of my head to keep from knocking my brains out on the headboard. Between his suit and the rubber, not one inch of his skin touched mine.

When he finished, he let out a choked sound, like somebody had him by the throat, then he pulled out, removed the rubber and, holding it delicately between his thumb and forefinger, dropped it in the trash can. By the time he zipped up, I was already putting on my panties.

He walked over to me and trailed a finger from my face to my breast to my belly. "Like fucking a statue," he said. He took his hand from me and reached into his breast pocket for a cigarette. "Not that I'm complaining, mind you. I enjoy knowing that the woman beneath me feels nothing, that's she's only letting me do what I want. That's why I limit my libidinal indulgences to transactions such as these."

He reached into another pocket, one in the lining of his jacket, and pulled out a silver flask. He poured two glasses of amber liquid and offered one to me. I sat on the edge of the bed in my black slip and stockings and drank.

"However," Alex began in the tone of voice I imagined he used when he lectured at the university, "most men do not share my tastes. Ridiculous as it may seem, Vestal, many men like to believe that they can move a woman of your sort to paroxysms of unbridled ecstasy. Perhaps with your future customers, you might consider indulging in some amateur theatrics."

I curled my feet under me the same way I'd do at home. For some reason, probably because I knew he saw right through me, I was comfortable with Alex Winter, even though I wasn't sure whether I liked him or not. "I don't think I know what you're talking about."

"I'm talking about pretending. Play-acting. Move your hips a little while the poor chump's inside you. Moan or sigh or call out his name...if you can remember it."

"That's what women do when they like getting screwed?"

"Well, isn't it what you do when you're doing it...not in a professional capacity?"

"No. I've never liked it, but I've never not liked it either. I guess I don't feel much about it one way or another."

Alex Winter looked fascinated. He sat down beside me on the bed. "Not even with your boyfriend, when you're doing it for free?"

"Nope. I had a husband once, and I didn't like it much with him neither."

Alex smiled. In a strange way, he seemed to enjoy talking to me more than screwing me. For him, sex seemed to be something he did because he got the physical urge, but once it was done he was just as glad to have it over with. He was like one of those people who eats because his body requires it but not because he enjoys food. "So," he said, "what happened to your poor husband, pray tell?"

"He killed hisself because he thought his daddy was screwing me."

Alex laughed deep in his belly like what I just said was the funniest thing he ever heard. "Well, I'll tell you what, Miss Vestal. I should probably pay you and send you on your way. I'm beginning to fear what will happen to me if I spend too much time with you." He picked up the telephone. "Do let me call you a taxi, though." Once he was off the phone, he slipped a couple of bills into my hand. "I failed to ask you what you charge for your services. I trust, though, that this is sufficient?"

I looked down and saw two twenty-dollar bills. "That's twicet what I usually get for an hour."

"Twicet?" Alex cringed. "Well, dear, in addition to that, I'd like to give you a tip. And here it is: learn to speak English. Even in this hellish little cow town, there must be some way you can lose that God-awful hillbilly accent. At the risk of sounding Shavian, speaking the proper English can get you quite far in the world. Of course, no one should ever turn you into a lady. With proper elocution, those theatrics I mentioned earlier and your natural beauty, though, you could be a world-class whore."

The next day when I went to the library to check out books on grammar and elocution, I also sat down at a desk with *Prometheus's Liver*, a book of Alex Winter's poems. Even though I must have jumped up from the desk to look up words in the dictionary twenty times, I still couldn't get a lick of sense out of it.

Chapter 20

One night I was sitting at my table at the Talk of the Town, wearing a new emerald green shantung silk dress and dyed-to-match pumps. I could feel dozens of eyes on me and was waiting for the owner of one pair to get drunk enough to come talk to me. To speed things up, I fished the maraschino cherry out of my Tom Collins and sucked on it, an act which usually made men knock each other down to get to my table.

I held the stem between my red-polished fingertips and opened my mouth just wide enough to pop the cherry inside it. When I looked up, there was a man standing in front of me, but seeing who it was made me suck the cherry halfway down my throat so I had to cough it up into my cocktail napkin, which didn't do much for my sexy image.

"Lord, missy, I know I'm a right ugly feller, but you don't have to gag at the sight of me."

"I just wasn't expecting to see you here." That was an understatement. Having Les Tipton bust into the nightclub where I was trying to drum up a little business wasn't that different than if C.R. had walked in, back from the dead, to tell me the error of my ways.

"I went to Diller's the other day when I thought it'd be about time for your dinner break. The girl at the perfume counter told me you didn't work there no more. She said if I wanted to see where you was working to try the Talk of the Town on Thursday evenin'. I thought you might be a cigarette girl or somethin'."

"I'm not a cigarette girl."

"You care if I sit down?"

"Go ahead." But of course, I did care. I had missed Les over the past few months and had been meaning to go see him. But I had wanted to see him at his store or at a diner or at someplace else where I could pretend I was still working at Diller's and was the same girl he'd known back in Bartlett. I wasn't ashamed of my new life, but Les was the closest thing to a big brother I had, and big brothers don't usually think much of their sisters turning to whoring.

"You talk different." Les was sitting stiffly at the table and fiddling with the lamp.

Ever since my evening with Alex Winter, I had been going to the library a couple of days a week and studying up on grammar and listening to records of people talking properly. "I've been studying elocution."

"Hell, I don't even know what that is. You talked fine before. And look at this fancy get-up." He looked me up and down, then shook his head. "Maybe I ort not to have brung you to the city."

"Shoot, Les, I'm still me." I let myself talk natural, which, after a few months more of studying, I decided to do anyway. Alex was right that I should pretend to enjoy getting screwed, but I finally decided to take issue with him on the subjects of grammar and elocution. No man in East Tennessee wants to screw a woman who sounds like his prune-faced high school English teacher. Plus, it was too hard for me to act sexy and worry about making sure my subjects and verbs agreed at the same time. "I'm just fixing myself up a little bit…some new curtains, a fresh coat of paint."

"If you ask me, the paint's a little thick. Listen, missy, I don't like this place. I never trust a place where men do their drinking in starched shirts. I know this place over on Central Avenue. How bout we head over there?"

The looks some of the men gave Les as we left the Talk of the Town said they didn't think we were going somewhere just to chat. I hoped Les didn't notice.

The Corner Lounge was dark, but not dark in a glamorous, romantic way; it was dark in a way that said. 'You don't want to know what's crawling on the floor.' Country music was blasting from the jukebox, and as soon as the unshaven bartender spotted Les, he hollered, "Hey, Les, what'll it be? A beer or nothin'?"

"A beer's better than nothin," Les hollered back.

Les bought me a beer, too, and we sat down at a rickety table. The other customers looked like factory workers or construction men in their coveralls or dungarees. I was the only woman in the place, and nobody seemed to notice me. It was a strange feeling.

Les drank half his beer in one gulp. "You ort to come down to the store tomorrow; we're having a big to-do with free hot dogs and ice cream for the youngun's. You wouldn't believe the business I'm doing, missy. Last week I stuck up signs all over the neighborhood that said, 'Hot Salted Peanuts, Free, All You Can Eat.' I set out a big barrel of nuts, and I bet two hundred people musta come and just eat and eat. 'Course, what they didn't know was that I put a whole pound of extra salt on them goobers. So before long, they commenced to getting thirsty. I charged them double what I usually charge for Coca-Colas, so giving away them free peanuts ended up making me a heap of money."

I laughed. "Les, you're awful."

"I never heard tell there's anything wrong with making a body pay for somethin' they want real bad." Les looked at me a little harder than I was comfortable with. "Far as I can tell, that's what this country's all about."

"I reckon you're right."

Les knocked back the rest of his beer, and I set mine down in front of him. Unless I was crawling across a desert, if somebody offered me beer or nothing, I'd take nothing.

"Missy," Les said, after drinking about half my beer, "even before I walked into that place tonight, I knowed you wasn't no cigarette girl."

I suddenly wished I had my beer back. I needed the booze to calm my nerves. "Is that a fact?"

"They was a feller come into the store last week that works for the Kern's Bread Company. He said he was out at a club and met up with the most beautiful girl he'd ever seen, real petite, with black hair and green eyes like a cat's. He said with the way you look and what you charge you probably make more selling...what you're selling...than I do selling groceries." Les lit a cigarette and exhaled with a sigh. "For a while I told myself it couldn't be you, even though I figured they wasn't another girl in Knoxville that could look like that. Finally, it got to eating me up so bad I went to Diller's to look for you." He studied the ash on his cigarette. "I don't like it, missy. It's a sad pass for a young lady to come to... selling herself cheap."

"I don't come cheap, Les. And I ain't selling my whole self neither. I'm just renting out a little part of me. It's like renting out a room to somebody...it don't mean you're letting 'em have the whole house. And besides, do you know how much money I make? I've got me a beautiful little apartment, I eat steak in good restaurants, wear pretty clothes. I've got a savings account, for heaven's sake, and I know I'm the first Jenkins to have one of them."

Les looked at me like he might cry. "There's more important things in life than money."

All I could think about was Les's card games, his rooster fights, his oversalted peanuts and overpriced Coca-Colas. I couldn't help it. I laughed. "Well, well, if you asked me the one thing I never thought I'd hear Les Tipton say, I reckon that'd be it. I don't want to call you a hypocrite, Les. Please don't make me."

Les slammed his empty beer bottle down on the table. "Goddamn it, missy! I ain't no hypocrite! But there's just some things in this world you don't stand for. You don't let nobody talk bad about your mama. You don't treat your dogs mean, and you don't let the sister of your best friend who died in service of this country sell herself to strangers!"

"I'd appreciate it if you kept your voice down."

"And I'd appreciate it if you'd kept that decent job I got you!"

"Les," I said softly, in hopes of calming him down. "It was real sweet of you to get me that job, but I couldn't spend the rest of my life selling paste pearls. I was meant for better things. Now I work less and make more. The fellers get what they want, and I get what I want, too. I don't see why you're so riled up about it. You was all for me marrying David for his money."

"That was different. He made an honest woman out of you."

"An honest woman? When every time I said 'I love you' to

him, it was a lie?"

"Missy, I used to think you and me was as alike as a man and woman could be, like we was two sides of the same coin. But…"

"But nothin', Les Tipton. Don't you go thinking you're better'n me. We are as alike as a man and woman can be, but being a man, you get to do all kinds of things I can't. How many women do you see opening their own grocery stores? Shoot, the girls at Diller's either worked the counters or cleaned the floors. The bosses in women's apparel and perfume and jewelry were all men. Now what does a man know about women's apparel? Mr. McGivney at Diller's couldn't tell the difference between a shift and a shirtwaist. Hell, he probably couldn't even tell you his wife's dress size. But he still gets to be boss over women's apparel because he's a man and a golf buddy of Mr. Diller's. The rules of this world ain't made for girls or by girls, Les. And so any girl that plays by 'em ain't nothin but a sucker. I make my own rules to get what I want, and if you was a girl like me, you'd do the exact same thing." I looked at Les's thick glasses and beaky nose. "Of course, you'd have to be a damn sight prettier than you are as a man, or you wouldn't get a lick of business."

Les's eyes were always weak and watery, so I couldn't tell if there were tears in them or not. "It breaks my heart, missy," he said, "to think of C.R. and to look at you and see that little ol' girl that used to set on the porch back in Bartlett, so full of dreams…" He shook his head like he was shaking off a bad memory. "I can't sit here and talk to you like this no more." He grabbed his hat, got up from the table, handed a couple of bills to the bartender and said, "Call her a cab."

As Les marched out the door, I hollered behind him, "Twenty bucks an hour, Les! I'm making more money than my mother and daddy ever seen!"

After I watched Les disappear around the corner, I turned around to see a man standing by my table. He had curly dishwater blond hair and was wearing coveralls. His hands were the size of baseball mitts.

"Looks like your friend left you high and dry," he said, with a crooked-toothed smile. "I was wondering if you might like some company."

He was rougher around the edges than my usual customers, but I took a chance and turned on the slow, seductive smile I had practiced in the mirror. "Do you know what kind of girl I am?"

He laughed. "Little lady, after the conversation you just had, everybody in this bar knows what kind of girl you are."

I broke one of my rules and let him screw me in his car. I didn't figure he could afford a hotel room, and he seemed like a nice fellow. He rolled up his jacket as a pillow for my head and eased into me with surprising gentleness, like he was sinking into a nice, warm bath.

When he was done he said, "Don't let your friend make you feel bad. I think it's awful nice of a beautiful girl like you to let an ugly ol' boy like me do it to you, and I'm more than happy to pay you for it. Hell, if I was a girl, I'd want some money for laying down with somethin' that looked like me."

"You look just fine," I said, taking his money. "And you know how to treat a lady." Unlike Les Tipton, I thought, who might as well give up selling groceries and become a Baptist preacher, for all the moralizing he was doing.

When I stepped out of the stranger's car, my taxi was waiting.

Around ten-thirty the next morning I was drinking my first cup of coffee when there was a knock at my door. I opened it to find a pimply-faced boy who couldn't have been much over sixteen staring at me pop eyed. His stare probably had something to do with the fact that I hadn't dressed yet and so was wearing my turquoise satin dressing gown, which was embroidered with a big peacock and had the tendency to slip open at the top. "May I help you?" I said.

"Um...um...um," he replied intelligently.

I adjusted my robe so that the good parts weren't quite so visible, and he managed to spit out, "Um? Les Tipton? Sent me over? To pick you up? There's a big to-do at the store?"

So this was Les's way of apologizing for walking out on me at the Corner Lounge. I had half a mind to screw his errand boy just to spite him, but since I was fairly certain this stammering kid was unlikely to have twenty bucks on him, I couldn't really get up the energy. "Won't you come in?" I said, using my best elocution.

He almost tiptoed in, holding his hat in shaking hands.

"You want some coffee while I get dressed?"

"No, um, thank you."

I reckon he figured he didn't need anything to make him jumpier. He stood there so stiff I could've hung my robe on him until I said, "Sit," and he did immediately.

I knew what Les thought of my line of work, that I degraded myself by letting men take advantage of me. Of course, that's how men always like to think of it. The truth was just the opposite. If anybody was being taken advantage of it was the fellows, especially in those days when a fellow was lucky to get anything more than a tight-lipped good-night kiss until he produced an engagement ring. The poor bastards would do anything I wanted in hopes that I'd give them the one thing they wanted.

Men have talked themselves into believing that they have all this sexual power because they don't like to think about the fact that the little dangly thing between their legs is doing the thinking for them about half the time.

Nothing could have prepared me for the scene at Les Tipton's Stop 'n Save. I had expected a booth with somebody handing out hot dogs and Coca-Colas and maybe some balloons for the youngun's, but I never imagined the spectacle that was spread out before me when we pulled up in the car. The vacant lot next to Les's store had been transformed into a carnival, or, as the hand-painted banner put it, Les Tipton's Fun Fair. There were the hot dogs and balloons I expected, but there were also pony rides, a stage with a country band playing 'You Are My Sunshine,' and a table heaped with watermelons with the sign, 'Les Tipton's World Famous Watermelon-Eating Contest, 12 noon.' All the signs had Les's name on them; even the pony ride sign said, 'Les Tipton's Playful Ponies,' though I figured he had probably rented the ponies from somewhere.

The lot was packed with men, women and children, many of them black, some white, a mix you didn't see much in those days.

I found Les himself at the dunking booth, laughing and

hollering, "Go ahead and try to hit me, Arthur! I bet you couldn't hit the broad side of a barn!" He was perched on a chair that hung over a big tub of water.

An older black man stood in front of him and hollered, "This is for sending that boy around to collect on my grocery bill last week!" He pitched a baseball which hit the bull's eye perfectly, and Les toppled into the water, glasses and all.

When Les's shiny head surfaced, he spotted me and hollered, "Hey, missy! Meet me over at the watermelon table in fifteen minutes!"

I said I would and wandered around the vacant lot seeing the sights, my high heels digging into the damp dirt of the vacant lot. At the hot dog and Coke stand, I saw a young man who looked familiar, with toasted almond skin and neat, short hair, but then I realized I was making the same mistake I made the first time we met.

"Treasure?" I said, smiling at the boyish woman who had shaved my pubic hair and brought me pot liquor...how long ago?

"Call me Trey. My mama's the only person who calls me Treasure. You're Vestal, right?" Trey was wearing an ironed, starched white shirt and pleated charcoal-colored pants. I looked down at her feet and saw polished penny loafers with shiny new pennies in the slots. You couldn't say she didn't dress well, but you couldn't say she dressed like a woman either.

"Vestal." It was then I became aware of another pair of eyes on me. Standing next to Trey was a pretty, light-skinned black woman with ironed hair and nails as long and red as mine. In her flowered dress, she was dressed as feminine as Trey was masculine, and she was looking at me with a glare I had been on the receiving end of many times. At first I couldn't figure out where the jealousy was coming from, but then it hit me: she was jealous because I was talking to Trey. The two of them were together, a couple. It's funny how a girl can make her living getting screwed and still be so innocent about some things.

Trey nodded toward her fiery-eyed friend. "This is Barbara. She's a friend of mine from the college. Barbara, I met Vestal—"

"Oh, I think I know how you met Vestal," Barbara said.

She was clearly trying to embarrass me, but you can't embarrass somebody who feels no shame, so I just went right on and asked, "How's your mama, Trey?"

"She's good," Trey said, looking relieved that I didn't take Barbara's bait. "I keep telling her she ought to slow down a little, but she won't listen to me."

"Well, you tell her I said hey, all right?" I figured I'd better move on before Barbara's eyes burned a hole in my dress. "Good to see you, Trey." I grabbed my hot dog and Coke and walked on. I didn't say a word to Barbara because I had already learned that trying to make a jealous female like you is a wasted effort.

The watermelon table was right in front of the stage where the band was playing 'Rocky Top.' As soon as they finished, Les, who was still drenched from the dunking booth, shoved the singer away from the microphone and hollered into it, "Hidy, neighbors!"

A bunch of folks hollered back, "Hidy, Les!"

"We're fixing to have the watermelon-eating contest up here," Les said. At the table, Les's wife, Peg, and one of the store's bag boys were cutting the melons into big wedges. "Whoever eats the most gets a silver dollar and a whole watermelon to take home with him. Course, you'll probably be right sick of watermelon by then." Les grinned. "Spit the seeds wherever you want to, neighbors. Maybe by next summer we'll have this whole lot turnt into a watermelon patch!"

The gleam in Les's eye was almost crazy; he looked like he used to on poker nights.

After he got off the stage, he came up to me and whispered, "Peg's judging the contest. Let's you and me go back to my office for a minute."

Les dripped a trail of water through the store all the way back to his dark, tiny office. "Ain't you gonna change clothes or somethin'?" I asked.

"I reckon I'll dry out directly," Les said. "Shoot, that makes me sound like a drunk, don't it?"

I wasn't expecting a regular apology from Les, which was a good thing because I didn't get one.

Instead, once we were sitting, he said, "You really make all the money you said you did...doing what you do?"

"Yep."

"But you...don't like doing it that much, do you?"

Since it was Les, I decided to be honest. "I like having that effect on men. I like feeling their eyes on me when I walk into a room. But the part that comes later, the part they pay for... well, I like it lots better than standing on high heels in Diller's department store for eight hours a day, but it still feels like work."

"They's girls that like it, you know."

"Standing in high heels in a department store all day?"

Les's face turned red. "Damn it, missy, you know what I mean."

"I do and I don't. What are you getting at?"

Les lit up a cigarette and offered me one. I shook my head no, since I had just read an article in *Glamour* that said smoking caused wrinkles.

"The way I figure it," Les said, "right now you're doing about like I was when I was playing poker and fighting roosters—you're making some pretty good money under the table. But the way you really make money, the way you get to be somebody, is to start a business. I didn't sleep a wink last night thinking about what you was saying about women not getting a fair shake in the business world."

Les tapped the ashes from his cigarette into an empty Nehi bottle.

"And then I got to thinking about this trip I made over to Bowling Green a while back. I was with a few ol' boys who wanted some female companionship, you know, and one of them said he knew a place where we could meet the prettiest girls in Kentucky. We drove out to the country, to this old brick house. A woman answered the door, she was a big, comfortable-looking woman, you know, and she said her name was Arlene, and why didn't we come in and make ourselves at home. It was quite a place, let me tell you, full of antiques, big, gold-framed mirrors on the wall, fresh flowers all over the place. Arlene fixed us drinks, and then she brought out four of just about the prettiest girls you ever did see, 'course, I don't reckon they was prettier than you, and told us to pick out who we wanted."

He shook his head and grinned. "Now I was already engaged to Peg, and I knew she'd kill me soon as look at me if she ever found out I'd been with another woman, so after the other boys had picked out their girls and gone upstairs, I told the girl that was left that I'd pay her for her time, but that I couldn't do nothin' on accounta a war injury I had."

I laughed. "You lying dog!"

"I didn't want to hurt her feelings. What I really wanted to do, see, was to set down and talk to Arlene about her business, which I did. And do you know, that woman was a millionaire?"

My jaw dropped. "Is that a fact?" I had never heard of a woman millionaire before, at least not one that had earned the million herself instead of marrying it.

"Missy, I've been buying up some property here and there, houses that's just about falling down. I buy 'em real cheap and fix 'em up myself, then rent 'em out to folks. A couple of months ago I bought this old farmhouse out toward Sevier County. It ain't but about eight or nine minutes from downtown Knoxville, but it's on a narrow little side road. Real private."

"Do you mean to tell me that after all that moralizing you done last night, you're fixing to set me up in a whorehouse?"

"Well, I done a lot of thinking last night, missy. I got to studying on how hard it is for a woman to get ahead in this world, and that got me to thinking about Arlene. Here's the offer: I make the payments on the house real cheap for you, plus I help you round up a few girls to work there and do a little advertising to all the businessmen I meet. There's two conditions, though."

"Go on."

"The first one is that all the work you do in that house you do standing on your feet. You manage the money, look after the girls and make small talk with the customers in the parlor. But you don't work on your back. You let the other girls take care of that, and they split the money with you."

"But I'll be the prettiest girl there. All the customers will want me."

Les grinned and kind of shook his head. "I reckon they will, but your looks is what'll get 'em in the door. After that, they'll be willing to settle for a girl who ain't quite as pretty. For most fellers, missy, willin' is more important than pretty."

"All right, but why would these girls be willing to split their money with me when they could work by themselves and keep it all?"

"Because you're giving them a nice place to live and feeding them three meals a day. You take care of their doctor's visits, and you talk to the fellers when they come in the door so you know they ain't crazy or on dope. I asked Arlene that same question when I talked to her, and she said the same things I just did, but the first thing she said was, 'Because you're giving them a family.'"

Part of me was scared to death of all the responsibilities I'd have, but another part of me was tingling with excitement. I also didn't hate the idea of charming the men when they hit the door and leaving the wallowing naked part to my employees. "So what's the other condition?"

"The other condition is that I give you the money to buy the house outright. You sign the papers, then you pay me back over time and under the table. I also wouldn't say no to ten percent of the house's profits, since I'll be doing some private advertising and keeping the police away from you as much as I can. But in public it's gotta look like you bought the house outright without me knowing what you was gonna use it for. I've got a few things in the works here in town that'd make it look awful bad if folks found out I was renting out a whorehouse."

"What kind of things?"

Les grinned. "Let's just say I've begun to take an interest in politics."

I laughed. "Shoot, Les, it sounds like you and me are going into the same business!"

CHAPTER 21

At first I felt like I had moving into that little house with David, picking out curtains and rugs and lamps, hanging pictures on the wall. For all my bustling around in an apron with my hair tied back, I could've been a happy little housewife. Except I was nobody's wife, and this was no ordinary house.

On the outside, it was ordinary enough, though, a two-story farmhouse, white with green shutters, with a wraparound porch already equipped with four rocking chairs. The acre of land it sat on was full of large, lovely trees, an oak in the front, and an apple in the back. The house didn't look any more like a whorehouse than a seventy-year-old lady dressed for church looks like a whore. I was glad it was remote and plain enough not to draw the attention of the police, but I hoped it wasn't so remote and plain that it would keep customers away, too.

After a week of hard work, things were looking pretty good. I had put the blue couch from my apartment in the living room and had picked up a couple of secondhand gold upholstered armchairs and an authentic-looking (but still fake) Oriental rug with shades of gold and blue. My bed and dresser and chifforobe went in the room beside the kitchen that probably used to be the dining room. I didn't want my quarters to be too close to the three upstairs bedrooms, newly furnished with secondhand double beds and dressers, that would belong to the girls.

The girls. They were what was worrying me. They were the one absolutely essential part of my business and the one thing I didn't have. Les kept saying he was making phone calls and putting out feelers, but I was beginning to have my doubts.

One afternoon I was sitting out on the porch, not feeling

much different than I used to sitting out on the front porch of the camp house in Bartlett. I was thinking how if I was going to live this far from town I was going to have to buy a car, but how was I going to buy a car if my business never took off? I'd be trapped, out in the country and broke, just like I'd started out in this world. My little pity party was interrupted by two cars pulling into the driveway, Les's car and a sharp, powder-blue Chevy I didn't recognize.

"Hidy, neighbor!" Les called as he slammed the car door behind him. "I brung somebody out to meet you...thought I'd let her follow me out so she wouldn't end up plum in the Smoky Mountains."

I watched as Les opened the powder-blue car's door and a slender brunette who might have been twenty stepped out. Her hair was a bland shade of brown, but it was thick and wavy and arranged in a pretty, shoulder-length style. Her eyes were big and brown and doelike, and she had on a cake-frosting pink dress that was fitted on top and flared to mid-calf on the bottom one of those numbers that used up yards of fabric, unlike the short, tailored fabric-rationing suits gals wore during wartime. I wouldn't go to a dog's funeral in a cake-frosting pink dress, but somehow it suited her. Also, unlike me, she had a light hand with the makeup just enough to darken her lashes and put a little color on her lips. My first thought was that she looked too much like a nice girl. My second thought was, well, some men do like the thought of 'corrupting' a nice girl.

"This is Rowena," Les said as they walked up on the porch. "She used to work in a house up in Clarksville."

Rowena looked me up and down. "Lord, girl, if you're who I've got to compete with, I might as well just get back in my car and head someplace where the girls are uglier."

I decided right then that I liked her. "No competition here," I said. "I'll be running this place. I'll mix the drinks and keep the books, but the only thing I'm gonna make with the customers is conversation." Having a girl there and talking about the business made it start to seem real. "Why don't you come in, and we'll have a little talk?"

Les doffed his hat at both of us. "I reckon this kind of talk is best left to you gals. I just wanted to escort Miss Rowena over here."

"Thanks, Les. You're a doll." Rowena gave Les a little peck on his cheek, which promptly turned fire-engine red.

"So," I began after Rowena and I were settled on the living room couch with bottles of Coke and a plate of store-bought cookies, "why did you leave the house where you'd been working?"

"Mostly I was tired of Clarksville," Rowena said, nibbling her cookie in a straight little line. "When you work in a house in a small town, you get the same customers over and over. After a while you feel like you're married to 'em." She rolled her eyes. "And then when new girls come into the house, which a couple just did in Clarksville, they get all the business because the same old customers get tired of screwing the same old girls. I thought it might be nice to be somewhere where I was the new girl for a change."

"You don't have any kinfolks around here, do you?" The last thing I wanted was an angry father or brother showing up with a shotgun.

"No, my family's all in Georgia, and I haven't talked to them in years. My daddy's a Baptist preacher, if you can believe it."

I grinned. "I believe it. You can't swing a dead cat without hitting a Baptist preacher in this part of the world. Is there any chance he might come looking for you?"

Rowena laughed. "Lord, no. And even if he tried, I don't think he could find me. I haven't used my real name in years. My real name is Mercy, but you can't really be a whore with a name like that, can you? Some fella'd be screwing you and hollering, 'Mercy! Mercy!' and it would sound like you was killing him."

It was my turn to laugh.

"No," Rowena said, chewing her cookie thoughtfully, "Daddy won't come looking for me. He knows he wouldn't like what he'd find."

I didn't say anything to Rowena, but I figured what she just said applied to my own daddy, too. "No jealous husband or boyfriend anywhere?"

Rowena grinned. "Lord, no. I'm not about to get married

anytime soon. And I don't believe I'll ever have kids. This doctor in Clarksville gave me this jelly to use so I won't get pregnant. Every time he gave me a fresh tube, he said the same thing: 'Don't put this jelly on your toast, now.' It was funny the first time."

The next question I asked was out of sheer nosiness. "So what makes a Baptist preacher's daughter go into this line of work?"

Rowena looked me over. "You've done it, too, haven't you?"

I nodded.

"Well, then, I probably went into it the same reason you did. I love sex. I can do it a dozen times a night with a dozen different men and love it every time. And getting paid for it, well, that's the frosting on the cake, isn't it?"

As far as I was concerned, getting paid was the cake, the frosting and all. But I didn't want Rowena to think I lacked the usual womanly desires, so all I said was, "You're hired."

After Rowena had a couple of days to get settled, she and I decided that you can't run much of a whorehouse with just one whore and one madam, and it didn't look like any other girls were going to be pulling into our driveway anytime soon. After we had our toast and coffee, we put on our nicest daytime dresses, Rowena's was a powder-blue shirtwaist the exact same shade as her car, and mine was a bright green sheath I had bought at Diller's because I could afford to shop there now. As we checked ourselves in the hall mirror, I thought that in our fresh spring colors, we looked like a particularly voluptuous pair of Easter eggs. We grabbed our purses, hopped into Rowena's car and headed into town to look for girls.

Of course, it's not an easy thing to approach a young woman you've never met before and try to lure her into a life of prostitution. For the first time, I wished I had made friends with some other girls when I had first moved to Knoxville, that I had gotten close to some girls who were like me. The trouble was, though, that I had never met another girl like me.

For a second or two I thought of Lucy as a possible girl for the house, but a second was all it took to determine that hiring her would be a disaster. True, she slept with lots of men who gave her money or presents, but she was always getting all tangled up with them, complaining about how this creep or that creep hadn't called her. Lucy let her heart get involved with men who only wanted her body. For this reason, she would always be an amateur.

As we walked down Gay Street downtown, I looked over every woman we passed, a petite young mother whose apple cheeks were the mirror image of her toddler daughter's; a tall, willowy woman with razor-sharp cheekbones who was wearing a hat with a pheasant's feather; a plump young woman with honey blond hair who was all softness and curves.

I was used to thinking of myself as the most beautiful woman in whatever place I was in, but when I started looking at different women, really looking at them and trying to figure out what I would find desirable about them if I was a man, I discovered that most women are beautiful. Some, like me, might have beautiful features and a beautiful body; others might just radiate goodness or elegance or sensuality, less obvious kinds of beauty, but beauty just the same. It seemed to me that there was something in most women to find attractive, and for a second, this thought scared me. Was I actually finding these women attractive myself?

Not for the first time since I had seen them, I thought of Trey and her girlfriend, but I quickly pushed them out of my mind. I was a businesswoman, and to be successful in my business, I had to look at women and imagine how my male customers would see them.

I pulled Rowena off to the side of the sidewalk. "This isn't gonna work. What are we supposed to do, just walk up and down Gay Street until we see a girl we both like and then grab her?"

Rowena laughed. "That's what we'd do if we were men." She chewed her lip thoughtfully for a second. "I was thinking we could maybe go to some diners and coffee shops, see if any girls working there might want a better-paying job. I used to wait tables, and it was awful. I never met a waitress who wanted to stay a waitress forever."

That day I drank so many cups of coffee in so many diners that my hands shook and I had to pee every five minutes. But every waitress we saw seemed better suited for pouring coffee than selling her body. A couple of them were grandmotherly types, with wide behinds and shelf-like bosoms. Others were young and pretty enough but were wearing wedding rings or cross pendants—jewelry that said right away that they weren't the right girls for the job.

By two o'clock we were so exhausted by our pointless searching that we decided to go see the Judy Garland picture that was playing at the Tennessee Theater. My caffeine-rattled nerves calmed a little as I sat in the cool darkness of the theater, watching Miss Judy sing and dance onscreen. I was just thinking that old Judy looked like she'd had a few too many cups of joe herself when the need to pee hit me again. I hated having to get up and miss some of a movie, but I also didn't want to leave a puddle on the Tennessee Theater's plush red carpet.

I excused myself past Rowena, squinted as I walked into the bright light of the lobby and made my way to the ladies' room. I was so focused on my goal when I walked in that I didn't notice that anybody else was there, but as I was on my way back out, I saw a girl slumped on the velvet couch by the door. She was crying.

"Are you all right?" I asked the way people do when the answer is clearly no.

"Sure, I'm just dandy. Never better." She looked up at me with a blotchy, tear-streaked face.

I reached into my purse for a lace-trimmed hanky. "Here, use this. It beats toilet paper."

She took it and looked it over. "It's too pretty to blow my snot all over."

"Keep it. You can take it home and wash the snot off."

She blew her nose with a loud honk.

"So," I said, "you want to talk about it?"

"About what?"

"About whatever…or whoever…has sent you crying to the ladies' room." Normally I would have just given the kid my hanky and hurried back to catch the rest of the show, but I couldn't help noticing that even though this girl's face was red and swollen from crying, her features were nicely arranged. She had on a shapeless blouse and skirt that looked like they'd come straight out of the Montgomery Ward catalog, but there seemed to be a nice figure under there somewhere, and she had a pretty wave of blond hair that put me in mind of Veronica Lake. Whether from nature or peroxide, we needed a blond in the house.

"I can't imagine why you'd care, but I lost my job today. I came to this town right after high school graduation and got a job at the bank as a secretary so I could save money for college. Anyway, my boss was all hands, if you know what I mean, but I put up with it because a girl does what she's gotta do to get ahead, you know?"

"Believe me, I know."

"So today he had me backed into a corner like usual when the office door swings open. It's his wife, who had popped into town to do some shopping. He blamed the whole thing on me, of course, and fired me on the spot." She blew her nose again.

I sat down on the couch beside her. "So why did you come to the show?"

"I always go to the movies when I'm sad."

I draped my arm around her companionably. "What's your name, hon?"

"Mabel."

"Well, we can fix that later. Listen, what if I told you I could offer you a job that isn't exactly to the letter of the law, but that could earn you your college money at least ten times faster than typing, filing and getting chased around a desk?"

"I'm listening," Mabel said.

I talked a good twenty minutes, and Mabel listened. I couldn't help thinking about how when I met Lucy I had been the crying girl in the bathroom, and she had been the experienced, worldly-wise woman. Now, just a little more than a year later, I was the woman, not the girl.

When I was finished talking, Mabel followed me into the darkness of the theater and sat with Rowena and me for the rest of the movie. When Judy had finished her big closing number, I leaned over to Rowena and said, "This is Mabel."

"Hi," Rowena said. "We're going to have to do somethin' about that name."

Mabel smiled. "So I've been told."

We drove Mabel to her shabby boardinghouse and waited while she got her things. In ten minutes she was out the front door, carrying a single battered suitcase. She hopped in the backseat. "What if I call myself Jezebel?"

"Nope," Rowena said. "Can't be scaring the Christians. They already feel guilty enough going to a whore as it is. Call yourself Jezebel, and they won't be able to get it up to save their souls."

By the time we pulled the car into the driveway, we had decided that Mabel's new name would be Honey. We were laughing and cutting up as we walked to the house, so we were startled when we saw a woman sitting on the porch.

"Thank God I got the right house," she said. "I kept worrying that some old farmer in overalls would pull up, and I wouldn't have the foggiest idea what to say."

"You could ask him if he wanted you to show him a good time," Rowena said, laughing. Rowena's comment seemed careless to me, what if our visitor was here for some reason other than the obvious one? I was relieved to see her smile.

In her own way, the woman was almost as beautiful as I was. It was a different kind of beauty, though. She was fine-boned, all elegant planes and angles, where I was soft and curvy. She was wearing an expensive tan linen suit with mother-of-pearl buttons and the prim white gloves that ladies wore back then when they traveled. A little tan cloche hat perched on top of her neat curls, which were mousy brown, I definitely had the advantage in the hair department. She looked like one of the ladies who shopped at Diller's and got bitchy with the salesgirls. She certainly didn't look like a woman in my profession.

"Sorry to keep you waiting out on the porch," I said. "I'm Vestal. This is my place."

"Oh, I was comfortable. And the view from the porch is lovely." Her speech was as perfect as a schoolteacher's. She must be from up North, I decided. "I'm Gwen," she said, rising to shake my hand. "I hope to find a position here."

"Well, given what kinda house this is, you'll probably find several positions," I said. "You do know what kind of house this is, don't you?"

"Yes, I know what's...involved."

"Have you done this kind of work before?"

Gwen's lips curled in the hint of a smile. "Not for money. But if I can do it for free, I think I should be able to do it for money. And I've never had any complaints."

"So," I said, figuring I'd get her to chitchat a little, "what made you decide to come looking for this kind of work?"

Gwen took a silver cigarette case from a purse, took out a cigarette and lit up. I thought she might be settling in for a good story, but all she said was, "If it's all the same to you, Vestal, I don't especially want to discuss personal matters. I am very discreet, which I feel makes me well qualified for this kind of work."

Gwen was a different breed than Rowena and Honey, who would both tell you their whole life stories within two seconds of meeting you. Honey and Rowena had their differences, of course, for one thing, Honey had more going on in the brains department, but they were both open, approachable girls, like friendly little dogs that craved attention. Gwen, though, kept her distance. She didn't give away anything about herself. She was an elegant cat, sleek and aloof. And while I could sense that Rowena and Honey didn't like her, I thought some of our customers would. Rowena and Honey would be the fun-loving girls who put nervous customers at ease, but Gwen would give the place some class.

With all the girls moved into their rooms, we were ready for business. But opening up a whorehouse isn't the same as opening up a grocery store, you can't just put an ad in the paper that says, 'Grand Opening-Come Sample Our Produce.' A whorehouse has got to build its business by word of mouth, and discreet word of mouth at that. Of course, this is where Les came in.

The Saturday we had decided would be our grand opening, Les invited me and the girls to yet another grand opening, the opening of his second store, this one in South Knoxville. He said that while he promoted his new business loudly, he'd promote our new business quietly to gentlemen who were well off enough to afford our services. So under my supervision, Rowena and Honey and Gwen got all dolled up on Saturday morning to go into town. I say 'under my supervision' because Rowena and Honey tended to paint the makeup on a little thick.

Gwen, though, always knew the right balance, how to put

on enough makeup to bring out her natural features, but not too much; how to choose a dress that showed off her figure but still left something to the imagination. That morning, Gwen unveiled another surprise which told me that even though she lacked experience, she already knew the business. As Rowena and Honey and I were fussing over our clothes in front of the big mirror in my bedroom, she emerged from the bathroom with her mousy brown curls replaced by deep auburn ones.

"Oh, my Lord!" Rowena exclaimed. "How'd you do that?"

"Henna," Gwen said, stepping in front of the other girls to survey herself in the mirror. "I should've done it years ago. I've never liked my hair."

"It suits you," I said. "And men go crazy for redheads. Look at Rita Hayworth."

"Or Suzy Parker." That month's issue of *Glamour* had had the famous redheaded model who was to become the Face of the Fifties on the cover. With her new flame-colored hair, Gwen was just about a dead ringer for Suzy.

Then, Gwen did something that left the other girls slack-jawed with shock. Still standing in front of the mirror, she let her dressing gown slide off her shoulders, down her arms and into a heap on the floor. She stood, looking at herself naked, in the same way you'd look over a car you were thinking about buying. Rowena and Honey and I had changed clothes in front of each other, but Gwen always changed with her door closed. Now, though, she stood before us naked for what seemed like minutes, staring into the mirror without even seeming to notice we were there. Finally, her eyes left the mirror and met mine. "So what do you think, Vestal? If you were a man, would you be willing to pay for this?"

I glanced at her long legs and her high breasts, her long, lean, elegant form. I wasn't sure why a girl with such a beautiful body would be worried that men wouldn't want her, but she must have been, or why would she have asked? "Sugar, they'll be linin' up out the door to pay for it."

Gwen let herself smile a little, then picked up her dressing gown.

"Hey," Rowena hollered, pointing below Gwen's waist. "What

happened to you? You don't have any hair down there!"

I couldn't believe I hadn't noticed it myself, but the patch above Gwen's pussy was as white and smooth as an egg.

"Well," Gwen said, "once I dyed my hair, my other hair didn't match, so I just shaved it off."

She strode out of the room, still naked, while Rowena and Honey collapsed on my bed in a fit of giggles.

Every head turned to stare at us when we arrived at the opening of Les's second Stop 'n Save. Four stunning women, one redhead, one blonde, one brunette and me with my blue-black hair, each of us wearing sleeveless sheath dresses the colors of jewels: sapphire, ruby, amethyst and emerald. Dowdy wives in their housedresses scowled at us and shushed their little girls when they said we were pretty. The men tripped over their own feet, lighting our cigarettes and fetching us Cokes. Rowena and Honey giggled and teased, while Gwen wore only a half-smile and carried herself like a princess. Even though Rowena and Honey were about my age and Gwen was probably several years older than me, I felt as proud of them as if I was their mother.

"Hidy, neighbors!" Les came up to us, then leaned in to whisper, "You girls better make sure your liquor cabinet's full this evenin', cause you're gonna have business like you wouldn't believe."

Seconds later, Les was standing on an outdoor stage next to a tall, skinny fellow in overalls.

"So," Les boomed into the microphone, "Mr. Sharp here has kindly volunteered to let us bury him alive for three whole days. He'll live on nothin' but the Heinz soup and the RC Cola that we'll run through a straw down to where he's buried. So over the next three days, you'uns come on down and see the Living Burial. We've even got a special two-way radio set up here so you can talk to Mr. Sharp in person, and while you're here, you'll want to take advantage of some of the special deals we've got going here at Les Tipton's Stop 'n Save. We've got Heinz soup and six-packs of RC Cola two for the price of one for the whole time Mr. Sharp's in the ground!"

Les's eyes were gleaming in that nearly insane way; considering this promotional stunt, I began to wonder if maybe he had gone all the way around the bend.

"And now, as some of you may know," he went on, "I can't turn down a good bet. So, Mr. Sharp, if you manage to stay down there three days, I'm gonna give five hundred dollars, cash money, to the East Tennessee Home for Orphaned Children!"

The crowd broke into wild applause.

Les looked over at his skinny friend, or victim, depending on how you thought about it. "You ready, Mr. Sharp?"

"Ready as I'll ever be," Mr. Sharp said into the microphone, grinning. I hoped Les was lining his pockets generously for his trouble.

"All right, then, get in your box!" Les hollered. "They's shovels for whoever wants 'em!"

I watched in disbelief as Mr. Sharp crawled down a ladder into a hole in the ground, and then into a box so small he could barely sit up in it. A hole with a large, long straw protruding from it was on the box's lid, which was soon secured onto the box itself. Okay, I thought, the straw and the hole are how he'll get air and food and water, but how will he go to the bathroom? It had to be a hoax, I decided. Les must have had a way to get him out.

But I started to have my doubts as I watched the crowd of men gleefully throwing the dirt back in the hole. I looked at the shock on the faces of Rowena, Honey and Gwen and the delight on Les's. I thought of my new business venture and wondered if I, like Mr. Sharp, was getting in over my head.

CHAPTER 22

"What'll you boys have?"

The two young men cast a nervous glance over at the couch, where Rowena, Gwen and Honey were sitting, Rowena in a pale blue silk evening gown, Gwen in a pearl-gray strapless and Honey in a gown that was cut so low that even though it was white, it was far from virginal. I looked at the wide, wondering eyes of the young men. They were both in their early twenties, but their kid-in-an-ice-cream-shop expressions made them look about ten.

"I was just talking about drinks, boys," I said. "You don't have to make any big decisions yet."

The first young man tittered nervously and said, "Oh...uh... bourbon."

The other one, who couldn't look me in the eye, muttered, "Same."

I did feel his eyes on me, though, when I bent forward to get the glasses. My red gown had a sweetheart neckline that my titties kept threatening to spill out of. At first I wasn't sure about buying the red gown. Just because I was a scarlet woman, I thought, did that mean I should dress in scarlet? But I've always looked good in red. And besides, if a customer knocked on the door, and I opened it wearing a red gown cut clear down to the equator, then he'd know he'd come to the right place. Nobody was going to mistake me for a farm wife.

I gave the boys their drinks. "Now," I said, "why don't I introduce you to the girls?" I took their free arms and half escorted, half dragged them to the sofa. "Looky here, girls," I said, grinning, "if y'all don't take a liking to these handsome fellas, I just might have to keep 'em both for myself."

The boys looked down at the fake Oriental rug; the quieter one of them was blushing. Dealing with these boys, I couldn't believe how nervous I'd been earlier in the evening, but I had quickly discovered the first rule of running a whorehouse: no matter how bad your jitters are, your customers' jitters will be worse.

"Now that's a pretty rug," I said, "but it's not near as pretty as what's sitting on the couch. Boys, meet Gwen, Rowena and Honey." Each of the girls gave a ladylike little wave as I introduced her. "Now, if y'all will excuse me," I said, "I think I'll put on a little music. It's as quiet as a funeral home in here."

I sashayed over to the secondhand record player and put on some Benny Goodman. Soon the more talkative boy was dancing with Gwen, and the shyer one was dancing with Honey. Rowena looked a little sullen to be the one left sitting on the sofa, but she tapped her foot in time with the music just the same.

The Baptists always put down dancing; some of them even say it's like fornicating set to music. As much as I hate to admit that the Baptists might have a point, I have to say that when running a whorehouse, you should never underestimate the value of a dance as the icebreaker that will lead to fornicating. The touching that two people do standing up, moving their bodies to the rhythm of the music with their clothes on, prepares them for the touching they'll do lying down, moving to the rhythm of their bodies with their clothes off. Of course, the Baptists would call this sinning. I call it good business.

Within fifteen minutes, the two boys were climbing the stairs, hand-in-hand with Gwen and Honey.

Rowena didn't have much time to sulk because within seconds there was a knock on the door, and a wildly grinning curly-haired middle-aged man looked me over and howled, "This must be the place!" He didn't even want a drink. He just took one look at Rowena and said, "Come to Daddy, you pretty little brown-eyed thing!"

Rowena grinned back at him as big as he grinned at her, and soon they went upstairs. When I lifted the needle from the gramophone, the house was filled with the music of squeaking bedsprings—a sound I soon happily associated with money.

That first night, men streamed in and out of the door of the house. The girls would entertain gentlemen upstairs, run to the bathroom to wash and fix their hair and makeup, and then run back downstairs to smile seductively at the next set of eager customers. I marveled at the girls' endurance; in my whoring days, I had only done one man a night and had felt exhausted and used up afterward. These girls' pussies must've felt like an aching tooth the dentist keeps right on drilling, but they smiled and flirted and went upstairs for more.

Another thing that amazed me was the camaraderie of the men in the house. On that first night and many nights after, there were times when there were more men in the house than there were girls to take care of them. We were a pretty small operation, after all. Men who would've hated one another if they had met in any other setting, diehard Republicans and yellow-dog Democrats, atheist college professors and Pentecostal preachers, sat and drank and played cards together like the best of friends while they waited for a turn with one of the girls.

A man who would've happily killed another man for screwing his girlfriend or even looking at her the wrong way could sit and drink beer with another man while they both waited to screw the same girl. I guess it all comes down to ownership. If you're a fellow's girlfriend, he feels like he has to defend you against anybody who might try to take you away from him. If you're a whore, though, you're not his in the first place, so there's no masculine pride at stake.

We made so much money I couldn't stop counting it. I'd count, laugh and count again. Even after I gave the girls their share, there was still so much money I couldn't wipe the smile off my face.

After the first month we were making more money than we knew what to do with. The house was open Wednesday through Saturday. Wednesdays were usually a little slow. On Thursdays, things picked up a little, and by Friday and Saturday we were packed to the gills. All kinds of men came to see us: traveling business men who were after a quick thrill while they were away from their wives; soldiers who had been penned up with only men for weeks and were desperate for female companionship; shy young men who claimed never to have 'been with' a woman before; preachers who were so filled with that delicious combination of guilt and lust that they'd sometimes do it with one of the girls, then wait half an hour and do it with another.

Rowena and Honey and I spent most of our days spending the money we earned at night. Gwen would usually stay at the house, saying she wanted to catch up on her reading or that she needed to write letters to her friends or that someone really ought to be around to supervise the girl who came in to clean the house and wash the come stains out of the sheets. Honey called Gwen 'standoffish,' while Rowena dismissed her as 'stuck-up.'

The way I saw it, though, Gwen just looked at life in a whorehouse differently than Rowena and Honey. For Rowena and Honey, the house was their home, and the girls in it were their adopted sisters. For Gwen, though, the house was just the place where she worked. If she wanted to spend her free time alone instead of listening to Rowena and Honey giggle about who had the smallest peepee they'd seen that week, then that was her business.

While Gwen was at the house, doing whatever she did (Rowena and Honey speculated on this a lot, figuring that Gwen couldn't really want to stay home just so she could read books or write letters and that she must be entertaining a secret lover instead), we went to town. With my new wealth, I had come to look at department stores like Diller's with the same distaste an old-money matron these days would have for Wal-Mart.

Instead, the girls and I shopped in elegant boutiques—the ones where they pour you coffee in a china cup as soon as you hit the door, and you sit on a fancy brocade sofa and watch girls model the latest fashions for you. It was like having *Glamour* magazine come to life before your eyes. Sometimes one of the models would be so pretty I'd be tempted to ask her to work in my house, but since discretion is key when you're traveling in classy circles, I'd keep my mouth shut and concentrate on the clothes, not the girls.

Rowena and Honey and I would usually eat lunch at one of the fancy hotels. The treatment we got in these places would depend on the waiter. Some waiters flirted with us and sneaked us free drinks; others made it sniffily clear that we were well below the station of the society matrons who usually lunched there and that the money that we paid for our overpriced finger sandwiches must be very dirty indeed. These sniffy, snobby waiters were happy enough to pocket our tips, though, and their roving eyes made it clear that they wanted to screw us just as much as every other man did; they just hated themselves for it.

One afternoon, after finger sandwiches at the Bentley but before a matinee at the Tennessee Theater, I popped into Klein's Jewelers. I hadn't been to Klein's since David's and my honeymoon, when he had lectured me about how he was going to change me into a pearl instead of the piece of grit I was.

Now I was changed, all right, but not the way David had wanted me to be. My grit had served me well. Maybe if David had been a little grittier himself, he would've had a better chance of surviving in this tough, old world.

I passed over the display case of pearls because looking at it made me sad. But then something else caught my eye. In the center of a small case, resting on the fourth finger of a stuffed black velvet evening glove was a two-carat ruby surrounded by small, sparkling diamonds. Mother always said that any woman who wore red was a harlot, and this bold, harlot's stone came a lot closer to saying what kind of girl I was than a dainty little pearl could.

The diamonds surrounding the ruby captured my heart, too, as I remembered Les looking at my engagement ring and telling me how every diamond starts out as plain old black coal. Looking at that ring, I felt like I had finally shaken off the coal dust of Bartlett and found the diamond that glittered inside me.

"Can I try that on?" I asked Mr. Klein, who clearly didn't recognize me as the wide-eyed newlywed I had once been.

"Certainly, miss." He opened the case and slipped the ring off the velvet glove.

I slid the ring onto the finger that used to hold my wedding ring. The glittering red stone stood out against my milky skin and matched the red polish on my long nails. The diamonds danced in the light if I moved my hand even slightly. "How much?"

When Mr. Klein answered, Rowena and Honey gasped out loud at the amount.

I just said, "I can give you a hundred today, and I should have the rest in a couple of weeks."

Within three weeks, the ring was mine. Like a different kind of wedding ring, I slipped it onto my left ring finger and thought about a Bible passage I had once heard my sister Myrtle rattle off: "A virtuous woman has a price above rubies." Admiring the ruby on my hand, I knew there wasn't a virtuous woman on earth who could afford to buy herself something so beautiful.

CHAPTER 23

Looking at my ring made me think of Bartlett. Maybe it's impossible for a girl who was raised like I was to see a diamond without thinking about coal and the men who eke out a living crawling underground to get it.

I didn't miss Bartlett, of course. Missing Bartlett would've been like missing a prolonged case of pneumonia. But I did miss C.R., and I saw his face in the face of every fun-loving, hard-drinking soldier who walked into the house. And while I didn't exactly miss Mother, Daddy and Myrtle, who I hadn't heard a peep from since I married David, I did feel something like pity for them.

Daddy got up every morning when it was still dark so he could be in the mines by six, and Mother got up with him to fix his breakfast and pack his dinner bucket. Daddy stayed in the mines until the sky darkened. Weekends were the only times he saw full daylight. And despite these exhausting hours of labor, hunched over in backbreaking positions in a dark hole in the ground, he barely earned enough to feed his family.

I, however, slept until ten or eleven every morning and did what I damn well pleased until eight o'clock at night, when I put on a beautiful gown, dangly earrings and lipstick and earned my living by laughing, pouring drinks and accepting the wads of money men handed me. Sure, Mother and Daddy would've said I was sinning up a storm, but it seemed to me that what it came down to was not the decision to be good instead of sinful, but the choice of living an easy life instead of a hard one. Myrtle would say that virtue lies in choosing the harder path, but I say, why break your back in a coal camp all your life, whether it's as a miner or a miner's wife, when you can barely lift a finger, and that finger will be ringed with diamonds?

Poor old infuriating Myrtle. I wondered if she was still living at home or if she had found a man who was fool enough to marry her.

Out of a mixture of pity and curiosity, I sat at the kitchen table one late morning and wrote on a sheet of expensive stationery, which I bought just to show Mother and Daddy I could afford it:

Dear Mother and Daddy,

I hope this letter finds you well. You may have heard that I am a widow now. I am living in Knoxville and have my own shop. Business is good. Mother, I have enclosed a little money so you can buy some fabric and patterns to make you and Myrtle some new dresses.

Well, I will close for now. Please write me now that you have my address.

Your daughter,
Vestal

I put a twenty-dollar bill in the envelope. At first I thought about sending fifty or even a hundred, but I knew it would be a slap to Daddy's pride for a daughter to send home so much money.

As I was licking the envelope, there was a knock on the kitchen door. Nobody knocks on the door of a whorehouse in the a.m., so I had no idea who it could be, and I hoped it wasn't some screwy customer who thought we operated around the clock. If so, he was in for a sorry sight. I was still in my dressing gown with no makeup on and uncombed hair. None of the girls had stirred from bed yet.

When I opened the door, though, it was not a man, but a mannish woman. It took me a second to place her, just because I couldn't figure out what she was doing at the house.

"Vestal?" She sounded shy, a little awkward, very different from when I had talked to her at her mother's and at Les's 'Fun Fair.' "You remember me?" she asked.

"Of course I remember you, Trey. It took pretty near three months for all the hair down there to grow back after you shaved it. Come on in and have a cup of coffee. How'd you find this place, anyway?"

Trey let herself smile just a little. "Everybody in town knows about your place, Vestal."

"Is that a fact?" I poured her a cup of coffee. "Well, I guess it's good to know I'm famous. Not much point in being famous if you don't know you are."

I gestured for her to sit down at the kitchen table and brought her the coffee. She looked into the cup for a moment, then asked, "Are we alone?"

I sat down at the table across from her. "Well, nobody's ever really alone in a whorehouse, but the girls are all asleep and probably won't be stirring for another hour or two. I reckon we're about as alone as we can be in this place. Why do you ask?"

Trey held her coffee cup in both hands but didn't pick it up to drink from it. "This is real hard to talk about," she said, looking at the cup like she had never seen one before, "but Mama said that since you're in...the kind of business you're in, you'd probably understand."

"Well, you've got me interested, anyway," I said. Usually, I could predict what people were going to say and be right about ninety-five percent of the time. But I honestly had no idea where this conversation was going.

"You remember I was going to school over at Frederick Douglass?"

"Uh-huh."

She smiled, but it wasn't a happy smile. "Well, I'm not anymore."

"What happened?" My first thought was that she was asking for money. I figured I could spare her some, but I didn't know if it would be enough to help her. I had no idea how much college might cost.

"Well..." she said, fascinated with her coffee cup again. "This isn't easy to talk about. You remember when you ran into me that time and I was with that girl, Barbara?"

"Uh-huh."

"Well, Barbara was my...she was my..."

I was tempted to snatch the coffee cup away from her so she'd quit fooling with it, but instead I said, "I think I know what she was to you."

Trey looked relieved and grateful. "Good. That makes this easier. A lot easier. All right, so Barbara is a student at Douglass, too. One Saturday night I went over to see her in her dormitory room because her roommate had gone home for the weekend. So after a while, me and Barbara are in her bed, you know, not sleeping, and then I hear the doorknob turn."

"The door wasn't locked?"

"I had meant to lock it, but the second I closed the door behind me Barbara was kissing me and calling me her sweet daddy and, well, I guess I just forgot."

Trey had gone silent, so I prompted her, "The doorknob turned?"

"The doorknob turned, and it was the dorm mother. We were in a position where we couldn't pretend we were doing anything else, if you know what I mean, so the dorm mother reported it to the dean of women, who called me into her office and very politely asked me to leave school."

"And Barbara, too, I reckon."

Trey laughed. "Oh, no, not Barbara. See, Barbara's story is she didn't want to do it; I made her. Never mind that she was the one who invited me over, she was the one who started kissing me...never mind that this was something we'd done at least a dozen times before. But look at Barbara, compared to me. She's got her neat little skirts and blouses, her lipstick and her beauty-shop hairdo. Plus, she's from a rich family from up North, and her parents give all kinds of money to the college. There's no question in the dean of women's mind who the real dagger is. So...I get thrown out. Barbara gets to stay, provided that she meets weekly with the dean of women and the college chaplain." She shook her head. "I guess I'm no better than a man who lets a woman walk all over him just because she's got a pretty face."

"Hmm...I guess you're not, at that." You'd think another woman would be able to see right through a coat of lipstick and a good pair of gams, but apparently women like Trey are just as helpless in the face of female beauty as any man who ever stumbled into a whorehouse with his just-cashed paycheck.

"I still haven't told you the reason I'm here." Trey looked in the direction of the kitchen window, probably so she wouldn't have to make eye contact with me. "I've always been an independent person. Stubborn as a mule, that's what my mama calls me. I never ask anybody for help, and I especially never ask white folks for help. But Vestal, everybody at school knows about me and why I got thrown out. All the folks in Mama's neighborhood know, too. As soon as I walk into a room, the whispering starts."

"I know that feeling," I said. "For different reasons, though." When I was working the clubs, as soon as I'd hit the door, the men would stare and the women would whisper.

"What I hate most about it is it's bad for Mama's business. One girl from the college came down the other day to, you know, get her problem taken care of, and as soon as she saw I was gonna be helping, she said, 'I ain't taking my clothes off nowhere near that bulldagger,' and ran out the door like she was afraid I was gonna chase her."

"I don't guess girls want you shaving their pussies if they think you're enjoying it."

Trey banged her fist on the table. "But I don't enjoy it! Not that way, anyway. And it shouldn't make any difference to them. Girls take their clothes of in front of man doctors all the time. How about you, Vestal? If you had known about me, and hell, anybody should know, just to look at me, would you still have let me take care of you like I did?"

"Of course I would. I'd know it was just a job to you. Business is business and pleasure is pleasure, and smart people don't get the two mixed up."

Trey grinned. "That's a funny thing to say, in the business you're in."

"It's especially true in the business I'm in. The only pleasure I've ever got from going to bed with a man is the money."

"Huh," Trey said. She looked like she was going to say

something else, but she closed her mouth.

"You still haven't told me why you're here."

"Well…Mama didn't throw me out of her house. She's always had a pretty good idea of what I am, and the main thing that bothered her about the big to-do with Barbara was that I didn't have sense enough to lock the door. But I knew I was hurting Mama's business, and Daddy had nothing to leave her when he died, so taking care of what she calls 'female complaints' is the only way to put collards and cornbread on the table. I know she'd let me stay there and work with her and not say a word even though business was winding down to nothing, but I couldn't do that to her. So I kissed her on the cheek and told her I was leaving to look for a job."

I got up and busied myself with the coffeepot, figuring it was best just to let her talk.

"Mama made me promise I wouldn't take a job as a cleaning lady or a restroom attendant. She wanted me to go to all the colored doctors' and dentists' offices to see if any of them needed a secretary. And I guess I would rather type and file than clean toilets and say, 'Yes, ma'am,' all day. But then again, I don't want the kind of job where I have to put on a dress and pretend to be something I'm not, where I have to keep so quiet about my life that the folks in the office start getting suspicious that I'm hiding something, where maybe I slip up and say something halfway truthful and get fired for it. Mama wants me to have a respectable job, but the way I look at it, the job's not respectable if the people there don't respect me."

"There's not a lot of respectable jobs for girls," I said, "let alone colored girls. Let alone colored girls like you." I didn't really have a name in my head to describe Trey's sexual identity, at least not a name that wasn't designed to hurt her feelings.

"I know. That's why I've given up on the idea of a respectable job. There's another house like this on my side of town, with all colored girls. I talked to Miss Lillian, the lady in charge there…"

"Trey, are you thinking of becoming a…"

"Of course not." Trey laughed. "Hell, I've never been to bed with a man for free, and I don't even know what you'd have to pay me to do it. I was just thinking I might be able to help out around the house...you know, maybe keep the books, mow the grass, run errands. Plus, I've got enough training from Mama that I could take care of any 'female complaints' that might come up. I made the same offer to Miss Lillian, but she just laughed at me. She said, 'A bulldagger in a whorehouse is about as bad as a fox in a henhouse.' So, this morning I walked over here, it took me two full hours, to ask you the same thing I asked Miss Lillian. And before you answer, let me just say that I've got much better sense than to ever lay a hand on one of the white women you've got working for you."

Keeping the books for the house had been taking away valuable time I could have been shopping or getting my nails done. The house could also profit by having somebody to run errands, I figured. Many was the night when we had run out of liquor or ice, and because I had to stay there and keep an eye on the girls, I had to call Les to send a boy over with the needed supplies. Sometimes the delay was long enough that the customers got cranky.

"I'll hire you," I said. "You're not gonna get rich but it does include room and board. I don't know where the hell we're gonna put you to sleep, but we'll figure something out. And you can wear pants, a suit and tie, a cowboy outfit, whatever you want. If any of the girls or the customers say anything about it, I'll give them a good talking-to. A whorehouse isn't a place where anybody ought to be judged."

Trey grinned. "I'll just go get my bag, then. I hid it under your porch. I didn't want to come in carrying it, looking like I was expecting something."

"You mean to tell me you walked two full hours carrying a full suitcase?"

"Yep." Trey grinned. It was like the smile of a cocky teenaged boy. "When I set my mind to something, nothing can stop me."

If you want to see some beautiful women looking their absolute worst, stop by a whorehouse the morning after an especially busy night. At ten after eleven, Rowena and Honey staggered into the kitchen looking like moles who had just tunneled their way into sunlight.

"Where's the coffee?" Rowena rasped.

"Where it always is," I said. "Y'all want me to fix some eggs?"

Both girls looked as if I had offered them a plate of squiggling worms. "Just coffee for now," Honey said, pouring a cupful.

When Trey walked back in, her suitcase in hand, I said, "Trey, this is Rowena and Honey. We've got one other girl that works here, Gwen, but she's still in bed. Girls, this is Trey. I've just hired her to help us around here a little."

"We've already got a maid," Rowena said after a quick glance at Trey.

"Trey's not a maid," I said. "She's gonna help me with the books, run errands, maybe do a little yardwork if she feels like it, but she's nobody's maid. She's got three years of college under her belt, which is more than I can say for any of us in this house."

"That's why we have to make a living from what we've got under our belts." Honey laughed and looked at Trey. "I'm saving up for college, though." It was important to Honey that people knew that for her, whoring was just a temporary stop on the road to better things.

"Of course, for all we know about her, Gwen could have half a dozen college degrees," Rowena said.

"No, just one." Gwen was standing in the doorway, stretching like a cat.

Trey proved herself to be valuable around the house. She was a much better bookkeeper than I was, she could drive to town for liquor on nights when we ran low, and once she even showed the door to a drunk who was playing a little too rough with Honey on the dance floor.

One evening I came in from an afternoon of shopping to find her busy in the kitchen. I watched as she dropped floured pieces of chicken into a cast-iron skillet, each piece hissing when it hit the hot grease.

"I don't pay you to cook," I said.

Trey wiped her hands on a frilly pink apron of mine that looked ridiculous over her trousers and shirt. "I know you don't pay me to cook. But I like to cook. And just between you and me, I couldn't stand the thought of eating those soup beans I knew you were gonna heat back up for tonight." She was grinning the way she did when she was giving me a hard time.

I put on a hurt tone. "You don't like my soup beans?"

"I do, but not when I've been eating on them for three days. I know you and the girls go have yourselves fancy lunches in town, but the way you eat at home, you'd think this place didn't make a dime. Ham sandwiches when you don't feel like cooking, beans and cornbread when you do. Plus, I just don't think it's safe to be feeding these girls soup beans every night. One of 'em's gonna end up letting out a fart that'll blow the man that's screwing her right out of the bed!"

I laughed. "You're awful. No wonder they threw you out of school for being an improper lady."

"Like you have room to talk."

"I don't guess I do." Trey and I were as different as two women could be, and yet we shared one thing in common: neither of us was anything close to the happy little homemaker women back then were supposed to be. "But listen, Trey. You can't be working in the kitchen all the time. I don't want people to think of you as my cook." I thought back to all those dinners at the Goldstein's and Cora, their black housekeeper who cooked all the food and stood by the table to serve seconds.

"I'm not gonna work in the kitchen all the time...I just want to cook supper maybe a couple of times a week. And I'm gonna sit down and eat with y'all, so it's not like I'm the help. Me spending some time in the kitchen doesn't turn me into a mammy any more than hopping in bed with a man turns one of your girls into a wife. If you feel so bad about me cooking, you can make it up to me by washing the dishes after."

That night, Trey, the girls and I sat down to a supper of fried chicken, mashed potatoes, corn on the cob, collard greens and hot biscuits.

If you work in a whorehouse, three a.m. is the earliest you can hope to get to bed...well, to bed to sleep, anyway. The same night Trey fixed the chicken, two soldiers came in around midnight.

Pretty lit already, they knocked back three shots of whiskey and then announced that they each wanted a girl for the whole night. Getting paid for a whole night is a mixed blessing. A girl gets a lot more money than for a standard, hour-long screw, but her beauty sleep is disturbed by having a strange, drunk man in her bed who she knows is going to demand more sex the second he wakes up in the morning. The two soldiers chose Rowena and Gwen for their all-nighters, leaving poor Honey alone to take care of the remaining customers.

Luckily, the fellows didn't come in all at once. It's bad business to have a parlor full of fellows and just one girl to go around. A balding, middle-aged man came in, and Honey took him upstairs. About fifteen minutes later, a talkative young salesman came in, and Trey and I got him involved in a game of poker while he waited. "I'm playing poker while I'm waiting to poke her," he said of Honey.

It's always the madam's duty to laugh uproariously at the customer's jokes, no matter how feeble.

Honey ended up screwing four fellows in two hours that night. At two a.m. she said, "Can we turn off the lights and call it a night, Vestal? My pussy feels like somebody drove a train through it."

I sent her up to bed and turned off the porch light that signaled that we were open for business. On the porch, the cold air hit my bare arms, and I thought of Trey, who, because of the lack of available bedrooms in the house, insisted on sleeping in the shed out back. I ran in the house, grabbed the mink stole I had recently bought myself, wrapped it around my shoulders and went out back.

"It's Vestal," I said, knocking on the shed door.

Trey opened the door. She had her clothes and shoes and a coat on, and from the rumpled nature of the cot's covers, I could tell she'd been trying to sleep this way.

"Listen," I said, "you're gonna catch pneumonia out here. Why don't you bring your cot on in the house?"

"And sleep where? You've got customers in the house. You don't want them to come downstairs in the morning and find me sprawled out in the parlor."

"You can set up your cot in my room, then. Come on. A body could freeze to death out here."

Nobody had shared my actual bedroom since David. Trey unfolded her cot, and I stepped behind the Chinese screen, which was usually just for decoration and not for privacy, and changed into my peach silk nightgown. As I slipped out of my things and stood naked behind the screen, I felt a little shock that wasn't too far away from embarrassment. But being embarrassed made no sense. I changed clothes, and not behind the screen, in front of Rowena and Gwen and Honey all the time. For that matter, I used to be in the nightly habit of stripping naked for men I had just met, so why the sudden attack of modesty?

When I stepped out from behind the screen, I saw that Trey had undressed for bed, too. She was wearing a white, men's undershirt and undershorts. From the back, as she bent over arranging the covers on her cot, she looked like a small man, with wiry muscles in her arms and calves and thighs. When she turned around, though, the curves of her breasts beneath her shirt made her sex obvious.

"What are you looking at?" She sounded accusatory, but she was grinning.

"I was just admiring your lingerie."

"Oh, it's the very latest thing," she said. "You should get some for the girls. Drives men wild."

She slid into her cot, and I crawled into bed. I didn't feel tired but told myself to be quiet so Trey could sleep.

After a couple of minutes, she said, "Not many white girls would let a colored girl sleep in the same room with them."

"I don't see why not. Everybody's the same color when the light's off."

"Not too many straight girls who'd let a bulldagger sleep in the same room with them either."

"What do you mean, straight?" She was using that word in a way I'd never heard it before, and it sounded like an insult, like calling somebody square.

"Straight means you like men."

I laughed. "Well, men like me, that's for sure."

"And you like them." I couldn't tell if it was a question or a statement.

"Sure, I like 'em. I liked my brother before he died, my daddy before he threw me out of the house. And I like Les Tipton, even though he's kinda off his rocker sometimes."

"Hell, I like my brother, too, and I liked my daddy before he died, but that's not the kind of liking I'm talking about. I'm talking about the kind of liking that makes you end up at my mama's doorstep with 'female complaints.'"

"Oh, yeah, that. Well, I guess I liked David. He was a nice fellow. I didn't love him exactly, but by God, he loved me. Or at least he loved the way I looked and the way he thought I was. When we was courting, he wanted to screw me so bad, but he wouldn't let himself. He wanted to marry me first, so he could preserve my 'virtue.' See, I figured marrying him was a way for us both to get what we wanted. He wanted unlimited access to my body, and I wanted to be paid for the inconvenience of getting screwed, with jewelry and a nice house and clothes and spending money."

"The inconvenience?"

"Well, maybe I shouldn't have called it that. It's more like the price you pay for getting what you want. See, Trey, you don't act like a real girl, so you don't understand what a regular girl's got to do to get a little piece of happiness in this world. The men hold all the keys, they've got the money, they run the businesses, they run the government. But the one thing that can bring them to their knees, that can make them cry like a baby or beg like a dog, is a beautiful girl. Flutter an eyelash, show a little leg, drop something accidentally on purpose and bend over to pick it up so they get a peep down your blouse, and pretty soon the men are loosening their grip on those keys to power and money because what they really want to get their hands on is you. So you give 'em a little of what they want." I sighed. "Marriage is a waste of time because it puts all your eggs in one basket, and it's too damn respectable to stay sexy. So you give a fellow what he wants for the evening, and in exchange, he uses his keys and opens a door for you, usually the door to money. He slips you some cash or buys you some jewelry. He gets a little piece of your ass; you get a little piece of his money."

"And you both live happily ever after?"

"Something like that."

"Not very romantic, is it?"

"Romance is what gets girls sweeping up a shack in a coal camp with six youngun's underfoot."

"Well," Trey said, "I wanted to know if you like men, and from the best I can tell, the answer is no."

I couldn't figure out how Trey had gotten a no out of what I'd just said. "The answer is yes. I like men. They're useful."

"Because they hold the keys?"

"That's right."

"But what if a girl doesn't want to borrow the keys from a man? What if she wants to get keys of her own?"

"Then she's got a hard row to hoe. But I guess if she's not beautiful like me and doesn't want to be somebody's wife, then she ain't got much choice. I wouldn't envy that girl, though. The things she'll have to do sound too much like work."

"The day I walked into this place you told me the only pleasure you'd ever gotten from going to bed with a man was money. Is that true?"

"Yeah. Even with David. Of course, what's a wife but an underpaid, monogamous whore?"

"A lot of women wouldn't see it that way."

"Well, I'm not like a lot of women."

"Neither am I."

I laughed. "That's true. You're not like a woman at all."

"But I must not be all the way like a man, or you wouldn't be having this conversation with me."

I laughed again. "Well, you've got me there, I reckon."

"We're different women, Vestal, you and I, different from the other women in the world. Even the girls in this house will quit their wild ways and get married and have babies one day, but not you and me."

"But you and me are different from each other, too."

"I think we might be more different from the other women in the world than we are from each other." She was quiet for a minute and then said, "Vestal, I want to ask you something, and if it makes you mad, you can send me right back out to the shed."

"Go ahead."

"Have you ever been to bed with somebody who touched you to please you, not just to please himself?"

"I don't understand what you're asking me."

"Has a man ever tried to give you pleasure instead of just taking his pleasure from you?"

"No, I don't suppose so."

"See, it's different with two women. A woman like me gets her pleasure from pleasing the other woman. Her pleasure is my pleasure, you understand?"

"Not really." The thought of getting pleasure from giving pleasure was new to me; I was ignorant of anything that had to do with unselfishness.

"I could show you."

"What?"

"If you let me share your bed tonight, I could show you what I mean."

It was a fearless and probably a foolish suggestion, a black woman asking a white woman to share a bed with her in a time when whites and blacks weren't even supposed to share the same water fountain. Trey broke more rules with that one sentence than I had broken in my whole lawless life. My heart pumped when I thought of the risk she was taking, and I did what a coward does in a dangerous situation. I pretended she was joking. "Lord, lord." I laughed. "You better be glad you said that to me and not to one of the other girls. They might not know you was kidding."

"I would never say that to any of the other girls. And I'm not kidding."

"Trey, you know I ain't like you, in your little tailored pants and penny loafers. You're a good-looking girl in your way, but you have to know that no man has ever looked at you. When men look at me, they want me. They always have."

"This isn't about what men want, Vestal. It's about what you want."

"I don't want like other women do. I don't know what I want." I couldn't believe what I'd just said. I'd always been the girl who knew just what she wanted, the girl with more ambition and dreams than anybody around her. It seemed ridiculous to say I didn't know what I wanted, but it must have been true, or why were tears sliding down my cheeks?

Suddenly Trey was beside me. "Come here," she whispered, and I did. She wrapped her strong arms around my back and shoulders and held me, her hands not straying from my back, for the longest time.

Sex with men was always like playing connect the dots. If you let him put his arms around you, then that was dot number one. From there, he could move to the number two dot, kissing. From there, to number three, a hand on a covered breast. I had always connected the dots in my head as the men connected the dots on my body, which they always did as quickly and efficiently as possible so they could get to the big dot at the end.

Trey didn't seem to have one big goal in mind. When she finally did kiss me, she didn't go straight for the lips. Instead, she brushed her own lips against my forehead, my eyelids, my cheeks, which were still damp from crying. When her lips touched mine, I could taste the salt from my tears. With her lips sealed to mine, with her weight on top of me, with my hands stroking the short, coarse curls on her head, I suddenly did something I'd never done in bed with anybody. I felt.

I felt her lips, I felt her touch, I felt her desire, not a desire to have or possess me, but her desire to please me. For once, I was not calculating in my head where I was in the process, thinking ahead to the next step and when it would be over; instead I felt her mouth on my breast, her tongue circling my nipple. I felt her hands stroking my feet, my calves, my thighs. When she reached between my legs, I couldn't have thought ahead to the next step even if I had wanted to because I had no idea what to expect.

What she did was touch a part of my body that, even though I had been to bed with dozens of men, I didn't know that I had. She didn't put a finger or anything else inside me; instead she put delicate pressure on the little nub that I was too ignorant to know the name of. With just one finger, she pressed rhythmically, rapidly, but with such lightness it felt like the flutter of a butterfly's wings. Soon I felt the dried, closed-up cocoon of me split wide open to release dozens of blue and gold butterflies. I must have cried out, because when I opened my eyes, Trey's free hand was clamped over my mouth.

Suddenly, I understood. I must have laughed for two full minutes before I said, "So that's what all the fuss is about."

Trey smiled. "That's what it's all about, all right."

"Hell, no wonder business is so good." I looked at Trey in her undershirt and shorts. "You didn't even get undressed."

"I don't have to."

"No, I don't reckon you do." Now that I was coming back to myself, I remembered the other people beyond the walls of my bedroom. "You know we can't tell anybody about this."

"Of course not. The girls wouldn't understand. Plus, it'd be bad for business if all the menfolks that come through the door thought you didn't have eyes for them." Trey kissed my forehead. "As a matter of fact, maybe it would be a good idea for me to move to the cot, just in case anybody was to walk in."

"You're probably right."

Once Trey was settled into her cot, I rolled over onto the warm spot her body had left in the bed.

"Trey?"

"Mmm?"

"Maybe you should just plan on sleeping in here for the next little while instead of out in the shed. It's supposed to be a cold winter."

"All right," Trey said, and I could hear the smile in her voice. "I'll just stay right here then."

CHAPTER 24

Every night when the house was open, Trey would keep her distance from me, fetching the ice for the ice bucket and then sitting in the kitchen counting up the evening's receipts. When she did step into the parlor, she'd watch as I laughed out loud at the men's jokes and allowed myself, giggling, to be dragged out on the dance floor. Not one trace of feeling showed on Trey's face as she watched me cut up and flirt with the customers. She knew it was all a show, all for business, and when the lights were out, I'd be hers.

Every night I lay back and let Trey do whatever she wanted to me, and every night she surprised and delighted me. I surprised myself, too. How could I have had all these feelings inside me and never known it before?

Between the business and the pleasure I wasn't getting much sleep, but I didn't feel tired. I just felt happy. I was usually up by ten, the crack of dawn at a whorehouse, making coffee and leafing though the mail.

One morning, a couple of weeks after Trey and I had spent our first night together, I looked through the mail and found an envelope with my own handwriting on it. It was the letter I had sent to Mother and Daddy, unopened and marked 'Return to Sender.' I might have thought it had been returned because Mother and Daddy had left the coal camp, if the words on the envelope hadn't been written in Mother's deliberate block print. I wondered, had she gotten the letter and hidden it under the mattress for a week or so while she tried to decide whether to open it? Did she keep the letter a secret from Daddy, or did he know about it and tell her to send it back?

I tried to have hurt feelings, but I just couldn't summon them up. I decided that the day I walked out of that awful little house in Bartlett was the day my family lost the ability to hurt me. I dropped the letter in the trash, but then on second thought, I fished it out, opened it and took out the twenty-dollar bill I had put in the envelope.

Honey was the first girl to wake up that morning. When she staggered in, feeling her way to the coffeepot, I said, "The first girl out of bed this mornin' gets twenty dollars...the early bird and the worm and all that." I pressed the bill in her hand.

"Uh, thanks. I've never made money for getting out of a bed before." She looked at me like she expected men in white coats to drag me off any second, but she stuffed the money in her robe before I might change my unbalanced mind.

Every month Les Tipton sent a pimply-faced boy, I could never decide if it was the same one or if Les just hired lots of skinny boys with poor complexions, to collect that month's house payment and Les's percentage of the profits. The girls always had a good time flirting with the poor boy until his face turned as red as his pimples. This particular month the boy handed me a flyer that said, 'Les Tipton for City Council,' and advertised a rally to be held that Saturday downtown.

I told the girls they could come with me as long as they dressed respectably. I thought that if we showed up looking like what we were, it might hurt Les's political chances. As it turned out, Gwen looked completely respectable in a good brown suit and medium-heeled pumps, and Rowena and Honey, with just a little too much makeup and too-high heels, ended up looking like a whore's idea of respectable.

Les's grocery store events were nothing compared to his political rally. Red, white and blue bunting was draped over every available surface, and people I recognized from the grocery store wore huge sandwich boards that commanded, 'SAY YES TO LES.' A fat woman on a red, white and blue-draped stage belted out 'America the Beautiful,' and a booth near the stage advertised free hot dogs and apple pie.

"Shoot," I whispered to Gwen as we made our way toward

the booth, "you'd think he was running for President."

We walked past a little girl no older than eight in a pink pinafore. Her hair was a riot of yellow ringlets topped with a huge pink bow. She was holding a sign that said, 'Keep our families safe from the evils of liquor. Vote for my Uncle Les.'

I leaned down so I could talk to her. "Les ain't really your uncle, is he, honey?" I had never heard Les mention any family members when we were back in Bartlett.

"Well," the little girl said, whispering like she was letting me in on a secret, "he's giving me five dollars and all the candy I can eat, so I reckon he can be my uncle if he wants to."

Just then, Les walked up, looking like he was choking to death from wearing an ugly green necktie.

I nodded toward the little girl. "You should send this one to me in a few years, Les. From what I can tell, she's got a great future ahead of her."

Les cackled. "She's a pip, ain't she?" He reached into his coat pocket and produced a handful of penny candy, which he tossed at the little girl the same way you toss feed to a chicken. "There you go, sugar. Keep up the good work."

As Les and I walked on, I leaned over and whispered, "So what's all this foolishness about the evils of liquor? I've seen you take a nip a time or two."

"Well, see, the other feller running for this seat is for liquor by the drink, so I figure if he's for it, I'm agin it."

Back then, the only places in Knoxville you could buy liquor was in liquor stores and private clubs like the Talk of the Town... and in illegal operations like mine, of course. "Fine talk from the man I used to call when my house ran out of booze."

"Missy, it don't matter what you like or what you don't like; you sell what you know people are gonna buy."

Up on the stage, a brass band of twelve-year-olds launched into a version of 'Stars and Stripes Forever' that sounded like cats in a sack fighting.

"Shoot," Les said, "I'd better get up on the stage. I'm supposed to give a speech here in a minute."

When the band screeched its last so-called note, Les took the microphone. "Hidy, neighbors!" he hollered.

A bunch of people clapped and hollered back, "Hidy, Les!"

"Now you'uns know," Les went on, "that my lovely wife Peg is serving up free hot dogs and her famous fried apple pies at that booth over yonder, so I don't want nobody to go away without a full belly." He loosened his tie and unbuttoned his jacket. He was clearly getting comfortable. "Some of you'uns may know," he went on, "that I'm an old coon hunter from way back."

A few men in the audience cheered and whooped. Coon hunters, too, I reckoned.

"There ain't nothin' I like better than going out in the black of night with my best buddies and my best dog and running one of them little ring-tailed fellers right up a tree. As a matter of fact, I got somethin' to show you."

Les turned his back for a minute and reached into a box. When he turned around, he was holding a live baby raccoon. It clung to Les with its funny little hands and looked at the audience with beady, curious eyes.

"Now this coon's a right nice little feller," Les said after the women and children in the audience had finished oohing and ahhing. "But there's somethin' about him that puts me in mind of Jack Hill, my opponent. Look at that little mask he's wearing! Jack Hill wears a mask, too, friends and neighbors. He may say he's out to help the people of this town. He may say he's a regular feller just like you and me. But look behind the mask, and what do you see? A blue-blooded lawyer whose sympathies lie with big business and hard liquor! Jack Hill don't care about the regular working people in this town. I'll tell you, friends and neighbors, I might not have me no college degree, and I might be wearing a suit that come from Sears and Roebuck, but I ain't wearing no mask. You know your buddy Les, and you know what he stands for: family, temperance and the right of the working man to get ahead in this town. And with your help, this ol' coon hunter's gonna run Jack Hill so far up a tree we won't see hide nor hair of him again!"

The crowd clapped and cheered, and Les introduced the curly-headed little girl, who sang a syrupy song about a little girl whose daddy comes home drunk every night.

Somehow I never got around to voting for Les. Politics and

religion have always been about the same thing to me—people get all heated up about them and act like they understand more than they do. Me, I didn't claim to understand either one of them, and I didn't let myself get heated up about things I didn't understand.

As it turned out, though, it didn't matter that I didn't vote for Les. On the night of the election, at about one a.m., when the girls were all upstairs with customers and Trey and I were sitting at the card table playing poker, there was a loud banging on the door. I opened it, expecting to see a customer, but instead it was Les, grinning from ear to ear.

"Guess where I've been all night."

"Out hunting poor, defenseless raccoons?"

"Nope." Les took off his hat and threw it so it hooked perfectly on the hatrack. "My victory party. I figured you already knew I'd won, but I wanted to come tell you face-to-face."

I hadn't known. "Les, that's the best news I've heard all night. Congratulations!" I stood on tiptoe and kissed his cheek.

"Uh, since you was feeling sorry for the coons, I thought I'd bring you somethin' as a way of saying thank you for your vote. Besides, Peg's gonna kill me if I don't get this thing out of the house." Les unbuttoned his overcoat, reached into his inside pocket, and brought out the sleeping baby raccoon he had used in his campaign speech. He handed it to me, and I cradled it in my arms. "I thought you and the girls might have fun taking care of it. You could build it a cage out back, or keep it in the house if you want to. It'll use a sandbox just like a cat."

"Is that a fact?" I cuddled the warm little animal close and took it over for Trey to see.

Trey grinned. "It's cute, all right, but you're taking care of it, not me. You been called a coon enough times, it doesn't exactly make you want to have one."

Les cackled. "I don't know, Trey. I been called an asshole plenty of times, but that don't mean I don't want to have one!"

"So, Les," I said, "what would you say to a game of poker and a drink?"

"Yes to the poker, no to the drink. I saw some cars parked out front, and I don't want none of my constituents to come downstairs and see me drinking."

"Well," I said, "any constituents you might have here is upstairs screwing whores. If they come downstairs and see you with a drink in your hand, it don't seem to me like they'd have much room to talk."

Les sat down at the card table. "Well, then, deal me in and pour me a stiff one."

Trey dealt the cards, and I poured the drinks. As I sat down next to Trey and across from Les, a wave of happiness washed over me that must be like what regular women feel when they sit down to Thanksgiving dinner with their husbands, their children and their children's grandparents. I felt content and loved and natural, here in the home I had made with my handsome secret lover, the girls and my secret business partner/adopted brother.

"Missy, you look like a kitten full of cream tonight," Les said. "I wish C.R. could see you this happy."

"I wish he could, too," I said. "And I wish he could see you on the city council. For two ignorant briar hoppers out of a coal camp, we've done pretty good for ourselves."

"We're doing pretty good for ourselves, missy. We ain't nowhere near done."

I smiled at Les and looked down at the cards I had been dealt.

PART III: REVELATION

CHAPTER 25

If I had a nickel for every man who walked in the door of the house and said, "You're the spitting image of Elizabeth Taylor," I could still be living off that money today. The Liz of the Sixties and I did look a lot alike-the black bouffant, the liquid liner drawn out in kitty cat curls from the corners of our unusually colored eyes. Like Liz, my figure had filled out a bit, but most of the extra padding went to my bust and behind, which Trey liked quite a bit.

She'd make fun of me when I insisted that she strap me into a girdle before I changed into my gown for work. "If you say, 'Tighter, mammy,' I'm gonna hook this thing so tight you'll pass right out," she'd say.

Girdle or no girdle, I was still beautiful. I might not have been as firm in some places as I was as a nineteen-year-old, but it didn't matter since I didn't have to take my clothes off for a living. I looked good enough in my purple, sequined gown to get men in the door, and the girls who waited for them in the parlor were enough to keep them coming back.

Rowena and Honey and Gwen were long gone, of course. Being a whore is like being a professional athlete. After you've been doing it a few years, your body's not what it once was, and the stress of daily, or nightly, physical performance takes its toll.

Rowena was the first to go, and she left under the worst of circumstances. One late morning we were all sitting in the kitchen drinking coffee. Rowena got up to get another cup and came to the table with the pot. She poured refills for Honey, Gwen and me, but when Trey held out her cup, Rowena snapped, "Get your own."

"I beg your pardon?" There was enough frost in Trey's voice

to chill all the coffee in the room.

"I said, get your own coffee. It's bad enough you sit at the table with us."

I was already on my feet. "Rowena, apologize to Trey, and pour her some coffee."

Rowena's eyes flashed with rage. "I wasn't raised to pour coffee for niggers." She threw the coffeepot so it landed in the sink, but not before hot coffee sprayed across the room and scalded my arm. "For God's sake, Vestal," Rowena yelled, "you've got her practically running the place. Some things ain't right, and what goes on between the two of y'all…"

"I have no idea what you're talking about," I said. I sounded calm, but I was simmering with rage. "Rowena, start packing. I want you out of here by noon. And I'm taking the price of that coffeepot out of what you made last night."

For a few seconds, she was too shocked to speak. Finally she said, "You can't fire me."

"Sure I can. It's my goddamn whorehouse; I can do whatever I please."

"You can't run a house with just two girls."

"I won't have to. I'll have somebody to replace you in less than twenty-four hours."

Rowena packed and drove off, and Honey cried. "I know what she said wasn't right, Vestal," she said to me, "but she can't help the way she was raised."

"Sure she can," I said. "She wasn't raised to be a whore, but she seems to have jumped over that hurdle."

Trey didn't say anything about Rowena that day; she just borrowed the keys to my Cadillac and went out to buy a new coffeepot. That night, though, she made love to me for hours, until I finally passed out from exhaustion.

Honey left about three months after Rowena did. She had saved enough money to start college. She sent me a note when she graduated, a note when she got married and a note and a photo when her daughter was born.

Gwen's story is the most interesting. She stuck around for several months after Honey left and helped "break in the new girls," as she put it. Then one day she knocked on the door of my room, came in and formally told me that she was giving me two weeks' notice, that it was time for her to move on. We parted with a handshake instead of a hug. Somehow I felt like I didn't know her well enough to hug her even though she had lived under my roof and eaten three meals a day with me for years.

As it turned out, I was right. I hadn't known Gwen at all. She sent me a letter a few months after she left that explained that she was married and had been using her income as a whore to pay her husband's way through seminary in California. The good reverend apparently thought his wife had moved south where the cost of living was lower to take a job as an executive secretary. In fact, she had moved far away so word wouldn't get out about how she was really paying for her husband to sit around and read the Bible all day.

All I could think was that Gwen's husband must have more of a head for spiritual matters than financial ones if he actually believed she could've made all that money just by being a secretary. The man's head was obviously so far in the clouds that he was already halfway to heaven.

I've gone through over a dozen batches of girls since then, bigger batches, too. In 1958, business was so good that Trey and a couple of her bulldagger friends built on a three-room addition to the house, three bedrooms, of course. But soon, she had to add on an extra bathroom, too. Six whores trying to get cleaned up in one bathroom led to more hair-pulling fights than Trey and me could stand to break up.

The girls who came after Rowena and Honey and Gwen are mostly a blur of painted lips, shiny hair and long legs. After I parted ways with the first batch of girls, I realized that I couldn't think of them as my family because the day would come when they would leave forever, some on good terms, some on bad. They were more like foster children; I took them into my house and looked after them a little while until they found new homes and new lives.

The only girls I remember very specifically were the ones who didn't work out. There was the girl who drank too much. There's nothing wrong, of course, with a girl enjoying a cocktail with a customer before they get to the real 'cock' and 'tail' part of the program, but a man doesn't want a woman he's paying to screw to be sloppy drunk. He might have to get a regular girl drunk to sleep with him, but a whore should be willing to do it mostly sober.

There was the girl who was a junkie, although I didn't even know what that meant until Trey told me. The girl was slow and stupid all the time, but I thought she was just, well, slow and stupid. One morning one of the other girls found her passed out in her room and couldn't wake her up. When Trey and I went in and I saw the bruises on the girl's thighs, I was afraid one of our customers had roughed her up. But Trey saw that they were needle marks and found the used hypodermic that had rolled under her bed.

We rushed her to the hospital, with me halfway worried about her life and halfway worried about mine: If a girl died on dope in my house, could the police keep accepting their payoffs and turning a blind eye to my activities? Thankfully, she lived. I paid for her week in the hospital, gave her an extra couple of hundred that I hoped she wouldn't spend on dope and fired her.

But the drinking and doping girls were nowhere near as bad as the girl who had eyes for Trey. She was this little wisp of a blonde, nineteen years old, less than five feet tall and less than one hundred pounds soaking wet, with big blue eyes and a silky Mississippi accent. It was all, "Trey, dahlin', could you zip up this dress for me?" and "Trey, dahlin', these pumps just kill my feet. How 'bout a little foot rub?"

Trey seemed amused by the Southern siren's flirtations and zipped her dresses and rubbed her dainty, size-three feet under the glare of my cold green eyes.

One day I heard the little alley cat holler from upstairs, "Trey, dahlin', could you come in the bathroom a minute? I'm having a little...plumbing trouble."

I had announced that I was about to go to town so my guess was that Miss Moonlight and Magnolias thought I was safely out of the house. Trey started up the stairs, but I grabbed her arm. "No, let me go."

"But you don't know anything about plumbing," she said.

"Oh, I bet I do."

When I walked into the bathroom, my foe was stretched out in the tub, her milky-white body on display, pink nipples, blond pubic hair and all. Her eyes were closed, and her head was leaned back, revealing the long, elegant neck I wanted to wring. "Trey, dahlin'," she purred.

"It ain't Trey."

Her eyes snapped open. I walked toward the tub, so mad I could barely see. My brain felt like flames were licking it. A radio was sitting on a shelf near by, and I picked it up. "I read a mystery one time," I said, "where a fellow dropped a radio in the tub with a girl. It fried her like a chicken." I could do it, I thought. It would be easy. She was estranged from her family, so they'd never miss her. And we could tell the customers she'd moved on to another house.

Her eyes widened, and she looked as if she might scream. But she didn't; she just sat there, paralyzed. When I got to the edge of the tub I held up the radio, but then threw it so it smashed against the wall. She did scream then, and as she sat in the water, frozen in fear, I stuck my hand in the tub, reached down between her legs and yanked out the drain plug. The only sound for a second was the water being sucked down the drain.

"This ain't the only thing I'm pulling the plug on," I said. "You're fired."

She snatched a towel from the rack and covered herself. "I bring a lot of money into this house, Vestal. Men love me."

"It ain't the men I'm worried about. A dyke in a whorehouse is as bad as a fox in a henhouse."

"What about Trey?"

"Trey ain't one of my girls."

"Well..." She was out of the tub now, wrapped in the white towel. "What about you?"

"I have no idea what you're talking about."

"Oh, come on, Vestal, you can fool some of those dumb country girls you've got working for you, but you can't fool me. They're all ignorant enough to think you're Les Tipton's mistress, but I know what you are."

Nobody since Mother and Myrtle had ever made me so mad. "You don't know a thing about what I am, but I know exactly what you are." I looked her up and down.

"And what's that?"

"You're a waitress. Before the sun goes down tonight every madam of every whorehouse in this part of the United States is gonna know you can't be trusted around other girls. Come next week, you'll be waiting tables in Tupelo."

That night in bed, Trey said, "You didn't have to go and fire her just 'cause you were jealous. I wasn't gonna touch her."

"I've seen you touch her...plenty of times."

Her hand rested on my breast. "Not the way I touch you."

I pushed her hand away. "I damn near killed the little bitch. I can't remember the last time I was so mad."

Trey laughed. "It's sweet that you're jealous of me." She moved her hand back to my breast. This time, I let it stay.

I never told Trey that I called every house in Tennessee, Georgia and Kentucky and told them not to hire that little Mississippi Mata Hari. I knew what Trey would say, that dykes were like sisters, and sisters should stick up for each other. But I didn't think of myself as a dyke. To me, a dyke was a man-hating woman no man ever looked at, and I owed my fortune to men, so how could I hate them? And as for sisterhood, well, if my experiences with Myrtle were any indication, then sisters were about as gentle and loving toward each other as two rabid pit bulls.

More girls worked out in the house than didn't, and the Fifties had been a great time for business as men fled their frilly-aproned wives and Dick-and-Jane kids for a taste of excitement on the weekends. Most of the men were so grateful for a little fun that they were well-behaved and courteous to the girls. Only the rare woman-hater had to be kicked out for being too obnoxious or too rough. I always think we were doing all those nice married men's wives a favor. Better the fellows should have their fun with a nice, clean whore who gets monthly medical checkups and who has sex as a business transaction than with a little gold digger who only pretends to be doing it for free. A whore doesn't threaten a marriage the way a mistress does.

The Sixties got complicated. For the couple of hours he

spends in a whorehouse, a man may find it free of all the worries and confusion of the outside world, but that's not really the way it is. It's the job of the girls and the madam to make men feel like the house is a safe haven from the world's problems, but this impression is as polite a lie as the whore's ecstatic gasps and moans. When life is complicated outside the house, it's complicated inside, too.

Trey started off the decade by getting arrested on a regular basis. Along with a bunch of black and white college kids and folks from the more liberal churches in town, Trey had gotten into all kinds of trouble. She would disappear in the morning and come back eight hours later, having spent the whole day sitting at the counter in a diner while the waitresses ignored her, 'accidentally' spilled coffee on her or sometimes got fed up and called the cops.

She and her friends would line up according to skin color at the box office of the Tennessee Theater with the whitest of the white folks in front, the olive-complected next, one cafe-au-lait mixed-race person next, and the darkest folks at the back of the line. They'd see how many people the cashier would sell regular tickets to before insisting that the next person in line had to buy tickets to the 'colored balcony,' and then they'd argue with his decision. How dark was too dark to sit with the white folks? What color, exactly, was 'colored?'

I never went out with Trey and her friends on their little adventures. I was the one who waited at home for the phone call to get them out of jail. Trey would always sound so calm on the phone; even if the police had roughed her up a little, she seemed unphased by it. She'd tell me how many of them had been arrested and how much they were being held for, and I'd put on a respectable-looking suit, fish the appropriate number of bills out of the JFG coffee can in the pantry and head down to the station to pay off the police-an activity I was already pretty familiar with.

Sometimes Trey would nag me about not sitting at lunch counters myself, but I told her somebody had to sit by the phone to bail her ass out of jail. That wasn't my only reason, though, and Trey knew it. If I made a public spectacle of myself over segregation, it would be disastrous for business. Those white business owners who 'reserved the right to refuse business to anyone' were some of my best customers. I hated their bigotry, of course, but instead of ruining my business by protesting the way they ran theirs, I took their money and used it later to bail Trey and her friends out of jail.

When Wade Robinson, a hardware store owner who was widely known to be the Imperial Grand Shithead of East Tennessee's Ku Klux Klan came to the house with a bunch of his loudmouth friends, I gave the girls their cut of the money, put the rest of it in an envelope and sent it to the NAACP.

Once Knoxville's business owners grudgingly allowed blacks to spend their money in their shops and greasy spoons, Trey still didn't rest easy. The desegregation battle had woken up something that had been sleeping inside her. The lunch counters and movie theaters had only been the beginning. The privilege of being allowed to eat a greasy hamburger in the same diner as white folks wasn't the full extent of equal opportunity, and she knew it. Trey took to wearing her hair full and natural and traded in her button-downs for loose-fitting, bright blouses. She looked beautiful, but not boyish the way she used to, and I missed that boy a little.

Trey worked for cause after cause. She and her friends were forevermore tooling around the ghetto to register voters and patrolling the university circulating petitions to end the war, which, Trey said, spelled genocide for her black brothers.

During nonbusiness hours, Trey and her buddies used the house as their headquarters. It was an unusual crowd. There was Odell Early, a black artist who had sold some of the lively street scenes he painted to galleries in New York. He'd done a fine painting of me in the nude, which hung over the couch in the parlor. There was Howard Franklin, Jr., the tall, gangly, college-student son of Howard Franklin, Sr., a local lawyer who had been the sworn enemy of Jim Crow and the KKK. My guess was that in the black radical circles in New York and California, skinny white boys like Howard wouldn't have been welcome. But in the South, where radicals are rarer than hen's teeth, creed matters more than color.

- There was also Celeste Wilkins, a high-yellow woman who, to her eternal frustration, could not get her soft, wavy hair to stand up in an Afro. Celeste, much to Trey's amusement, was the lover of the new dean of women at Frederick Douglass.

Trey was always trying to get me to make friends with Celeste; she said it would be good for me to have a woman friend I could talk to. But I wasn't about to reveal any secrets about myself to Celeste or to anybody else. A house like mine was built on a shaky foundation, one careless word to the wrong person, and it could all come tumbling down. Besides, I didn't like the way Celeste looked at Trey.

A couple of times a week, around lunchtime, they would all gather in the kitchen, Odell and Howard and Celeste plotting out their next 'action' at the table, while Trey stood at the stove, making country ham biscuits for the revolution. All the girls pretty much stayed out of their way, going outside for sunbathing or to town for shopping, except for the girl who called herself Fawn.

When Fawn had first shown up at the house, she looked like a starving kitten, all bones and big eyes. She was barefoot and had on what looked like boy's blue jeans, and her hair was clearly not on speaking terms with shampoo and hot water. After a bath and an hour and a half in my room with me, a bottle of Aqua Net and a fishing tackle box full of makeup, though, she was absolutely stunning, like a lighter brunette Audrey Hepburn. Her big brown eyes and delicate features were how we came up with the name Fawn.

Despite her nighttime glamour, though, Fawn still spent her days bare-faced, blue-jeaned and barefoot. I could never figure out how she got her feet so dirty just walking around in the house.

Fawn would sit at the kitchen table, listening, often taking a puff off the joint that Odell would pass around. I'd take a few puffs myself occasionally, but I could never figure out how Trey and her friends could smoke that stuff and then talk so serious. After three puffs, I thought everything in the world was absolutely hilarious.

One day when the kitchen was filling with the salty and sweet smells of country ham and grass, I was sitting at the table with

Gypsy Rose Lee, the tiny toy poodle I'd gotten after Tippy the raccoon died of old age. "I swear," I said, "I'm gonna have to buy Gypsy a gas mask. Y'all get the poor little thing so high she don't know whether she's coming or going."

Odell laughed. "Vestal, I love to hear you talk after you've had a couple of tokes. A little weed sends you all the way back to the coal camps."

"Hell," I said, "nothin' could send me back to the coal camps."

"So," Celeste said in a half-serious tone, "why don't we storm the Sequoyah Country Club? This town isn't really integrated as long as the only blacks you see some places are in the kitchen."

Howard laughed. "They'd beat us to death with their golf clubs." He smiled up at Trey as she set a plate of ham biscuits in front of him. "I figure the Sequoyah Country Club will welcome black members about the same time that Trey here realizes I'm so devastatingly attractive she can't live without me."

Celeste laughed. "Poor Howard. Such a lost cause."

Howard bit into a ham biscuit. "I never could resist a lost cause, though."

"Hell, Howard," Fawn said, "if it's a girl you want, come on upstairs with me. No charge."

I shot Fawn a dirty look for trying to give away the merchandise, but she didn't seem to notice.

"That's very kind of you, Fawn." Howard wiped his fingers on his napkin. "And you're a beautiful girl, but not my type, I'm afraid. I've always had a strong attraction to women who are a bit...well, masculine."

Odell hooted. "Well, it seems to me you should just take that impulse a little further till you arrive at its logical conclusion."

Howard looked sheepish. "What? Oh, you mean sleeping with men? Well, that thought's never done much for me."

Odell laughed. "Well, honey, it's not the thought that counts!"

I liked being in the kitchen with Trey and her friends when they were teasing one another and laughing, but when the conversation got too serious, as it always did, I'd usually discover that I needed to restock the bar or wash out my stockings before business hours. I had never been a very serious person, had never thought too much about the unfairness of the world, and so all their talk about how messed up the world was and how the responsibility to fix it rested on their shoulders and maybe mine, too, made me nervous. Plus, I was scared that I'd say the wrong thing and make Trey mad.

Making Trey mad was an art I had mastered over the past several years, and I always did it not by criticizing her personally, but by saying whatever popped into my head about world events. The terrible day that we watched Lyndon B. Johnson being sworn in after Kennedy's assassination, my heart went out to Jackie, a girl who always knew just what to wear. "Lord, lord," I said, staring sadly at the TV screen, "I can't imagine how much that little suit of hers cost, and I bet there's no way to get bloodstains that bad out of it."

Trey, horrified that I could be worried about Jackie's suit during a time of national crisis, stalked out of the house and slammed the door behind her.

When the news announced the U.S. troops were being sent to Vietnam, I sighed. "Oh, well, a war's always good for the whorehouse business, anyway."

Trey slammed the door on me then, too, but I never understood why. I had just been stating a fact.

So I learned that there were some subjects about which Trey had no sense of humor. I knew the causes she fought for were fair and right, but sometimes her missionary zeal put me in mind of Miss Taylor and Myrtle back in Bartlett. Missionaries may do a lot of good in this world, but they don't laugh enough.

I loved to laugh. And I loved to dress up in my green Givenchy gown and diamond bracelet and earrings and open the front door and let the boys and their money come rolling in. Why think about napalm and riots in the streets when thinking about those things did nothing but make you feel bad?

After business hours, around two-thirty a.m. or so, Les, who as far as I could tell had given up sleeping as a bad business, would sometimes stop by for a visit. It's funny, while I came closer to agreeing with Trey and her friends when I forced myself to think about politics than I did with Les, who for fifteen years had fought progress daily from his seat on the City Council. I still felt more comfortable with Les than I did with Trey's friends. Maybe it was because I always felt so uneducated around them, or maybe it was because Les, for all his faults, was the closest thing I had to family.

When Les came over, he and Trey would bait each other continually. He would tell Trey her hair looked like a Brillo pad, while she'd say that at least she had hair, unlike some old honkies she could name. When Trey would talk about her latest antiwar demonstration, Les would start rattling on about how he was the guest speaker at the next meeting of the Knoxville branch of the Young Americans for Freedom. Trey and Les would play cards and drink bourbon and egg each other on like two siblings. I sat with Gypsy on my lap, smiled, listened and played my cards close to my chest.

The one place where I insisted that politics stop was in the bedroom. One early morning as we got ready for bed, I backed up to Trey and asked her to unhook my girdle.

"I don't know why you wear these things," she said as she fussed with the hooks and eyes. "Your body is beautiful. Girdles just make you conform to an artificial male standard of beauty."

"Well, I hate to break it to you, Trey, but I've made my living for twenty years by conforming to an artificial male standard of beauty. If I'm not mistaken, that's what pays your salary, too." My girdle unhooked, I turned around to face her in my black push-up bra, black garters and black panties. "And don't tell me you want me to burn my bra because I know damn good and well you like the way it makes my tits look."

Trey stared down at the white of my breasts against the black of my bra. "Well...uh..." She never finished whatever that thought was, though, because I pulled her head down for a kiss, and soon, she had pushed me back on the bed, her face buried in my cleavage, her hands sliding over my stockings. I tangled my fingers in her hair and wrapped my legs around her hips. At that moment, all our differences were forgotten. Whoever said 'the personal is political' was apparently never faced with a beautiful woman who could care less about politics, wearing a size-D, black lace, push-up bra.

CHAPTER 26

What they say about a full moon is true. It drives sane people crazy and makes crazy people crazier. It's not just superstition. Ask anybody who works at night-policemen, nurses, and whores.

One time Trey got to sitting down and calculating, and she figured out that every time she had to throw out a customer for drunkenness, rudeness or violence, there was a full moon. Finally, we took the measure of hiring additional security for full moon nights. Billy Ray Johnson, a twenty-two-year-old overgrown farm boy Les often employed for heavy lifting, would come over to stand around in gigantic overalls and look intimidating. Billy Ray was six foot six and probably weighed more than three hundred pounds, but when one of the whores would smile at him, he'd blush.

This particular full moon night started off pretty normally. A couple of local businessmen had brought in some out-of-town clients and were drinking and whooping it up. A lawyer was sitting on the sofa with Fawn on one knee and blond-haired Betty on the other, trying to decide which one he wanted. And four boys who had just gotten their draft notices were preparing to drown their fears in alcohol and sex. Soon all six of the girls were busy upstairs or out back, and I was left to entertain some of the soon-to-be soldiers.

I was in full madam mode, telling funny whorehouse stories, bending over for them to light my cigarettes (which I had taken up because I figured I spent so much time breathing other people's smoke in the evenings that I might as well breathe my own) and letting them get a good look down my dress. The poor little bastards could be coming home in body bags within the year. If flashing them a little cleavage made them feel better, I figured it was the least I could do. Never mind that I was old enough to be their mother.

When the doorbell rang, I said, "Excuse me, boys. Think of me while I'm gone," and went to greet my next customer. The disappointment probably showed on my face when I saw who it was.

Thomas Murphy was a writer. He taught over at the university, and he always wore a slouchy brown corduroy blazer and a sad-sack face. He was one of our most regular customers. You could always count on him coming around once a week, but most of the time he didn't look like he was having a bit of fun. To look at his face when he was sitting in the parlor, he might as well have been sitting in the waiting room of a dentist's office.

Until he'd see Betty, then his mouth would turn up at the sides, and his thin lips would part to show small, mousy teeth. Betty was the only girl he wanted to see. I tried to discourage favoritism, so one night I offered him a twenty-five percent discount if he'd see Fawn or Dixie instead.

"No," he said. "It's Betty or nobody."

Not surprisingly, when I opened the door that evening, Thomas said, "I'm here to see Betty."

I felt like a mother greeting one of her daughter's young suitors, except that Thomas had about six or maybe seven years on me. "Well, come on in," I said. "Betty's busy right now, but you can see her after a while. Or if one of the other girls is free first, you can see her."

"No," Thomas said. "Just Betty." He helped himself to a drink and slumped in a chair in the corner. I decided to ignore him and go back to entertaining the troops. But before I could finish the story I'd started telling before Thomas arrived, the doorbell rang again.

The young man standing in the doorway did not look like our usual type of customer. His wavy brown hair hung down to his shoulders, and his bell-bottom jeans, tie-dyed T-shirt and blue denim jacket had all seen better days. He had an honest-looking face, though, so I gave him a cheerful, "What can I do for you, hon?"

"Um...I'm looking for Annie."

"Nobody by that name lives here, hon."

He looked confused and panicky. "But...but she gave me this address. And I hitched all the way from Cincinnati today."

I couldn't just run the kid off. Where would he go? "I'll tell you what. Why don't you come in a minute? You can sit in the kitchen, and we'll fix you a sandwich and coffee."

In the house, he looked wide-eyed at the gilt mirrors, fresh flowers and Oriental rugs.

"Trey, honey," I said, "would you put on a pot of coffee for my friend here? He's had a long walk today."

Trey smiled at our guest's hippie getup and went to put on the coffee.

One of the soon-to-be soldier boys wasn't as happy, though. "Vestal, I can't believe you'd let a freak like him in here! I thought you supported our boys."

"You know I support our boys, honey," I soothed the soldier. "This feller's just had a little misunderstanding. We'll have it cleared up here in a few minutes."

But the misunderstanding turned out to be cleared up in less than five seconds because right then Fawn walked down the stairs with the businessman she had been entertaining. Her eyes fixed on the hippie immediately. "Jerry!"

Jerry looked at her in the same awed, puzzled way he'd looked at the gilt mirrors and Oriental rugs. She must've been almost unrecognizable in her pink evening gown with her upswept hair and elegant eye makeup. "Annie?"

Fawn had never told me her real name. I started into my speech about how I didn't allow personal visits during business hours, but I might as well have been speaking Chinese for all the good it did because Fawn had already abandoned her confused customer and was enfolded in Jerry's arms.

Jerry looked down at her and smiled. "You ready, babe?"

She grinned. "You bet I am." She pulled up her skirts, ran up the stairs and was back down in three minutes in the ratty jeans she'd worn the day she came, her long hair stringing down and tangling with her duffle bag strap. "Well...bye," she called, taking Jerry's hand and nearly skipping out of the house.

"Probably made enough here to pay her boyfriend's way to Canada," one of the soldier boys muttered.

"You know," Fawn's final customer said, adjusting his necktie, "I screwed that girl seven times, and I never knew she was a hippie."

"Well, she wasn't a hippie during business hours," I said. "There's no such thing as free love in a whorehouse."

I thought the night was bad enough, what with me being one girl short, but as it turned out things hadn't even gotten wound up yet. Just seconds after Fawn had headed for the hippie hills, Betty sashayed into the living room, ready for her next customer. The tallest of the soldier boys stood up and announced, "There's the girl I want!" Betty was Hollywood blond and statuesque, and lots of men responded to her that way.

Betty grinned back at him until Thomas, who had been helping himself to more liquor than we usually allowed, pulled himself out of his chair and said, "Sorry, kid. Betty's mine." Soldier Boy whipped around to face Thomas, who was a good head shorter than he was. "Look, buddy, I was here first. You wait your turn like everybody else."

For the second time that night, Billy Ray and Trey stood, ready to spring into action.

"No, you don't understand," Thomas said. "Betty and I...we have a relationship."

I looked over at Betty to see if she really had taken a shine to this funny little man, but she just looked shocked and embarrassed. Some people might think it's impossible to embarrass a whore, but it's not. An unwanted emotional display will do it every time.

"Now listen, Thomas," I began.

"No, you listen, Miss Jenkins," Thomas said, "and you, Betty. I hadn't planned on doing things this way, but if I must, I must." He took a few steps closer to Betty and then dropped down on one knee. He opened his stubby-fingered hand, the palm of which held a diamond ring (not a very good one). Some highly predictable words were about to roll off his tongue, but they never did because right then, Betty screamed. She screamed like the object in his hand was a deadly snake, screamed so loud that one of the customers came running down the stairs in his boxer shorts to see what had happened.

"It's okay," I said, partly to Betty and partly to the terrified customer. "Come on," I said, pulling Thomas up by his outstretched hand. "You and me are going for a little walk."

"No," Thomas said, "I'm going to stay here and talk to Betty."

"Billy Ray, honey, why don't you help Thomas up?"

Billy Ray pulled Thomas to his feet and dragged him as he kicked feebly out the front door. As I followed them out I heard Betty say to the tall soldier boy, "Sorry about that little interruption, honey. Now what was it you were saying about me being the girl you want?"

As I stood on the porch with Thomas, with Billy Ray standing guard, I looked down at the ring I had taken from Thomas's hand. It wasn't even a full carat. I looked up at Thomas and shook my head. "You honestly thought you could impress a whore with something this little?"

Even though Billy Ray was standing guard, he turned his head away for a second. I was pretty sure he was trying not to laugh.

"I wish you wouldn't call Betty that name," Thomas said.

"Whore's not a name, Thomas; it's a profession. But it's more than that, too." I looked at his glasses, at the ink stain on the pocket of his tweed jacket. "I bet the first time you made up a story you knew you were a writer, and that nothing anybody did or said could change that."

Thomas's eyes widened. "How did you know that?"

"Because being a whore's just the same. You know what you're meant to do. I bet you'd be pretty damn miserable if somebody tried to make you stop writing and be an accountant instead."

"Of course." Thomas was looking at me in shock. Men like him always believe you've got to have a college education before you can think. And then they go off and do some foolish thing an uneducated person would have better sense than to do, like falling in love with a whore.

"Well, Betty would be pretty damn miserable if you tried to make her a wife."

"Now wait just a minute." Thomas shook a stubby finger at

me, and Billy Ray took one step closer to him. "You can't compare what I do to what Betty does, and you can't compare Betty to those other girls in there. She's different."

"Is she? Then how come she was leading that soldier boy up to her room the second you were out the door? You can't change her, Thomas. You'd drive yourself crazy trying. A whore ain't a wife. I tried to be a wife once, and the poor feller went so crazy trying to change me and trying to keep the other men away that he went and put a bullet through his brain."

I tucked the dinky little diamond into Thomas's jacket pocket. "Why don't you take this ring and see if you can find some nice lady teacher over at the college who'll marry you? A little diamond like that would thrill a schoolteacher to death."

Thomas's eyes were wet. "None of the women at the university look like Betty."

I looked at Thomas's balding head and potbelly and thought that the smartest man can still be shallower than the vainest whore. "Well, hon, I don't know if you realize this, but you're not exactly Steve McQueen yourself. You need to learn how to play in your own ballpark. If most men could marry girls who looked like the ones in this house, then I'd be out of business. Girls like Betty are like sinful desserts you treat yourself to now and then; they're not supposed to be the main course. What you need, Thomas, is to go over to that college and find yourself a real meat-and-potatoes kind of girl."

Thomas opened his mouth like he was going to argue, but I put my finger over his lips to shush him.

"But," I said, "if you ever feel the need to treat yourself to a sinful dessert again, you're gonna have to do it somewhere else because you're banned from this house. Billy Ray, why don't you walk Thomas to his car?"

That night, I did something I'd never done before, I turned off the porch light a full hour before our usual closing time.

"If anybody else wants some pussy tonight, he's gonna have to find a girl who's willing to give it away," I said, flopping on the couch with a bourbon and sliding my feet out of my punishing pumps.

"Hell of a night, huh, Billy Ray?" Trey poured a drink for

him and one for herself.

"Worst I've ever seen," he said, gulping down his bourbon. "Say, Vestal, that story you told Thomas, the one about having a husband that shot hisself, is that true?"

I smiled my madam's smile, the one that seems to say a lot but reveals nothing. "True or not, it was a hell of a story, wasn't it?"

Trey's eyes met mine for a second.

The other girls had turned in for the night, but Betty padded into the parlor, barefoot and freshly bathed and wearing a very unsexy flannel bathrobe. "I thought I might come down for a nightcap. Settle my nerves."

"How you doing, girl?" Trey asked. "That was quite a scene tonight."

"Tell me about it." Betty sat cross-legged on the floor and held her bourbon in both hands like a little kid holding a big glass of milk. "Of course, it's my own damn fault for feeling sorry for the guy. His wife left him last year, and he was so lonely and pitiful. The weird thing was, he never fucked me."

"What?" Trey and I yelled at the same time.

Betty laughed. "It's true. He came once a week, but he never came, you know? He'd just sit and look at me and write down things in his little notebook. He said I inspired him. He called me something...I don't remember what it was. It started with an M."

"His muse?" Trey said, laughing.

"Yeah, that was it." Betty took a big swig of bourbon. "So I'd just sit there while he scribbled away. He never let me see what he was writing."

"And he never touched you?" Billy Ray sounded truly amazed.

"Nope. It was real important to him, though, that everybody thought we were screwing. Sometimes he'd ask me to bounce up and down on the bed and make, you know, sounds."

Trey lost it on that one and spat bourbon across the room.

"One time, just to see what would happen, I unzipped my dress and slipped it off real sexy," Betty said. "I sat on his lap and kind of felt him up. It was as soft as biscuit dough."

"My guess is he's got the kind of dough that can't rise," I said.

"Well, I feel sorry for him, but I'm sure glad to be rid of him." Betty drained the rest of her glass. "So, Billy Ray, you want to come upstairs?"

Billy Ray's big face was as red as a strawberry. "Well, I reckon if Miss Vestal says it's all right."

"Y'all do what you want," I said, lighting up a cigarette. "You're off the clock."

After we heard the door of Betty's room shut, Trey sat next to me on the couch and draped her arm around me. "Baby?" she half-whispered.

I laid my head on her shoulder. "Mm-hmm?"

"Do you ever think of doing something else?"

"What do you mean?"

"Something besides running this house."

"Oh, on nights like tonight I do. But tomorrow morning when I'm taking the money to the bank I'll feel a lot better." I laughed. "And I know what you're gonna say. 'Vestal, there's more to life than money.' And then what am I gonna say?"

Trey grinned. "'That may be, honey, but when you ain't got no cash it's awful hard to remember what those things are.'"

I snuggled closer to her. "We know each other."

"Yeah," Trey said, but she didn't sound happy.

"You all right?"

"Yeah. Just tired."

I squeezed her thigh. "You're not tired of me, are you?"

I expected playfulness, but I didn't get any. "No, but sometimes I get tired of pretending all the time, acting like I'm nothing but your faithful employee during business hours, not even letting myself look at you until we've closed up shop and everybody else is in bed. People like us aren't hiding as much as they used to, Vestal, especially if you go to the big cities. Plus...I don't know... sometimes I just feel like there's so much happening in the real world, and none of it is happening here. There are other ways we could live."

"Not with this kinda money coming in."

"Vestal, you act like the only way to make money is running

a whorehouse. I was thinking we could take some of the money we've saved and get a little place somewhere away from the South, maybe California. I could get a job, and you could get one, too, if you wanted to. In the evenings we could sit down and have dinner together. We could make friends with other women who…"

"I'm nobody's wife, Trey. No man's and no woman's either."

"Did I say you were? I'm not talking about an old-fashioned marriage, Vestal. I'm talking about two women loving each other out in the open. There are plenty of people in this world who are throwing away the old rule book on how to live their lives and creating something new."

"I kinda like the old book. That way I know what rules I'm breaking." That was the big difference between Trey and me: she wanted to change the whole world, and I just wanted to be able to keep on doing what I liked. As a result, I spent a whole lot less time being angry and frustrated than she did. She always wanted to change the laws about how the world worked, but I was content to roll my eyes at the laws and keep on doing as I pleased. I needed the laws; you can't be an outlaw without them.

Trey sighed and went silent, which was one of the two ways she gave up on winning an argument with me. The other way was marching out and letting the door slam behind her, but I knew after the night we'd had she wasn't going anywhere.

There was no use talking, so I took Trey's hand. Trey's hands were beautiful, not like a woman's, but not exactly like a man's either, wide and long-fingered, the color of almonds. She didn't take her hand away, but she didn't grasp mine with it either. She just let it lay there, limp. Clearly, hand-holding wasn't going to be enough to bring her out of her sulk.

I stood over Trey where she sat on the couch, then sat down on her lap straddling her, face to face. When I sat, there was a loud rip as the split in my silver evening gown went from thigh-high to hip-high. The sound of the rip got Trey's attention, and I leaned over and whispered in her ear, "Here. Now."

"What?" she said. "For years it's been nothing but behind locked doors in the dark. What if one of the girls comes in and sees us?"

"Then she'll have a little surprise, won't she?" I let the shoulder straps of my evening gown drop. "Here, Trey." I breathed. "Out in the open."

Compromise was not a specialty of mine, but I was giving it a try. Okay, Trey, I thought, I won't move to California, the home of earthquakes and lots of women who are just as pretty as I am, to be a big dyke with you, but I will run the risk of letting you fuck me on the parlor couch after all the girls have gone to bed.

Trey kissed me hard and forced her hand up my dress as I straddled her. In the past few years, Trey's lovemaking had grown more gentle, but this was different. Fueled by a crazy mixture of anger and attraction, Trey moved inside me like her old butch self, with the kind of cockiness that didn't require a cock. When my muscles clenched around her hand, I bit her shoulder to keep from crying out, tearing a small hole in her shirt.

I sat on her lap, my head snuggled against her shoulder, her arms around me, floating on the soft cloud of well-being that good sex can bring. But you can't work in a whorehouse without knowing that the calm, safe feeling that comes after sex can be as deceptive as the calm before a storm.

"Trey?" I whispered, not sure what I was going to say next, but pretty sure it was going to be something foolish.

"Mmm?" she answered, stroking my hair.

But the foolish words, whatever they might have been, never got to spill from my lips because at that moment, even though it was a little after three o'clock in the morning, there was a knock at the door.

CHAPTER 27

At first we were going to ignore the knocking, since the porch light had been turned off and the girls were asleep. But then I heard the high, whiny voice I knew so well. "Vestal, I know you're in there! It's me, Les!"

"Christ on a raft," I muttered, getting up from the cozy nest of Trey's lap. My dress had split plum up to my hip, but I decided to answer the door like I was. It wasn't like Les expected me to be a paragon of virtue.

When I got the door open, I saw Les standing next to a tall, handsome man who looked to be in his early forties. With his full head of neatly cut brown hair, his broad shoulders and his sharp, tailored suit, he was everything that scrawny, bald-headed, sloppy Les wasn't. Les punched his handsome friend on the shoulder and said, "I told you she was pretty."

By this time I was feeling a little confused, but I also knew that Les only complimented my looks when they were going to play a part in some business venture. Interested in hearing his latest scheme, I said, "Come in."

"Vestal," Les said, "this is Michael Kingsley. I was telling him you might be just the person for him to meet."

"Is that a fact?" I shot Trey a look that said I had no idea what the hell was going on.

She just said, "Why don't I go make us some coffee?"

"Coffee would be lovely," Michael said. "And I apologize for coming here at such a ridiculous hour, but Les promised me you'd be awake."

"Oh, I'm always awake around this time," I said. "It's part of the nature of my business. I don't know what Les's excuse is."

"I ain't got time to sleep," Les said as we settled down on the couch. "Sometimes I go the whole week without getting more than two hours of sleep a night. Come Sunday, Peg puts me to bed and makes me stay there. She says, 'Even the Lord rested on the seventh day, Les Tipton.'"

I smiled politely and helped Trey serve the coffee, wondering what the hell all this polite chitchat was leading up to.

After Les took a couple of loud slurps of coffee, he said, "Michael here ran for city council this last election."

"Is that a fact?" I said. Michael, I noticed, was showing an unnatural amount of interest in his coffee cup.

"He sure did," Les said. "Didn't win, though, which was a damn shame. He's a fine feller and has some fine ideas about what's wrong with this city."

I wondered if Michael minded being talked about like he wasn't in the room.

"See," Les went on, "what hurt him was the rumors. Rumors was being spread that Michael here was...a little light in the loafers, if you know what I mean. There was even some young feller, who was lying his head off, I'm sure, who said that Michael approached him in a public park for...for reasons you wouldn't want to tell your granny about." Les set down his coffee cup. "Now, I think we'd all agree that it's a terrible thing for a man's political career to be dead in the water just because somebody starts spreading rumors about his personal life."

"Yes," Trey said, "especially since, even if the rumors are true, the fact that he likes men shouldn't make him unworthy to hold a political office."

"Well, that's one way of looking at it, I reckon," Les said as though he was talking to a crazy person. "But what I was thinking was that if Michael's gonna build up his reputation so he can win the next election, he's gonna have to start looking like more of a ladies' man."

I looked at the prim way Michael held his cup and saucer.

"Now isn't that the most hypocritical thing you've ever heard?" Trey said. "It ruins a politician's career to be thought of as promiscuous with men, but it improves if he's thought of as promiscuous with women."

"Most people are born hypocrites and stay that way all their lives," Les said. "If you can make yourself look like the kind of person they want you to be, they'll vote for you. And then you can do anything you want to. Vestal," Les said, shutting Trey out of the conversation, "being a big high-society lawyer, Michael gets invited to all these fancy parties. Now, usually he just goes to 'em by himself, or takes his mother. But that ain't gonna do nothin' for his reputation. If he was to take you to a party or two, though, can you imagine how tongues would start to wagging?"

"Sure, I can imagine it," I said. "But I don't see how being seen with a madam is gonna do much to enhance Michael's reputation."

"See, that's where you're wrong," Les said. "Nothin' would make Michael look more like a ladies' man than being the escort of Knoxville's most notorious madam...a beautiful woman who could have her pick of men, and the man she picks is Michael Kingsley. Pretty soon, Michael, fellers'll be punching you in the shoulder and calling you an old dog."

Michael jumped when Les punched him in the shoulder. The only old dog he put me in mind of was my little French poodle.

"I don't know, Les," Michael said, rubbing his arm. "It's a wonderful thing you're trying to do here, but I just don't think people will believe it."

"Sure they will," Les said. "A good-looking feller like you? Besides, people believe what they want to believe."

"That's right," Trey said, her voice hard and cold. "And the world isn't going to get any better until people stop believing what they want to believe and start accepting things for how they really are." She looked at me with a directness she usually saved for when we were alone. "Vestal, I've hardly ever asked you for anything, but I'm asking you now. Please don't say yes to what these men are proposing." She got up, said, "I'm going to bed," and marched out of the room.

"What got into her, do you reckon?" Les asked.

I tried to laugh it off. "Oh, you know Trey. She's got all these principles."

"How come she went into your bedroom?" Les said.

"She's got a cot in there. We're using all the other bedrooms for the girls."

Michael looked pale and afraid. I knew how he felt, knew how it felt to have a secret that could ruin your livelihood and strip you of your power.

"If you agree to be seen in public with me from time to time," Michael said, "I will, of course, pay you handsomely. You can set the price, in fact. And if you require a special dress to wear to one of these functions, I can cover the cost of it, too. We would be seen together once a month, twice a month, at the most. And, of course, it would be a strictly professional arrangement."

His businesslike tone didn't disguise the desperation in his voice. I knew Trey would be mad at me, but she'd been mad at me before. Michael's eyes were so sad, and the money he was offering was so good. I could buy Trey a new car and send her back to finish college. "All right," I said.

"See there, buddy." Les cackled. "I told you a little bit of money was all it would take to get you a girlfriend."

After Les and Michael left, I went into the bedroom to find Trey sitting in the chair in the corner with her knees hugged to her chest. "You're going to let him take you out, aren't you?" she said, her voice just a whisper.

"Just a time or two. He told me I could set the price."

"I asked you not to." She wasn't looking at me as she talked, just staring straight ahead.

"I thought we could use the money to send you back to school."

"Do you think I want any part of that money? I feel bad enough living off the money women make from selling their bodies, but this is worse."

"How is this worse? Me going to a party or two with Michael, it don't mean nothin'."

"It does mean something," Trey said, her voice rising. "Vestal, being a whore's a lot more honest than what you're doing with Michael. If you're a whore, a man pays you for a fuck, you let him fuck you, and that's that. It's a private business transaction, and except for deluded people like Betty's friend who got kicked out tonight, nobody's ever going to mistake what goes on between a whore and a john for anything more than what it is." She sniffed and ran a finger under her eyes. "When you go out with Michael, though, and people see you dancing together, talking together, you're telling a lie. You're telling the world that this man, who has probably never kissed a woman except his mother, and you, who has never been with a man except as a means to an end, are together, that you're lovers, that you just might quit the whorehouse business and let him make an honest woman out of you. Whoring isn't about telling lies, Vestal. But this is."

"So what if people think me and Michael are together? Since when did you care so much about what people think?"

"Vestal." Trey's voice was heavy with exhaustion. "A couple of months ago, when Howard and Celia and I went down to Atlanta for that rally, Celia took me to this bar. It was in a rough, rundown section of town in a building that had seen better days, but when we got inside, even though it was dark and damp and furnished with rickety secondhand tables and chairs, it was still the most beautiful place I'd ever seen. It was full of women together in pairs, dancing, talking, laughing. I saw this one couple at the bar, one of them had on a button-down shirt and pleated pants like I used to wear; her girlfriend had on a red dress. The one in the pants leaned over to light her girlfriend's cigarette, then reached up with her other hand to stroke the girl's cheek, and she gave her this look of...I guess adoration is the only thing you could call it. And I thought, wouldn't it be something to be with a girl you could take out, a girl who'd be proud to be seen with you? And I realized that with you, I'd never know what that was like."

I didn't know how long the secret nature of our relationship had been eating at Trey, but I suspected it had started a long time before she saw those women at the bar in Atlanta. Finally, stupidly, I said, "I am proud to be seen with you."

Trey shook her head at the ridiculousness of my statement. "How can you be, Vestal? We've never been seen together, not as we really are. When I saw those women together, I thought that's how we ought to be. But I knew if I asked that of you, I'd be asking you to choose between me and this house, and I'd never ask that because I know what you'd choose."

In all our years together, I'd never seen Trey cry, and now I watched, mesmerized, as a single tear slid down her cheek.

I knew what the right answer was, the thing that would make

things all right between Trey and me again. I would put my arms around her and say, "I choose you."

But if I did that, what would I be choosing? Days spent working straight jobs and making next to nothing? Evenings spent sitting in a dreary, cheap apartment, having serious political conversations with serious women who needed to tweeze their eyebrows and put on some lipstick? Early nights spent sleeping because we were too tired to make love after spending all day at our backbreaking, low-paying jobs?

I would have liked to tell Trey I chose her, but I didn't want all the horrible changes that would go along with that choice. So instead of saying those three words, I put my arms around her without saying anything. I had hoped she would melt under my touch, but she hardened under it instead.

As I held Trey's rigid body, I wondered how she could possibly think our lives would be better if we told the world about our relationship. People were arrested for setting foot in a gay bar, gay couples were beaten up on the street, faithful employees who turned out to be gay were fired from their jobs, and gay politicians had to find a beard if they hoped to get elected. That was the way of the world, and I had no idea why Trey thought she could change it.

"You'd better go on to bed, Vestal. I'll stay on the cot."

It takes a lot to make tears come to my eyes, but that statement was enough. I had thrown around the sheets on that cot every morning for over fifteen years so it would look like Trey had been sleeping there, but this was the first night she actually did.

I don't know if she really slept, though. I didn't for the longest time, but when the sky outside was turning from black to gray, my exhaustion finally took over.

When I woke up a few hours later, the cot had been folded up and put away, and there was a piece of paper on the bedside table. Looking at it made me sick to my stomach; I might not know what it said word for word, but I knew the gist of it well enough. I lay in bed and stared at it a few minutes, on the verge of crying and throwing up, before I finally picked it up and read it.

Dear Vestal,

When I was in college I remember reading this part of Homer's Odyssey where Odysseus's ship lands on the island of Circe, a beautiful enchantress. Odysseus is charmed by Circe, and even though he and his men are supposed to be sailing for home and slaying monsters and doing other heroic things, they stay on the island a full year, safe from the troubles of the world, basking in the pleasures of Circe's luxurious food, wine and lovemaking.

It's been way more than a year since I washed up on the shores of your island, Vestal, seeking refuge from a world that had grown too hard for me. And you took me in and gave me your friendship and the pleasure of your company, and later, your love and the pleasures of your beautiful body. You enchanted me, and I have been happy here.

But I can't stay on this island forever, not while the world is in such a big mess on the one hand and on the verge of so many exciting changes on the other. When I was a little girl, Mama used to say, 'Girl, you're gonna be one of them that grows up to make a difference in this world.' So far I haven't. At least not enough of a difference. I keep telling myself, though, that it's not too late.

For years I've been hoping I could get you to leave with me, to take an active role in the world. But I realize now that you can't ask an enchantress to sacrifice herself by leaving her island, where she can arrange everything to suit her, the rest of the world be damned. So, my beautiful enchantress, I leave you on your little island, so I can venture forth into the world, perhaps to do heroic things. Please know, Vestal, that your spell over me is not, and probably can never be, broken.

Love always,
Trey

I don't know how many hours passed before a couple of the girls knocked on the door to check on me. I looked bad, I say this not because I could see myself, but because I could see it on the girls' faces.

"Are you okay, Vestal?" one of them, I don't remember who it was, asked.

"Mm-hmm," I muttered, shoving Trey's letter under my pillow. "Today's the anniversary of the day my brother got killed, so I'm a little down."

Of course, it was nowhere near the time of year that C.R. died, but I must've sounded convincing because the girls brought me toast and coffee and piled into the bed with me like it was a big slumber party. I tried to give the appearance that they were comforting me, but there was only one woman I wanted in my bed, and not one of them was her. The coffee they gave me was sour, and the toast was as dry as sawdust in my mouth.

CHAPTER 28

That was the last morning I ever gave the girls a reason to think I was sad. After that, I was the same old Vestal when I was around them, or at least they thought I was.

They thought I was the same old Vestal because that was who they needed me to be, their livelihoods relied on it. So they didn't look at me too close and didn't ask me many questions, and I did my part by smiling and pretending to care when they talked to me about their little personal problems.

People want you to be okay because they don't want to have to deal with your problems in addition to their own. If you're ever falling apart but make even a small effort to convince the people around you that you're just fine, they'll believe it because they want to believe it.

When the house opened up in the evening, I was even better than the same old Vestal. My dresses were louder, and diamonds, emeralds and rubies sparkled on each of my manicured fingers. I flirted and laughed with all the customers, and I felt their adoration sink into every pore of my flawless skin. As the fellows lit my cigarettes or pulled me up from my chair to dance with them, I'd think, Trey could never have a roomful of men eating out of her hand like this. That just goes to show that I'm not like she is.

The new, even more fabulous Vestal who appeared in the house every night was brought to the public courtesy of Kentucky's finest bourbon. I had been a lightweight before, keeping a drink in my hand to appear sociable but nursing it all night. Now I had one bourbon when I was fixing my face for work and then steady stream of it throughout the evening. The drink filled me with a warm well-being that cleared my mind, relaxed my body and loosened my tongue so I could talk to customers.

And could I talk! After three drinks, I could talk the ears off a billy goat. When a fellow told me how beautiful I was—and one always did, I'd say, "You know, I was a runway model in Paris when I was a teenager. They kept hoping I'd get taller so I could get the real big modeling jobs, but as you can see, I stayed petite." Or, "I did a screen test in Hollywood one time, but they didn't want me because I looked too much like Liz Taylor and they didn't want her throwing a fit."

No matter how wild my stories got, the men always seemed to believe me. Men are fools that way. They'll believe anything a beautiful woman tells them.

By the time we'd shut down for the night, I'd be so soused I'd usually just kick off my shoes and crawl into bed in my evening gown and jewelry. There, in my empty bed with nobody but Gypsy the poodle for company, I would finally let myself have the cry I'd been holding in all day, facedown on the bed, biting the pillow to muffle my sobs.

I hated to leave Dixie in charge of the house, but I had no choice, since the Christmas party at the country club that I was to attend with Michael fell during our regular business hours.

I had a hell of an outfit to wear to the party, a crimson velvet cocktail dress, cut off the shoulders, which Michael had done me the kindness of paying for. I decided I would take Gypsy along with me, I had gotten so I found it nearly impossible to be without her, and dressed her in a crimson velvet doggy coat to match my dress.

Fortified by bourbon, I met Michael at the front door, holding Gypsy in one hand and my evening bag in another.

"You look lovely," he said, like somebody who had been told he was supposed to say "you look lovely" to a woman when he picked her up for a date.

As he opened the door of his black Cadillac for me, he cast a nervous glance at Gypsy. "She won't piddle on the upholstery, will she?"

"Of course not. I can't make any promises for myself,

though."

It took a minute for the joke to dawn on him, then he smiled. "I hope we can pull this thing off."

"Don't you worry," I soothed him as I slid into the Caddy's plush seat. "As much as you're paying me, I plan to spend the whole evenin' looking at you like you hung the moon."

The inside of the country club reminded me of all the movies I used to see with beautiful, elegant women and men at beautiful, elegant parties. Of course, the women and men here weren't that beautiful. In fact, some of them were downright dumpy, but they were dressed nice. And the club itself was both beautiful and elegant, with white cloths on the tables and a big marble dance floor and tiny fairy lights sparkling everywhere for the holiday.

"Would you like me to get you a drink?" Michael asked.

"Champagne, please." I really wanted another bourbon, but I knew I'd look prettier holding a glass of champagne. A waiter passed by with a tray of shrimp, and I took one for me and one for Gypsy. I looked around to see who I knew and spotted Les, standing in a corner by himself, wearing a crooked necktie, and I made a beeline for him. "Les Tipton, I didn't know you was a member of the country club!"

"I ain't. Michael just wangled me an invitation for tonight. It was Christmas, so I reckon they was feeling charitable. It's good to be seen at these things from time to time. But all things being equal, I'd rather be coon hunting." Michael came back with my champagne, and Les said, "Well, I'd better make myself scarce before I start looking like a third wheel," and wandered off to another corner. For somebody who was famous for his ability to work a crowd, Les seemed shy and miserable in this situation.

I sipped my champagne and smiled at Michael like I was delighted to be in his presence. I could feel people looking at us and knew we were going to be the talk of the party.

As I was busy with my fake flirting, though, Gypsy started to quiver. Her little puffball tail started wagging, she let out three yips, and then leapt out of my arms and darted across the floor.

"Come back here, girl!" I called, but there was no stopping her. Her little toenails click-click-clicked across the marble floor as she ran to jump up on the pants legs of three prominent

Knoxvillians: a doctor, a lawyer and a banker, all of whom were regulars at the house. Gypsy danced around the ankles of her old friends, wagging and yipping and probably trying to figure out why they weren't picking her up and playing with her the way they usually did.

The three men stood frozen in terror, trying to figure out what the whorehouse poodle was doing at the country club.

I ran as fast as my heels would carry me and scooped Gypsy up in my arms. When the fellows saw me, their faces turned as white as Christmas snow. Here they were, surrounded by their colleagues, with their wives no doubt nearby, and here I was, with a dog that might as well be calling them 'daddy.'

"You fellas must be dog lovers," I said. "She can smell one a mile away. I'm sorry she jumped on you like that. My name's Vestal Jenkins, by the way. I'm here with Michael Kingsley."

The color returning to their faces, the men all managed to blurt out, "Nice to meet you," and, "A pleasure to make your acquaintance, Miss Jenkins."

Walking away from them with Gypsy held securely in both arms, I spotted Les in his corner, laughing so hard he had to wipe away tears.

Back in Michael's corner, a society matron bustled up to us and said, "I don't think you two have noticed that you're standing under the mistletoe."

I smiled, stood on my tiptoes and gave Michael a very genuine-looking kiss. He kissed me back, tight-lipped and mechanically, and the partygoers applauded, rewarding him for his obvious heterosexuality. Michael laughed and took out a white hanky, muttering something about getting my lipstick off his mouth.

He wasn't fooling me, though. I knew he was wiping off the girl germs.

On the way back to the house, Michael said, "You were great tonight."

"Usually when a feller tells me that, we've been doing somethin' besides drinking champagne at the country club."

Even in the dark, I could tell he was blushing. "What I mean is," he finally said, "I really appreciate what you're doing for me."

"Well, it ain't like it's charity work."

"That's true, but I still appreciate it, especially since I got the idea that Les's proposition was causing some tension between you and the woman you live with."

I decided to pretend I didn't know what he was talking about. "Which woman? I live with a bunch of them."

"The pretty black woman who was there when Les and I were over."

"Oh. Her. She's no longer in my employment."

"Oh. So she was just an employee? I thought she might have been...something more."

"Well, you thought wrong."

When you spend most of your days about half drunk, time doesn't fly exactly, but it flows. One day flows into the next, like bourbon from the bottle to the glass.

Just like any other job, drinking creates a routine. Mornings are spent nursing a hangover with coffee, aspirin and, when you can choke it down, food. By early afternoon, it's acceptable to pour a discreet nip of bourbon into your coffee. Five o'clock is cocktail hour, and so is every hour after that, until it's time to stumble into bed.

I didn't need a shrink to tell me that I was pouring down liquor to fill the hole Trey had left inside me. I knew exactly what I was doing, and I figured it was all right because the booze made me a friendlier, funnier madam. And if the girls and the customers took notice of the hollow leg I'd developed, they didn't say anything about it. After all, wasn't I supposed to be boozy and brazen?

So, unlike with Trey, I found that I could have a relationship with my new partner, bourbon, out where everybody could see. In East Tennessee it's a lot more acceptable for a nice white girl to drink herself into a stupor every night than it is for her to go to bed with a black girl.

And business was great. Going out with Michael had cast me as a colorful local celebrity. Fellows came to meet me and stayed for the girls. With the money pouring in, I started ordering my clothes from New York instead of wasting my time with Knoxville's tacky little so-called 'boutiques.' I bought a full-length mink coat and used it like an afghan to curl up under on the couch while I watched the news.

Of course, I never watched the news without a drink in my hand. How could anybody watch those burning Vietnamese villages and those poor, mutilated soldiers without having a little something to calm her nerves? Every time I saw the piles of body bags of our boys being shipped home, I thought of C.R's funeral and Mother, deranged with grief. But at least C.R. had died in a war people could understand.

Every night I wanted to turn off the news, wanted to put on my best gown and ignore everything that was going on in the world. But I couldn't. Maybe it was because if I shut out the world entirely, then everything Trey said about me would be true. Or maybe it was because somewhere among all those wild-haired people they showed on the news, protesting the war, proclaiming that 'black is beautiful,' I hoped to see Trey's face.

When the moon landing happened, all the girls gathered around the TV with me, giggling about spacemen and green cheese and which one of the astronauts was the cutest. When Neil Armstrong took those first, floaty steps the girls cheered and clapped, while I sat silently. The astronaut looked so alone there on that barren surface. Those rocky craters surrounded by black sky looked like nothing to me but the landscape of my loneliness.

CHAPTER 29

Some people might say it's impossible for a whole decade to whoosh by without you hardly noticing it. But those people didn't drink as much as I did in the Seventies. Surely I'm not the only person who can't quite piece together all of that decade in my mind. Shoot, with all the booze and blow and ludes and weed making the rounds, it's a wonder anybody can remember anything about those years.

I'll tell you one thing, though: it was damned hard to run a whorehouse in the Seventies. You're probably thinking, it can't have been that hard, everybody was screwing. Well, that's exactly the problem.

In the Fifties, when it was damned hard to find a nice girl who would let you screw her for free, what I was selling was quite in demand. But in the Seventies, a fellow could go out to a bar and find a girl who'd screw him if not for free, then for the price of one brandy alexander. Or he and his wife could go to the next-door neighbor's cozy, shag-carpeted suburban house, and he could violate one of the Ten Commandments by screwing his neighbor's wife while his neighbor screwed his own, without paying so much as one red cent for the privilege. So how does a whorehouse compete with all this free fucking?

Well, you have to do what any other business owner would do in a highly competitive situation. You specialize. You have to think, what kind of sex is hard to come by for free these days?

And of course, the answer was kinky sex. Now, I'll tell you I didn't even know what kinky sex was until I traipsed down to the Town and Country adult bookstore and started reading up on it. And, well, I didn't really feel like I understood half of it after

I finished reading about it, but I did understand one key thing: if you lived in New York or California, you could probably ring your neighbor's doorbell and they'd show you their collection of whips and leather. But in East Tennessee, where most people probably thought S&M was the name of a cafeteria, it must be hard to satisfy your appetite for such things.

So the new girls I hired had specialties. Diana, who had chestnut hair that fell to the tops of her thighs, used her large collection of whips and riding crops to make men call her 'Mistress.' And Crystal, a pretty blonde, told me during an interview that she had lots of experience 'fucking guys with a strap-on.'

"With a what, honey?" I asked.

"A strap-on dildo. It's a fake…"

"Oh, I know what you're talking about." I recalled Trey telling me about butches who used those on their femmes. "So you put that up their rear ends, do you?"

"Yes, ma'am."

"And they like it?"

"They love it."

"Well, I tell you what, honey. I'll hire you and your dick on a two-month trial basis."

Somehow I couldn't imagine any of our customers in that position, but I didn't want to lose out on money just because I lacked imagination.

I also hired two girls, both petite, one blonde and one brunette, who described themselves as 'best friends' and who specialized in putting on 'dyke shows' in which they'd kiss and touch each other while the customer watched. "Guys love that shit," they said, giggling.

Looking at the two of them, I wanted to ask if they liked it, too, if they might kiss and touch each other without a paying audience. But I didn't ask, of course. This was business, and there was no room for personal questions.

The house profited hugely. We started advertising in national sex magazines, and men would fly in from all over the country and pay astronomical sums to get whipped or buttfucked or to watch two women go at it. I was moving away from being just financially comfortable and toward being genuinely rich. But it wasn't fun. The new girls were cynical and businesslike, and the new customers wanted to get right down to the business of getting their kinks worked out and had no time to dance or joke with an aging madam.

As I refilled my glass and counted the night's receipts, I'd get nostalgic for the days when a girl just taking her clothes off and lying down was enough to make a fellow happily open his wallet.

I still went out with Michael once or twice a month. His political career was flourishing, and my salary as his date had gone up as a result. We were seen dancing at parties and leaning over the table in 'intimate conversation' in restaurants. Of course, usually these intimate conversations consisted of us talking about some movie we had both seen and disagreeing about it (I had loved *The Godfather*, while he shuddered at the thought of 'all that blood and marinara sauce'). Our quiet little arguments about movies must have looked romantic enough, though, because our names kept popping up in the tittering little gossip column on the society page of the *Knoxville News-Sentinel*. My least favorite of these columns asked the question, 'Is a certain dashing city councilman turning Knoxville's most notorious lady of the evening into a one-man woman, now that her looks have started to go?'

I cried into my bourbon over that sentence long after that issue of the paper was off the stands. Michael marched down to the *News-Sentinel* office and demanded that Mary Davis print an apology. She did, but it was a biting one: 'A knight in shining armor rode into my office and chastised me for making disparaging remarks about his lady love in my column last week. My apologies to the lady in question.'

I have to admit I was touched by Michael's defense of me. "Lord," I said when he told me about it, "you'd think you was my boyfriend."

"Pretending to be your boyfriend has nothing to do with it. I just know how upset I'd be if some busybody old crone like Mary Davis said my looks were going."

The fact was that Mary Davis was right. The rose of my

beauty had not only lost its first bloom, the petals were drying up and falling off. Part of it was my age, but a lot of it was the drinking. My face was puffy, and even my free hand with the makeup couldn't conceal the bags under my eyes. Also, the liquid calories I was pouring down my throat made my evening gowns require some extra yardage. I still spent a great deal of time on my hair and makeup, but the effect was like spreading beautiful frosting on a cake that has started to dry up and crumble. Mary Davis's words hurt me not because they were mean, but because they were true.

But what was I going to do? I wasn't going to stop drinking, that was for sure. And it wasn't like my beauty was an asset to my business anymore. All the regular old customers who had come to the house at least in part to see me had gotten too old to risk the erotic excitement of a whorehouse. The customers I was getting now, who came from parts unknown and did God knows what when they actually got upstairs, only required two things of me: that I let them in the house and take their money.

Maybe my beauty was dying not because of age or alcohol, but from neglect. From the time I was a tiny girl, there had always been somebody, Daddy and his friends, then David, then dozens of other men and, of course, Trey, even though she was different from the others somehow, who worshipped my beauty, who made me feel special for it. And now there was nobody. Maybe it was just the old rule of supply and demand. There was no demand left for my beauty, and so my body had stopped supplying it.

My only other distinct memories from the Seventies, besides the mean-spirited mention of me in the gossip column, is of two deaths. The first was Gypsy, whose death from cancer shook me so much I swore I would never have a pet again. The second was Les's wife, Peg.

Les never went to the doctor much ('Never had a sick day in my life,' he'd always claim), and I guess Peg didn't either because by the time she figured out she was really sick, the doctors couldn't do much about it. The cancer had started in her ovaries and spread so that there was hardly a part of her that was cancer-free.

I never went to see her in the hospital because I knew she

didn't like me, but I had flowers sent to her room every day until Les told me I had to stop because it was getting so he couldn't find his way to her bed for all the damn flowers.

The night she died, Les came over to the house, his hat in his hands. "She's gone," he said before I could say so much as hello. "I meant to go home, but I started driving here instead."

I hugged Les close, it was the first time I'd touched him since the day he'd helped me run away from home, and he stood still and let me, but he didn't hug back.

I led him to the couch and poured us each a bourbon. He drank his in one gulp, so I poured him another. "She was a good woman," he said finally.

"Yes, she was."

"When we first got hitched, they was a lot of people said I coulda done better, I coulda married a prettier woman or a rich woman. But I loved her and she loved me."

"Then you couldn't have done better."

"No," Les said. "I couldn't have." He looked down at his empty glass, and I filled it up again and topped mine off a little. "And now," he said, "I don't know what I'm gonna do. Seems like nothin's any good no more."

"Well, you've got your seat on the city council."

"And you can have it as far as I'm concerned. These new boys on the council treat me like I just fell off the farm truck. All them young little rich boys with their university degrees and their good bloodlines. You'd think they was talking about hunting dogs the way they go on about who their daddy is and who their grandaddy was. I figure I'll serve a few more terms. I ain't gonna get voted out 'cause everybody knows I'll vote for business, but I ain't going nowhere from here but down."

"You don't know that, Les."

"Sure I do. I've gone as far as a person who starts out with nothin' can go. So have you, I reckon. You really want to get to the top of the ladder, you can't start out on the bottom rung." Les drained his glass and sat quietly for a minute. "Vestal, I never woulda asked you this with Peg alive, but have you ever thought about...you and me?"

"Me and you how?"

"Now don't do me thisaway, Vestal. You know damn good and well how."

"Les Tipton, are you coming on to me when your poor wife ain't even in the ground yet?"

"I ain't trying to court you. I was just...wondering."

"Well, I don't know, Les. I guess for me, you know, I always liked you, and then when C.R. died, it was like you stepped in to fill his place."

Les nodded gravely. "That's how I thought it was." We both sat quietly for a minute or two, then Les said, "You know, my mama was in your line of work."

In nearly fifty years of knowing Les, I had never heard him mention his family. "What do you mean?"

"She worked in a whorehouse that house out in western Kentucky I told you about that time. I was raised in that house, around all them women. That's where I learned to play poker and make money. I reckon that's why I've always felt so comfortable here. It's like coming home."

"Well, shoot, Les, no wonder you never said nothin' about your people when we was back in the camps."

"You know how people are. If they think they've got somethin' on you, they'll never give you the time of day. It wasn't because I was ashamed. My mama took good care of me. She was a good woman." He was silent for a minute. "I don't know if she was ever really happy, though. She was kinda like you."

I scooted away from Les. "What do you mean?"

"Well, it just don't seem like she ever had anybody to love her the way she needed to be loved."

"Well," I said, using getting the bottle as an excuse to get up off the couch, "that ain't me. I had somebody once that loved me like that."

"Did you?" Les said. "I never knew that. But yeah, I reckon David was an awful nice feller."

It took me a second to even remember who David was. I looked at Les, amazed that somebody could know me so well yet not know me at all.

CHAPTER 30

Years go fast when they're empty. They blow past like paper bags in the wind.

The house prospered. Girls left, and I hired new ones whose names I couldn't keep straight. When the house wasn't open I left the girls to their own devices and sat in my room, drinking my bourbon and watching old black-and-white movies on my color TV. I watched the news some, too, so I knew that a former star of old black-and-white movies (one that I'd never cared much for, although his little ex-wife would've been cute enough if she'd ever figured out what to do with her hair) was President now and doing his dead-level best to drag the country back into the Fifties. Oh, well, I figured, it would be good for my business.

And it was for a while. Whenever the times demand that people act good, they're dying to sneak and be bad for a night. Business in the house was booming. There was just one problem.

I got careless.

A lot of it was the bourbon. My mental faculties weren't what they used to be. I couldn't concentrate, and large blocks of time disappeared from my memory. So it was mostly the bourbon, but it was also the times. The way things had loosened up in the Sixties and Seventies made me forget the need for discretion when the so-called 'moral code' tightened back up again.

Starting in the late Seventies, we got into the business of doing outcall. Some men wanted a girl for the night without wanting the whole whorehouse experience. This type of gentleman, usually a businessman staying at one of the downtown hotels, would call me up and ask for a girl. I would talk to him long enough to determine that he wasn't a maniac, and then I'd send the girl who seemed to match his tastes the best, dressed fairly discreetly so as not to call attention to herself, to meet him at the hotel.

One evening I got a call from a gentleman at the Hilton who wanted two girls, one for himself and one for his friend. This wasn't a particularly unusual request, so I sent Candy and Brandy, two slender, blond-haired, blue-eyed girls who claimed to be sisters and who had only been working at the house a couple of months.

Two hours later, the phone rang. I picked it up and heard nothing but sobs. "Who is this?" I said.

After several more sobs, the voice finally choked out, "It's Candy. Me and Brandy...we're at the police station. Those men were cops."

"Cops? What the hell are the cops doing picking on me all of a sudden? I've been in the same damn business for over thirty years, and they ain't bothered me yet." Needing something to vent my anger on, I picked up the pencil from the telephone table and snapped it in two. "Well, you won't be in jail for long. I'll send down one of the girls to get you out. What's your bail?"

I told Tiffany, the girl who wasn't occupied, to wash off her makeup and put on a plain dress while I fetched a stack of bills from my secret stash in the JFG coffee can in the pantry.

When Candy and Brandy returned from their little adventure, their pretty faces were puffy and streaked with mascara tears. "You girls sit down," I said. "Let me fix you a drink."

Candy and Brandy liked girl drinks—sticky-sweet concoctions that masked the taste of the alcohol. I fetched some lemonade from the refrigerator, mixed it with vodka and even threw in a few maraschino cherries. I, of course, stuck to bourbon.

They tearfully sipped their drinks. Finally, Candy said, "Vestal, there's something else you should know...besides me and Brandy getting booked for prostitution, I mean."

I sipped my bourbon, knowing what was coming wouldn't be good. "What's that?"

"Well, when the cops arrested us, they asked us for ID. We showed them our driver's licenses, but the thing is, neither of us is exactly eighteen."

My hand tightened around my glass. "Well, then, exactly

how old are you?"

Candy fished her maraschino cherry out of her drink and twirled it by its stem. "I'm seventeen; Brandy's sixteen."

"So you girls lied to me about your age?"

"We never lied; you just never asked us about it."

She was right. In all my years of running the house, I'd never asked a girl to tell me her age (after all, isn't that the rudest question you can ask a woman?) or to show me her ID (what whore wants her madam, or anybody else in the business, to know her real name?). I always figured that if a girl looked grown up and filled out and knew enough to come ask for a job at a whorehouse, then she was old enough to be hired.

"Well," I said finally, "don't you girls worry about a thing. I'll get this all taken care of."

"I don't know if you can," Candy said, while Brandy started sobbing beside her. "They'll be coming after you, too."

"Don't you worry about me. I was taking care of myself before your daddy was a gleam in his daddy's eye. I'll tell you what. You girls go get some rest, and I'll call Michael Kingsley first thing in the morning. I'm sure he'll be willing to help you. And don't worry about the money; I'll take care of it."

The girls thanked me and climbed the stairs with slow, heavy steps. But in the morning there was no need to call Michael on the girls' behalf. Candy and Brandy, and all their belongings, were gone.

Like a lot of heavy drinkers, I was good at pretending a problem was gone when it actually wasn't. When I saw Candy's and Brandy's empty closets and stripped dressers, I thought, good. One less thing for me to take care of.

That night a couple of forty-something guys in cheap knockoffs of Lacoste shirts came by and asked if they could meet some ladies. I invited them to sit down and have a drink, and soon they were talking and laughing with Tiffany and Melody (or Melanie? I could never get that girl's name straight). The four of them made their way upstairs. But within five minutes they were coming back downstairs again, with both the girls wearing handcuffs, but not in a recreational way.

"Vestal Jenkins," one of the men said, "you are under arrest for aiding a house of prostitution. You are also charged with two counts of contributing to the delinquency of a minor for employing underage girls."

I was up out of the chair. Would they shoot me if I tried to run? I wondered. "You can't just barge into my house and arrest me!" I yelled.

One of the cops grinned. "Well, when your house is a house of prostitution, we sure as hell can. You invited us in."

"You got invited in by lying to me about who you were. You ought to be ashamed of yourself, lying like that. This is an honest business."

The taller of the two cops snapped the cuffs on my wrist. "If you don't mind, ma'am, I'd rather not be lectured on my morals by somebody in your line of work."

"What's immoral about my line of work? I sell pussy. I've been selling pussy for more than thirty years, and once I get out of this I'll be selling it for thirty more. Pussy's better for you than liquor and cigarettes, and it's legal to sell them!"

As the cops pushed us out the door, Tiffany said, "Vestal, would you shut up? You're gonna get us all the electric chair!"

"I will not shut up! Everybody's known what line of work I've been in all these years. Why are you people picking on me now?"

"Because you're breaking the law." The cop opened up the back door of the police car and, in a less-than-gentlemanly way, barked, "Get in."

"Well, these charges won't stick, I'll tell you that! I've got some real powerful friends in this city."

The cop laughed. "If you're referring to Les Tipton, that old coot's been in on so many shady deals, we could probably book him, too." He slammed the car door in my face.

At the station I used my one phone call to call Michael.

"What did they charge you with?" he asked.

"Running a house of prostitution."

"No surprise there."

"And two charges of contributing to the delinquency of a minor."

"How was that?"

"Well, apparently a couple of the girls I had working for me were underage."

"Shit."

I had never heard Michael cuss before. He was the only person I'd ever met who actually said, "Oh, fiddlesticks" when he got frustrated. "That's bad?"

"It's pretty bad. But listen, let's take this one step at a time. Right now we've got to concern ourselves with getting you and the girls out of jail."

"Well, they've made it pretty clear that we're not going anywhere till morning. But if you can get over to the house, there's enough money for bail in the JFG coffee can on the top shelf of the kitchen pantry. Maybe you can get one of the girls to come with you in the morning. There's still three girls in the house; they hid when they saw it was a bust."

"Well, we'll come get you first thing in the morning, then. I'm sorry you'll have to spend such an uncomfortable night."

"No sorrier than I am. Michael, if this was gonna happen, why didn't it happen before now?"

"City politics. A lot of these new city officials love to talk about 'cleaning up the city,' getting rid of sex and drugs and anything racier than a church ice cream social. It's an easy cause for politicians to embrace, and it makes for great headlines."

"Your time's up," the big cop standing behind me barked. Really, the worst thing about being arrested was the complete lack of manners displayed at every step of the process.

Tiffany and Melody/Melanie got put in a cell with other whores, but of the common, streetwalking, soliciting-outside-the-Greyhound-bus-station variety. To be honest, those poor girls were so hollow-eyed and greasy-haired that I was amazed anybody would pay to screw them.

They put me in a cell by myself across from the other girls. I don't know if they thought I was a more dangerous criminal than the two girls working for me or if they thought putting me by myself would increase the chances I might shut up. I didn't shut up for quite a while, though. I yelled about freedom and justice and a woman's right to do whatever she wants with her body, including renting it out by the hour.

I didn't shut up when the guard told me to, but when one fellow inmate yelled, "We ain't gonna get no justice here, so we might as well get some peace and quiet," I gave up and slumped on my hard cot.

This was, of course, the second time in my life I'd sat in a jail cell, waiting for somebody to come to my rescue. The difference was when I'd been in jail before, I'd been innocent of the crime I was charged with, and this time, I supposed, I was guilty. So why was it that I had felt so much guiltier in that jail cell in Morgan than I did now?

That morning, after a sleepless night, I watched my tray of powdered eggs and coffee turn cold and wondered where the hell Michael was. Finally, around ten a.m., the guard came wielding his keys to let me know I'd been bailed out.

"I'm sorry it took me so long," Michael said when he met me outside the door that led to the cells. "But I'm afraid I've got some news that's... well...not so great."

"Is there any other kind these days?"

"I went to the house like you asked this morning, but all the girls were gone. So was the JFG coffee can."

"What? Those bitches! That was my secret hiding place!"

"Well, it wasn't that big a secret apparently. So that was the reason for the delay. The bail money had to be obtained from another source."

It was then that I saw Tiffany and what's-her-name talking to a young, prematurely balding man I recognized as the assistant manager of Les's south Knoxville store. So Les had come up with the bail money. He just didn't want to cause a scandal by showing up to pay it in person.

"I'll pay Les back," I said to Michael.

"The source of the money wished to remain anonymous," Michael said. "Let's get your paperwork done and get you out of here. We have a lot we need to discuss."

By that evening, the story was all over the papers. 'NOTORIOUS LOCAL MADAM CHARGED WITH EMPLOYING UNDERAGE GIRLS IN SEX RING,' the *News-Sentinel's* headlines blared. Never mind that I wasn't even sure what they meant by the phrase 'sex ring.' It seemed like if I was running one, I would know what it was. The picture they ran of me was awful. It was one they took of me at the police station, and I looked as old as Methuselah's mother. Of course, they wouldn't run a flattering picture of me because the goal of the article was to paint me as a degenerate old crone who preyed on innocent teenaged girls for her own personal profit, despite the fact that an innocent girl had never crossed the threshold of my house. To my shock, they even printed some of what I said to the cops when they busted me, except the way they worded it was, "I sell [sexual intercourse]. I've been selling [sexual intercourse] for more than thirty years, and once I get out of this, I'll be selling it for thirty more."

Now honestly, if the purpose of the article was to make me look bad, and it clearly was, then couldn't they have quoted me directly and written 'pussy'? Or at the very least, 'p___y'? That way I would have at least sounded like a proper madam and not like a damned fool. I bet there's not a madam alive or dead who has ever used the phrase 'sexual intercourse' to describe what she's selling. At least not with a straight face.

CHAPTER 31

I spent most of the days before my court date sitting in the empty house with a bottle of bourbon, sometimes staring at the TV, sometimes just staring. Michael would come over from time to time to check on me and discuss the case.

Les called me once a week to see how I was holding up (I wasn't) and sent a boy over every so often with a bag of groceries because he knew I couldn't so much as go out to buy milk and bread without ending up in the papers. Les didn't come over in person, I was too controversial now for a city council member to openly fraternize with. So I never really saw Les, and I hardly touched the groceries he sent because I could barely force myself to eat. The boy would set the bag down on the kitchen table, and sometimes I wouldn't notice it until a week later, when the milk started to stink.

I couldn't understand how my life had changed so quickly. How had I gone from being a glamorous madam with a gorgeous secret lover and a house full of pretty, laughing girls, all of them making me pots of money, to a bloated, wrinkled old crone, drinking alone in an empty house and awaiting trial on criminal charges? As far as I could tell, I hadn't changed, at least not on the inside, so something in the world must have. How else could I explain the fact that I had gone from being the butt of affectionate but risque jokes to being regarded as a criminal in the town I considered my home? My line of work was once considered amusing and a bit naughty; now, to judge from the papers, you'd think I was as bad as a child molester.

A child molester. I thought of Candy and Brandy, the girls who had started all this trouble. Was I no better than a child molester for making these teenagers sexually available to grown men? Surely it wasn't the same thing. After all, I didn't know the girls were underage, and neither did their customers. And besides, those two girls were about the same age I was when I started using my sexual powers to get what I wanted from men. Of course, when I was Brandy's age I got married instead of becoming a whore, but really all that says is that Brandy caught on a lot faster than I did about the easiest way for a girl to get ahead.

The morning I was to enter my plea I had a shot of bourbon, brushed my teeth and gargled with Listerine and dressed in a plain gray suit, with only my most modest diamond brooch as jewelry. Despite my respectable duds, when I stood before the judge with Michael at my side and half-whispered, "Not guilty," I might as well have been wearing a red satin dress slit to the hip, given the way the old man with the gavel was looking at me. He set the trial date for two months away. I dreaded the trial less than I dreaded the waiting.

Over the next month, between the bourbon and the TV and the solitaire, Michael would come over to coach me on my upcoming courtroom performance. He'd bring me fashion magazines and food from the best restaurants in town, the places we used to go on our 'dates.'

"Look," he'd coo as he opened a Styrofoam box with a slab of prime rib from Regas or a pile of fettucini from Naples. "Now eat up, you need your strength."

I'd force myself to swallow a few mouthfuls of baked potato or a few nibbles of noodle so as not to be rude, but really, I had no appetite for anything but bourbon, me, a girl who used to be nothing but a mixture of beauty and appetite.

"Now," Michael said one afternoon when I had finished picking at a salad and had gotten up to pour myself a drink, "let's pretend you're on the stand. I'm going to question you like the DA, and I want you to give the answers we talked about, okay?"

"Yes, sir," I said sarcastically, flopping down on the couch.

"Now, Mrs. Jenkins," he began, pacing the parlor floor.

"That's Ms. Jenkins," I said. "Jenkins ain't my married name."

Michael looked exhausted but went on, "Ms. Jenkins, in your 'business,' you employed two young women who called themselves Candy and Brandy, did you not?"

"They was two of my girls, yeah."

"When Candy and Brandy came to apply for a…er…'position' at your business, did you ask them to show any identification?"

"I never ask any of my girls to show ID. If you're old enough to come to a whorehouse asking for a job, then you're old enough to know what you're getting yourself into."

Michael's hands fluttered in exasperation. "Vestal, that's not the answer we discussed. You were supposed to say, 'They mentioned that they had graduated from high school, so I figured they were at least eighteen.'"

"But they didn't say nothing about graduating from high school. You think I ask a girl about her educational experience before I hire her to be a whore? If she knows how to lay down, then she's educated enough to do the job."

"That's not the point, Vestal. The point is that Candy and Brandy are long gone and can't verify your story. This way, it'll at least sound like the girls gave you the impression that they were of age."

"Shoot, Michael, I can't remember none of the stuff you tell me to say."

"Well, maybe if you weren't pouring bourbon down your throat every waking hour, you could remember some of it."

I held onto my glass tight. "You expect me to face what's happening sober?"

Michael sat down on the couch beside me. "Look," he said, making his voice real calm, "all I'm saying is you'll have a much better chance of getting out of this, or at least of getting a light sentence if you sober up enough so you can think straight."

"Sober up enough so I can remember how to lie, you mean? Michael, I'm not gonna get out of this. You're a real good lawyer and a real sweet man, and I know you're doing the best you can for me. But I'm not gonna get a fair trial in this town. Everybody's already got their minds made up about me. So I might as well go up on that stand and be who I am instead of saying what you told me like a damned trained parrot."

"Vestal," Michael said with a sigh, "if you're not going to take my advice, then why are you even bothering to have me as a lawyer?"

"Cause you look so pretty standing up there in the courtroom in your Armani suit."

Michael laughed a little, but then put his head in his hands and rubbed his eyes.

The next time I saw Michael I was lying in a bed in Saint Mary's Hospital. Apparently Michael had come to see me at the house and had found me unconscious on my bedroom floor, my right temple bruised where I had hit the nightstand when I fell. Terrified that I was dead (I later told him he just didn't want to lose the client who paid for his Armanis and kept his name in the paper), Michael called an ambulance.

When I finally came around, a prissy little doctor told me I was suffering from severe dehydration and malnutrition and explained that the IV in my arm was to restore the fluids in my body. He also told me in his sensitive-doctor voice that my liver would not be able to withstand the amount of damage I was doing to it and asked, sounding like a waiter asking if he could recommend the wine that would best complement my meal, "Might I recommend an alcohol treatment program?"

"Might I recommend that you mind your own business?" I snapped.

Michael came in carrying a vase of yellow roses. "You scared the living daylights out of me," he said.

"I like to keep you on your toes."

"Well, you do that all right. You're the reason I keep getting my Valium prescription renewed." He sat on the edge of the bed. "Listen, Vestal, I had lunch with Judge Campbell yesterday. I told him about your...illness, and we had a very interesting conversation about whether you're competent to stand trial for these charges."

"What do you mean, 'competent'?"

"Well, you admit yourself that you have problems with your memory. And even if you won't admit it, you do drink too much. One could make a case that for the past several years, maybe you haven't always thought as clearly…"

"You're saying I'm crazy?"

"Not crazy exactly, just…not at the top of your game. If we can convince the judge that you're ill, and this hospitalization certainly helps out on that front, and that because of this illness you've experienced some cognitive problems…well, you might not have to face these charges at all."

"You mean after all these months you've been preaching at me to stop drinking and face my problems, that me being a drunk could actually save me from going to jail?"

"Well, I'm not exactly comfortable when you put it that way, but I suppose that's fairly close to what I mean."

Just then a surprisingly pretty nun who was one of the nurses came in with a bottle of shampoo and a plastic wash basin. "You wanted someone to wash your hair, Mrs. Jenkins?" she asked.

"That's right, honey," I said, then I turned to Michael. "Just look at her. Such a sweet little thing and so good at seeing to a person's needs. I told her if she ever got tired of this line of work, she oughta give me a call."

Michael laughed. "Good lord, Vestal. Sometimes I think I should just let them throw you in jail."

Judge Campbell agreed to consider the matter of my competency if I would 'submit to a battery of psychological tests,' and so just three days after I was released from the hospital, Michael drove me down to a big building downtown where they had all kinds of services for crazy people. Speaking of crazy, I wasn't crazy about the idea of being declared incompetent. I had prided myself on my competence all my life. In my prime, you could've dressed me in a flour sack and dropped me in any town in America at eight o'clock in the morning, and I would've had a pretty new dress and a source of income by noon. I didn't want people to say I was too crazy to do my job, but if the choice came down to spending my so-called golden years in prison or being called crazy, you could call me crazy all day long.

Michael sat me down in the lobby of an office that looked just like a regular doctor's office, with its uncomfortable furniture and year-old magazines. He told me he'd be back for me in three hours when the tests were over.

I looked at the other people waiting in the lobby, a white woman in her thirties with bleached blond hair and a few extra pounds on her and a bearded black man who wasn't much younger than me. They waited calmly, just like they were in any other kind of office.

After a while the secretary called my name and led me down the hall to a room that was decorated in ferns and flowered furniture. The woman behind the big oak desk had shoulder-length, stick-straight dishwater blond hair that had been cut off in a straight line at the shoulder.

"Good morning, Ms. Jenkins," the dishwater blonde said, smiling and revealing an overbite that put me in mind of a mule. "I'm Dr. Vaughn. I'll be administering your tests today. Please sit down wherever you're most comfortable."

I could tell that where I chose to sit was the first test, and I thought about climbing on top of her desk and sitting there, but instead I chose the overstuffed armchair directly across from her desk.

Dr. Vaughn was already looking me over, so I decided to look her over, too. Her fingernails were short and unpolished, and she wasn't wearing a wedding ring. The only piece of jewelry she had on was a big, clunky necklace made out of wood, of all things. Now honestly, if you can't do any better than wooden jewelry, then why bother wearing jewelry at all?

"Nice necklace," I said, in hopes that she'd stop staring and start talking. "Did you whittle it yourself?"

"No, I bought it at a shop in D.C. that sells ethnic jewelry."

"Oh," I said. Poor girl. If she'd get those teeth fixed and put a little curl and color in her hair, I thought, then maybe she wouldn't be stuck buying sad little necklaces for herself.

"Ms. Jenkins, you're going to take several tests today. Some of them will be written tests, and for others you'll just tell me the answers. This first test is one in which you just talk. I'm going to show you some pictures, and you tell me the first thing that pops into your mind when you see them."

But, of course, they weren't real pictures; they were just big black blobs. I knew this was called a Rorschach test because I'd seen it on TV before. When she held up the first blob and asked me what it made me think of I said, "Spilled ink."

She flashed me a less-than-genuine bucktoothed smile. "Now, Ms. Jenkins, I'm sure you can do better than that."

So I said it made me think of clouds or something like that, and she moved on to the next blob. There were only two blobs that really reminded me of anything, one was kind of an oval blob with a round fuzzy blob around it that made me think of Trey's hair when she let it grow out all bushy and natural. So when I saw it I said, "An Afro."

"I beg your pardon?" Dr. Vaughn said.

"An Afro-you know, the hairstyle."

"Oh...oh, yes, of course," she said, writing down my answer in her little notebook.

The only other picture that reminded me of anything was a bunch of blobs that kind of looked like a poodle.

After the doctor had used up all her ink blobs, she took me to a little room and sat me down at a desk to take the first written test. I hadn't taken a test since high school.

As I read through the test, it was clear that some of the answers were what a really crazy person might say, like, 'True or False: Sometimes voices in my head tell me to do bad things.' I wondered, if I was trying to get declared incompetent, should I mark the crazy answers on purpose? The problem was that the crazy answers were so crazy they'd make me sound like a serial killer instead of just a drunk old madam, and if I wasn't careful I might end up in a soft room for the rest of my life, which wouldn't be any better than prison. I decided I'd answer most of the questions honestly, but if I saw any answers that were sort of crazy but not off-the-scales crazy, I'd mark those, too.

By the time I got about halfway through the second test, I was getting pretty tired. There were all these questions that started out like, 'If Jack weighs twice as much as Fred and Joe weighs half as much of Fred...' questions I thought I'd seen the last of in high school.

By the third test I was in pretty sorry shape. My concentration was fading, and I had the shakes real bad. I looked at my watch; it was almost one. I would like to say that my shaky stupidity was because I needed some lunch, but I knew what the real reason was. I needed a drink. Actually, I needed more than just one drink, but one would've been a start—enough to steady my shaking hands and my rattled nerves.

Nothing was required of me at my competency hearing except to sit quietly, this time in a respectable-looking blue suit, while everybody discussed whether I had gone 'round the bend or not.

The smarmy doctor who had treated me at the hospital was there, telling the judge about how I had been hospitalized after a fall and blackout and how I had been suffering from the dehydration and malnutrition associated with severe alcohol abuse.

Dr. Vaughn was there, too, wearing a necklace that looked to be made of dried beans. After the judge was done with me, I decided, he should hold a hearing to declare that woman incompetent to wear jewelry.

Dr. Vaughn was holding a Manila envelope. "What I have here," she said, "are the results of the psychological tests that I administered to Vestal Jenkins."

"Could you talk to us about those results?" Judge Campbell asked.

"Certainly." Dr. Vaughn let Judge Campbell get a good look at her big mule teeth. "Well, to use everyday language, these tests concluded that Ms. Jenkins is of above average intelligence, but she displays some basic cognitive problems. Her performance showed an inability to sequence information, and her performance on a relatively simple memory test was...well, abysmally low."

I remembered how shaky I was by the time I got to the memory test. I wondered if I answered a single question right.

"Dr. Vaughn," Michael asked, "do you have a sense that Ms. Jenkins' cognitive difficulties could be caused by years of alcohol abuse?"

"They certainly could. Long-term alcohol abuse can definitely impair cognitive function. Ms. Jenkins' advanced age could be another factor."

I pictured myself choking Dr. Vaughn to death with her bean

necklace and making my own necklace out of her big mule teeth. Advanced age, my foot! I wasn't that damn old.

"But, Dr. Vaughn," said the DA, who puffed out his chest like a big toad, "isn't it possible that a person with cognitive damage can still distinguish right from wrong, could still understand the consequences of her actions?"

"It's possible," Dr. Vaughn said. "However, when one's memory is severely impaired, it's difficult to grasp the consequences of one's actions. After all, one may not be able to remember what her actions were in the first place. Also, we all know that alcohol, even when consumed in moderate quantities, can impair one's judgment. Alcohol consumed in large quantities on a daily basis over the course of several years...well, it could erode one's judgment entirely."

It's a strange feeling to have a roomful of people talking about you like you're not there. To tell the truth, I wasn't sure why I was there; my presence didn't seem to make one iota of difference to anybody. My mind floated away for a while, as it had taken to doing, and for a few minutes I was that teenaged girl sitting on the porch of that house in Bartlett, staring out at the mountains and dreaming of better days. Suddenly I heard a male voice say, "Vestal Jenkins," and felt an insistent tap on my shoulder.

"What?" I jumped a little and looked around. I was in the courtroom. It was Michael who had been tapping my shoulder, and it was Judge Campbell saying my name.

"Vestal Jenkins," Judge Campbell repeated, "after hearing the testimony of medical authorities, it is the opinion of this court that you are incompetent to stand trial on the charges that have been brought against you. However, given the nature of the offenses you have committed and the serious physical and psychological problems our experts have discussed, I feel it would be irresponsible of me to let you go scot-free and thus return to getting both yourself and other people into trouble. Therefore I am requiring that you spend a period of no less than thirty days at Lakeside Psychiatric Hospital for further observation and for treatment of your alcoholism. After that thirty-day commitment, arrangements will be made through your assigned social worker to release you into the custody of a family member or to place you in a halfway house, where you will remain for no less than six months." He dropped his formal manner, leaned over and looked straight at me. "That way, I can know for sure you'll stay out of trouble for seven months, anyway. Now, Vestal, if you violate any of these conditions, you'll be seeing me in court again, and this time I won't be inclined to listen to a bunch of doctors who tell me you're too sick and crazy to go to jail. Do you understand?"

"Yessir."

"And if I ever hear of you operating a brothel again, I'll see to it that it'll never happen again because the only money you'll be able to earn will be from making license plates in prison. Do you follow me?"

"Yessir. I've got no plans to open my house back up. I'm getting to be about retirement age anyway. I had been planning on retiring—I ain't just doing it because you're making me. But I've got no regrets—ow!" This last comment was the result of Michael kicking me under the table. The judge shook his head at me like I beat all he ever seen and then banged his gavel.

When we got up to go, Michael draped his arm around my shoulder. "Well, it looks like I actually managed to get you out of this, despite your best efforts to the contrary."

I knew I should be relieved, but I couldn't be too happy about where I'd be spending the next thirty days. "But they're sending me to the funny farm."

"The funny farm for a month beats the work farm for six years."

"I've seen that *Cuckoo's Nest* movie. I know what it's like in places like that."

Michael laughed. "Sweetie, with your personality, you'd have Nurse Ratched out turning tricks for you."

CHAPTER 32

Lakeside Psychiatric Hospital was indeed by a lake, but the fence separating the ugly red brick box of a building from the lake was so high that nobody, no matter how crazy, could climb over it. The front lobby of the building looked like the lobby of a regular hospital, all white and shiny clean. The lady at the front desk showed me where to sign the form, and I signed without even reading it. Dr. Vaughn signed, too, and a fat nurse with a gray ponytail took me by the arm and led me away.

She took me into a room lined with lockers that adjoined a tile room full of showers. "What, am I supposed to get ready for PE class?" I asked.

She looked at me with cold, flinty eyes. She was a person with a small position of power, and people with a little power never have a sense of humor. "You have to take a shower," she said.

"I took one this morning." I raised my arm. "Smell me."

"All patients must shower upon arrival. And you'll have to take off your valuables and give them to me."

I looked down at my diamond and ruby ring and the diamond tennis bracelet I had bought myself for my birthday one year. "Give them to you?"

"I'll put them in the safe. You can have them when you leave the hospital."

I didn't trust her not to hock my ring and bracelet. I did know she wouldn't be wearing them, though. Her forearms were as big as Popeye's, and her fingers were as fat as Polish sausages. I gave her the jewelry. "You see that this gets taken good care of, now. This ring alone is worth four months of a nurse's salary."

"Your earrings and necklace, too."

"Are you a nurse or a mugger?" She didn't crack a smile. I took the diamond studs out of my earlobes and shakily unlatched my necklace, a whisper-thin gold chain with a pendant of the letter V.

"Now undress all the way and get in the shower." I stood there for a minute and waited for her to leave, but she didn't move. "With you here?"

For the first time, she smiled. "Well, in your line of work I can't imagine that getting undressed in front of somebody would bother you."

But it did bother me. Being young and beautiful and naked in front of somebody who wants you is completely different than being old and naked and used up and stripping down in front of the cold, watchful eyes of a psychiatric nurse. I put my clothes in the wire basket she held out for me, and she handed me a bar of soap and a bottle of cheap shampoo.

I stood with my head outside the spray of the shower, so as not to muss my hair and makeup, and lathered up while the nurse watched me. As I ran my soapy hands over my body, I remembered what my body used to feel like, the high, firm fullness of my breasts, the sweet curve of my hip. Now everything that had been high hung low, and the soft curves had turned to flab. For the first time in my life, I was ashamed of my body.

"Wash your face and hair, too," the nurse barked.

"Now, look," I said. "My hairdresser's the only person who can get my hair looking like anything once it's been washed. And unless you want to call him, I ain't putting my head under that water."

"Mrs. Jenkins, if you don't wash your hair, I'll call in a couple of orderlies to wash it for you."

Defeated, I let the water run over my face and hair.

When I got out, she gave me a pair of ugly green pajamas and some house slippers. When I looked in the mirror, I saw a pale old woman with deep wrinkles on her forehead and dark circles under her eyes. My wet hair hung lank around my shoulders. There was nothing of me in the face in the mirror. The woman in front of me might as well have been somebody's granny in the coal camp.

The nurse led me, or what was left of me, to an elevator down the hall and took me up to the room where I'd be staying. It was a plain white room with two single beds, like a regular hospital room. "Well, at least the walls aren't padded," I said.

"Gladys is your roommate. She's seeing the doctor right now," the nurse said. "The day room is down the hall. You can go there to watch TV or visit with the other patients. You'll be seeing Dr. Silver first thing in the morning." She turned around and was gone. I was glad to see her go, but when the aloneness of being in that room hit me, I almost wished she'd come back.

I sank to my narrow little bed. Tears of rage burned my eyes like acid. I cried and I shook because I was alone, because I was in the nuthouse, because I wanted a drink so bad. I cried and I shook and I shook and I cried. After a while I realized my hands hurt. When I looked down I saw that my fists had been clenched so tight that my fingernails had dug bloody crescents into the meat of my palms.

I looked up from my bleeding hands and saw a woman in her early sixties standing before me. Her gray hair was cut in a short, straight pageboy, and she was wearing hoot-owl glasses and an ugly brown cardigan. "Goodness," she said, "look at those scratches. There's some ointment in here somewhere, I think." She dug around in the chest of drawers. "Here we go."

She sat down next to me on the bed, smeared a little ointment on each of my palms, and topped the ointment off with a Band-Aid.

"Are you a doctor here?"

She smiled. "Oh, mercy, no. I'm a patient, too. I'm your roommate, Gladys."

"I just thought since you were in your regular clothes…"

"Oh, they'll give you your clothes, too, in a couple of days."

I shook my head at the ridiculousness of it all. How could they 'give' me something that already belonged to me? I looked at Gladys and said what hundreds of people in the place had probably said before me: "I'm not crazy, you know."

"Why, of course you're not," Gladys said, like the question of my sanity wasn't even an issue. "Lots of people here aren't crazy. They just come here because they need a little rest. Like me."

"Well, this doesn't seem like much of a vacation spot."

"Oh, it's not so bad, really. Once you get used to this routine, you'll find it quite relaxing. Why don't you let me show you around a little?"

Since I had nothing else to do, I followed where Gladys led.

We ended up in the day room, a lounge with worn-out couches and a TV blaring an obnoxious game show. Nine or ten people, some in pajamas, some in street clothes, sat on couches and chairs, some staring at the TV, some just staring.

A tall, skinny pop eyed man whose pajama top was buttoned the wrong way darted up to me. He pointed his finger at my chest and yelled, "Hot Lips! Hot Lips! Hot Lips!"

I took a step back, looking around for a nurse or somebody to rescue me. But Gladys just looked straight at the guy and said, "That's right, Hawkeye. Now you'd better move on. The colonel wants to see you."

"Colonel Potter, Colonel Potter," he said and headed off across the room.

"He thinks everybody's a character on M*A*S*H," Gladys whispered to me. "I'm kind of disappointed, though. Yesterday I got to be Hot Lips. I guess the part just suits you better."

"Well, I thought I'd met some crazy fellers in my line of work, but I guess I didn't know the half of it," I said.

"What line of work is that?" Gladys asked.

I figured there was no reason to lie. "I run—well, I ran a whorehouse. And I got busted. The judge sent me here."

"He thought you were crazy just for that?"

"Well, my lawyer convinced him I was crazy. He figured a short stay in the nuthouse is better than a long stay in prison. The jury's still out on that one, though."

"Oh, I'm sure this is much better than prison," Gladys said. "Just look around." She swept out her hand to take in the whole room, like she was the cruise director showing me all the fun that could be had on a luxury ship. A slump-shouldered old man in baggy pajamas shuffled across my line of vision, muttering about the Masons. God, I wanted a drink. "We've got TV and magazines and board games and cards. Do you play cards?"

"Sure."

"Great! Let's play, then." She sat down at a rickety card table. "What's your game, Vestal?"

"Poker."

"All right. I'm more of a bridge player myself, but I can play poker." She called across the room, "Hey, Jane, you want to play poker?"

A girl who couldn't have been more than twenty made her way across the room. Her hair was long and naturally blond and lustrous. She had enormous ice-blue eyes and a little pink cupid's bow of a mouth. If she could just smile and laugh a little, I thought, she was the kind of girl who could bring untold amounts of money into a whorehouse. But she didn't seem like the smiling and laughing kind. As she slumped into her chair, she sighed. "Yeah, whatever. Deal me in."

As Jane picked up her cards, I noticed a long, angry scar running from the base of her hand almost all the way up to her elbow. I wondered what a twenty-year-old girl could be so sad about. For a beautiful young girl, the world is a big, fat, juicy peach, ripe for the picking. It's only when you're old and your looks go that the world turns against you.

I had always prided myself on being a pretty good poker player, but as I sat holding my cards, my hands shook and I couldn't concentrate. I tried to remember the last time I had held cards in one hand without holding a drink in the other. I lost to Jane once and to Gladys twice. Les would've been ashamed of me.

As Gladys was putting the cards back in the box, a frenzied-looking woman with several missing teeth leaned on our table and said, "Have I missed the bus? Have I missed the bus?"

"No, honey," Gladys said soothingly. "The bus isn't here yet, but I'll let you know just as soon as it comes." After the woman left, Gladys whispered, "It's best just to play along with the ones who are delusional. If you try to talk sense into them, it just confuses them."

Jane shook her head. "Buncha fucking loonies."

That night, after the nurse had given me a tranquilizer, which helped me shake less, I lay in my narrow bed in the dark. "Gladys?" I whispered, not sure if she was still awake.

"Mm-hmm?"

"You never did tell me what you're doing here. You seem like such a nice, normal lady."

"Well," she said with a sigh, "I guess I am a nice, normal lady, but sometimes it all just gets to be too much for me. I have a very difficult relationship with my son."

"A bad boy, is he?"

"Oh, no, he's a good boy. The best, some people might say. But just because he's good, that doesn't make him any easier to live with."

"Well, sometimes it is hard to live with a good person." I thought of Trey and how she was always trying to make me better than I ever could be.

"You know," Gladys said, "you actually reminded me of him today, when I first walked in here and saw your hands were bleeding. His hands bleed all the time, but you can't stop it with a Band-Aid like I did for you. Big gouts of blood just pour out of his palms all the time. You ought to see the armrests of the chair where he watches TV. I put new doilies on them every day, but they always get soaked through."

Maybe her son was a hemophiliac, I thought. The stress of having a seriously ill child could be enough to send an otherwise sane woman to the bughouse. "Does he have to go to the doctor a lot?"

Gladys laughed. "A doctor? What could a doctor do for a person that's already been raised from the dead? Oh, and that's another thing. He loves to raise other people from the dead, too. We can't even drive past a cemetery; you can't imagine the commotion!"

Gladys had stopped talking, which probably meant it was my turn to say something, but I had no idea what to say. Then I remembered what Gladys had said just a few hours ago: It's best just to play along with the ones who are delusional. "Well," I finally said, "children sure can be a trial, can't they? I'm not sorry I never had any myself." I took a breath and said, "Good night, Gladys."

The next morning, after I sat staring at a plate of eggs that looked like it had been imported from the county jail, a nurse came to take me to the doctor.

I was expecting another bucktoothed woman who smiled at me without meaning it, but Dr. Silver was a man, balding, bearded, maybe ten years younger than me. Something about him put me in mind of David, what David might've looked like if he'd lived to be in his fifties.

All right, I thought. A man I can handle. I may not have the looks anymore, but with a man in my age range, I could still turn on the charm.

"Good morning, Ms. Jenkins," Dr. Silver said. "Please sit wherever you're comfortable."

"Sit wherever you're comfortable" must be a standard trick of headshrinkers, I figured. "Good morning to you." I flashed him a slow, wide smile. I knew my teeth were still good. I sat down in the chair across from him and crossed my legs like I always did in front of men. Of course, it's hard to show off your gams in a pair of loony-bin-issued green pajamas.

Dr. Silver looked down through his half-glasses at a folder on his lap. "Well, Vestal. Do you mind if I call you Vestal?"

"You can call me anything you want."

He didn't smile or bat an eye. "Vestal, I have the results of your psychological tests here. And one thing that's apparent is that we're going to need to do some more testing to assess your levels of cognitive functioning."

"Shoot," I said, smiling at him, "I don't even know what those are."

This time, he smiled back. "Vestal, I have a feeling that you probably know more about a lot of things than you let on."

I shifted a little in my seat. "I wouldn't bet on that, Doctor. I'm really just a dumb old country girl."

"Well, your IQ scores say you're not dumb," Dr. Silver said. "So we can clear up that little misapprehension right now. As I was saying, there'll be more tests for you, but I'd also like to make sure that you and I have plenty of time to talk."

"Talk about what?"

"Well...about you. About whatever you feel we need to talk about."

"Oh, I know what you want us to talk about."

305 THE KIND OF GIRL I AM 305

"And what's that?"

"Well, I reckon the judge or somebody told you what business I was in."

"I am familiar with your line of work, yes."

"So you want to spend a bunch of time preaching to me about how running a whorehouse is wrong."

"Do you think it's wrong?"

That stopped me for a second. "If I thought it was wrong, would I do it?"

"I don't know. Would you?"

"Do you answer every question with a question?"

"Do I?" He smiled. "Look, Vestal, aside from the legal risks involved, with which you are no doubt familiar, I don't have a problem with how you've made your living if you don't have a problem with it."

"Well," I said, "I don't have a problem with it. So does this mean we get to talk about you instead of me now?"

"No, it just means that we won't focus on your career in our conversations. Instead, we'll talk about other areas of your life... your drinking, your relationships."

I flashed him another one of my smiles. "Shoot, all things being equal, I think I'd rather just talk about running a whorehouse."

"Therapy isn't about talking about things that make us comfortable." He scooted forward in his chair. "Vestal, if I asked you to tell me the three people over the course of your life that you've been closest to, who would they be?"

I scooted forward in my chair, too, and made eye contact with him. "Me, myself and I."

"Besides yourself, I mean."

"Well..." It was a hard question. I certainly wasn't going to tell him about Trey. I already felt like he had sawed off the top of my skull and started poking around in my brains, so I wasn't about to let him take my relationship with Trey and make something dirty out of it. "I guess my brother would be one."

"Do you still see your brother?"

"If I did, then I'd actually belong in this nuthouse. He got killed in World War Two."

"I'm sorry to hear that. How old were you?"

I wagged an index finger at him. "Now, now, Dr. Silver, a lady never tells her age. You've got my files right in front of you. If you're all that curious, you can do the math yourself."

"Who else are you close to?"

"Well...Les Tipton. He was my brother's best friend, and him and me have always stayed in touch. But you know, he has his life; I have mine."

"Anybody else?"

I pictured Trey's big, strong hands, but I said, "No."

"Do you drink because you're lonely?"

I laughed. "Lonely? I've had people around me my whole life. Running a whorehouse don't give you much chance to be lonely. I drink because it makes me feel good."

"But the next day, after you've drunk too much, you don't feel good, do you?"

"Of course I don't. But that's just the way life is, ain't it? There's always a price to pay for feeling good."

Dr. Silver scratched his beard, like men do when they want to look thoughtful. "I don't know. I walk for my health, and that makes me feel good, but there's not a price to pay for it afterward."

I shook my head. "Oh, you're one of them health nuts, huh? You people are always fooling yourselves, aren't you? Trying to convince yourself that taking a two-mile walk makes you feel better than drinking two martinis, telling yourself that granola tastes better than chocolate. Exercise, eating yogurt and wheat germ...that's about being good, not about feeling good, and there's a big difference between those two things. I could tell you a lot of times I've felt good, Doctor, but I can't think of the last time I've been good."

Dr. Silver took off his glasses and rubbed his eyes, and I could tell I'd won the first round.

Nearly every day I'd have to take some kind of test they'd come up with, a personality test, a memory test, an intelligence test. I didn't need a test, though, to know that there were big chunks missing from my memory. In my meetings with Dr. Silver, I noticed that I could talk in great detail about everything that had happened to me from the 'thirties to the 'sixties, but once I hit the 'seventies, the pictures in my mind were vague and fuzzy-edged, like images from a half-forgotten dream.

When I wasn't taking tests or having my head examined, I played poker with Gladys, who was tolerable company as long as you could keep her off the subject of her son, the Savior. I still wanted a drink, but as the days went by, I shook less and felt less sick. Even though I would've killed for bourbon, I knew there were no drinks to be had in this place, and I didn't see any point in sitting around pining for what I couldn't have, like a foolish man who falls in love with a whore.

I wasn't exactly happy in the nut house, but I did settle into the routine, and time passed quicker than I thought it would. When my thirty days were nearly over, I was called in to Dr. Silver's office and was surprised to see Michael and a little college girl there, too.

Michael gave me a kiss on the cheek and told me I looked fabulous, which, I'm sure, wasn't true, although I did look a damn sight better now that they were letting me wear my own clothes and fix my hair and makeup.

"Vestal," Dr. Silver said, "this is Cassie Bowden, the social worker who'll be helping you make the transition from Lakeside back into the real world."

"Hi," Cassie said. She had long, chestnut-brown hair and would've been a pretty girl if she'd worn something to show off her figure instead of the loose, flour-sack-looking jumper she had on.

"A social worker?" I said. "Why, honey, you ain't old enough to be a whore, let alone a social worker."

Her cheeks flushed. "I'm older than I look."

"I've heard that one before," I said.

Dr. Silver cut off our entertaining little conversation to say, "Vestal, since you are due to be released on Monday, I wanted to take some time to meet with you and your attorney and your social worker so we could discuss your diagnosis and your future after leaving Lakeside."

I sat up straight to hear what he had to say about my diagnosis and my future, figuring that I didn't have a bit of control over either one of them.

"The results of the tests Ms. Jenkins took here," Dr. Silver said, looking down at some papers inside a Manila folder, "very much concur with the earlier tests she took, showing enough memory damage to seriously call her competence to bear responsibility for her actions, or even to remember her actions, into question. The type of damage Ms. Jenkins displays is typical of many long-term alcoholics, especially once they start getting on in years."

I felt like I was sitting in that courtroom all over again. "Excuse me," I said, "could you at least talk about me like I'm in the room?"

"I'm sorry, Vestal." Dr. Silver gave me a half-smile. "From now on, I'll just address my comments to you and let the other folks listen in, okay?"

"All right."

"Vestal, our conversations in your therapy sessions have revealed that you have a tendency toward what is known as borderline personality disorder. People with this disorder have difficulty forming intimate relationships, in large part because they themselves lack a core identity. Instead of having her own true identity, the borderline changes her personality to suit whoever's she's with, like a prostitute who decides what kind of woman a particular customer would most like and then transforms herself into that woman. A borderline is a chameleon who changes to blend in with or to please the people around her."

"But that ain't a sickness," I argued. "That's just good business."

"Well, it can make for good business, that is true," Dr. Silver said. "But it makes for dishonest relationships and a poor sense of self. Because the borderline is so busy adapting herself to suit those around her, she becomes incapable of having a truly honest, intimate relationship with anyone. And Vestal, from what you've told me, you've never had a truly close relationship with anyone, except possibly your late brother."

"That's not true. I…" But I couldn't tell him about Trey. "Never mind."

"But I'll tell you something, Vestal. I don't believe that borderlines are incapable of forming intimate relationships. I believe that given the right kind of care, they can change. And so when Cassie and I were discussing your case, we decided it would be best for you not to serve your six-month probationary period in a halfway house. In that kind of environment, you would simply fall back on your old habit of blending in with the group, and the fact that the other people in the halfway house would also be recovering from substance abuse problems might make you fall back into some bad habits as well. So we decided it would be best for you to be released into the care of someone with whom you'd had a past connection, someone with whom you could form a true relationship. Of course, we had no idea who this someone would be until we got a call from Michael, telling us about someone who turned out to be, well, a godsend."

I hadn't noticed anybody else sitting in the room until then, but in the chair in the far corner was a lady who was probably a few years younger than me but who was so dowdy-looking she could have passed for ten years older. Her dull brown hair was arranged in a stiff bubble around her face in the style of old ladies who get their hair shampooed and set on Saturdays and sleep in a hairnet for the rest of the week. She was wearing a mint green polyester pant suit that hadn't been in style for a decade, and she held a cheap gray vinyl handbag on her lap.

I tried to focus in on her face to see if there was anything familiar about it. I noted the deep lines around her mouth, the kind that came from frowning too much, and her heavy-lidded brown eyes, which did seem a little familiar; I just couldn't figure out from where.

Suddenly, the woman stood up. "Vestal," she said in a voice that was familiar and strange at the same time, "it's me, Myrtle."

At that moment I did something I'd never done in my life, except when I was dead-dog drunk. I passed out.

When I came to, Dr. Silver, Michael, the little social worker and Myrtle were all gathered around the chair where I was slumped. The social worker held out a glass of water. I took a sip, looked up at Myrtle and said, "How...how did you find me?"

"It wasn't hard," Myrtle said, smiling in this insulting way. "I live in Camden County, that's just three counties over, and I saw a story about you in the Knoxville paper. I called up that judge that had you on trial, and I said, 'Your honor, Vestal Jenkins is my long-lost sister, and I want to save her soul.' He said that sounded like a good idea to him."

"So," the little social worker said, just as chipper as you please, "on Monday, Myrtle will come pick you up and take you to stay with her at her home in Camden County for the next six months. I can't imagine how much you two have to catch up on!"

"Now wait just a minute here," I said. "Isn't the punishment supposed to fit the crime? Did I do something a lot worse than running a whorehouse and just can't remember it on accounta my memory being so bad?"

"Now, now, Vestal," the little social worker said, "I'm sure you don't mean that. You've just forgotten the natural bond that you have with your sister."

I remembered Myrtle's self-righteousness, her tattling, her showing Mother and Daddy my secret engagement ring. "No," I said, "I remember my sister real well."

"Myrtle," Dr. Silver said, "are you sure you're up for this challenge?"

Myrtle smiled. "With the Lord on my side, I'm up for anything."

When it was time for me to leave, Michael patted me on the shoulder and whispered, "It's better than jail."

I glared at him with such heat it's a wonder I didn't burn a hole in his necktie. "The hell it is," I said.

CHAPTER 33

Myrtle came to get me that Monday, this time wearing an outdated pink polyester pant suit. We loaded my two suitcases into her tacky little economy car. "I've got more things back at the house," I said.

"Well, you'll just have to get by with the things you have with you," Myrtle said. "I'm not stopping to get your ill-gotten gains from that house of sin."

My life was going straight down the toilet, and I knew it, but I couldn't help laughing anyway. "You know what, Myrtle? For the past thirty years or so, I haven't even believed in God. But I think you coming back into my life has made a believer out of me."

"Is that so?" Myrtle sounded pleased.

"Yep. Now I believe that there is a God, and he has one sick sense of humor."

"God doesn't have a sense of humor." Myrtle was steering us onto the interstate.

"Then why the hell did he make you and me sisters?" I stared at the wide gray stretch of highway before me. "You know, I ain't been out of Knoxville since they built the interstate. We're headed toward Morgan, ain't we?" Even on this big, modern highway, I felt like I was traveling back in time.

"I live about twenty miles from Morgan, just before you cross the Kentucky state line. Me and Charlie, my husband, God rest his soul, lived up in Ohio for eleven years, but we moved back down here when Daddy got sick."

Part of me felt bad for knowing nothing about my family, but since when had they known anything about me? "When did

Daddy get sick?"

"Sixty-eight. Emphysema. He died in seventy. Mother lasted till seventy-five. Cancer. Daddy lost his mind toward the end, what with all the different drugs they had him on, but he never stopped talking about you."

"If I'd known, I'd've come to see him."

"You might have, but you wouldn't have been the you he wanted to see. He kept saying, 'Vestal, come sit on your Daddy's lap,' and 'Vestal, show these fellers how you dance like Shirley Temple.' He wouldn't even have knowed the grown-up you. And Mother spent the whole time she was dying calling for C.R." She shook her head. "I was the only one who was there for them when they was breathing their last, and neither of them remembered who I was."

"I wrote them, you know. Even sent some money. But they sent it back to me."

"Well, of course they did. They could've been starving to death and wouldn't have taken so much as a penny from you. Mother could never figure out why you turned out the way you did. But that's the way it is with children, you try to raise them up knowing right from wrong, and you send them to church every Sunday, but how they're gonna turn out once they're grown is anybody's guess."

"Do you have any kids?"

Myrtle sighed. "One daughter. Lisa. She's thirty-one. She just lives in Atlanta. It looks like she'd make it home to see her mother more than once or twice a year."

No, it doesn't, I thought, but I kept my mouth shut. The only thing I could imagine that could be worse than being Myrtle's sister was being her daughter.

The seat of Camden County was a little wide place in the road called Tucker. Downtown Tucker, such as it was, boasted a Hardee's, a dingy IGA grocery store and a red brick funeral home. "Well, I guess I don't have to ask what there is to do here," I said. "You eat, and then you die."

"It's a nice, quiet town," Myrtle said, "a good place to raise children."

It was quiet, all right. It was just four o'clock, and the streets were as empty as they would be if the town had been leveled by an atom bomb. I've never understood why people like Myrtle always think these dried-up little towns are good places to raise children.

Of course, Myrtle didn't live near downtown Tucker, probably the excitement of living that close to Hardee's and the funeral home would've been too much for her, so we had to wind down curvy country roads, past cow fields and Pentecostal churches.

It was strange to see the mountains up so close again. I could see mountains in Knoxville, but from a distance. Unlike here, they weren't closing in on me so tight I couldn't breathe.

"Here we are," Myrtle said finally, pulling into a gravel driveway beside a low-slung ranch-style house. Red brick with white shutters, the house was identical to four others we'd already passed.

The living room walls were covered with dark, cheap paneling. On the coffee table was a Bible that was bigger than the Knoxville telephone book and a porcelain figurine of Jesus talking to some blond-haired, blue-eyed children.

"Well," Myrtle said, "I guess this is your home for the next six months. And after that, well, we'll figure out what to do. They're fixing to break ground on this apartment building for senior citizens over near the IGA…"

"Now wait just a minute," I broke in. "We need to get this straight. After six months there is no 'we.' After six months I walk out of this place, and I do as I damn well please. I'm doing my time here the same as I would in jail."

I looked at the big TV in the corner; it was the kind that's in a big wooden Mediterranean case so it'll look like furniture. "You got cable?"

"Oh, no," Myrtle said in the same tone as if I'd just asked her if she had any cocaine I could have a little toot of. "Why, the preacher was just talking the other day, saying you wouldn't believe some of the stuff they show on cable."

"I bet they couldn't show me nothing I ain't seen before."

Myrtle shook her head sadly. "Vestal, I swear, when I think of some of the things you've seen and done, I just cry and cry."

"My life ain't nothing for you or anybody else to cry about.

I've had some troubles the past few years, I admit that, but other than those, I wouldn't trade my life for nobody's, especially yours. Have you ever taken a bath in champagne, Myrtle? Have you ever had a man decorate your naked body with diamonds? Have you ever put on a seafoam green evening gown and stayed up all night, laughing and dancing? Well, those things were all in a day's work for me, Myrtle...and I mean, that was work. If I told you what my idea of play is, you'd probably have a stroke and die." The image of Trey's brown, sure hands moving over my young body flashed in my mind.

"That's what I'm talking about, Vestal. You've spent your whole life mired in a swamp of sin." Myrtle tried to take my hands, but I snatched them away from her. "And that's why I've made it my job to save you. You don't have a lot of years left, Vestal, and if you don't accept the Lord into your heart, you're gonna go straight to hell."

"Gonna go?" I looked around the paneled living room, resting my gaze on a picture of a little girl in a pink frilly dress, kneeling in prayer beside a stained-glass window. "Seems to me like I'm already there."

The next morning Myrtle got me up at six and made fried eggs and sausage patties and canned biscuits and the worst coffee you ever put in your mouth.

"You always get up this early?" I nibbled at a biscuit but couldn't touch the greasy eggs that were staring up at me.

"Charlie got up at six every morning. I'd get up with him and make his breakfast and pack his lunchbox."

"Just like Mother did for Daddy, except she called it a dinner bucket."

"Yeah. And of course for years I'd get Lisa ready for school, too. Even after Charlie retired, he still got up every morning at six. Since he's been gone I can't sleep past six to save my life. It's like I've got an alarm clock in my belly."

"I can't remember the last time I was up this early, without having been up all night." Actually, I had been up most of the night the night before, until three or four in the morning, feeling the little glass eyes of the creepy china dolls in Myrtle's spare bedroom watching me in judgment.

"Charlie always said a good man gets up with the chickens, but a bad man stays out with the dogs all night."

"Well, I've never claimed to be good or a man, either one."

Myrtle shook her head as she cleared away my mostly untouched plate. "It's a big job the Lord has laid out for me."

I decided to pretend not to understand. "What, washing the dishes?"

"You know what I mean, Vestal Jenkins," she said. "Listen, if you get yourself cleaned up we'll go over to the beauty shop after a while. Then I thought we might run over to the Wal-Mart in Taylorsville to get you some clothes."

My hair was in fierce need of the beauty shop treatment, but Wal-Mart clothes? "I've got clothes in my suitcase."

"But you ain't hardly got nothin' to wear around the house. I thought we might get you a housecoat and a couple of sweat suits."

"I've got three closets of the most beautiful clothes you ever seen back at my house. Les has a key. I'll get him to box some up and send them to me."

"Well, I don't see as there's any need to do that. You're here to get away from your old life, not to have it sent to you."

"Damn it, Myrtle, just because I have a few of my favorite dresses sent to me don't mean I'm gonna turn this mausoleum of yours into a whorehouse."

"I would thank you to watch your language while you're under my roof."

"And I would thank you for not being a pain in the ass, but I don't think that occasion will ever arise." I marched down the hall and slammed the bathroom door, cussing Myrtle all the way.

The hair salon I went to in Knoxville was in a downtown high-rise and was decorated in modern chrome and glass. The beauty shop Myrtle took me to was in a trailer, with a portable sign outside that said, 'The Kountry Kurl.'

The dumpy middle-aged woman inside the Kountry Kurl wore a pink sweatshirt with a goose on it and had bottle blond hair that put me in mind of cotton candy. She looked right at me, then looked at Myrtle and asked, "Is this her?"

"Sure is," Myrtle said.

The woman's face lit up. "Why, come over here and sit in this chair, Miss Jenkins. I've never fixed a famous person's hair before!"

Myrtle's eyes narrowed to slits. Here we were again, just like when we were kids, with me getting all the attention.

By the time the beautician got done with me, my hair was arranged in a hard bubble around my head, exactly as I had worn it in 1964. Myrtle ended up with the same style, and so, I'm sure, did every other customer of the Kountry Kurl, whether she was six or sixty.

The Wal-Mart scared the hell out of me. The fluorescent lights blinded my eyes, the smell of cheap fabric dyes made my nose itch, and my ears ached from the constant squawl of all the sticky, grimy children. In the women's wear section where racks of cheap rags were shoved so close together you could hardly move, Myrtle kept pulling pastel sweatshirts off the rack and saying, "Well, isn't this nice?" and "This one's so soft" and "What about a pink one and a light blue one?"

"Good God, Myrtle," I half-shouted, "those things look like baby pajamas. You'll have me sleeping in a crib next!"

When an old lady in a housedress turned to stare at us, Myrtle smiled at her sweetly, mouthed the word "senile" and nodded in my direction.

"Christ on a raft!" I hollered. "You don't care a damn thing about saving my soul. All you want is to make yourself look good and make me look bad." I pushed myself past the racks of clothes.

"Vestal, where are you going?"

"You can stay in here and buy me pink footy pajamas and diapers if you want. I'm going outside to get some air."

Outside a beefy, red-cheeked man in a denim workshirt stood smoking. He had a nice face, so I said, "Excuse me, could I have a cigarette?"

He gave me a nod, reached into his pocket and said, "Yes, ma'am."

The 'ma'am' hurt a little. Thirty years ago, this man would've given me a ride away from this place and maybe even slipped me a little cash if I let him screw me. But no more. All I could get from him now was a cigarette.

"Vestal, what in the Sam Hill are you doing?" Myrtle was carrying three plastic shopping bags filled with God knows what.

I looked at the man I had bummed the cigarette from getting into his truck. "I always smoke after sex. Don't you?"

Myrtle's face turned nearly purple. "Why...why...I'm just so embarrassed I don't know what to say. Foul language, and smoking…"

"It ain't like I'm smoking a joint in front of the Wal-Mart. Not that I wouldn't smoke one if I had one, mind you."

Her eyes glazed over. "Merciful Father in heaven, give me strength…"

I threw down my cigarette butt. "Now you're embarrassing me."

But if I didn't want to spend the rest of my old age in the Wal-Mart parking lot, I didn't have much of a choice. I gave my smoking buddy a nod of thanks and followed Myrtle to her car.

"Well…" Myrtle sighed as she backed out of the parking space. "I was gonna take you to Hardee's, but now I'm not so sure."

"Do you really think you'd be punishing me by not taking me to Hardee's? Do you honestly think that a woman who has lived my life would find a trip to Hardee's so exciting that she'd be disappointed by not going? If you really want to punish me, act like you're gonna take me to the liquor store, then tell me you've changed your mind."

"There are no liquor stores in Camden County."

I had suspected as much, and I knew that even if there was a liquor store, I'd have no way of getting to it. Still, this knowledge made my stomach sink in disappointment.

We went to Hardee's. Before Myrtle unwrapped her hamburger, she bowed her head and said, "Bless this food for the nourishment of our bodies and make us fit for thy service, amen."

I made it a point to start eating before she finished praying. I hadn't had a hamburger in years, and I have to say a rare steak and a bourbon would've suited me better.

Myrtle insisted that I go to bed at ten o'clock just like she did, but I'd go to my room and wait to hear her snores from across the hall. She had always been a sound sleeper, so I knew that after she was out, it was safe to roam a little.

Not that there was anywhere to roam, mind you. Myrtle kept her car keys hidden, so my roaming was limited to the inside of that dark, tacky house. I poked through the kitchen cabinets for a while, moving around cans of Campbell's tomato soup and Luck's pinto beans in hopes that Myrtle's late husband had kept a bottle of liquor stashed somewhere. God knows if I was married to Myrtle I'd have to take a snort every now and then. But of course, there was no booze to be found. Charlie had probably been just as big a Holy Roller as his charming wife.

I tried to watch *The Tonight Show*, but it was too depressing. A beautiful, black-haired actress was perched on the guest chair wearing a gorgeous purple cashmere sweater with a black leather miniskirt. The audience laughed at her jokes and applauded. I had been like her once, and now here I was, being held hostage by my sister in the ass-end of the universe.

I turned off the TV and picked up the phone. Myrtle would shit when she saw the long-distance bill, but hell, it would probably be good for her; she had been constipated since birth.

"What can I do for you?" the crackly voice answered the phone.

"Les?"

"Missy? That lawyer of yourn told me your sister had come to get you at the nut hatch and dragged you plum up to Camden County."

"Yep. And you wouldn't believe how bad it is here. I'm sitting in a room full of pictures of praying children, wearing this God-awful pink sweatshirt she got me with fuzzy white kittens on it."

Les cackled. "She's as bad as she used to be, huh?"

"Worse. She orders me around like I'm a slow-witted six-year-old, and she prays more than the Pope. I feel like I'm living in that movie where Bette Davis serves Joan Crawford a rat for supper."

"You want me to come up there and get you? I can't drive too far these days on accounta my eyes, but I could get a boy to drive me up there tomorrow."

"If you come get me, the judge'll have my hide. He's the one making me live with Myrtle for the next six months."

"Six months with Myrtle might be worse than six months in jail."

"I know it. Listen, Les, you still got a key to my house?"

"Sure do."

"Why don't you go over there tomorrow and pack up a box of my clothes and shoes and send 'em to me? None of the evening stuff...just a dozen or so daytime dresses and suits. Myrtle will have a fit, but I'll be damned if I'm gonna spend the next six months dressing from the Wal-Mart."

"You want me to send your jewelry, too?"

"Lord, no. Why don't you take it and put it in the safe at the store? I can't have my diamonds here; Myrtle'd be boxing them up and sending them to that prune-faced man on *The Seven Hundred Club*."

Les cackled. "I'll get you your clothes, missy."

The clothes arrived in a big box labeled "Chiquita Bananas" three days later when Myrtle was out on her weekly trip to the IGA. I opened the box and pulled out my pearl-gray suit and my green shirtwaist dress. Seeing my pink and black Chanel suit again was like hugging a long-lost friend.

But what Les had left for me at the bottom of the box made me laugh out loud. It was the most whorish dress I could still fit into, a red, V-necked Halston number from a few years back that my old titties still looked pretty good in when I wore a sturdy enough bra to hold them up. The dress was slit up to mid-thigh on the right side, which I could get by with if I wore my support hose. That dress was the opposite of everything Myrtle stood for, and I'm surprised the walls of her house didn't crumble just because it was under the roof. When I lifted the dress from the box, I had another surprise: ten one-hundred-dollar bills were pinned to its hem.

CHAPTER 34

You want to know what a true sign of being crazy is? You have to have church services in your house because there's not a free-standing church in the whole town that's loony enough to fit your belief system.

When I dragged myself out of bed on Sunday morning, Myrtle had moved the living room couch and coffee table up against the wall and was arranging metal folding chairs in rows on the carpet.

"What are you doing?"

Myrtle looked at me, annoyed. "Getting ready for church. You better get cleaned up. The service starts at ten."

I put on my Chanel suit because I was looking for an excuse to wear it. Plus, I didn't figure there'd be a chance that anybody at Myrtle's wacko church would be wearing one, too.

At twenty till ten, the members of the First Church of Myrtle started to arrive. They were all women around Myrtle's age and so dowdy it was a wonder they'd ever found a man to screw them. There was about a dozen of them, all wearing pastel polyester pant suits or out-of-style floral dresses and carrying big vinyl handbags. Their names all ran together, but Myrtle introduced me to each of them, saying with a tone full of insinuation, "This is my sister, Vestal, who I was telling you about."

Whichever dowdy woman it was, her eyes would widen for a second, and then she'd say something like, "Well, Vestal, we think a lot of your sister around here. She sure loves the Lord."

"She always has," I'd say.

One of the faceless dowdy women, this one in a lilac polyester pant suit, looked me up and down and said, "Well, that's an unusual outfit."

"It's Chanel," I said, like that would make a lick of sense to her.

"You know, you really ought to get Myrtle to drive you down to the Fancy Flair in Taylorsville. They've got some real cute little outfits there that look just right on ladies our age."

"Chanel," I said, "is ageless." I figured my suit probably cost more than every piece of clothing in the Fancy Flair put together.

The women stood around and clucked like chickens pecking around a henhouse, but they fell silent when the rooster arrived.

The rooster was Brother Gary, a tall, ruddy-faced, fiftyish man with reddish brown hair that was roached up on his head in the closest thing I'd seen to a pompadour since 1964. His teeth were huge and white (I was trying to figure out if they were dentures or not), and he showed every one of them when he spread his lips in a grin and boomed, "Good mornin', ladies! It's a beautiful mornin' to worship the Lord!"

The women all said "Amen" or "It sure is," but from the looks of some of them, it was really Brother Gary they were interested in worshipping.

And Myrtle, of course, was the most obvious one of them all. She had him by the hand as soon as he hit the door and was babbling, "Do you want some coffee, Brother Gary?" and "Do you want a doughnut, Brother Gary?" and "Brother Gary, there's somebody I want you to meet." She led him over to where I was standing and said, "Brother Gary, this is Vestal, my sister that I was telling you about. The one I'm bringing to the Lord."

Brother Gary looked at me strangely for a second with his small, piggy eyes, then turned on his brilliant smile and took one of my hands in both of his. "Vestal." He drew out my name long and smooth. "Your sister is a wonderful woman, so I know you've got some of that goodness in you, too. It's a blessing that you've come back home."

This was not my home, and I was fixing to tell Brother Gary so, but he had already moved on to kiss up to other old ladies before I could say anything. Nobody can work a room like a country preacher, except maybe a madam.

The "church service" was like a scene straight out of Lakeview Psychiatric Hospital. As Brother Gary rambled on about love of the Holy Spirit, the old ladies cried and hugged and held hands while they sang one of those awful songs about Jesus's blood. I was forced to hold hands with the woman who'd been bitchy about my outfit, so I made a point of digging my long thumbnail into her palm.

I've never paid attention to a sermon in my life, and Brother Gary's was no exception. I watched him pace back and forth in his chocolate brown, three-piece suit and caught enough phrases like 'kids on dope' and 'pregnant teenagers' and 'recruiting homosexuals' to know it was a good thing I wasn't paying closer attention.

If you spend the better part of your life running a whorehouse, you see so many preachers come in and out the door, you feel like you're running a seminary. Now, I know there are some preachers who'd never darken the door of a whorehouse unless it was in a serious attempt to save the poor, wayward girls' souls, but more often than not, when a preacher crossed the threshold, he was interested in something a little more tangible than the girls' souls.

Brother Gary was a type I'd seen in the house a hundred times, grinning and gladhanding and sitting on the parlor sofa with a whiskey in his hand and a girl on each knee.

I looked at Brother Gary as he paced pompously across Myrtle's living room, talking about the poor sinners who "try to fill up the hole in their hearts with sex and drugs and liquor." As I stared at the ruddy face, the reddish, poufy hair and the big teeth, I realized that the image that had flashed in my poor, memory-impaired brain had not been a composite of all the preachers who had ever walked in the door; it had been a memory of Brother Gary himself, who clearly had some firsthand knowledge about 'filling up holes.'

He had come to the house two, maybe three years ago, dressed, I believe, in that same chocolate brown polyester suit. He drank whiskey in the parlor and talked about how he was a widower but how even when his departed wife (God rest her soul) had been on earth, she hadn't been woman enough to fulfill the huge sexual appetite that the Lord gave him. He asked me if he could take two girls upstairs instead of just one, and I said, "Sure, honey, if you can pay for 'em."

He paid me with a big wad of small bills, ones and fives and tens, that I was sure had come out of an offering plate. Talk about a love offering!

He went upstairs with two blondes, Tiffany and Crystal. The reason I remembered was probably because of what Crystal, a quick-witted girl who only worked for me a short time, said about it afterward. After Brother Gary left, she turned to me and said, "You know, Vestal, that preacher man was truly Christlike."

"How's that?" I asked.

"Well, he did it to Tiffany, and then he rose again and did it to me."

Looking at Brother Gary now, sweating and praying, I knew my memory was right. No wonder he had looked at me so funny. Shoot, I thought, trying to hold back the only case of church giggles I'd had since I was a teenager, if I could remember dirt on people this good, maybe there were some advantages to staying sober.

After the service Myrtle laid out a sad little buffet in the kitchen: assorted lunchmeats of the scary pink variety, white bread, potato chips and off-brand sodas. Everybody stood around eating pickle loaf sandwiches and talking about Jesus and about all the people in Camden County who, unlike them, were going to hell.

Myrtle hovered over Brother Gary, refilling his paper cup with soda, laughing at his jokes and patting him on the arm. Biting my cheek to keep from laughing out loud, I wondered if Myrtle was enough of a woman to satisfy the huge sexual appetite God gave Brother Gary.

I stood in the kitchen with everybody else, but I ate nothing. Instead I kept my eyes on Brother Gary at all times, smiling at him with an I-know-something-nobody-else-knows smile. One time when he caught my eye, he choked so hard on a potato chip I thought Myrtle was going to have to do the Heimlich maneuver on him.

For the rest of the day Myrtle went on and on about how

wonderful Brother Gary was. My tongue itched, but I didn't say anything.

That night around nine-thirty the phone rang. Myrtle already had on her high-necked cotton nightgown and the pink showercap-looking thing she slept in to make her shampoo-and-set last the whole week.

Whoever was on the phone, Myrtle blabbed to him or her for a full ten minutes about Brother Gary and his wonderful sermon before asking, "Are you going to church anywhere?" Then she said, "Well, it looks like with all the churches they've got to choose from in a city that big, you could find one you liked."

She had apparently given the person on the other end a chance to get a word in edgewise because there was silence.

Then she said, "Well, that would be all right. It's sure been long enough since you've been up for a visit. It looks like you could at least come up for Thanksgiving and Christmas and Easter like other people's children."

So this must be Lisa, I thought. My heart filled with pity for her.

Then I heard Myrtle say, "Yes, she's here. That's why you're coming, isn't it? You want to see her."

There was only one person Myrtle could be talking about. I marched down the hall and shut myself in the bathroom so I wouldn't have to listen to her.

When I came out, Myrtle was waiting for me. "That was Lisa. She's coming for a visit this weekend. I'm sure she'll find some excuse to leave before church, though."

"Well," I said, "that'll be nice. I'd like to meet my niece."

"As far as I'm concerned," Myrtle said, "this is your first test. I expect you to be on your best behavior and to try to be a good influence on that girl. She's always been weak in the spirit, and I don't want you leading her further astray than she already is."

Myrtle spent the next week forcing me to help her clean the already-clean house. She took particular pleasure in making me clean the bathroom.

"I bet you ain't never cleaned a toilet in your life." Myrtle stood over me as I kneeled before the porcelain bowl, a can of Comet in one hand and a toilet brush in the other.

"No, but I've not done it for forty years or so." The last toilet I'd cleaned myself was in the little apartment I lived in when I first started whoring.

"I bet you've always paid somebody to clean for you because you think you're too good to do it yourself."

"No. I just figure if a girl's gonna get down on her knees and clean the toilet, she might as well get paid to do it. A girl ought to get paid for anything she's got to get down on her knees to do, whether it's housecleaning or screwing."

Myrtle stamped her foot just like she used to when she was a little girl. "Why, I ought to wash that filthy mouth of yours out with soap!"

I stood up and threw the can of Comet against the pink tile wall. White powder dusted our heads like snow. "And I ought to slap your self-righteous little face, but it wouldn't be worth breaking a nail!"

Myrtle stared at me with hard brimstone eyes. "Sometimes I think the Lord made you my sister just to test me."

My next words shot out like poison from a spitting-mad snake. "And sometimes I wonder why the Lord saw fit to take C.R. instead of you. I reckon it's true what they say about only the good dying young. C.R.'s long gone, and here you and me stand."

Myrtle shook her index finger in my face. "Don't you ever make it sound like you and me are cut from the same cloth, Vestal. If it wasn't for my good heart, you'd still be locked up in the crazy house right now."

"I am locked up in a crazy house."

Myrtle's fists clenched. "Ungrateful! That's how you've always been, ungrateful for your daddy's love, ungrateful to me!"

"And what should I be grateful to you for? For dragging me back to your godforsaken lair? For getting me kicked out of the house when I was fifteen?"

Myrtle's face was right up against mine, and her hands squeezed my shoulders. "You know good and well it was your own whorishness that got you kicked out of the house. I was just trying to save you, like I always do."

The voice that came out of me was calm and even but

dangerous. "Myrtle, you'd better take your hands off me."

She didn't let go; instead she shook me back and forth in rhythm to her words. "Always trying to save you...to drag you up out of the dirt!"

"Damn it, Myrtle, I said to let go of me!" I pushed her chest, a little too hard maybe, and she stumbled backward into the towel rack.

She rubbed her back where she'd hit it, and her face clouded over for a second. But then she looked at me, her eyes gleaming with a mixture of rage and zeal. "I'm gonna make you clean!" She took a step toward me.

"I know you are. You're gonna make me clean your toilet, clean your bathtub!"

"No, Vestal. You're gonna be clean. That's why the Lord made me your sister, because I'm the only one who can make your filthy soul clean!" She tackled me like a football player and started shaking my shoulders and yelling, "Clean! Clean, do you hear me?"

She had me pinned with my back against the bathroom sink. "Goddamn it, Myrtle, get offa me!" This time she had me tight, and I couldn't get free. I was still weak and shaky from drying out, and between Myrtle's clean living and younger age, she for the first time in her plain, homely life, had the physical advantage over me. "You crazy bitch," I added. I might not have had too much physical fight left in me, but by God, I could still cuss.

"That's the devil talking in you," Myrtle said. "But we're gonna wash him out. You've always had the devil in you." Her eyes were wild, and spit gathered in the corners of her mouth.

She was starting to scare me. I managed to shake one shoulder out of her grip. I reached down, picked up the toilet brush and slapped her across the face with it.

She let go of me, spat, "You little...," then clamped her hand over her mouth. "That's how it is with you," she said, giving me a shove that made me stumble backward. "Always trying to drag folks down in the gutter with you. But it's not gonna happen again." She pushed me down on my knees onto the fuzzy pink bathroom rug. "Pray with me, Vestal. Pray." Her hands were forceful on my shoulders.

I looked up at her hateful face. "Myrtle, I'll get down on my knees and scrub your toilet, but I'll be damned if I'll get down on my knees and pray to your God."

Something inside Myrtle must have snapped because before I knew what hit me, she had grabbed me by my hair and was pushing my head into the toilet bowl. From my position inside the porcelain, I could hear her quoting Bible verses about the wages of sin and the dogs eating Jezebel. I tried to elbow her but missed. Finally, I got my foot at an angle so I could donkey kick her from behind, and since I was wearing high-heeled mules, it was a hard enough kick that I heard her say "oof" and felt her let go.

When I got my head out of the toilet and turned to face her, I saw that I must have knocked her backward into the tub. She sprawled there, looking stunned, her housecoat hitched up to show her big, white granny panties.

When Myrtle pulled herself out of the tub, she whispered, "Father, forgive me," and handed me a bottle of that cheap Suave shampoo she insisted on buying at the dollar store.

Later as I passed her bedroom, I could hear her sobbing and praying, but all I could do was laugh. My crazy Jesus-loving sister had tried to baptize me in the toilet.

Friday afternoon Myrtle fried chicken and made potato salad, which I told her needed more mustard, but she wouldn't listen. At five o'clock she put the food on the kitchen table and sat beside it, waiting. An hour passed.

Finally I said, "Myrtle, she'll get here when she gets here. Why don't you just come in the living room and watch some TV or something?"

"This is just like her." Myrtle didn't budge from the table.

"She's got a long way to drive. She coulda got stuck in traffic or something."

"Just like when she was a teenager. Every Saturday night I'd wait up for her when she was out with those friends of hers doing heaven knows what."

"They was just out being kids, probably. Driving around, flirting. She never got in bad trouble, right? It sounds to me like she turned out pretty good. Got a college degree, a good job."

"Well, it might seem like she's doing pretty good in this life," Myrtle said from her station at the kitchen table, "but she won't be doing so good in the next one. The girl ain't darkened the door of a church since she was eighteen years old."

"Oh, there's a movie coming on with that Susan Lucci," I said, flipping channels with the remote. "She's a pretty little thing. Could stand to put on a few pounds, though."

I watched the TV movie. Susan Lucci was being stalked by her ex-husband and was falling in love with a cop played by that cross-eyed boy from that show about that talking car. Myrtle sat at the kitchen table and sighed dramatically every two minutes or so.

During a commercial I said, "You might as well put that potato salad in the fridge. There's no use for Lisa to get here only to die of food poisoning."

"I'm calling the highway patrol, is what I'm gonna do," Myrtle said, not budging from the table. "I've got her license plate number somewhere."

"Oh, for God's sake, Myrtle." I jumped up off the couch and put the potato salad in the refrigerator myself. "You can't get the cops following her; you'll scare her to death."

"There's no reason for you to take the Lord's name in vain."

"I've got plenty of reasons."

Myrtle was rising from the table, about to either slap me or preach me a sermon, when there was a knock at the kitchen door. "It's the police," Myrtle said. "She's dead."

"Oh, just answer it, for God's sake," I said, throwing in the Lord's name again on the theory that she wouldn't smack me while somebody was at the door.

As anybody with a lick of sense would have figured, it was Lisa. I heard her before I saw her. She said, "Hi, Mom," and Myrtle, her usual cheery self, said, "I thought you were dead."

"Mother, I told you I didn't get off work till four. How could I have gotten here any earlier?"

Lisa was in the door now, and I was so startled I took a step back when I saw her. Her dark hair was cut like a boy's, short over the ears and clipper-cut in the back. She had on a plain white T-shirt tucked into nice-fitting Levi's, which flared over her black cowboy boots. But what startled me about Lisa wasn't that she was butch, butch enough that I felt like I probably knew what kind of girl she was, it was her mischievous blue eyes, her keen nose, her sharp jaw. The girl was the spitting image of C.R. about the time he was going off to war.

"You must be Vestal," Lisa said, flashing a lopsided grin that was so much like C.R.'s it gave me chills. "I've always wanted to meet you."

"I've been wanting to meet you, too, honey." I held out my hand for her to shake, but she hugged me instead. It was a tight, warm hug, and it made me feel a little shy somehow. It was the first time I'd been touched with affection in I couldn't remember how long.

"Well," Myrtle huffed, "I reckon we might as well eat." We sat down at the table and Myrtle pronounced, "Bless this food for the nourishment of our bodies, and may all those gathered at this table come to know the glory of Thy name. In Jesus's name we pray, amen."

Lisa took one bite of her potato salad, got the mustard from the refrigerator, squirted more on the salad and stirred it up before taking another bite. I looked at Myrtle, but she wouldn't look back at me.

"I hope you can stay till Sunday afternoon so you can hear Brother Gary preach," Myrtle said, ignoring me and looking at Lisa.

"I don't know, Mother. We'll see."

"You always say 'we'll see,' and then you always manage to leave before church starts."

"I've been going to a Unitarian church in Atlanta every once in a while." Lisa bit into a drumstick.

"The Unitarians?" Myrtle yelped. "I've heard Brother Gary talk about them. He says they're a secular humanist cult! They're probably brainwashing you."

"I don't know how they can brainwash me if they can't even make up their own minds about what they believe," Lisa said and turned to look at me. "So, Aunt Vestal, how do you like it here in scenic Camden County?"

"Well…" I pushed my plate away "I reckon it's better than jail."

Lisa laughed. "It's good to keep things in perspective, isn't it?"

Myrtle, obviously mad that I was trying to have a conversation with her daughter, butted in and said, "Lisa, you remember Sharon Silcox, your friend from high school?"

"She wasn't really my friend, but I remember her."

"She just had her third baby, a little boy this time. Her husband's got a real good job over at the coal company."

Lisa sighed. "Well, I'm glad she's happy."

"I reckon you're the only girl from your high school class that ain't settled down yet."

"I am settled, Mother. I'm as settled as I'm ever going to get."

Myrtle shook her head as she cleared the dishes. "If a woman's got no husband and no children, it's untelling what kind of trouble she can get herself into. Why, you could wind up like Vestal here."

Lisa patted my shoulder as she walked past me. "Aunt Vestal seems all right to me."

There was a ballgame on TV, which let the rest of the evening pass in relative peace, until Myrtle announced that it was bedtime, not just for her, but for all of us. That was the whole problem with Myrtle's personality. I wouldn't mind a bit if she went to bed early and loved Jesus and left everybody alone, but she had to force everybody around her to do what she did, too.

I went to my room knowing I wouldn't be able to sleep and stretched out on the bed with one of the fashion magazines I'd started buying at the grocery store with the money Les had sent me. Looking at the beautiful, flawless women in their beautiful, flawless clothes made me sad for a time in my life I knew I'd never get back. But the magazines were a comfort, too, just like my movie magazines had been back in Bartlett, a reminder that there was life beyond the mountains.

Around ten-thirty there was a gentle tap on my door. "Hey," Lisa whispered, "I saw your light on." She sat down on the foot of my bed.

"I don't go to sleep with the chickens like Myrtle."

Lisa smiled. "Me neither. Listen, I just wanted to let you know that the me you were seeing at dinner tonight, that's not how I am all the time. When I'm around Mother, my whole personality changes. She makes me crazy."

"Listen, hon, you don't have to explain yourself to me. That biddy's been driving me crazy since the day she was born."

Lisa laughed. "Say, I was going to get out of here for a couple of hours. You want to come with?"

"You mean you're gonna sneak out?"

"If I hadn't learned the art of sneaking out of this house while Mother's asleep, I never would've survived my teenage years."

At that moment, it was like Lisa and I were sisters, rebelling against a mean and unreasonable mother. "Just let me get my shoes on," I said.

Lisa had a sharp little car, a silver convertible. Clearly, whatever business she was in, she was doing all right.

"Where are we going?" I asked, once Myrtle's ranch-style prison was out of sight.

"I thought we might get the hell out of this dry county," Lisa said. "Drive over the county line, maybe grab a couple of beers."

I laughed. "Myrtle'd have a shit fit if she knew."

"Mother's probably not had a shit in years," Lisa said. "Her sphincter's too tight." She popped a tape in the tape player and turned it up loud. It was some woman with a low, growly voice singing with a lot of electric guitar. Now me, I would've taken Miss Peggy Lee over that any day, but it was still fun to hear loud music and to know that in a few minutes I would be able to feel the warm buzz of alcohol in my blood.

As soon as we crossed the county line we pulled in front of a white, concrete block building with a black, lettered sign that said, 'CHARLIE'S TAVERN FIRST STOP, COLD BEER.'

"I don't drink much back in Atlanta," Lisa said as we slid into a sticky vinyl booth in the dark tavern. "But there's something about being at Mother's that brings out the rebellious teenager in me, makes me want to sneak out with my fake ID and drink myself sick. Back when I was in high school, this place was called the D and M Tavern. The women in Mother's church used to say that the D and M stood for the Devil's Mansion."

I looked around at the drunk coal miners shooting pool at the broken-down pool table. I shifted my behind from where I was sticking to the seat. The floor was even stickier. "Looks like the devil could afford a better place than this."

Lisa laughed. "I'm going up to the bar. What can I get you?"

"Just a Coca-Cola." I was surprised to hear these words coming from my mouth. I had been looking forward to a buzz, even a cheap beer buzz, but then if it hadn't been for all the alcohol that had been humming through my brain for the past God knows how many years, I wouldn't have lost control of my life and my business and ended up living with my shrew of a sister. Life with Myrtle had done for me what drug and alcohol counseling couldn't, but not for the reasons Myrtle wanted.

"Are you sure that's all you want?"

"I figure you can drink all the beer you want, and maybe I'll get to drive you back to the house in that snazzy little convertible."

"It's a deal." She tossed me the keys.

Lisa came back to the table with a Bud longneck and a plastic cup of Coke and ice.

"So," she said, "I've got a perverse desire to hear what it was like growing up with my mother. To hear her tell it, she was a perfect little angel, and that pretty black hair of yours was just there to cover your horns."

With great pleasure, I told her every time Myrtle had irritated or betrayed me when we were growing up, leading up to the big moment when she showed Mother and Daddy my engagement ring and got me kicked out of the house.

Lisa shook her head. "She never changed, did she? When I was sixteen she caught me making out with my boyfriend. We were fully clothed, mind you, just kissing. Even so, she pulled me out of public school to get away from him and put me in this psycho-Christian church school where everybody had to wear baggy polyester uniforms and diagram sentences from the Bible."

"You poor thing." I sipped my Coke. "Did Myrtle ever say anything about what I did with my life after I left home?"

"She said that you were dead to her. That you were living in a swamp of sin."

"Well, it was a successful swamp, anyway." I laughed. "Did you ever hear that I was the madam of a whorehouse?"

"I'd heard rumors. Is it true?"

I didn't say anything, just smiled my sly kitty-cat smile.

"Oh, my God, this I've got to hear."

Lisa knocked back three more Buds while I told every whorehouse story I could remember. My drinking years were cloudy, but I still had plenty of stories from the early days, some of them so funny that Lisa smacked the table when she laughed. Something about the way she laughed put me in mind of C.R., too, that, and the way her eyelids drooped when she started to get tipsy.

"Damn!" she said when I was done talking. "I obviously got the wrong Jenkin's sister for a mother."

"I wouldn't say that. I would've been just as bad as Myrtle, but in a different way. Some women just ain't cut out for marriage and motherhood."

"Yeah," Lisa said. "Yeah, that's true."

"So you're a business owner, too?" I said.

Lisa laughed, "Yeah, I run a restaurant."

"A restaurant's a good business, too. People got to eat just as sure as they've got to screw."

"I guess so."

"So do you like living in Atlanta? So far all I really know is that you're in the restaurant business and you don't love Jesus the way your mama wants you to."

"Well...my life is good. Not like yours, maybe, but there are plenty of parts of it that Mother wouldn't approve of."

"Do tell."

She grinned a sheepish C.R. grin. "Well, I actually turned out to be a pretty good student, and so when I graduated I got offered two full scholarships, one to East Tennessee State and one to Bethany College, a private Christian college for women. You can guess which scholarship Mother made me take."

"I bet I can."

"One night I overheard her telling Daddy, who wasn't all

that hot for me to go to college in the first place, that at least if I went to Bethany College he could rest easy knowing I'd keep my virginity." Lisa laughed. "And I guess she was right. If you go by the technical definition, I'm still a virgin these thirteen years later."

"What?" I couldn't even begin to wrap my mind around the idea of a virgin over thirty who wasn't a nun.

Lisa laughed. "I just mean I've never been with a man. See, my first year at Bethany I met this girl named Amy, a blue-eyed blonde no bigger than a minute. She was from a family that was just as controlling and fanatical as mine, and she had a great sense of humor. And believe me, at Bethany College, humor was hard to come by. We got really close really fast. By the start of spring semester we were sharing a bed. We knew we'd be nailed if the housemother ever caught us; I always figure the reason we weren't more careful is that we wanted to get caught, wanted to get thrown out of that God-awful place so we could start a real life together. Which we did. All of the above."

I raised my Coke to her in a toast. "Good for you."

Lisa touched her cup to mine. "Actually, we ran away from the school before they could throw us out. The night the housemother caught us, she ordered us to report to the dean of women first thing the next morning. Instead, we pooled our money, packed a suitcase apiece, climbed down the fire escape and walked to the Greyhound bus station where we bought two tickets to Atlanta."

"Why Atlanta?"

"It was the biggest city we could afford tickets to. We figured since it was so big, there were probably other people like us there, although we were both so innocent we hardly knew what 'people like us' meant. We both got waitressing jobs and rented a crappy one-room apartment on a street full of drug dealers and prostitutes, sorry, no offense."

"None taken, but it does pay better than waiting tables."

"I'm sure it does. But we were happy. We had a tiny apartment and low-paying jobs, but we were together, and for the first time, we were free to do as we pleased. Mother would raise a big stink from time to time and threaten to come down to Atlanta and get me, Amy's parents would make the same threats. But when it came down to it, we were of age, so they couldn't really do jack shit. Eventually Amy and I got better-paying jobs and a less roach-infested apartment and managed to go to Georgia State part-time until we finished our degrees."

"So what happened to Amy? Do you know?"

Lisa grinned. "She's in Atlanta, in our little pink stucco house in Midtown."

"You're still together?"

"Yep. She's the only person I've ever been with and the only person I've ever wanted to be with. For all of Mother's yapping about how I ought to settle down, my relationship with Amy has lasted longer than most marriages."

"So Myrtle just pretends you're some dried-up old maid who lives by herself?"

"She goes to great lengths to believe that, yes. If she calls and Amy answers, she just hangs up, and she won't have Amy in her house, which is why I don't visit more often. She bitches to high heaven that I only make it to Camden County once or twice a year, but she's lucky I visit her at all."

"I don't believe I would. I never went back to see Mother and Daddy after they threw me out of the house."

"Do you regret it?"

"No. They never understood a thing about me, and I never understood a thing about them. I have no regrets." But even as I said it, regret washed over me like a bucket of ice water. Not regret about how I treated my blood kin, but about how I drove away the one person who was kin to my heart.

"That's what I need, Aunt Vestal. Your freedom from guilt. I don't guess you can grow up with Martyred Myrtle for a mother and not feel some guilt, though. She was programming it into me in the womb. Amy's got the guilt thing, too. She still goes to see her crazy family every Easter weekend, leaving me to spend Easter Sunday at the dyke bar."

"You can't let yourself feel guilty, though," I said, sounding a lot more fired up than I'd expected to. "There's two kinds of people in our family. There's the ones like my mother and Myrtle who spend their whole lives doing what they think they're supposed to do and making themselves and everybody around them miserable. Then there's the ones like you and me and your uncle C.R. who've gotta have their freedom or die trying. C.R., who you look just like, died trying. People like us can't let people like them drag us down."

Lisa nodded. "Maybe those aren't just the two kinds of people in our family. Maybe they're the two kinds of people in the world."

"Maybe so."

Lisa was peeling the label off her beer bottle and speaking without even looking at me. "Aunt Vestal, I was thinking...what if on Sunday morning you and I got up early, way before time for Mother's infernal church service, and you came back to Atlanta with me?"

"Is that the beer talking?"

"I never say things I don't mean just because I'm drunk."

"I don't know...I wouldn't want to get you in trouble. I was released into the custody of a family member, and Myrtle..."

"I'm a family member, too. And Mother will pitch a fit when she finds out you're gone, but she won't come after you because deep down she'll be glad to have you out of her hair. This is something I know from experience."

"Well, you'll have to talk to Amy about it first."

"I will, but she'll say yes. We've got a three-bedroom house. The master bedroom is Amy's and mine, and the second bedroom belongs to Ralph and Winston...they're a couple, too. The third bedroom is kind of small, but it's all yours, if you don't mind living in a house full of homos."

"I spent the better part of my life living in a house full of whores, so a house full of homos is nothin' to me." A strange wave of feeling swept over me, and I found myself saying, "Lisa, I told you a lie tonight. I told you there was nothing in my life that I regret, but there is one thing. One time, years ago, I was put in a position where I had to choose between love and money. I chose money, and I've been sorry ever since."

Lisa nodded. "As poor as you and Mom were growing up, I guess it's not surprising that you chose money." She peeled the label on her beer bottle for a few seconds. "So who was it who made you choose?"

Not wanting to give away all I had left that was just mine, I said, "It was the only person I've ever taken to my bed for the sake of pleasure."

Lisa looked like she wanted to ask me something else, but instead she said, "It's late. We'd better go."

On the way back to Myrtle's I put the top down on the silver convertible. The sky was full of stars, the wind was whipping through my hair, and my sweet little niece was beside me, looking for all the world like my long-lost brother. For the first time in a long time, I felt good.

The next morning Lisa and me were so nice to Myrtle that it should have made her suspicious. We got up early and ate the fried eggs and sausage and canned biscuits she made. I could tell the grease wasn't doing much for Lisa's hangover, but she choked down her food all the same. Then we got dressed and rode out in Myrtle's car to put plastic flowers on Lisa's daddy's grave. Lisa went along dutifully, even though she told me when we were alone that she thought it was fine for people to visit their loved ones' graves if it made them feel better, but it didn't do anything for her, and besides, those plastic flowers her mother always insisted on setting out would take a thousand years to break down. People's time on earth was short, but that wasn't so for plastic flowers.

I went along with everything—the breakfast, the cemetery trip, the trip afterward to the Dollar General Store and Hardee's, without complaining. Like a convict who's just about finished digging a tunnel out, I wanted to appear to be a model prisoner for my last few hours of confinement.

Lisa and me got up Sunday morning before it was even light outside. The night before I had packed my suitcases and my box of clothes from Les and painted my nails candy-apple red. My traveling dress, I had decided, would be the red dress Les had sent me, the one that stuck out in Myrtle's dumpy little closet the same way I stuck out in Myrtle's dumpy little house. The dress was a little much for a car trip, I knew people didn't dress up to travel anymore, but I couldn't get the picture out of my head of me in my red dress in the passenger seat of that convertible, tearing down the highway with the wind in my hair.

"Wow," Lisa whispered when she saw me, "you're beautiful."

"Not no more I ain't. Wait till we stop at my old house in Knoxville. I've got pictures there. I'll show you what beautiful is." I held my pumps in my hand and tippy-toed down the hall so as not to wake Myrtle.

But Myrtle was already awake. When we walked into the living room, she was sitting in the La-Z-Boy recliner just like she was waiting for her teenage daughter to come home from an all-night date. "You'uns is up awful early," she said.

"Um, yeah. Well, I need to get back to Atlanta," Lisa said. "And Aunt Vestal, well, she was seeing me off…"

"I'm going with her." No way was I gonna let Lisa get scared of her mother and leave me behind.

Myrtle pulled herself up out of the chair and stood nose-to-nose with me. "You ain't going nowhere. That social worker said you had to stay with me!"

"She said I had to stay with a family member. Lisa's a family member, too."

Myrtle looked at me with the same hateful eyes she had when she was eleven years old. "Lisa can't help you. She can't bring you to the Lord."

"Well, neither can you, Myrtle," I said. "People can't just be one way all their lives and then switch around to being another. I may be old enough to be somebody's granny, but I'm still the same wild girl I've always been, even if you can't accept it. And your daughter here's a big old dyke, and I don't reckon that'll change either." Lisa blushed but didn't say a word. "And Myrtle," I went on, "you're just the same as when we were kids, once you found out you were a Holy Roller, you stayed that way. People are what they are, and you can't change them."

"You just stay here till Brother Gary gets here," Myrtle ordered. "Brother Gary will…"

"Brother Gary used to be a customer in my whorehouse. He'd bring in money he took from the offering plate. Bought himself two girls one night…"

The flat of Myrtle's hand hit my cheek, but I didn't flinch.

"You liar!" she yelled. "You bald-faced liar!"

My hand balled into a fist, but suddenly Myrtle seemed too pathetic to hit. Here she was, like always, denying the uncomfortable truths of life, shrinking her world until it was small enough to fit her view of the way things ought to be. My cheek stung from her slap, but when I looked at her, I felt not anger but pity. "You ask him when he gets here if it's a lie," I said. "See if he can look you in the eye and say it is. Don't judge him for it, though, Myrtle. Nobody can live up to your standards of behavior...nobody but you, and living that way makes you so damn miserable that nobody can stand to be around you."

I looked at Lisa, who was frozen in shock.

"Well, I reckon we're heading to Atlanta," I said. "You know where I'll be if you want to find me. And if you really want me back and you come down there to get me, I promise I'll come back here with you without saying a word. But I expect you'll have too good a time here, playing the martyr to all your church lady friends, talking about how you tried to save me but I had done sold my soul to the devil. Let's go, Lisa."

Lisa followed me to the door. Myrtle looked like she might follow us, but she didn't. Instead, she stood in the doorway, looking old and small in her housecoat, and called out, "I'll pray for your souls."

"You do that," I said. "We'll pray for yours, too."

After Lisa pulled out of the driveway, she asked, "Are you okay?"

"I'm great. I feel great."

"I couldn't believe you two yelling at each other like that. I've never seen anything like it."

"That's because you don't have a sister. All them hairy-legged women back in the Seventies who used to go on about how great sisterhood was...I figured they all must be only children."

When we got to Knoxville, I gave Lisa directions to Les's main store.

"Come in with me," I said after we'd parked under the big lighted Les Tipton's Stop 'n Save sign. "Les'll be tickled to meet you."

We got some stares in the store, the boyish girl in her vest and jeans and the old lady in the slutty red dress, but we ignored them as we walked back toward Les's office.

I tapped on the door. When there was no answer, I opened it. Les was leaned back behind his desk, snoring an old man's wheezing snore. He was thinner than the last time I saw him, and his liver-spotted head and scrawny, wrinkled neck put me in mind of a baby bird. He seemed almost helpless, snoozing there, but I knew that as long as Les was breathing, he wasn't helpless.

I touched his shoulder lightly. "Les? It's me, Vestal."

"Missy?" he mumbled, his eyes still closed. "Me and your brother's going to the cockfights." He opened his eyes, focused on Lisa, and said, "C.R.?"

"It ain't C.R., Les," I said. "Ain't she a dead ringer for him, though? This is Lisa, Myrtle's girl."

"Myrtle's…oh…" He was waking up. "It was the most peculiar thing. I was dreaming about you and me and C.R. back in Bartlett, and then here you come. Ain't you supposed to be in Camden County?"

"Since when did you know me to do anything I was supposed to do? If I had to be cooped up in that house one more second with Myrtle, I'da been guilty of murder instead of just selling pussy. Lisa here's taking me to Atlanta to keep me from committing further criminal acts." Les cackled. "Well, Lisa, I'd tell you to make sure she stays out of trouble, but that ain't no way possible."

"I came by to get my jewelry out of your safe," I said.

"I've got it right here." Les turned around, moved an apple crate aside and turned the dial on the metal box, stopping to hack a dry, hollow cough.

"If that ain't a miner's cough, I don't know what is," I said. "You sound just like my daddy."

"I know it," Les said. "Doctor said I ort to take some time off work, but you know me. I ain't took a day off since I was born. Wouldn't know what to do with myself." He handed me a big, red velvet-lined box. "There you go, missy."

I opened the box and smiled to see my diamonds, emeralds and rubies winking at me.

"Holy shit," Lisa said. "Do you know how much all that stuff is worth?"

"Naw," I said. "It sure is pretty, though, ain't it?" Of course, I could've told her what it was worth to the penny. "Les, you might want to tell the fellers down at the bank I'll be sending for my money once I get settled in Atlanta. And I'm gonna leave the key to the house under the mat for you. All the papers on the house is in my bureau drawer in the bedroom."

"What do you want me to do with it?"

"Keep it. Or sell it to some young couple that thinks it's a hoot to live in what used to be a whorehouse. If you do that, keep the money. Or split it with me. I don't care."

"You take care of yourself, missy." Les tried to rise from his chair, but a coughing fit took him. Lisa fetched him a glass of water.

Once he was calm again, I bent down and kissed his soft, wrinkly cheek. "Les," I said, "I'll see you."

But I never saw him again.

We picked up a few things from the old house: the nude portrait of me that hung over the couch, some photo albums, a few outfits and pairs of shoes. But I didn't want to stay long. It made me sad, like being in the house of a person who had died.

Lisa looked around at the dust-covered antiques and the closets full of clothes. "Are you sure you don't want to take anything else?"

"I'm sure. These things used to mean the world to me, but when I look at them now I don't know why. They're just things. I do want to show you one thing, though." I had been thinking a lot about the night before, about what I had left unsaid. If I didn't tell Lisa the whole truth, I decided, I'd be no better than Myrtle. I picked up an old photo album and flipped it to my favorite picture a grinning, handsome black woman dapper in a starched shirt and pleated pants. "You know how I told you about me choosing money over love? This is who I lost."

Lisa's eyes were wide. "Aunt Vestal, this is a woman!"

I smiled. "Yes. I didn't know that the first time I saw her, though. I just thought she was the prettiest boy I'd ever seen. Trey...that's her name. Short for Treasure, which is what she was."

Lisa looked down at the photo. "She's gorgeous. But Aunt Vestal, does this mean you're saying you're a…"

I closed the book and hugged it close to my chest. "I'm not saying I'm an anything. I'm not like you young people. I don't have to wear a big sign saying, 'I'm a this' or 'I'm a that.' What I am saying is that I loved this woman, but I said no to her. That's why I'm saying yes to you."

We drove all the way to Atlanta with the top down and the music blaring.

When we hit the city, my jaw dropped at the sight of the skyscrapers. "Well, here I was all my life thinking I'd made good in the big city. This place makes Knoxville look like Bartlett."

"Everything's relative," Lisa said. "I thought Atlanta was huge until I saw L.A."

We turned down a street and passed a Japanese restaurant and a pizza place and a bar that Lisa informed me was 'a dyke bar.' Then we turned onto a narrower street lined with old Victorian houses that put me in mind of the house David's parents had lived in all those years ago. Some smaller, less old houses were a little ways down the street, and Lisa pulled into the driveway of a stucco cottage that looked like it was made of cake covered with pink frosting.

When the car door slammed, a blond girl ran out on the porch in her bare feet. She was one of those naturally blond, naturally tan, natural beauties who would've been an absolute knockout if she lost the blue jeans and fixed herself up a little bit. Nature can always be improved upon. She met Lisa on the porch steps and kissed her right out in the open. Then she turned to me and said, "Vestal, that dress you're wearing is a Halston, isn't it?"

"It sure is, honey. And bless your heart for knowing it."

"Are you kidding?" Amy took my arm and helped me up the stairs. "It'll be great to have another woman with some fashion sense in this house. If I didn't pick Lisa's clothes out for her, she'd dress like somebody's dumpy old uncle." She swung the screen door open, nudging a calico cat aside with her bare foot. "Come on in."

It's hard to explain how much my life has changed since I walked in that door. That first night there, Amy had cooked some dish with shrimp and rice and vegetables, and she and Lisa and Ralph and Winston and me sat around the big dining room table and ate. Ralph's a dog groomer, and Winston works in a nightclub, and they're both as cute as they can be. It reminded me of the old days when Odell, Celeste and Howard would come over to the house, except this time I felt a little awkward because it wasn't my house.

"Now, if you'uns ever get tired of having me around, just let me know," I said, declining the wine Ralph offered to pour for me. "I know you ain't running a nursing home for old whores."

"Don't talk that way," Winston said, patting my hand. "We couldn't be happier. This is like having a great movie star come to retire at your house. Of course, you realize we'll have to introduce you to everyone we know!"

And so I settled in and let myself feel welcome. And I have met everybody Lisa and Amy and Ralph and Winston know, lesbians and gay men and a few of those Christine Jorgenson-type people. Nice folks, all of them. And happy. Back in our day, they always said homosexuals had tragic lives, but maybe that was just because there were a lot of people working real hard to make sure that their lives were tragic.

In June, when it was time for the Gay Pride parade, Winston came up with this idea for a float. He said he could decorate the bed of a truck like the parlor of a whorehouse, with red flocked wallpaper and gilt furniture. I could sit on the sofa as the madam, and all the 'girls' from the club where he worked, he called them girls, but they weren't really, of course, could dress in sexy lingerie and evening gowns and be my girls. I told him that nobody would want to look at a dried-up old thing like me in a parade, but he insisted. I wore this great gown he found for me, red sequins with marabou trim, and stretched out on a chaise lounge while a dozen drag queens in garters and nighties danced around me, moving their lips to that song that goes 'kitchy kitchy ya ya da da' or something to that effect.

Like I said, at first I hadn't wanted to do it. My looks were gone, and I felt like I had nothing to show off anymore. But you know what? When I sat up there, smiling and waving at the crowd, surrounded by 'girls' who were at least as pretty as the girls who used to work in my house, I felt proud. Proud to be among these people who were happy to be the way they were. Proud to have lived the life I've lived. And proud to have spent the time I spent with you, Trey, even though I wish it had been longer.

When Lisa started encouraging me, well, nagging me, really, to write all this stuff down, she kept telling me what a bestselling author I could be, like Xaviera Hollander in the seventies and that Mayflower Madam in the eighties. But that's not why I finally sat down to write. I've got all the money I want.

I wrote these pages for you, Trey. I wrote them to explain my life to you, if you're even still on this earth, or if you're at least somewhere where you can know what's in my heart. When we were together, I never talked to you enough about real things, never told you why I did the things I did. But now I've told you. I've given you my life in these pages, Trey, a life with many adventures, lots of money and more than its fair share of troubles, but with just one love.

EPILOGUE

Vestal lived with us for nearly five years. She put a great deal of her energy, which was considerable for her age, into these memoirs. She'd talk into her tape recorder when Amy and I were at work, and then she'd give us the tapes to transcribe. When the manuscript was finally done, she insisted that the woman who obsessed her, Trey, should receive a copy, if she was still living.

As it turned out, finding Trey wasn't as hard as I had thought, thanks to the wonders of the Internet, which indicated that she was still very much alive and running an independent bookstore in California. We sent a copy of the manuscript to her, and Vestal received several letters from her, though she would never tell any of us what they said.

During her fourth year with us, Vestal's health started to deteriorate. The long-term effects of her years of alcoholism started to catch up with her, and she suffered a series of strokes that left her partially paralyzed. Eventually we were not able to provide the care she needed and were left with no choice but to move her to an assisted-living facility. Amy, Ralph, Winston and I took turns visiting her each day, and she, with her stroke-slurred southeastern Kentucky accent, took great pleasure in telling us outrageous tales about the youthful exploits of her roommate, Mildred, the widow of a Nazarene minister.

The best that we could tell, Vestal's roommate was only capable of making garbled, infant-like sounds, but Vestal was always saying things like, "Why, Mildred was just telling me the other day that when she was sixteen year old, she could suck the chrome off a trailer hitch, weren't you, Mildred?" and "Winston, Mildred was just saying as how she'd love to have her some dick, but I told her you didn't go for girls."

Even in her final days, Vestal was her funny, flamboyant self. In our last conversation, I asked her if she'd like me to find a publisher for her memoirs.

"Sure, honey," she said. "Just as long as I'm dead. You can't sue a corpse. And listen, when I go, I don't want what's left of me laid out in a casket like a dried-up old husk. I want you to cremate me, and I want them letters from Trey I keep in the dresser drawer over yonder to burn with me. If you feel like you've got to have a service, you can set out some old photographs of me for people to look at. None after nineteen-seventy, though. I started to go downhill then." She grinned. "And you can put out that oil painting of me, too."

I couldn't help smiling. "The nude?"

"That's the one. When people remember me, I want them to remember me beautiful."

-Lisa Bryant

Publications from Spinsters Ink

P.O. Box 242
Midway, Florida 32343
Phone: 800-301-6860
www.spinstersink.com

MERMAID by Michelene Esposito. When May unearths a box in her missing sister's closet she is taken on a journey through her mother's past that leads her not only to Kate but to the choices and compromises, emptiness and fullness, the beauty and jagged pain of love that all women must face.   ISBN 978-1-883523-85-5 $14.95

ASSISTED LIVING by Sheila Ortiz Taylor. Violet March, an eighty-two year old resident of Casa de los Sueños, finally has the opportunity to put years of mystery reading to practical use. One by one her comrades, the Bingos, are dying. Is this natural attrition, or is there a plot afoot?   ISBN 978-1-883523-84-2 $14.95

NIGHT DIVING by Michelene Esposito. *Night Diving* is both a young woman's coming-out story and a 30-something coming-of-age journey that proves you can go home again.
                    ISBN 978-1-883523-52-7 $14.95

FURTHEST FROM THE GATE by Ann Roberts. *Furthest from the Gate* is a humorous chronicle of a woman's coming of age, her complicated relationship with her mother and the responsibilities to family that last a lifetime.   ISBN 978-1-883523-81-7 $14.95

EYES OF GRAY by Dani O'Connor. Grayson Thomas was the typical college senior with typical friends, a typical job and typical insecurities about her future. One Sunday morning, Gray's life became a little less typical, she saw a man clad in black, and started doubting her own sanity. ISBN 978-1-883523-82-4 $14.95

ORDINARY FURIES by Linda Morgenstein. Tired of hiding, exhausted by her grief after her husband's death, Alexis Pope plunges into the refreshingly frantic world of restaurant resort cooking and dining in the funky chic town of Guerneville, California.
ISBN 978-1-883523-83-1 $14.95

A POEM FOR WHAT'S HER NAME by Dani O'Connor. Professor Dani O'Connor had pretty much resigned herself to the fact that there was no such thing as a complete woman. Then out of nowhere, along comes a woman who blows Dani's theory right out of the water.
ISBN 1-883523-78-8 $14.95

WOMEN'S STUDIES by Julia Watts. With humor and heart, *Women's Studies* follows one school year in the lives of three young women and shows that in college, one's extracurricular activities are often much more educational than what goes on in the classroom.
ISBN 1-883523-75-3 $14.95

THE SECRET KEEPING by Francine Saint Marie. *The Secret Keeping* is a high-stakes, girl-gets-girl romance, where the moral of the story is that money can buy you love if it's invested wisely.
ISBN 1-883523-77-X $14.95

DISORDERLY ATTACHMENTS by Jennifer L. Jordan. The fifth Kristin Ashe Mystery. Kris investigates whether a mansion someone wants to convert into condos is haunted. ISBN 1-883523-74-5 $14.95

VERA'S STILL POINT by Ruth Perkinson. Vera is reminded of exactly what it is that she has been missing in life.

Visit

Spinsters Ink

at

SpinstersInk.com

or call our toll-free number

1-800-301-6860